"Would you let me hold her so you can eat?"

"You're sure?" The blue of Eli's eyes darkened with emotion. "Even though you said goodbye to me?"

"I was upset that night," Brianna answered honestly. "Your daughter is so precious, Eli. Of course I want to hold her, but I'll try not to wake her."

"Don't worry about it." He walked over and placed Libby in her arms.

The motion caused her eyelids to flutter open. Her blue eyes were so much like her father's.

"Hi, darling. Do you remember me? I'm Brianna."

The little girl put her arms around her neck and clung to her. Brianna held her against her heart and felt her breathe. "I'm so glad you're feeling better." She rocked her back and forth, loving the feel of those arms holding on to her.

Though he sported a slight beard and looked exhausted, Eli stood there watching them with a sweet expression on his rugged face. "I do believe you're the reason she's suddenly acting normal."

Brianna smiled up at him. "Her daddy is all the medicine she needs."

FALLING FOR THE COWBOY'S BABY

Rebecca Winters

&

Heidi Hormel

2 Heartfelt Stories

A Valentine for the Cowboy
and *The Kentucky Cowboy's Baby*

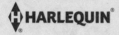

ISBN-13: 978-1-335-44885-9

Falling for the Cowboy's Baby

Copyright © 2022 by Harlequin Enterprises ULC

A Valentine for the Cowboy
First published in 2017. This edition published in 2022.
Copyright © 2017 by Rebecca Winters

The Kentucky Cowboy's Baby
First published in 2016. This edition published in 2022.
Copyright © 2016 by Heidi Hormel

This edition published by arrangement with Harlequin Books S.A.

For questions and comments about the quality of this book, please contact us at CustomerService@Harlequin.com.

Harlequin Enterprises ULC
22 Adelaide St. West, 41st Floor
Toronto, Ontario M5H 4E3, Canada
www.Harlequin.com

Printed in U.S.A.

CONTENTS

Rebecca Winters lives in Salt Lake City, Utah. With canyons and high alpine meadows full of wildflowers, she never runs out of places to explore. They, plus her favorite vacation spots in Europe, often end up as backgrounds for her romance novels—because writing is her passion, along with her family and church. Rebecca loves to hear from readers. If you wish to email her, please visit her website at rebeccawinters.net.

Books by Rebecca Winters

Harlequin Romance

The Baldasseri Royals

Reclaiming the Prince's Heart

Secrets of a Billionaire

The Greek's Secret Heir
Unmasking the Secret Prince

Escape to Provence

Falling for Her French Tycoon
Falling for His Unlikely Cinderella

The Princess Brides

The Princess's New Year Wedding
The Prince's Forbidden Bride
How to Propose to a Princess

A VALENTINE FOR THE COWBOY

Rebecca Winters

Dedicated to my fantastic parents,
who somehow managed that I would be born
on Valentine's Day. They made that birthday
special for me all the years that they
were alive. What a blessing!

Chapter 1

"Hey, Brianna—I keep telling you I wish you'd come home. You could *never* be in the way. When you said you wanted to stay with Aunt Joanne and Uncle Clark in Montana, I thought you'd only be gone a few weeks. It's now been six months!"

"I know." She looked at the Cattlemen's Association calendar on the wall. It was already the twenty-seventh of December. "But I've been doing well here working for them. I like being busy and was afraid if I came home for the holidays, I'd be overwhelmed with memories and I can't deal with that yet."

The car crash that had killed her beloved parents seven months ago had been so devastating that Brianna was amazed she'd survived this long.

"I hear you," he said in a mournful voice, "but I

want you to realize that Carol and I miss you more than anything."

"I feel the same way." But Doug, her elder brother, who was as blond as she was and sounded like their father, had only been married to his longtime girlfriend a few months before their parents had been killed. They were now running their parents' fruit farm in Marysville, California, and making a success of it. This early in their marriage they shouldn't have to worry about Brianna. Not when they'd had so much responsibility thrust on them.

The aunt and uncle she adored and who'd been so close to their family had never been able to have children. They'd begged her to come and live with them for a while.

"If you stay away any longer, you'll probably forget you have an older brother." He was twenty-seven to her twenty-three.

"Don't be silly. I love you to death and promise to fly home soon." The nearest airport was in Missoula, a half hour away from Stevensville. An hour if the roads in midwinter were bad. According to her uncle, this winter hadn't hit them too hard and business had been good. Today was a beautiful day with a lot of sun that had brought in the customers.

Four or five times a year since she was a little girl, Brianna had come to Montana with her family to visit her aunt and uncle. They often took in a rodeo because her father and uncle once did bull riding themselves and Brianna loved it. In fact the three of them were going to the Stevensville rodeo tonight. While she stood there swamped by sweet memories, she heard the front door open. It was closing time, but she hadn't locked up yet.

"Doug? I've got a customer. I promise to phone you next week and we'll have a good talk after I'm off work. Give my love to Carol."

"Will do. Talk to you later, sis."

Brianna hung up. An attractive male, probably in his late twenties, had just come into Frosts' Western Saddlery, one of Stevensville's oldest and most well-known stores. They sold everything cowboys and cowgirls could possibly need. A lot of men young and old came in all the time, but she'd never seen this guy before. He had light brown hair and wore a gray North Face half-dome hoodie and jeans.

His hazel eyes twinkled as they fastened on her. "I can see you're new here. Where's Clark?"

"He left for home ten minutes ago." Their ranch house was only a mile away. "What's your name? If it's an important matter, I'll call him and tell him you're here."

"I'm Roce Clayton, but please don't bother him."

That name caught her attention in a hurry. "One of the legendary Claytons?" The Clayton Ranch was one of the oldest and most famous ranches in the Bitterroot Valley. It lay between the Bitterroot and Sapphire Mountains outside Stevensville. What a coincidence! Brianna was planning to drive there later to visit the Sapphire Mine Gem Shop owned by the Clayton family.

"Well, now, that all depends." His smile made her chuckle. "What's your name?"

"Brianna Frost."

She could hear his mind working. "You're Clark's niece!"

"Yes. How did you know?"

"I'm a vet. I've taken care of their dog, Taffy, for the last year."

"Aha. So that's where I've heard your name."

"He just called me to take a look at her. I'm afraid her hip is bad."

Brianna loved that dog. "She's getting worse."

"It's a shame. You know, whenever I make a visit, all he talks about is you and your brother."

"You poor man."

"Not at all. I heard about your parents' death. Clark took losing his brother very hard. I can only imagine the pain you've suffered. I'm so sorry."

His sincerity touched her. "Thank you." She cleared her throat. "I understand your father passed a little while ago, too. My uncle really misses him. It couldn't have been an easy time for your family, either."

"You're right about that. He died thirteen months ago. Thank Heaven my mother is still alive. My older brother Wymon is head of the ranch now, but, between you and me, we'd all fall apart without her."

Tears stung her eyes. "I know what you mean. You're lucky to have her."

"That's for sure, but I don't see her often enough."

"Why is that?"

"I work at an animal hospital in Missoula and only come home when I can take an odd weekend off." He gave her a half smile. "Anyway, I just thought I'd drop in to buy a pair of driving gloves while I'm on my way to the ranch."

"For yourself or someone else?"

"For me." He gave her the size. "My old ones are falling apart. Maybe I'll pick up a pair for my mom, too."

"We've got some great gloves." She walked him over to a display case and showed him several styles. He found the gloves he wanted and went back to the counter to pay for them.

After handing him the bag she said, "If you're going to the ranch, could I follow you? I've never been there and I want to visit your family's gem shop. Uncle Clark wants to give my aunt a gift for their wedding anniversary coming up next week. I told him she'd love a ring. I'd like to see what's available."

"Then you're welcome to trail me."

"Thank you so much. Let me just grab my jacket and purse from the back, then I'll meet you in front."

After she'd locked up, Brianna stepped outside and was greeted by clear blue skies, the temperature hovering around a chilly thirty-four degrees. She climbed into the Ford pickup her uncle let her drive. It helped that the sun had melted the ice on the windshield. Roce Clayton waved to her from his black Escalade and she followed him down the snow-packed road in the direction of the ranch.

He seemed like a great guy—it was too bad she wasn't attracted to him. While Roce had been buying his gloves, she'd noticed he didn't wear a ring. With a smile like his and his classic good looks, she figured he wouldn't be single much longer. Her brother had been like that. Attractive and sweet. Carol had fallen for him in high school. Brianna hadn't found that kind of connection with anyone yet.

She'd had a series of boyfriends in college, but she'd never been in love before. Not really. Her feelings toward the guys she'd dated had never been that strong. Brianna's mom had told her, "When you meet the right one, you won't have to wonder. You'll know it in every atom of your body."

She let out a sigh and followed the car in front of her around a curve in the road. Light glinted off the magnificent snow-capped mountains studded with pines. It really was a spectacular drive. Five more miles and they reached the entrance to the Clayton Ranch with its tall arch of antlers. Somewhere on their property was the entrance to an old sapphire mine.

Her uncle had told her stories about the first two Clayton brothers, who'd hailed from Lancashire, England. In the late 1800s they worked and slaved to bring a big herd of Texan longhorn cattle to Montana, where they bought land and built their business into one of the most successful ranches on the western side of the state. They also bought mining rights as sapphires had been discovered throughout these mountains. Apparently Elias, the elder of the two brothers, neither married nor had children, so the legacy came through Wymon. The present-day Clayton brothers all had old English names to preserve their heritage, Roce being one of them.

She tried to remember the other brothers' names but failed. She thought she would ask Roce when they arrived at the ranch. The Sapphire Mountains were looming closer, and she figured they mustn't be far now.

The section of the Sapphire Mountains known as Gem Mountain was also called the "Quiet Giant" because it had produced over 180 million carats of sapphires over 120 years, yet it didn't receive a lot of publicity. According to Brianna's uncle, people in the early part of the twentieth century used to dig for larger sapphires that could be polished and sold for a lot of money. The fractured stones were sold for industrial purposes and many of them were shipped to Switzerland to be turned into watch bearings.

After World War II the rock hounds came. The Claytons had sapphire gravel brought out of their mine and they opened their own gem shop. People would sift through the material and often find a special sapphire to buy. Today you could still visit the mine, but it was much easier to shop at the store owned and run by Roce's mother, where you could see the sapphires on display.

Brianna's thoughts were still concentrated on finding the perfect sapphire for her aunt when the large, two-story ranch house sitting at the base of one of the foothills came into view. When the Escalade pulled up in front, Brianna slowed to a stop and waited for Roce. He got out and walked over to her.

She lowered the window. "Your ranch is fabulous."

"It is to me because it's home."

Home. How would it be to go back to Marysville and find her parents there? She could only hope that one day she'd stop hurting so badly.

"I'll go inside and find Mom. Be right back."

"It's okay. I'm not in a rush."

She expected to wait a while, but to her surprise Roce came back out in no time. "I just spoke to the housekeeper, Solana. It seems Mom decided to take advantage of this warm break in the weather and went up to the gem shop this afternoon."

Brianna smiled. "I guess thirty-four degrees in Montana in December *is* warm."

He grinned back. "Yup. Why don't you get in my car? I'll drive you and bring you back here. It'll be easier than giving you directions."

"If you're sure, that would be great."

"Of course."

She climbed down from the cab and got into the passenger side of his car. Her aunt and uncle had been so wonderful to her that she really hoped to find a stone that her uncle would be excited about to give his wife.

After working all day in the winter pasture, Eli took care of his horse and then left the barn and drove his blue rattletrap of a truck down to his house to shower and change his clothes. He made himself a couple of peanut butter sandwiches before leaving to pick up his daughter at the main ranch house. The ranch foreman, Luis, and several stockmen waved to him from a distance.

When Eli pulled up to the house, he saw an unfamiliar Ford pickup truck parked in front. It could be someone here to talk business with Wymon, except his brother's truck wasn't around. Neither was the Land Rover.

Anxious to give his little girl a hug, he hurried inside, but no one seemed to be about. There weren't any voices coming from the front office. No patter of little feet. He walked through the foyer and down the hall to the kitchen where he found the dark-haired housekeeper at the sink, washing vegetables.

"Solana? Whose truck is out in front?"

She looked over her shoulder. "Roce came home from Missoula and brought a woman with him. I suppose they've gone up to the gem shop in his car."

Whoa.

Maybe his brother had finally found the perfect woman to settle down with. He'd certainly had his share of girlfriends over the years. Roce had probably invited her to tonight's rodeo. Their brother Toly and his partner, Mills, were competing in the team roping event. "Did you meet her?"

"No."

"Where's Mom?"

"She took Libby to the shop with her. They'll be back soon."

He checked his watch. "She'll need to be since we're leaving for the rodeo in an hour and a half. Are you sure it won't put you out to watch Libby while we're gone?"

"Of course not. I love her."

"She loves you, Solana. Even so, I'm trying to find the right person to take care of her so you and Mom don't have to shoulder the whole load. Libby's my responsibility after all."

"Stop your worrying," the housekeeper said. "We're happy to help."

"And I appreciate it," Eli said. "But I want you to know that I am looking." Now that his daughter was fourteen months old, she was a real handful. His mother insisted that taking care of Libby helped her deal with her husband's death, but it was still hard work and no one knew that better than Eli. "I'll drive up there and relieve her." He grabbed a bottle of water from the fridge to wash down the sandwiches and went back out to his truck.

After starting the engine, he took off up the road past the barn and outbuildings, but a great weight had descended on him. It wasn't fair for his mother to be taking care of Libby when she'd already raised four sons and had found fulfillment running the gem shop. Though he was trying to be a good father and pull his weight on the ranch, his guilt about the impossible situation was growing heavier with every passing day.

Sadness filled Eli's soul when he thought about his ex-wife, who'd become too ill to raise their daughter and had suffered a nervous breakdown. He'd loved Tessa and they'd had a good marriage. Yet after the baby was born, she'd become a different person. He fought hard to keep their love alive and would have done anything to make their marriage work.

When she'd said she wanted a divorce, he was shattered. The word itself—the whole painful thought of it—was the last thing he'd wanted to hear, but she didn't relent. It left him with no choice since her happiness had to come first. Paying for it had been costly.

He'd been saving money to pay for a woman to watch Libby. But it couldn't be just any woman. She'd have to be a saint! Could there ever be a replacement for Eli's mother? She was so wonderful with Libby, but it pained him that she couldn't spend more time at the gem shop she owned and loved while she was taking care of his daughter.

Before he reached the shop at the base of the mountain, he spotted Roce's Escalade parked in front next to his mother's Land Rover. He shut off the engine and climbed down, eager to take his little girl back to his house. She'd become his whole world.

As he opened the shop door and felt the warmth envelop him, he saw his precious Libby in the arms of a shapely woman in a light-colored sweater and jeans standing at the counter talking to his mother. She had to be Roce's girlfriend. There was no sign of his brother. Where was he?

Eli couldn't help staring. She had the kind of otherworldly gossamer hair he'd always longed to run his hands through. While he was still mesmerized by her, Libby saw him and called out, "Dada!" His brunette daughter started squirming to get to him.

He moved toward her as the woman turned around. Eli was almost blinded by eyes that were the same deep blue as some of the sapphires in his mother's shop. Libby reached for him and hugged him around the neck, breaking the spell that had held him captive.

"All the light bulbs have been replaced." Roce's voice came from the back room. He emerged and gave their mother a kiss. "Hey, bro." He smiled at Eli. "How are things going? Libby gets bigger and cuter every time I see her."

"I think so, too," he muttered, caught totally off guard. "She's my little cowgirl. Aren't you, sweetie?" After kissing her cheek, he eyed his mother. "Thanks, Mom. Just so you know, I'm headed home. If you're going to the rodeo with us, you need to be at the ranch in an hour." On that note, he headed for the door.

"Wait—don't forget this." His mother held up Libby's little parka.

He'd forgotten because he couldn't get out of there fast enough. Eli reached for the coat and put it on his daughter, aware of the younger woman's engaging smile.

"Bye-bye, Libby."

He suffered another shock because his daughter smiled back. "Bye."

Their exchange trapped the air in his lungs because Libby had never said that word before. Once back at the truck, he fastened his daughter in the car seat and started down the mountain road.

Eli knew he'd been rude to leave like that. *So* rude, in fact, that he hadn't even answered his brother's question about his welfare. But the sight of Libby in that woman's arms had jolted him. Normally his daughter wasn't comfortable with strangers, but she'd seemed perfectly content with this one just now.

As for Eli, he hadn't been involved with another woman since meeting Tessa two and a half years ago. After a quick marriage and early pregnancy followed by a divorce, he'd devoted his life to Libby and had lost all interest in women, or so he'd thought.

So what in the hell had just happened to him? He'd stood there helplessly assessing her attributes as if he'd never seen a beautiful woman before. What made it worse was the fact that she was Roce's girlfriend.

Had his brother noticed Eli's behavior?

Of course he had! Roce didn't miss anything.

Damn and damn.

Brianna tried to concentrate on the reason why she'd come to the shop in the first place, but the arrival of the little girl's gorgeous daddy had brought a tension she couldn't shake. Was it anger she'd felt as he pulled his daughter away from her?

She'd offered to hold her while Mrs. Clayton showed her the sapphires. The little fourteen-month-old was so adorable and Brianna had loved entertaining her. Yet the father had seemed anything but pleased. Brianna wasn't exactly pleased, either.

Not only had she felt a strong and immediate physical attraction to Roce's brother—something that rarely happened to her just by looking at a man—it wasn't until he was putting the parka on his daughter that she noticed he wore a wedding ring.

Life played mean tricks on you. Roce Clayton didn't wear a ring, but he hadn't caused her heart to race when they looked at each other.

Time to snap out of it, Brianna.

After a moment's hesitation, she chose the stone she

loved the most from one of the trays. "Can you set this dark pink sapphire aside? My uncle will come to pick out the setting he wants and pay for it then. Will you be open Monday evening? He can be here by six. Their anniversary is on Wednesday."

"We'll take care of all of it on Monday," Mrs. Clayton said, smiling kindly. Brianna could see where her two sons got their good looks. They all bore a resemblance to each other.

The pretty dark-blond widow whose short hair was cut in a becoming style also possessed a charming nature and was wonderful with her granddaughter. She turned to Roce. "I'm ready to go if you are."

"See you back at the house, Mom." After he gave Libby a hug, they walked out to his car and started down the mountain.

"Thank you so much for bringing me here. I found exactly what I wanted for my uncle. Your mother is so knowledgeable about these stones. It was fascinating listening to her."

"Dad had the gem shop built for her to run. What started out as a hobby turned into a career for her. Over the years she's made quite a name for herself. She brings in business from all over the country."

"With your father gone, I'm assuming it has become even more important. She's a lovely woman and her granddaughter clearly adores her."

He nodded. "Dad fell for her the first time he saw her."

"That's so wonderful. It was the same with my brother and his wife. Love at first sight."

He grinned at her. "I would say it doesn't exist, but then I see it happen to other people all the time."

Brianna was thinking the exact same thing. Her mind flickered back to Roce's brooding brother. Did he have a fairy-tale love story, as well? When they reached the ranch house and Roce pulled up next to her truck, she opened the door. "Thanks for driving me up there. I really appreciate it."

"It was my pleasure. I guess you heard us talking about the rodeo. Have you ever been to one?"

"Yes, actually. Plenty of times. My father and uncle were both bull riders years ago. We're going to the arena tonight."

"Then you'll see our baby brother, Toly, and his partner, Mills, competing in the team roping event."

"Uncle Clark said one of the Clayton boys would be in the lineup. We'll be rooting for them."

"I have to be there early to check over their horses. Why don't you and your family join ours in the bleachers? We'll save seats for you down in front."

"That's very generous of you. Thank you."

"Good."

"One thing, though, Roce. Can you please not mention that I went to your ranch today, and ask your brother and mother to do the same? Uncle Clark wants to keep the ring a secret."

He winked. "Understood."

She jumped down. "Thanks again for everything. See you there."

On the drive to Stevensville she wondered if she was crazy to have accepted his invitation. It couldn't be construed as a date since it was meant for the whole family. That was the problem. His brother would be there, the *married* one with the piercing blue eyes. The *angry* one with the darling daughter. Brianna didn't even know his name. Would his wife be there? Roce had provided no explanation for his behavior. Of course it was none of her business.

An hour later she and her aunt and uncle bought their tickets and made their way through the crowd inside the noisy enclosed arena. Excitement was high because Stevensville's favorite son was competing. Brianna scanned the bleachers down in front and picked out Roce's mother right away. There were empty seats on either side of her.

"Brianna?"

She turned her head. "Hi, Lindsay!" Her married friend worked at the bookstore a block away from the saddlery. They often ate lunch together during the week.

"Come on," her uncle murmured. "The parade is beginning. Let's just sit here for now."

She waved to her friend and followed her aunt and uncle down a nearby aisle. The three of them found seats and watched the horses prance around, ridden by the contestants carrying flags. Brianna loved the fanfare and the smell of the horses, but tonight she was distracted and kept her eyes on Mrs. Clayton. After the national anthem had been sung by a local country singer, she watched three tall, hard-muscled men file into the row and sit next to their mother.

Brianna had never seen three such handsome brothers. Brianna couldn't distinguish who was who in their Stetsons.

A minute later one of them stood and began walking up the stairs. As he approached, she could tell it was Roce. She waved to him and he walked over and shook hands with Uncle Clark and Aunt Joanne. "I'm glad you're here. Why don't you all come with me?"

Her uncle and Roce talked about Taffy's condition as they followed Roce to where his family was sitting. The poor dog was on her last legs, a sad fact of life that couldn't be ignored.

The saddle bronc riding event was announced. Everyone shook hands quickly before it started. Brianna's aunt and uncle knew all of the Claytons and greeted Roce's mother warmly, calling her Alberta.

Roce explained that he'd been to the saddlery earlier in the day to buy gloves and had met Brianna there.

He went on to introduce Brianna to his brothers Wymon and Eli. But the first contestant was out of the box, stalling the conversation for the time being. Brianna sat on the end next to her aunt, but, instead of concentrating on the rodeo, her thoughts were on the brother named Eli, who'd come without his wife.

Roce was conventionally handsome and Wymon, whom Roce had introduced as the eldest brother, had light gray eyes that stood out in striking contrast to his black hair. Still, it was Eli with his rugged dark looks and his black Stetson who made Brianna's pulse quicken. She silently cursed herself for always being attracted to the bad-boy type.

All rodeos thrilled a crowd and this one was no exception. She held her breath throughout the team roping event and whooped and hollered along with the rest of Stevensville when the best time went to Toly and his partner. The celebrating went on for a long time. According to her uncle, the Clayton family hoped Toly and Mills would go to the Pro Rodeo National Championship in Las Vegas next December.

Brianna could only imagine how much the Claytons missed their father at a time like this. Her own parents would have loved this rodeo, too. She wished they were here and missed them terribly. It was especially hard not to have her mom to talk to after what had happened at the gem shop earlier that day. Her awareness of the man sitting five seats away had dominated her thoughts all night.

She was relieved when the barrel racing ended and the winners received their gold buckles. With the rodeo over, everyone got up to head outside. While her uncle stood talking to Roce, Brianna put an arm through her aunt's. "I'll walk out to the car with you."

"He could be a while. Clark lives for nights like this."

"Dad did, too."

Brianna thought they'd evaded any more socializing and was happy when they reached the car and got in. But then along came her uncle with Roce, who walked around the front of the car and knocked on the window. She asked her aunt to turn on the ignition so she could lower it.

He smiled down at her. "You got out of there too fast for me to say good-night."

"Thank you for allowing us to sit with your family. It made the whole evening that much more exciting and we're so proud of your brother."

"It was fun. Too bad I have to get back to Missoula tomorrow. But when I come to visit again, I'll drop by the saddlery. If you're not busy, maybe we could go out to dinner."

"That would be great," she said, blushing.

"Good. I'll look forward to it."

After they drove off, her uncle glanced at her through the rearview mirror. "I do believe you've made a conquest of Roce Clayton."

"I don't think so, Uncle Clark," she said. "If he were truly interested, he would have asked for my phone number and said he would call me. He was just being nice because he lost his father and knows I lost mine."

Her uncle made a turn and followed a line of cars out onto the highway. "The girls around here have been after him for years. He was a great bull rider before he gave it up to go to veterinary school. Can you honestly tell me you're not the slightest bit interested in him?" he teased.

Her uncle knew she'd spent time with him earlier in the day, but he'd made assumptions that were way off base. "Yes," she said without hesitation. The memory of Eli was constantly before her eyes.

"That sounded definite," her aunt said.

"He's a fine man, honey."

"Clark—" her aunt cautioned him. "Leave the poor girl alone."

Brianna leaned forward and patted his shoulder. "You sounded like Dad just now and I love you for it. But as Mom once told me, when I meet the right man for me, I won't have to question it. I'll know he's the one." *But please, don't let him be a married man...*

"Of course you will," her aunt concurred.

"I'm just saying you couldn't do any finer than a Clayton."

Both she and her aunt laughed the rest of the way home.

Chapter 2

Eli drove to the ranch house with Wymon and their mother. He raced upstairs so he could take his daughter home, but Solana stopped him at the door to the bedroom.

"She's asleep. Don't wake her up now. I'll watch her tonight and you can come get her in the morning. You've been going nonstop for months. It's time you had a break."

He reached out and hugged her. "You already gave me one. Toly won another gold buckle tonight. He's racking them up! Thanks so much for watching Libby so we could all be there to support him."

"She's a little angel. Luis and I couldn't have children so there are no grandchildren. Libby fills a hole in my heart."

He nodded. "She's my whole heart."

"I know. Luis and I promise to take good care of her tonight."

"You don't have to tell me that." He shoved the cowboy hat back on his head. "If you're sure you're okay, I'll be over at seven to fix her breakfast."

"Why don't you sleep in?"

"Even if I want to, I'm always awake by six anyway."

"You're still too young to be saying things like that."

"Didn't you know I've aged since my divorce?" he teased, but there was a kernel of truth in what he'd said.

Solana's expression sobered. "I *do* know," she murmured. "So does your mom. Now go on home and relax."

Eli walked back down the hall to the stairs. He could hear voices coming from the living room and found Roce talking privately with their mother. They appeared almost secretive. Wymon must have gone home to his own ranch house, and Toly would probably be out celebrating late with Mills after their win.

"You two are so quiet that I'm beginning to wonder if something's going on that I don't know about."

His mom stared at him in surprise. "Why would you say that?"

"I don't know. When I walked into the ranch house earlier today, I learned you were up at the gem store with Libby. A strange truck was outside." He eyed Roce. "Solana told me you'd brought a girl home with you. When I drove up there, I found you and a woman I've never seen before holding my daughter while picking out a stone." A drop-dead gorgeous woman. "Are you with me so far?"

Roce broke into a grin. "Mom? Shall we tell him?"

She nudged him. "Oh, don't be such a terrible tease."

Somehow Eli didn't feel like laughing. Anything but.

His mom moved toward him. "Eli? What's eating at you?"

"I just wondered if you and that girl might be serious."

Roce's eyes narrowed. After a silence he said, "Not yet, bro, but I have to admit she's a hottie."

"Oh, for Heaven's sake, Roce—" their mother chastised him. "Brianna Frost came up to the shop to pick out a stone for her uncle. He plans to give his wife a ring for an anniversary present. Roce had been to the saddlery for some gloves. She asked if she could follow him to the ranch because she'd never been to the shop before."

"Maybe you didn't know I've been caring for her uncle's dog, Taffy," Roce chimed in. "To be friendly, I asked her if she and her family would like to join ours to watch the rodeo. Nothing more, nothing less. Let me tell you something. The day I find the woman of my dreams, everyone will know about it."

Ridiculous as it was, those words caused some of the tension to leave Eli's body.

Their mom turned to Roce. "What day will that be, my second born? How many more years do I have to live before that happens?"

"I'm not ready to settle down yet. You know that." He gave her a hug.

"You're impossible," she muttered. But she said it on a burst of laughter.

The need to escape drove Eli out of the room. "Solana's watching Libby tonight," he called over his shoulder. "I'll be back in the morning."

By the time he reached his truck, he was out of

breath. He pressed his forehead against the steering wheel. Seeing Brianna Frost at the rodeo in her white cowboy hat convinced him he hadn't imagined his attraction to her at the gem shop.

Damn, was he ever glad she wasn't Roce's girlfriend.

Monday night, Brianna drove to the gem shop with her uncle. Her aunt thought they'd gone grocery shopping. They'd have to pick up a few items on their way home so she wouldn't get suspicious upon their return.

Mrs. Clayton greeted them when they walked into the warm, brightly lit store. But the first thing Brianna saw was little blue-eyed Libby with her floppy brunette curls, toddling around in front of the counter with her helicopter push toy. She was dressed in pink camo Wrangler jeans and a white-and-pink top with a ruffled hem. With Libby's matching pink cowboy boots, Brianna thought she'd never seen such an adorable child in her life!

"Hi, Libby."

The toddler recognized Brianna and pushed her toy toward her. Brianna got down on her haunches to examine her outfit. "Don't you look good enough to eat. Uncle Clark? This is Libby Clayton, Eli Clayton's daughter."

He tousled her curls. "She's a picture all right."

When he reached the counter Brianna heard him say, "Alberta? What a blessing to have such a beautiful granddaughter."

"Don't I know it!"

Brianna encouraged Libby to push her toy around. After a minute of doing an excellent job, Libby dropped it and held up her arms. "You want me to hold you? Oh, you little darling." She scooped her up and walked over to the counter with her.

Her uncle was examining the 1.5-carat pink sapphire solitaire. The way his eyes glowed as he looked at it told Brianna she'd chosen a winner. "I've never seen such a brilliant stone. I didn't know a pink sapphire could be such a deep color. Joanne will love it."

"It's definitely an eye-catcher. Which setting would you like?" Mrs. Clayton had put half a dozen rings on the velvet. He studied them.

"Which ring do you like, honey?"

"I like the white gold, but don't let what I think influence you."

"I think that would be my choice, too," the older woman concurred.

"Then let's do it, Alberta."

"Give me Joanne's size and I'll go in the back. It will only take me a few minutes to mount the stone. While you're here, maybe you'd like to look at some other stones."

She put out a display of sapphires sorted by colors in trays that looked like cupcake tins. The natural stones mined from the Sapphire Mountains came in every color. When they were heated, their colors grew more intense. Some were already a deep hue, but those like the one Brianna had picked out were rare.

While her uncle stood looking at the sapphires, Brianna walked around the shop with Libby, who was back to pushing her toy. Each time the propeller spun, the little girl laughed. "You must love to come up here with your grandmother. It's fun, isn't it?"

Two hands patted Brianna's cheeks. Libby had an endearing way. Brianna couldn't help kissing her. "I love those little cowboy boots on your top." She touched each one, causing the girl to giggle. In the midst of it, Libby called out, "Dada!"

Brianna looked up, unaware that Eli Clayton had entered the shop. Her pulse started to race. In a sheep-skin jacket and boots, he looked the spitting image of the tough, quintessential cowboy.

He's married, remember?

"It's Brianna, right?" His deep voice reverberated through her body. She nodded. "I can see my daughter is very taken with you. She seems perfectly happy to stay in your arms."

She had to admit she was surprised that Libby hadn't reached for him yet. Did it upset him? Yesterday he'd been angry. Brianna moved closer to the tall male to hand him his daughter, but Libby stayed where she was. "I'm enamored with your little girl," she said. "She's too precious for words."

His eyes played over Brianna's features. "The feeling appears to be mutual. Come on, Libby. Time to go home for your dinner." He plucked her from Brianna's arms. His daughter made a sound of protest.

"You've got competition," his mother spoke up.

"You're right." He picked up the push toy and walked over to the counter to talk to Brianna's uncle. Libby clung to her daddy's shoulder, never taking her eyes off Brianna. The two men chatted briefly about Toly's performance at the rodeo.

"Sorry to barge in like this, Mom. I'll trade you this toy for her parka and we'll get going so you can get on with your business."

"We're finished," Mrs. Clayton said.

"I do believe my wife is going to be a happy woman." Uncle Clark smiled.

Mrs. Clayton handed Brianna's uncle the wrapped package. "I have no doubt of it."

"It's good to see you, Eli." He turned to Brianna. "Shall we go?"

"Yes. Don't forget we have to stop for some groceries on the way home." She waved to Libby. "Bye-bye, sweetie."

The little girl's lower lip wobbled and she started to cry. Uh-oh. Brianna's instinct to comfort her had to be squelched. She hurried out the door with her uncle behind her. They climbed into the truck and started heading down the mountain.

"It's a damn shame about Eli," her uncle muttered.

At the mention of his name, Brianna's heart leaped to her throat. "What do you mean?"

"Of course you wouldn't know. His wife had a nervous breakdown after their baby was born. Roce said it was brought on by severe postpartum depression. She just couldn't get over it. It got to the point where Eli was playing both father and mother. His wife went back to her parents in Thompson Falls. She was too sick to handle being a mom and filed for a divorce Eli never wanted."

The air froze in Brianna's lungs. That explained the wedding band he still wore on his ring finger. He obviously still loved her and held out hope she'd recover so they could get back together. "How awful. That sweet little thing without her mommy."

"Life can throw you for a loop sometimes. Your aunt and I would have given anything to have a baby. The first time we tried to adopt, it fell through right at the end. On our second try, the birth mother lost the baby at seven months. Joanne couldn't bear the thought of another setback so we didn't try again."

"I'm so sorry."

He reached over and patted her arm. "We've been lucky your parents were willing to share you with us once in a while."

Too many emotions converged at once and tears trickled down Brianna's cheeks. "I'm the lucky one," she said.

Since his mother was ready to go home, Eli walked her out to the Land Rover. After giving Libby a kiss, she got in behind the wheel but didn't pull the door closed. Instead she stared hard at him the way only a mother could do.

"You've acted strangely the last two times you've come to the shop for Libby. The first night I saw a rudeness in you I didn't recognize. At the rodeo you didn't say two words. Tonight it was all you could do to be civil. I'm worried about you. What's going on? Don't tell me it's nothing."

Eli drew in a deep breath. "It's killing me that you're having to sacrifice so much for me. Before the week is out I'll contact an agency to help me find someone to watch Libby during the day. It won't be much longer before you have your freedom back."

"Libby is a joy! I don't ever want to hear you say that again, but I don't believe that's the reason for your behavior."

He held his daughter tighter. "I'm not sure I understand it myself."

Another silence followed. "Don't you think it's time you figured it out?" Streams of unspoken words flowed between them. "It's cold out here," his mother finally said. "Get Libby home and I'll see you two at breakfast."

Eli shut her door before getting in the truck with Libby. Once he'd fastened her in, they started down the snow-covered mountain. He passed Wymon's house and then Luis and Solana's. Eli's small ranch-style three-bedroom house sat closest to the main ranch house, two minutes away on foot.

After getting his daughter fed and bathed, he held her while they read her favorite story, *Goodnight Moon*. That was the book she always wanted him to read to her. Eli said the words over and over, hoping she'd repeat them. She fell asleep in his arms and he put her down in her crib.

Except for her hair color and eyes, his little girl resembled Tessa more than she resembled him. Eli had put photos of his ex-wife around the room so Libby would grow up knowing her. He leaned over the bars to watch her for a minute. A week after her birth, the nightmare had begun. Since then he'd experienced every range of human emotion while he grieved the breakup of his marriage. It had meant Libby had lost her mother.

For so long he'd been living in denial about everything. But tonight his mother's question about his state of mind had brought him up short. *Don't you think you'd better figure it out?*

The first sight of Libby so happy in Brianna Frost's arms had acted like a catalyst, jolting him out of the limbo in which he'd been wallowing. The anger he'd felt because it should have been Tessa holding their daughter had made him see red.

Worse, throughout this pain-filled year, he'd been blind to women. But, out of the blue, he'd found himself eating up Brianna Frost with his eyes when he knew his brother had brought her to the gem shop. Something earthshaking had happened to him over the last three days.

He left the nursery and walked across the hall to his bedroom. Deciding to take his mother's advice, he sat on the side of the bed and called his in-laws in Thompson Falls. It was the same time there. Quarter to nine.

They'd remained friends through all the grief and had stayed in touch. Diane and Carl Marcroft had driven down to Stevensville dozens of times in the past year to see their granddaughter. The divorce had been the last thing they'd wanted, but naturally they had to give Tessa their full support.

"Eli—" Diane had picked up on the second ring.

"Is this a bad time to call?"

"No. Tessa's downstairs in the TV room with Carl."

His hand tightened on the phone. "How is she?"

After a silence, "There's no improvement. Dr. Rutherford in Missoula has her on a new medication, but he thinks her condition may be chronic."

So nothing had really changed. That was the news Eli had needed to hear tonight in order to see things clearly.

"How's our Libby?"

"Growing cuter every day. Before bed tonight I took a picture of her in that pink outfit you sent her for Christmas. It should be on your phone."

"Oh, wonderful. I'll check it in a few minutes. How's Alberta?"

"Mom's just been terrific, as always."

"She's amazing. We feel so guilty for not being able to help more, but—"

"Don't go there," he broke in. "Tessa needs you full-time."

"What about you? We admire you so much, Eli."

"Thank you. To be honest, things are looking up. I've been saving money and am now able to pay for someone to watch Libby during the day. Hopefully by next week Mom will be able to get on with her own life."

"That's very good news, for both your sakes. We'll try to help all we can."

"You already do. Give my best to Carl. I'll call you again soon."

"We love you, Eli."

"Same here. Good night."

Eli clicked off. Diane didn't know it, but this call had given him the push to let go of the past and move in a new direction. No more hoping for something that wasn't going to happen. He looked down at his wedding ring. *Time to take this off for good, Eli.*

After removing it, he walked over to the dresser, where he put it and the picture he'd displayed of Tessa in the bottom drawer. He stared at the white skin where the ring had been. In the last year he'd experienced his father's death and the death of his own marriage. He'd suffered enough pain to last a lifetime. No more.

Before getting ready for bed, he phoned Luis and arranged to take Wednesday off work to check out employment agencies in Stevensville and Missoula. By next week he hoped to find a satisfactory nanny who could come to his house every Monday morning and leave after he got home from work every Friday evening.

The woman would need to have a car and could make the spare bedroom her own. She'd share the guest bathroom with Libby. He would expect her to prepare meals and do some light housekeeping. Her age didn't matter to him as long as she was the right fit for Libby.

As he climbed under the covers, the vision of his daughter patting Brianna Frost's cheeks replayed itself in his mind. Disturbed that he couldn't turn it off, he punched the pillow to get comfortable before oblivion took over.

The Justin Boots supplier came on Wednesday afternoons. Brianna opened the rear door of the saddlery to let him in while her uncle was out front dealing with a customer looking for the right saddle.

"How are you, Antonio?"

"Things are good, senorita, but they'd be better if you'd agree to go out with me tonight."

The rodeo celebrity from twenty years ago was probably in his midforties. According to her uncle, he'd been married and divorced twice. He had a certain reputation with the ladies. Brianna imagined he had several children with different women.

He lifted the last box off the dolly and put it on the floor. "What's it going to take?"

His bold approach and persistence annoyed her. "I've got a boyfriend," she lied.

"But you're not married yet."

All women were fair game to him. "That's true, but I'd like to be." Brianna counted the delivered inventory and signed the paper on his clipboard. "Accepting a date with another man would spell the end of my dreams, so I'm not taking any chances. Do you have any other business? My uncle's out front if you want to talk to him." She handed him the clipboard.

"No other business, *chica*."

Good. She'd angered him. Without wasting another minute, she walked over to the back door and opened it. "See you next week."

He pushed the dolly out the door. "*Hasta la vista.*"

She shut the self-locking door and got busy unpacking boots and other items of clothing. Her uncle was whistling when she went out front with the delivered items. "I take it you made a sale."

"That's the third Dakota saddle this week. I'll have to place more orders."

"Your business is booming."

A smile broke out on his face. "We keep getting repeat customers. You're part of the reason."

"Nice one, Uncle Clark. You know I'm indebted to you."

"That works both ways. Your aunt can teach school without worrying about me running the saddlery alone. But any time you're ready to use that college degree to start a real career, you need only say the word."

"I know, but I'm very happy working here with you. To be honest, it makes me feel closer to Dad."

Her uncle squeezed her shoulder. "Same here."

She checked her watch. Ten after four. "Since today is your wedding anniversary, why don't you leave now so you can get ready to sweep Aunt Joanne off her feet. What's your plan?"

"I'm going to surprise her and pick her up at school. We'll drive to Missoula and grab some dinner and then go country dancing."

"Ooh, I'd love to see the look on her face when she sees that ring."

"I'm excited, too."

"Then go home. I'll close up and see you two in the morning at breakfast."

"Thanks, honey." He gave her a hug and left the store. She had two more customers before it was time to lock the front door and put the closed sign in the window. With that done, she started for the back room but paused when she heard a knock on the window.

Brianna whirled around and almost fainted when she saw Eli Clayton's tall form through the glass. "Will you let me in for a minute?" he called out to her.

She nodded but couldn't imagine why he was there. Her heartbeat pounded in her ears as she unlocked the door. He stepped inside, bringing the cold air with him.

"If you've come to see my uncle, he left early."

He removed his hat. "I came by to talk to you."

Brianna smoothed her palms against her denim-clad hips. "Why?"

"After the way I treated you, you've got every right to ask that question." Those piercing blue eyes stared into hers. He was building up to something. "I want to apologize for my rude behavior at the gem shop last Saturday. Don't bother to deny it," he said before she could make a sound.

"I won't."

"At least that's honest," he muttered. "Several reasons were driving me at the time, but nothing excuses the way I acted. If my daughter had been old enough to express an opinion, she would have asked, 'Why are you being so mean, Daddy?'"

Brianna couldn't help smiling. "I realized something was wrong, but you didn't have to come here to explain."

"I disagree. If we could start again, I'd like to make

up for it by taking you to dinner this evening. If you have other plans, then how about tomorrow night?"

Her second invitation of the day.

She couldn't say yes to him either, but for an entirely different reason.

Eli might be divorced, but he was still in love with his ex-wife. That made him off-limits to her. There was no way she dared accept an invitation to get to know him better.

"I accept your apology, but dinner isn't necessary."

"Then I did more damage than I thought," he said, his voice husky.

She shook her head. "Don't be silly." She took the few steps needed to open the front door so he would leave. "My aunt and uncle said your father was a true gentleman. Your visit here to make things right means it runs in your family. Consider that achieving your objective and have a lovely evening with your daughter, Eli."

He shoved the cowboy hat on his head at an angle and moved toward her. Beneath the brim, his shadowed gaze studied her features. "We'll meet again soon. Good night, Brianna."

"Good night."

After locking the door, she rushed through the store to the back room, where she turned off all the lights except for the ones in the display windows. Her legs were still trembling when she got into her truck and headed home. On the way she stopped at a drive-through for some pizza and a soda.

Once she got back, she didn't go inside the house right away. Instead she ate in the truck and called her brother, hoping he was available to talk. Carol answered and told her he was out in one of the sheds, but she'd have him call her ASAP.

No sooner did Brianna go inside the house than her phone rang. Seeing the caller ID, she hurried into the study and sat down on the couch. "Doug?"

"Hi, Brianna. You kept your promise to call me this week. What's up?"

She loved her brother so much. "Can you talk?"

"That's what we're doing, aren't we?"

"You know what I mean."

"I have all the time in the world for you. Carol's fixing dinner. Go ahead and tell me what's on your mind."

Brianna bit her lip. "I may have made a mistake tonight, and now I don't know what to do."

"Do I dare assume this has to do with a man?"

Clever Doug. His instincts were razor-sharp. "Yes."

"I take it he's a good one."

"Yes, I know he is. He has the most adorable fourteen-month-old daughter."

"Is he single? A widower? Divorced? Wait—he's not married, is he?"

"Doug—"

He chuckled. "You've got to give me more than a couple of yesses."

"I'm sorry. Let me ask you a hypothetical question. If you lost Carol—Heaven forbid if you did—how long do you think you'd stay in love with her?"

"I would always love her, but I don't think you can stay 'in love' forever because life has a way of evolving. I take it you've met a widower."

She breathed in deeply. "No. His ex-wife is alive, but he still wears his wedding ring."

"Yeah?" This after a brief silence. "That's a tricky

one." It was not the response she'd been hoping for. "What mistake have you made, aside from falling for him?"

"I haven't fallen for him!"

"Then why ask me for advice?"

Brianna jumped up from the couch. "I barely know him, but I—I find him very attractive," she stammered. "That's all."

"Don't forget the adorable daughter."

That wasn't possible. Libby had his eyes.

"I don't want to be attracted to him."

Hearty laughter poured out of him. "Poor Brianna. After all those years of tying guys up in knots without compunction, you've found one who has turned the tables on you. What do you know..."

"Please don't make me feel worse."

"Now that I know a little more about the situation, how about telling me the nature of your second mistake?"

There was no getting around this with Doug, not when she'd phoned him. "He came to the saddlery a little while ago to apologize to me for something and asked me out to dinner. I told him I forgave him but that dinner wasn't necessary. Then I opened the door so he'd leave."

"And *did* he?"

"Yes."

"Good for him."

She winced.

"Why don't you tell me what happened for him to come to the store wanting to tell you he was sorry?"

"It's complicated."

"With you it usually is. Go on."

She told him everything that had gone on since the night Eli had been so rude at the gem shop. Quiet reigned after she'd finished explaining. "Doug?"

"You're frightened. Can't say I blame you, but he could still be wearing his wedding ring for a variety of reasons. At this early stage there's only one question you have to ask yourself. Is he so important to you that you won't be able to eat or sleep until you talk to him again and find out what's going on with him? In a few days you'll know if you can't get him off your mind."

"I'm afraid I already know." Her brother was right. "Thanks for listening to me."

"Anytime. Call me soon, okay?"

"I promise."

"Don't make promises you can't keep."

She chuckled. "Love you."

"Love you, too."

She hung up, hugging her arms to her chest. Yes, she was afraid. Eli had loved another woman, married her, had a baby with her. How did you compete with those memories? Did Brianna even want to try if it turned out he was interested in her?

Haunted by too many unanswerable questions, she went to her room and watched TV. Why did she have to meet a man who'd been married and had a past? A man who was still living in that past. A man with a darling little girl, who would remind him of his ex-wife every minute of their lives.

Brianna had no idea how long she stayed awake, tormented. It was a miracle that she finally slept. But when she awakened, she discovered her pillow drenched in tears.

Chapter 3

Eli cut a banana into pieces and put them on the tray of Libby's high chair. He ate one and then she ate one. Everything was a game with her.

"Mom? Are you sure you don't mind the applicants coming here this morning? I want to get your opinion before I take them up to my house." He'd narrowed the list down to three women. They'd be arriving in hourly intervals. The first one would be there in a few minutes.

"It's important we all meet, honey, and that includes Solana." The two of them sat at the kitchen table of the ranch house, enjoying coffee with their pancakes. Wymon had already left to meet up with Luis and the stockmen.

With Toly on the rodeo circuit and Roce in Missoula, Wymon needed Eli's help, but he'd taken this Wednesday morning off to conduct the nanny interviews. Life was about to change around here.

His mother eyed him with concern. "What's wrong?"

"Maybe none of them will be right and Libby won't like any of them."

"If things don't work out today, we can always interview more applicants." She eyed him over the rim of her coffee cup. "I didn't realize you'd removed your wedding ring. When did that happen?"

"Last week, after you advised me to get my act together. I phoned Tessa's family and had a talk with Diane. Nothing's changed with Tessa. The psychiatrist believes she might have chronic depression. I'd hoped in vain that she'd get better and want to come home." He shook his head. "It isn't going to happen, so I took the ring off and started looking for a nanny."

"You're very courageous. I'm proud of you, son."

"And I'm more grateful to you than you'll ever know for helping Libby and me through this last year."

He didn't hear his mother's response because Solana came into the kitchen. "Your first appointment has arrived. I showed her into the living room."

"Thanks, Solana." Eli got up from the chair. "Be right back." He tousled Libby's hair and headed for the other part of the house with little expectation that this could actually work.

By noon he'd found Sarah Giles, a cute young woman with an appealing personality whom everyone agreed would be great. Most important of all, Libby didn't cry when she picked her up and played with her.

She was twenty-eight and was living in Missoula with her grandparents while her husband was deployed with the army for the next fifteen months. They were saving their money and hoped to buy a house after his tour of duty was over.

Sarah had been trained as a cook and had worked as a sous-chef until recently. Cooking was her passion, but the restaurant had closed and she needed a job.

Eli decided that fifteen months with a nanny who could cook and keep his daughter happy sounded perfect. Sarah was ready to move in and would start work the next morning.

He was so relieved that he no longer had to rely on his mother for everything that he raced his horse Domino to the pasture. After telling Wymon his news, he did the job of three stockmen. They looked at him as if he'd lost his mind.

In a way, he had. Freed from a great source of worry for the first time in a year, he could concentrate on a plan to approach Brianna Frost again.

He'd never been shown the door before and was still smarting from the experience. In order to break through the barrier he'd caused her to erect, he needed backup. If anyone knew the way to Brianna's heart, Libby did.

When Saturday came around, he'd load his daughter in the truck just before closing time at the saddlery. On the pretext of wanting to buy her a child's cowboy hat, he'd ask Brianna for help. If he knew his little girl, she'd love the attention and wouldn't want to leave the shop. She might even start to cry, which would be a plus.

Eli would take it from there and suggest the three of them go for a bite to eat at a place where he could take Libby. A new sense of excitement filled him on his way back to the barn at dark. Tomorrow would be a new day and he had a good feeling about Sarah.

The last time Eli could remember looking forward to the future had been the night of Libby's birth. He'd felt such wonder as he held her in his arms. They'd started their family. At the time he couldn't have comprehended that they wouldn't live out a rich, full life together with more children.

The onset of Tessa's depression followed a week later and never went away. Eli had never suffered from chemical depression. But to watch it take hold of his wife and change her into someone he didn't know had devastated him. He'd been helpless to alleviate it or bring her comfort. She didn't want to hold Libby, let alone take care of her.

His whole family had pitched in to help and had been doing it ever since. Though Tessa's parents tried to do it long-distance, it was difficult.

On the night Tessa begged to go home, she didn't say, "I need to go back to my parents in Thompson Falls for a while." She'd made it clear she wanted to go *home*. That deliberate choice of words cut him to the quick and spelled the end of his dreams.

At the lowest point of his life, Eli packed up her things. After asking his mother to watch the baby, he drove Tessa back to her parents' house. The phone call asking for a divorce soon followed. What he'd feared most had come to pass, but the fact that it came as another shock proved to him he'd been living in denial.

He'd still been in denial until the day he'd seen Libby so happy in Brianna Frost's arms and realized he couldn't go on as he had been any longer. His mother's warning had acted as the catalyst for things to change, and he couldn't be more glad of the fact.

Brianna met Lindsay at the entrance to the Italian restaurant. "I'm glad you could meet me here for dinner.

Ken works the night shift in the ER on Saturdays and I didn't want to go home to an empty house after work."

"I hear you. My aunt and uncle have gone to their monthly Cattlemen's Association dinner. This was a great idea."

They went inside. Naturally the restaurant was crowded, being as it was a weekend night. The hostess showed them a table and handed them menus. Brianna opened hers. "So what do you think you're in the mood for?"

Her friend looked over her own menu. "I think I'll order the alfredo with mushrooms."

"Mmm, that sounds good, but so does the chicken Tuscany."

"Let's get both and share. Now that I'm over my morning sickness, I eat like a horse."

Brianna chuckled. "Perfect."

They gave the waitress their order. "That book on Elon Musk you were asking about came in. I'll save you a copy if you want."

"I'll come by Monday on my lunch hour to buy it."

"Why don't you just buy a Kindle?"

"I could, but I like a book in my hands, you know?"

"I do, too."

They were still talking books when the waitress brought their meal. Lindsay's eyes lit up. "Wow, this looks good."

"It does. I'm starving."

Halfway through their meal Lindsay leaned forward. "Don't make it too obvious, but you've got to get a look at this cowboy who just walked in carrying an adorable little girl wearing a cowgirl hat," she whispered. "If I weren't married…"

Brianna tried to turn her head inconspicuously and almost slid off her chair. Catching her breath, she faced her friend once more. "Even if you were single, you wouldn't want to get involved with him."

Lindsay blinked. "You know him?"

"I've met him several times. His name is Eli. He's one of the Clayton brothers."

Her friend sat back in surprise. "You're talking *Toly* Clayton's brother?"

"That's right."

"Wow."

"My uncle told me Eli's wife divorced him. But he still wears his wedding ring."

"He probably does that to keep all the women away. Otherwise there'd be a line a mile long."

A piece of chicken lodged in Brianna's throat. She had to take a drink of water to clear it. "I was thinking he can't take it off because he's still so much in love with her."

Lindsay went quiet. Brianna found herself the object of her friend's gaze. "What aren't you telling me?"

"It doesn't matter."

"I think it does," Lindsay said right back. "You're interested in him."

"Well, like you, I find him attractive."

"And?"

She averted her eyes. "And nothing."

"Has he asked you out?"

By now Brianna was squirming. "Yes, but I turned him down."

"Brianna—why?"

"I told you."

Lindsay kept at her. "Is it because he has a daughter?"

"No! She's wonderful."

"So you've met her, too." Her friend smiled. "If you want my advice, which I know you don't, I would tell him yes if you get another chance."

"That's not going to happen."

"Don't be so sure. He's walking this way."

What? Her heart thundered in her chest.

"Brianna?"

She looked up and her gaze collided with Eli's. At the same moment his daughter tried to get to her. Brianna pushed her chair back. "Hi, Libby. Have you come out to dinner with your daddy?"

By now the little girl was twisting to escape Eli's arms. Brianna had no choice but to reach for her. His little girl wrapped her arms around Brianna's neck, warming her heart.

Eli's blue eyes glittered with amusement. "When we came in for dinner, she spotted you out of all these people. Your hair is unmistakable. I gave up any hope of peace until we came over to say hi first."

"Why don't you join us?" Lindsay spoke up with a knowing smile Brianna had already deciphered. "We have two more chairs."

Brianna moaned inwardly.

"I don't want to intrude."

"It's no intrusion, is it, Brianna?"

"No, of course not. Please sit down."

"I'm Lindsay Turner, Brianna's friend," Lindsay said as he pulled out a chair. "And you are…"

"Eli Clayton."

"Well, Mr. Clayton, I have to say that's the cutest little girl I ever saw in my life, especially in that cowgirl hat. I'm expecting in four months and can't wait to start dressing my daughter."

"Congratulations. I'm happy for you. We bought this hat at the saddlery before coming here. She went right to the one she wanted and put it on her head. That was it."

He'd come by the store? Had her uncle told him she'd be at the restaurant?

"It's my favorite one," Brianna admitted. The white felt with the pink trim and star looked as if it had been designed for his daughter.

"But it needs to come off while we eat, or you won't be able to finish your dinner." Brianna watched as Eli leaned over and undid the tie before lifting it off his daughter's head.

His ring.

It was gone!

Libby didn't seem to mind being relieved of her hat, but Brianna sat there in shock to see the white skin where the band had been. From Brianna's lap the little brown-haired princess wanted to touch everything and reached for Brianna's roll. She darted Eli a glance. "Is it all right?"

"If it is with you. She eats everything. I'll order you another one with her mac and cheese." He signaled the waitress to come over and asked for a high chair.

While Brianna fed Libby a spoonful of linguine from her plate, Eli and Lindsay discussed Toly's recent wins. Soon Eli's order arrived, but, to Brianna's consternation, Lindsay had finished her meal and stood up.

She smiled at Brianna. "If you'll excuse me, I'm going to take what I didn't finish to my husband while it's still kind of warm. I promised him." Brianna had feared this would happen. "Thanks for having dinner with me. I'll see you on Monday at noon."

"I'll be there."

Eli got to his feet. "It was nice to meet you."

"I'm so glad to have met you and your daughter, Mr. Clayton. Wait till I tell my husband that I had dinner with Toly Clayton's brother. We're both great fans."

"I'll tell him," Eli said and smiled.

After she walked away, Eli plucked his daughter from Brianna's lap and put her in the high chair. He set it right next to Brianna so Libby wouldn't complain and started feeding her macaroni while he ate his spaghetti and meat balls.

He eyed her. "Would you believe I had intended to ask you to have dinner with me and Libby tonight at this same restaurant? I was disappointed you'd left the saddlery early so I didn't get the chance to ask. Seeing you here was fortunate for us, but I didn't mean to break up your plans for the evening."

She sat back in the chair. "Please don't worry about it. Lindsay works at the bookstore in the mall and we eat lunch together a lot. She was just anxious to take her husband, Kenneth, a treat. He's a doctor doing his internship in emergency medicine at the hospital and has been working a lot of nights lately."

"Lucky man to have such a devoted wife."

Brianna nodded. "They're a great couple."

"A baby will change their lives," Eli said. A wealth of emotion lay behind his words. "Libby sure has changed mine."

"I can only imagine."

"As you've learned, my mother has been watching her since the divorce. But a few days ago I hired a nanny so I can get on with my ranching duties. She seems to be working out well." He drank part of his coffee. "Speaking of the ranch, did your aunt like the ring you purchased from the gem shop?"

"She loves it. My uncle is definitely in her good books after that gift."

A smile broke the corner of his mouth. "Maybe I should give you a sapphire so I can get in yours."

Heat filled her cheeks. "I'm sorry if I gave you the wrong impression."

"You had every right to turn me down, but I still have a problem because I would like to get to know you better. Are you dating someone?"

She could lie about it, but she didn't want to because he was a good man who deserved the truth. "Not right now."

"So it *was* my bad manners that ruined my chances." *If he only knew the truth...*

"Since my nanny is willing to do some babysitting at night if I want to go out, I'm going to try this once more. Will you have dinner with me next Tuesday? If the answer is no, then I'll never bother you again."

The finality of that remark drove her to a quick response. She had to take that chance, even though it scared the living daylights out of her. "Sure," she said. "I'll have dinner with you next Tuesday."

A look of satisfaction entered his eyes. "Good. I'll pick you up at your uncle's house. I thought we'd go to Chez Maurice, the new French restaurant. Shall we say seven o'clock?"

"That will give me time to leave work and get ready." Brianna hadn't been to that restaurant yet, but she'd heard it was pretty fancy. On that note, she reached for her purse and got up from the table. When he made a motion to stand, she said, "Please, Eli, stay where you are so it won't upset your daughter. I'm just going to slip away. Enjoy your dinner and I'll see you on Tuesday."

Before Libby realized what was happening, Brianna hurried over to the counter to pay her bill and left the restaurant for home. She felt shaky—and more excited than the situation warranted. Libby had provided a buffer tonight, but the next time she saw him, he'd be without her. The thought made her nervous.

Don't forget, Brianna. Just because he's removed his wedding ring doesn't mean his heart has stopped longing for the woman he married.

A huge winter storm front moved in Monday night. On Tuesday Eli and Wymon spent the day with the stockmen, rounding up strays and making certain the cattle had enough food. They talked about the lawsuit against the Bureau of Land Management that their father had taken out while he was still alive because they'd been charged taxes for the acid mine drainage coming out of their mine.

They had little time left to clean up before a larger tax would be levied against them. A good chunk of their ranch money was tied up because of it, something that worried the whole family. Eli didn't get back to the house until ten after six and had to rush to get ready for his evening with Brianna.

Libby didn't like being denied the usual time he spent with her. He didn't like it either and could hear her fussing as he walked out the door. But Sarah would cheer her up. She had a great way of handling his daughter.

He left the house, knowing Libby was in good hands, and headed for the Frost home.

It was hard to believe he was going on his first date with a woman in years. He'd thought he'd put all that behind him when he'd married Tessa. Some of the divorced guys he knew said that dating again was just like riding a bike. Once you got on, it all came back to you. The hell it did. He was nervous, an emotion he'd never experienced around women in his life.

When he pulled into the shoveled driveway, Clark Frost was just putting his snowblower away in the garage. The two men greeted each other before Eli went to the front door and rang the bell. A German shorthair squeezed into the opening first.

Brianna looked like a vision in a belted, camel-hair wool coat that ended above the knee. In the hall light her collar-length blond hair took on an ethereal quality. The creamy pink lipstick drew his attention to round, full lips.

"You made it here." She sounded slightly breathless.

"I haven't yet met a storm I couldn't handle."

She laughed. "Good night, Taffy," she said, patting the dog's head. "See you later." The shorthair's low moan sounded as she closed the door.

Eli cupped her elbow and walked her to his truck. The small, gold side buckles on her black high-heeled ankle boots completed her classy outfit. He couldn't take his eyes off her. A flowery fragrance wafted past him as he helped her into the cab, nearly undoing him.

Most of the streets had been plowed. They drove across town to Chez Maurice and discussed what their day had been like. She cast him a sideward glance. "How did Libby handle you leaving her?"

"She made sounds like your dog."

"It's no fun being left behind."

"You should have heard her after you walked out of the restaurant Saturday night. I'm convinced people thought I was a child beater. Any thought of a fun evening with my daughter went up in flames."

"I'm sure you're exaggerating."

"Maybe a little, but clearly she didn't want you to leave. Luckily, the nanny's working out well, so my mother can lead her own life again."

"Tell me about your nanny."

"Sarah Giles is married," he started by saying. He filled her in on the woman's background. "She's good with Libby. When her husband gets back from his deployment I'll have to find another nanny, but for now I'm really happy."

"If Libby likes her, that's all that really matters."

He pulled into the plowed parking lot and walked her inside. The maître d' led them to a candlelit table for two by the fireplace. After the freezing cold outside, he felt Brianna breathe in its warmth with pleasure.

The simple act of removing her coat caught him off guard. He wanted to pull her against him and knew he was already in trouble. There was nothing like firelight. The glow outlined her feminine figure dressed in a simple knee-length black dress with cap sleeves.

They sat across from each other. "I took the liberty of ordering our dinner ahead of time." He poured the white wine brought to their table and lifted his glass. "To you, Brianna. I haven't been on a date with another woman in almost three years."

She took a sip. "How did you meet your wife? I hope you don't mind my asking."

"Not at all. We met at college in Missoula."

"Was it love at first sight?"

"No. We grew on each other after studying together. Pretty soon we were spending so much time together that we decided to get married. Her breakdown after the baby made me realize we don't always know everything about each other, even if we think we do."

"I'm sorry, Eli."

"It's life." He took a swallow. "Now it's your turn to reveal the unadorned truth about yourself."

Her features sobered. "Unadorned, huh? Hmm. Well, I was proposed to twice, but I didn't get married because I never met the right man for me." She finished her wine and put the glass down.

"How old are you?"

"I'll be twenty-four on February 14."

"A *Valentine* baby." Amazing.

"It's the best birthday on earth. Everyone remembers it and I'm given so much chocolate I have to go on a diet for a month."

He loved it. "I've never known anyone born on that day before."

"I know of three: Jimmy Hoffa, Jack Benny and Carl Bernstein."

He chuckled. Her personality was growing on him like mad.

"How old are you, Eli?"

"I'll be twenty-seven on the Fourth of July."

"You're kidding!"

"Nope! Same birthday as Calvin Coolidge."

A smile lit up her lovely face. "That has to be the birthday of all birthdays."

He grinned. "It probably comes close to yours."

Brianna laughed gently before the waiter brought their chateaubriand to the table. Once he had left, they were alone once more and began to eat. "This is delicious, Eli. To get good French food back home, we used to drive to the Napa Valley, but it was a hundred miles away."

"Who is 'we'?"

"My parents and brother. Now that my parents are gone, he and his wife live in our family home and run the fruit farm."

He studied her features. "I'm sure you miss them."

She nodded. "But they're newlyweds and deserve some time to themselves."

The answer to his next question was of vital importance to him. "How long are you going to stay with your aunt and uncle?"

"I'm not sure. I graduated from college with a business degree right before my parents were killed. My aunt and uncle saved my life by asking me to come and live with them for a while. One of these days I'll get my act together and do something with my degree. But to tell you the truth, I like my job at the saddlery. Uncle Clark is so much like my dad that it helps lessen the pain just being around him."

"I can relate. My brothers are made up of parts of my father. Family means everything." While they talked about their families, the waiter brought them their dessert.

As soon as she saw the chocolate mousse, she flashed him a wide, natural smile that lit up his universe. "How did you know I love chocolate?"

"The truth is I guessed. Who doesn't love chocolate?"

Between the wine and the warmth of the fire, he felt pleasantly relaxed for the first time in ages. He could tell she'd been affected, too. Her eyelids fluttered and there was a pretty flush on her cheeks. If they were alone at his house, he wouldn't let her leave. How unfortunate that all good things had to come to an end and he would have to take her home soon.

"Eli Clayton—it *is* you!" declared a male voice from the past, snapping him out of his endorphin-induced haze.

Chapter 4

Eli turned his head. "Don—" He got to his feet. "How are you?" They shook hands. "It's been a long time."

"You can say that again."

"Haven't you been working in Missoula all this time?"

"That's over since I've just been promoted to bank manager here."

"Congratulations."

"Thanks. You're still ranching, I presume?"

"Always," Eli muttered. He was acutely aware of the way Don kept staring at Brianna. His old nemesis was still single and it showed.

"I heard Tessa divorced you and went back to Thompson Falls." Don never did understand boundaries or show sensitivity. "I take it the baby is with her?"

"No. Libby lives with me."

Don rocked on his heels. "I didn't realize. Who's this heavenly creature?" he asked, speaking directly to Brianna.

"A friend."

"You're not on the rodeo circuit anymore, yet you still manage to find the hotties, eh?"

Eli bristled.

"Aren't you going to introduce us?"

"Sure." He darted a glance at her. "Brianna Frost, meet Don Shapiro. He's the new manager of the Bitterroot-Sapphire Bank Branch here in Stevensville."

She nodded. "How do you do?"

"It's my pleasure. Frost? That name is familiar, but you're not from Stevensville or I would have remembered you. I was born here and went all through school with the Clayton boys."

"I see. I'm from Marysville, California. I'm just living with my aunt and uncle for a while."

"Now I remember. Clark Frost. He does business at the bank and owns the saddlery. Is he your uncle?"

"Yes. I work at the saddlery."

"Well, what do you know. I'll have to drop by."

Eli had taken all he could and put some bills on the table. "If you'll excuse us, Don, we were on the verge of leaving. Ready, Brianna?" He walked around and held her coat whether she wanted to leave or not. She stood up so he could help her put it on.

"I was going to ask you to join me and my friends at our table."

"Another time maybe. Thanks anyway. I imagine I'll see you again." *But not if I can help it.*

They said good-bye and he ushered Brianna out of the restaurant into the frigid night air. After the contentment he'd felt being with her, the unwelcome intrusion had turned their dinner into something else, leaving a bitter taste in his mouth. In the foulest of moods, he drove them back to her family's home.

"I take it he wasn't a close friend."

His hand tightened on the steering wheel. "What an irony. Tonight I wanted to explain the reasons why I was so rude when we first met. Now I find myself needing to apologize again. I'm afraid I'm not fit company, Brianna. Your instincts were right the first time." He pulled into the driveway but kept the engine running so they'd stay warm.

"If it will make you feel any better, he reminded me of Antonio Perez, the salesman who comes around the saddlery every once in a while and annoys the heck out of me. I was glad we left when we did. Somehow I can't see him as the manager of a bank. The poor tellers. Was the transfer a demotion, do you think?"

Eli threw his head back and laughed. "He'd be crushed to hear you say that. The dude couldn't take his eyes off you, but I suspect that happens to you on a regular basis."

"Of course it doesn't. If I may be so bold, what is the history between you two?"

"He comes from a prominent local ranching family, but he couldn't cut it on the rodeo circuit."

"Ah—" she exclaimed. "According to Uncle Clark, the Clayton boys are rodeo legends in Montana. He told me you were a champion bull rider like your dad."

"I was average. Toly's the best bull rider of all of us."

"Well, if Mr. Shapiro wanted to compete and couldn't make the grade, then that had to be tough on him. But mentioning your wife and daughter in front of me was rude. I thought you handled the situation well. If I'd been you, I would probably have knocked his block off."

The woman sitting next to him had a way about her that calmed the beast in him. "Thanks for your understanding."

"Thank *you* for a lovely evening and delicious dinner. What I'm waiting for is the explanation you promised me about your feelings the first time we met."

Eli sucked in his breath. "You mean now? In the truck?"

"Why not. It's cozy and warm in here and no one will bother us."

He grinned. "I wouldn't count on that. If your uncle thinks I've been here long enough, I wager he'll make his presence known."

Her chuckle made its way inside him. "I can take care of him," she said, and he had no doubt of it. "Seriously, Eli, what happened? I didn't know Libby belonged to you when you first walked in, and I couldn't understand why you were upset simply because I was holding her for your mother."

"The night I entered the gem shop and saw Libby so happy in another woman's arms, it killed me that it wasn't Tessa holding her."

"Oh. That would have been painful."

"It was. At first I was in denial about the seriousness of Tessa's postpartum depression. We'd been so excited about the baby coming and had outfitted the nursery, but a week after the delivery she turned into a completely different person. Those dark days ran into a month. She lost interest in the baby, in me. That never changed."

"Oh, Eli. I'm so sorry."

"I was sorry, too, but mostly for our daughter, who

wasn't able to bond with her mother. The psychiatrist said her depression was severe and she might never want to be with the baby. I was horrified. It was up to me, Mom and Solana to take care of Libby.

"Soon after, Tessa told me she wanted to go home to her parents. I had no choice but to drive her to Thompson Falls. Two weeks later I got a phone call from her asking for a divorce. I fought it in my heart."

"Of course," Brianna whispered. "I can't even imagine."

"I wanted us to be a family. Libby needed her, but all the wanting in the world didn't change anything. Her parents urged me to agree to it. They hoped it might help her to calm down. The psychiatrist thought it was for the best, too.

"So I signed the papers. She gave up all parental rights to Libby."

"Eli? Does it mean that if she got better and wanted to be a mother, she couldn't?"

"Legally, yes, but it's just a piece of paper. I'd give anything if she wanted to see Libby, and I would do anything to make it happen. Every child deserves his or her own mother."

"Who could blame you for wanting that?" A troubled sigh escaped her lips.

"I was a mental wreck that night at the gem shop. I'd stopped at the ranch house earlier. Solana told me my brother had brought a woman with him from Missoula and they'd gone up to the gem shop. There you were with Roce. My mind jumped to the wrong conclusion that you were his girlfriend."

"It's all making sense," she murmured.

"What I'm about to tell you will convince you to avoid me at all costs."

"Why don't you let me be the judge of that?"

"This last year I've been functioning in a dark cloud of pain and anger. When I saw you with Libby, several things struck me at once. You were beautiful and I found myself attracted to you, even though Roce had met you first. I was so disgusted with myself over my thoughts that I couldn't get out of the shop fast enough." He ran a hand over his face. "Now that you know the truth, I'll walk you to the house."

"Wait—" she said as he reached for the door handle.

"There isn't any more, Brianna."

"You've had your turn. Now I need time to explain my behavior to you."

"What do you mean?"

"When you apologized to me at the store and asked me to go to dinner, I turned you down. But it wasn't because I couldn't forgive your rudeness."

"Then I don't know what you're getting at."

"A man who asks out a single woman while still wearing his wedding ring sends her one clear message—he doesn't honor his marriage." When Eli started to say something, she put up her hands to stop him. "I know. At the time you'd wanted to apologize to me in the nicest way possible, but I couldn't risk it."

"I don't understand."

She lowered her head. "I'd had thoughts, too. Thoughts that disgusted me."

Intrigued, he leaned closer. "Why?"

She sighed. "You've been so honest that I have to do the same. The truth is that first time I saw you at the gem shop I felt an instant attraction to you, too, but you were a married man. There was a ring on your finger. At the time I didn't know you were divorced."

What? His heart started to thud.

"To get involved with a married man goes against my principles and I got angry because I hadn't been able to control my emotions. I asked myself why I didn't feel that way about Roce, who didn't wear a wedding band on *his* finger and who couldn't have been kinder to me."

Good grief. They'd both been so wrong about everything. "Did he ask you out?"

"No. But he said the next time he came through Stevensville, he'd drop by the saddlery and we'd go out for a meal."

Roce had been interested. Any red-blooded man would be.

"Before you jump to any more conclusions, I can tell you now that he was only being nice to me. If he'd been serious, he would have asked for my phone number and made a definite date."

Eli sat back. "Do you still feel it's a risk to go out with me?"

"Yes. After what you've admitted to me tonight, I know it is."

He ground his teeth in reaction. "What exactly did I say?"

"I heard the intensity of your emotion when you said you'd give anything if your ex-wife wanted to see Libby. You said you'd do anything to make it happen. If ever a man sounded like he was still in love with his wife, you do."

"Brianna—"

"Let me finish. No woman would want to compete with the woman who holds your heart. Your Tessa might improve enough to want you and your daughter back. Anything is possible in this world. Miracles do happen. I will pray for you and Libby that it does."

She unexpectedly opened the door. "I loved this evening and the time spent so we could be honest with each other. One thing I've learned in the short time we've had together—you're a great father. I had a great one, too. Libby is luckier than she'll ever know. Don't give up on winning your wife back. The chemistry in the brain can change. Good-bye, Eli Clayton. You're the best."

He sat there in shock as she got out of the truck and hurried to the front door. When she let herself inside and turned off the porch light, he felt pain rip him apart as if a bull had stomped on his heart until it was a pulpy mess. Her admission that she'd been attracted to him, too, was negated when in the next breath she'd accused him of still being in love with Tessa.

Eli backed out of the driveway and headed home while the question over his feelings for his ex-wife forced him to dig deep in his soul. He would always love Tessa and the memory of her. But they hadn't lived as man and wife since the baby came. The flame that had kept their love alive had been smothered by illness.

Had it gone out completely? He would have to be with Tessa again to feel if there was any love coming from her before he could answer that question.

Once inside the house he walked to Libby's room and stood over her crib for a long time. His precious daughter lay flat on her back. Her favorite white polar bear was jammed against the top of her head. In her pink-and-white sleeper pajamas, she looked like a little angel with tangled brown curls who'd just popped out of Heaven.

His thoughts returned to Brianna and he lowered his forehead to the crib railing.

Brianna had said good-bye to him tonight and she'd meant it. He had no choice but to give her the space she wanted. But he didn't have to sit around and wonder what his heart was telling him about Tessa. Despite their divorce, he needed to see her a final time. It was vital he look in her eyes and talk about their daughter. Eli had stayed away from her more than long enough.

Saturday morning Eli stopped by the ranch house with Libby. "Mom?"

"Hi, honey. I'm in the kitchen." He walked through, carrying his daughter in his arms. "Oh, what a wonderful surprise!" She reached out to hug her. "What brings you here? I hope you're going to stay a while. I've missed you."

"We've missed you, too, but today we have plans. I'm going to be gone most of the day and wanted you to know why in case you tried to find me for some reason."

His mother gave him the discerning eye. "This sounds serious."

"It is. I'm leaving for Thompson Falls. I know Tessa and I are divorced, but I feel it's necessary that she sees us again. Perhaps nothing will ever change with her, but I'm giving it one last chance."

His mother waited a beat before she said, "You haven't put your ring back on."

"No. I want *that* plus the sight of Libby in my arms to be a surprise, along with my unexpected visit. I'm not the tormented, crushed man she remembers divorcing. Since she wouldn't have anything to do with Libby after being home a week, this will be my own version of shock therapy to find out if seeing her again changes anything. I owe it to our daughter to make this last attempt."

"And to you," his mother added. "Her parents don't know you're coming?"

He shook his head. That would take away the element of surprise, the one thing he was counting on.

She put a hand on his arm. "Tessa's a very lucky woman to have had such an honorable husband. Drive safely. Whatever happens, remember that you're doing a very unselfish thing today. When your daughter is older, she will bless you for trying."

Her comment let him know his mother didn't place a lot of faith in anything changing, but she still supported him. Eli's throat swelled with emotion. "Thanks, Mom. I love you."

He gave her a kiss and left the house for the truck. His little cherub sat in the back, strapped in her car seat. She had no clue where they were going and didn't care while she played with one of her doughnut toys.

Thompson Falls was located in a beautiful valley in northwest Montana along the Clark Fork River, two and a half hours from the ranch. He and Tessa had done a lot of fishing there with her parents.

The sun peeked in and out of the cloud cover all the way. Snow blanketed the familiar landscape, but he didn't feel the pain he'd felt the last time he'd made this journey without the baby.

His world was different now. He had a daughter who was growing up fast and needed all his love. There was also a blonde woman he wasn't ready to walk away from at this early stage, not by a long shot. Brianna's words continued to resound in his head. *Don't give up on winning your wife back.* It was good advice, if not for him, for Libby. But this would be his last attempt.

Eli sat back and turned on the radio to a soft rock station. This was the longest trip he'd taken with Libby to date. Every so often, he stopped to change her diaper and give her snacks. He noticed she'd been sneezing. Maybe it was a winter allergy of some kind, but he didn't think a great deal about it.

In St. Regis he stopped for gas and bought a couple of Snickers bars for himself. Then, at ten after eleven, he pulled into the Marcrofts' driveway.

It was a Saturday, and Eli imagined Tessa's family would likely be at home with her. Their cars were probably in the garage. He got out and reached for his daughter, whom he'd dressed in the pink outfit they'd sent.

"This is it, sweetie. You're going to see your mother for the first time since you were a tiny newborn." Her answer was another sneeze.

"Hey, what's going on with you?" He kissed her cheeks and then approached the front door and rang the bell. After a minute it opened.

Tessa stood in the entrance, looking like a person who'd seen a ghost.

"Eli—" she gasped. "My parents aren't here."

Maybe that was just as well. She clung to the door. He had the feeling that she was ready to close it on him.

"Naturally, I would enjoy seeing them, but Libby and I came to visit you."

The last time they'd been together was when he'd driven Tessa to her parents' house for good. Since then she seemed to have lost about five pounds. He could tell because her jeans were loose on her. Otherwise she was the same woman who'd given birth to their little girl, who was a replica of her with that brown hair and heart-shaped face.

Tessa's features froze. "If you're here to tell me you want me back—"

Even though Tessa had spoken in a low voice, Libby hid her face in his neck like she did when confronted by a stranger. It brought out his protective instincts and he held her closer.

"Not at all," he interjected quietly. "I came to grips with our divorce quite a while ago." She couldn't help but see he'd removed his wedding ring.

"Then I wish you'd leave."

Eli saw no sign in her brown eyes that she'd missed him or thought about him. Was it the medication, or her depression, or both that produced that vacant stare?

He supposed he'd never know. A wealth of memories bombarded him, but oddly enough the only emotion he felt was one of sorrow for his daughter, who would never know her mother.

"I realize this has come as a complete surprise. I didn't let your parents know my plans, either, but I thought you might want to see Libby just this once."

He saw her flinch, whether in fear, regret, anger, resentment, he couldn't tell.

"Now that you've accomplished your goal, I'm going to shut the door."

"Before you do that, I just want to be sure you haven't changed your mind about giving up your rights to her. Though you signed them away, I would never keep her from you. Wouldn't you like to hold Libby for a moment?"

Eli waited for her to answer, hoping that her hesitation meant she was considering it.

She acted nervous. "I can't believe you had the nerve to come here like this unannounced and uninvited." Her voice faltered.

Eli took a deep breath. "It will never happen again. Good-bye, Tessa."

Turning on his heel, he walked toward the truck with his daughter's head bobbing against his shoulder. After strapping Libby in her car seat, he got behind the wheel and backed out of the driveway just as Tessa's parents were pulling in.

They got out of their car and hurried toward him. "Eli?" Carl spoke first while Diane opened the back door to give Libby a hug. His little girl sneezed again. "Bless you, darling. We didn't know you were coming."

"I meant it to be a surprise. I needed to be certain that, after seeing Libby this time, Tessa still felt the same about signing away her rights. She didn't show any interest at all."

Tessa's father shook his head sadly.

"I got my answer for myself, Carl, and promised she'd never see me again. I'll make that same promise to you. Please forgive me. I realize it was taking a risk to show up uninvited. No doubt she'll need to talk to her therapist about what happened today."

Diane came around to the driver's side of the truck. "There's nothing to forgive. I'm glad you forced her to face Libby. Tessa's therapist had suggested a visit before but Tessa was always so indifferent to the advice. Seeing her daughter again after all this time is something she has needed no matter how much she has pushed you away. We love our Libby and you."

"The feeling's mutual."

Carl patted Eli's shoulder through the window.

"We'll drive to Stevensville soon to spend time with the two of you."

"We'd love that. You'd better go in to Tessa. Thanks for being so understanding."

After giving Libby more hugs and kisses, they stepped away from the truck and he drove down the street anxious to get back to the ranch. His little girl would need to run around and stretch her legs after another two-and-a-half-hour trip in the truck.

To his surprise her sneeze had turned into cough. She'd definitely picked up some kind of bug. When they arrived at the house, he'd take her temperature. If she got stuffed up, he'd put the old steamer in her room to ward off a full-fledged cold.

His mind relived today's visit. It had probably set Tessa back, but Eli wasn't sorry he'd made the trip. It amazed him what a year away from her had done to his feelings for her. She'd retreated to a place he couldn't go and wasn't welcome. He couldn't relate to the woman she'd become.

Eli had talked with Tessa's therapist at the beginning. The doctor had told him there were physical reasons behind postpartum depression that had to do with a change in hormones. Hers had turned out to be a severe case. More important, she'd become sleep deprived and anxious about her ability to care for the baby.

Add to that a feeling of being less attractive. The doctor suspected Tessa struggled with her sense of identity and the fact that she'd lost control over her life. Hearing that explanation, Eli had suffered greatly because of his feelings of hopelessness, but those days were over now.

He was glad that he'd taken Brianna's advice. Seeing his ex-wife today had not only proved to him that his heart was whole again, but he'd also accepted the truth. Tessa had left him and would never be coming back. From here on out he was going to make a brand-new life with his little girl and embrace it.

Once back at his house, he fixed dinner for Libby and himself. She wasn't very hungry and still had a cough but not a temperature. His mother came over and they played with his daughter until it was time to put her to bed. After setting up the steamer near the crib, they crept out of the nursery into the living room.

His mother darted a glance at him. "You seem good."

"I *feel* good. Diane said she was glad I forced Tessa to see Libby. When I drove away from the house, I knew in my gut it was the right thing to have done."

"I agree. What made you decide to do it?"

"It was something Brianna Frost said to me the other night after I took her out to dinner."

"What was that?"

"Don't give up on your wife. Then she said good-bye to me."

"As in—"

"Good-bye for real."

"I see. Does she know your history? That you're divorced?"

He nodded.

"That's interesting."

"Not really. She thinks I'm still in love with Tessa. Because I was wearing my wedding ring when we first met at the gem shop."

"That's right. You were."

"Yup, but she's wrong about my feelings. Tessa was my first love, but I've known for a long time that I'm no longer in love with her. I hated admitting to failure. That's why I kept wearing the ring. But today's visit helped me see that our marriage wasn't a failure. It just couldn't succeed. I drove away with the knowledge that it was truly over and it has steered me in a new direction. I feel so liberated."

"That's the best news I've heard in a very long time. Good night, honey. Don't forget Sunday dinner tomorrow, but if Libby gets worse, call me if you need me, even if it's the middle of the night."

He walked her to the door. "You know I will. Thanks, Mom."

Eli gave her a hug and watched her walk out to the Land Rover. Tomorrow evening he had a phone call to make to Brianna and would be counting the hours until then. He expected pushback, but he wasn't going to let that stop him from being with her again. She'd lit a fire in him the first time he'd laid eyes on her. He knew himself too well. The flame was far too strong for anything to extinguish it now.

Chapter 5

Late Tuesday afternoon the saddlery phone rang while Brianna was finishing up with a customer. Her uncle had already gone home. She handed the rancher his box of new boots before picking up.

"Good afternoon. Frosts' Saddlery."

"Brianna Frost?" The male voice was familiar, but it wasn't her brother or Roce Clayton or Antonio Perez or Asa Harding, who worked on a nearby ranch. It certainly wasn't the cowboy she'd made certain she would never hear from again. Big mistake, as she'd found out after too many sleepless nights.

Her hand tightened on the receiver. She hated it when a caller started out by blurting her full name that way. It made her nervous. "May I help you?" she asked.

"I'm planning on it."

The man's arrogance rang a bell. Don Shapiro from

the bank. "I'm sorry, but I don't know who this is," she lied.

"It's Don Shapiro."

"Oh, Mr. Shapiro. I'm afraid my uncle isn't here. If this is urgent bank business, I can reach him at home and have him call you."

"Whoa, whoa, honey. I'm calling to ask you out to dinner. Are you free tonight?"

"No, I'm not," she said so fast it surprised even her.

"In other words I'd be stepping on Eli's territory."

Suddenly she heard her cell phone ring. The timing couldn't have been more perfect. "Mr. Shapiro? I have to take another call and can't talk now. I'm sorry. Good-bye."

Brianna hung up before clicking on her cell without checking the caller ID. "Hello?" she said.

"Hi, it's Lindsay."

"Oh, I'm so glad it's you." She leaned on the counter in relief.

"What's wrong?"

"Nothing really. I just hung up on a nuisance caller."

"Oh dear."

It was too late to worry that she'd offended the bank manager her uncle did business with. Don Shapiro had been way out of line the first time she'd met him, let alone now. "What's new? How's the pregnant mom feeling?"

"I'm fine, thanks, but I thought you might want to know what Ken told me before he left for work."

Brianna went on alert. "Go on."

"While he was on duty last night, Eli Clayton brought his little girl into the ER at four in the morning with a bad case of croup."

"Oh no—" Poor Libby… Brianna's body broke out in perspiration.

"That's what *I* said. Ken knew I'd met them when you and I went out for dinner recently. He said she's been hospitalized. I don't know anything else, but I thought that maybe you'd want to know, if you hadn't heard already."

"I do!" she cried. "I'm going over to the hospital right now. I'll get back to you later. Thanks so much for letting me know." She clicked off.

It was closing time anyway and Brianna quickly closed up the store, and then got in her truck and drove to the hospital a mile away. She took the elevator to the pediatric wing and approached the male nurse working on a chart at the nursing station.

"Excuse me. Do you know if Libby Clayton is still a patient here?"

The nurse lifted his head. "She is. Are you a relative?"

"No. I'm Brianna Frost, a friend of the Clayton family. May I see her?"

"Sure. She's in room W1124 down that hall."

Brianna thanked him and walked past five doors. When she opened door to Libby's room, she saw Eli walking around, holding his sleeping daughter in his arms. Her breathing sounded noisy. It wrenched her heart.

Eli looked across the short distance and stared as if he couldn't believe Brianna was standing there.

Her mouth had gone dry. "Lindsay called me at work. Her husband told her you'd brought Libby in."

"That's right. He was the attending physician."

"Yes. Is it okay that I've come?" she whispered without moving.

"There's no one we'd rather see." His words filled her with relief. "Please, sit down."

Brianna took off her parka and hung it over the back of a chair. "Is she better than she was in the middle of the night?"

"Yes, even though it sounds bad. They took an X-ray and gave her medication in the emergency room. The pediatrician advised keeping her overnight just in case. Around seven this morning she was given an oral corticosteroid to reduce the inflammation and swelling. If all continues to go well, I'll be able to take her home tonight."

"Thank Heaven. Do you know how she got it?"

"No. It's a virus. Hers grew worse, but at least she's resting more comfortably now."

"I take it you haven't left her for a second. Has your mother been here?"

He nodded. "You just missed her and Wymon. They went out to buy a cool mist steamer for her room."

"I'm glad they've been here for you. Have you had dinner yet?"

"The orderly left a tray, but I haven't touched it."

She noticed it on one of the tables. "Would you let me hold her so you can eat?"

"You want to?"

"I'd love it." She'd tried without success to keep the tremor out of her voice.

"You're sure?" he asked. The blue of his eyes darkened with emotion. "Even though you said good-bye to me?"

She deserved that. "I was upset that night," Brianna answered honestly. "Your daughter is so precious, Eli. Of course I want to hold her. I'll try not to wake her up."

"Don't worry about it." He walked over and placed Libby in her arms. She was viscerally aware of the difference between his hard-muscled physique beneath his white T-shirt and jeans, and the tiny slip of a thing that was his daughter, dressed in a fuzzy onesie dotted with teddy bears.

The motion caused Libby's eyelids to flutter open. Her blue eyes, so much like her father's, stared up at Brianna.

"Hi, darling. Do you remember me? I'm Brianna."

"Bree," she croaked out the first part of her name and squirmed to sit up.

"Yes. Bree." She helped her to get up. The little girl put her arms around her neck and clung to her. Brianna held her against her heart and felt the breaths she took. "I'm so glad you're feeling better." She rocked her back and forth, loving the feeling of those arms holding on to her.

Though he sported a slight beard and looked exhausted, Eli's face broke into a smile as he stood there watching them. "I do believe you're the reason she's suddenly acting so normal."

Brianna smiled up at him. "Her daddy is all the medicine she needs, but you'd better sit down and have something to eat so you don't pass out from fatigue."

"I look that bad, huh?"

She averted her eyes. Brianna didn't dare tell him how good he looked to her, even now.

He walked over to the table and lifted the cover off the dinner plate before sitting down a few feet from her to eat.

Libby swung her head around and pointed at him. "Dada."

"Yup! That's me, sweetheart." He handed her half of his roll. She reached for it and took a bite.

Brianna squeezed her. "It looks like you're hungry."

He nodded. "That's a good sign she's getting better."

He'd just finished his meal when a man entered the room. Eli stood. "Dr. Ennis? This is my friend, Brianna Frost. Her uncle owns Frosts' Western Saddlery."

The older man nodded. "Of course. I've been in there many times." He walked over and hunkered down in front of Brianna. "Don't move. Just keep holding her while I check her lungs." He put the stethoscope to his ears and moved it around. Libby tried to squirm away.

In a minute the doctor got to his feet. "It's clear she's improving, Eli. You can take her home and keep the cool steam going. Sleep in her room tonight to listen for any changes in her breathing. I'll go out to the desk and sign the release papers."

Eli looked relieved. "That's the news I've been waiting for. Thanks, Dr. Ennis."

"My pleasure. The miracle is that children rally fast." He smiled at Brianna. "It was nice to meet you. Libby seems very fond of you."

"She's a darling."

"When she was born, she was the cutest baby in the nursery. Now she's even cuter." He patted Eli's shoulder. "Call the office tomorrow and give me a report."

The two men walked out into the hallway.

Brianna kissed Libby's cheek. "The doctor's right. With that heart-shaped face, you *are* the cutest thing in the world."

"Let me just check her diaper and then we can leave." Eli had come back in and plucked her out of Brianna's arms. His daughter protested as he carried her over to the crib.

"I'll find her parka." It was hanging in the closet

along with his sheepskin jacket. "If you want, when we go down to the lobby, I can hold her while you get your truck and warm it up."

"I'd like to take you up on that on one condition." He snapped up Libby's sleeper suit and put the parka on her. Brianna's heart thudded while she waited for the rest. "That you follow us back to the ranch in your truck and help me put her to bed. Now that you've made an appearance, she's going to be very upset if you leave. But if you have other plans. . ."

"No. I'll just phone my aunt and tell her I'll be home late tonight so they won't worry," she said, hoping her face didn't give away just how happy she was that he had asked.

"That's good to hear." Eli shrugged into his jacket and then reached for Libby. "Come on, sweetheart. We're all going home."

We're all going home. The sound of that sent a thrill through Brianna's body.

A hospital orderly appeared with a wheelchair.

"Really?" Eli questioned. The look on his face was comical.

"Sorry," the man said. "Hospital rules."

Eli sat in the chair and held his daughter. One dark brow lifted. "You'd think I'd just given birth," he muttered.

Libby chuckled as she walked alongside them to the elevator.

The woman keeping pace with them looked sensational in her melon-colored sweater and designer jeans. Eli felt like a fraud being wheeled out in the chair, but Brianna's gentle laughter sweetened the experience.

"I'll hold her," Brianna said when they reached the hospital entrance. Libby went right into her arms with no fuss. Eli thanked the orderly and took off for the parking lot. He started up the truck and brought it around to the entrance. When he felt it was warm enough, he left the engine running and went inside to get Libby. But the second he took her from Brianna's arms, she started to cry.

"It's okay, sweetheart. She's coming home with us."

Brianna walked with them out to the truck and waited while he strapped her inside and gave her some plastic, colored keys to play with.

"I'll see you in a minute, Libby. I promise." She kissed her cheeks before he shut the door on her croaky cries.

"Where's your truck?"

"Right down this row. I'll hurry."

"Drive safely. I couldn't handle another emergency tonight."

"I'll be right behind you."

Eli waited for Brianna and then pulled out of the parking lot and headed for the ranch. His daughter whimpered while he kept an eye on Brianna's truck in the rearview mirror. Before he'd been able to phone her Sunday evening after his trip to Thompson Falls, his daughter's condition had deteriorated. On Monday she'd gone from bad to worse. When he'd seen Brianna enter the hospital room tonight, he'd thought he was hallucinating.

Without this crisis bringing them together unexpectedly, there was no telling how long it would have taken him to get Brianna to talk to him. He silently thanked her friend Lindsay for letting her know what had happened.

For some reason, Libby had responded to Brianna from the very first time she'd seen her at the gem shop, and those feelings were obviously reciprocated. Otherwise she would never have come to the hospital after telling him good-bye. Now she'd willingly agreed to come back to his house.

When they reached the driveway, she pulled up her truck alongside his. They both got out. His family had left the porch light on. He went around to pluck Libby from her car seat, while Brianna gathered the diaper bag and little toys that had fallen on the drive over, and then they walked inside the house.

Wymon had made a fire and left more lights on to welcome them. Eli carried Libby through the living room and down the hall to the nursery. The room held a twin bed, a dresser, her crib and a rocking chair.

"Is Sarah here?"

He removed Libby's parka and put her in bed with the white polar bear she loved. "No. She goes home on weekends. On Sunday, when I realized Libby was sick and I'd have to stay home from work on Monday, I told her not to come in for a few days. I'm planning to stay home tomorrow, too."

After taking off his jacket, he switched on the new steamer his mother had set up and turned to Brianna. She'd removed her parka, too, and had put it on the bed with the diaper bag and other things. "If you'll stay with her, I'll go in the kitchen and get her a bottle of apple juice."

"Mmm, juice. That sounds good, doesn't it, Libby."

His little girl had gotten to her feet and clung to the crib railing. "Dada," she called to him as he left the room.

When he returned a minute later, he discovered Brianna holding her in the rocking chair. To his relief he could tell her coughing was much less severe and she seemed animated.

Eli walked over and handed the bottle to her. She put it right in her mouth and drank. Brianna looked up at him. "I think she's happy to be back in her own room."

That wasn't all she was happy about. "Yup. There's no place like home." Eli reached for a book sitting on the small pile on the dresser. "This is her favorite. When she's through drinking, she'll love reading it with you."

"Ooh. *Goodnight Moon.* Can you say *moon*, Libby? Mooooooooon."

Libby pulled the bottle away and he heard her say "Mooooooo," in a croaky voice.

The moment was so precious that both he and Brianna burst into laughter. "That's her sixth word," he said.

Their gazes collided. "You've been counting them?"

"Yes. She can say *Dada*, *Nana* and *Sol*. Around you, she has now said *Bree*, *bye* and *moo*. I'll have to get her a cow so she knows the difference."

"Maybe you'd better buy a wolf, too. You know. Howling at the moooooooooooooooooon?" As Eli chuckled and Libby said the word again. Brianna kissed the top of her head. "You're a very smart girl, you know that? But I think it's time you went to bed."

Eli gathered Libby in his arms, aware of Brianna's sweet fragrance on her. He lay her down in the crib to change her diaper one more time. He didn't realize Brianna had left the nursery until after he'd finally gotten his daughter to sleep. Leaving the small night-light on, he tiptoed out of the room to the bathroom across the hall to wash his hands.

His breath caught when he walked into the living room and saw Brianna sitting by the fireplace, her pale hair illuminated by the glow from the flames. She appeared deep in thought.

"Brianna?"

She turned to him and stood. Her parka lay across the end of the couch. "I hope your crisis is over."

"I'm sure it is, and you had a part in her fast recovery, but there's another crisis I need to deal with now."

He could tell she was the slightest bit out of breath. That was how he felt whenever he was around her.

"What's wrong?"

"You and I need time alone together. By Sunday, Libby ought to be much better. Mom will want to spend time with her. I'd like to take you out for dinner and talk. It's important. Last Saturday Libby and I went to see my ex-wife."

Her face blanched. "She saw Libby?"

"Yes. There are things I need to tell you about what happened. If I come pick you up at five, will you be ready?"

Several seconds passed before she nodded.

Now he could swallow. "It's getting late. If you'll wait a moment, I'll phone Wymon and ask him to follow you home."

"Thank you, but please don't. We don't live that far apart."

He rubbed the back of his neck in frustration. "Then will you let me put my phone number on your cell? I want you to call me when you've reached your uncle's."

"All right." They exchanged numbers. Before he could help her, she'd already put on her parka and started for the door.

Eli walked her out to her truck and made certain she was safe. He tapped on the window so she'd lower it. "You coming to the hospital tonight meant more to me than you know. I guess you don't need to be told Libby was a new little girl after you walked in the room."

"I'm glad she's doing so much better," Brianna said. "Take care of yourself, Eli. I'll see you on Sunday at five."

Her warm breath in the cold night air made him want to reach through that window and pull her into his arms. He hoped she was having the same feelings and thought maybe that was why it took her a whole minute to start the engine.

Eli stood there and watched until her truck disappeared around the bend. A new chapter in his life had begun. He could feel it. Though dead on his feet from worry and lack of sleep, he felt exhilarated as he walked back into the house to get ready for bed.

Five minutes later his phone rang. She couldn't have reached her uncle's yet. Something had to be wrong. He picked up without checking the caller ID. "Brianna?"

"Brianna, huh?" his brother teased. "So that's what has been going on while I've been getting the tar knocked out of me on the circuit!"

"Toly!"

"Yeah. You *do* remember me, but you sound out of breath." Eli needed to calm down. "Mom said Libby had been in the hospital with croup. Is she all right?"

"Yes. I brought her home earlier tonight."

"That's a relief. So who's Brianna?"

His heart raced. "Brianna Frost is a woman I recently met."

"Hmm. She must be very new if I haven't met her."

"She actually came to the rodeo with her aunt and uncle to watch you and Mills."

"You're talking Clark Frost?"

"Clark's her uncle. She works at the saddlery."

"Is she blonde?"

He blinked. "Yes."

"Then she's the one Asa Harding has a crush on!"

Eli had to bite his tongue. Asa and every other man in Stevensville.

"He came to see me in the stock pen after the rodeo and told me about this gorgeous babe he met when he went to buy some new shirts. How did *you* meet her?"

"At the gem shop. Mom was showing her some stones. I went up there to get Libby. Listen, Toly—it's good to hear from you and congratulations on another first last Saturday night, but I've got to hit the hay because I'm ready to pass out. I'll call you tomorrow and we'll talk."

"I'm going to hold you to that and you know why." They clicked off.

Yup. Eli was afraid he did.

The Clayton family had been worried about Eli for a long time. He knew Toly was shocked to hear another woman's name pass through his lips besides Tessa's. There'd been a huge change in Eli's life.

While he stood there in a daze, the phone rang again. This time he checked the caller ID before clicking on. "Brianna? Are you home?"

"I promised I'd call. I'm in the house. How's Libby?"

Libby who? For a moment Eli's mind had been in a different place. "She's still asleep and sounding better."

"Oh, that makes me so happy! Now you go to bed or you'll end up in the hospital."

"Yes, ma'am."

Her chuckle was the last sound he heard before she hung up. That chuckle invaded his body and accompanied him to the twin bed in Libby's room, where he collapsed as soon as his head touched the pillow.

Chapter 6

On Saturday after store hours, Brianna tried on the Wrangler two-piece suit in formfitting denim that had just come in. With a white scooped-neck top underneath, the outfit seemed perfect. She wrote up the invoice and paid cash for it using the discount her uncle gave her. Since coming to Montana, she hadn't bought anything new for herself and thought it was time.

Her uncle figured out why after he saw her walk into the living room Sunday evening carrying her coat. Her aunt was in the kitchen fixing their dinner. "Where are you going?"

"To dinner with Eli Clayton."

An odd expression broke out on his face, reminding her of her dad when he was pondering something serious. "Somehow I didn't expect Eli to come out the winner of the Clayton brothers. So it was *Eli* all along, not Roce."

"I—I didn't intend to see him again," she stammered, "but Lindsay told me his little girl was in the hospital with croup, so I went to visit her."

"And now he wants to thank you."

"Yes." She wasn't ready to talk about it yet.

"I take it she's better now." He cocked his head. "Are you sure about going with him? From what I understand, he's the complicated one."

Complicated?

"Clark," her aunt called out. She'd just walked into the living room with Taffy at her heels. "What a question to ask. Dinner's ready. Come in the dining room and let Brianna do her own thing. That suit looks terrific on you, by the way."

Her aunt Joanne gave her a hug before reaching for her husband's hand. The gorgeous pink sapphire on her finger flashed in the lamplight, reminding Brianna of the first time she'd met Eli.

Not thirty seconds later the doorbell rang. Brianna put on her coat and hurried to the foyer, thinking about what her uncle had just said. When she opened the door, Eli's striking blue eyes swept down the length of her, making her heart ricochet all over the place.

"Thanks for being ready on time. I couldn't have waited any longer." The things he said gave her a fluttery feeling in her chest. Eli wore a tan jacket and cream shirt with beige pants. Today he was clean shaven and smelled wonderful. He walked her out to the truck. When he helped her get in, she noticed he'd left his overcoat on the backseat.

"How's Libby?"

"If you'd seen her toddling around the ranch house

a little while ago, you would never know she'd been so sick. There's only been one problem."

She dared a look at him.

"Every so often she says 'Bree' to me. Libby keeps looking for you."

"She does?" Eli shouldn't have told her that.

"Surely you're not surprised." He started the engine and they left. "I hope you like Italian food. The Italian owner cooks the food himself. I've never been to Italy, but I don't see how the food would taste any better there."

"That sounds good to me." Last week she hadn't thought she'd be seeing Eli again. Now here she was going out to eat with him. She shouldn't be this elated, but she couldn't help it.

Before long they reached the small restaurant and were shown to a table. "You look stunning," he murmured after removing her coat.

So did he. "Thank you."

They were fed one delicious course after another. While they chatted about their work and sipped coffee, he said, "Thanks to what you said, my trip to Thompson Falls accomplished two things."

The sudden change of topic caused her pulse to race. She stared at him. "What do you mean?"

"You told me not to stop trying to win my wife back. I took your advice and drove down to Thompson Falls with Libby to see Tessa again. After a year I was curious to find out what would happen when Tessa saw us again. But the woman who answered the door looked through me as if I weren't there. As for Libby, Tessa had no desire to hold her. I promised she'd never see me again."

Brianna groaned. "I'm sorry."

"Don't be. She was a stranger to me and has been for a long time, but I didn't want to admit that our marriage was one of those that didn't make it. That was the reason why I wore my ring as long as I did."

"I do understand, Eli."

"Then you're one woman in a million."

She shook her head. "Hardly."

"The important thing here is that I know in my soul it wasn't anyone's fault. The doctor can't give me the exact reason for her illness, but it wasn't something preventable."

"Of course not," she whispered.

"I returned home a new man and planned to call you Sunday evening, but by then Libby was so sick that I was preoccupied. I'd like to thank your friend for telling you she was in the hospital. It meant the world to me and Libby that you came."

Brianna drank the rest of her coffee. This was the time for honesty. "It meant a lot to me, too."

He leaned forward. "I hope by now you understand that I've asked you to dinner because I want to start over again with you. Let's not have any secrets or concerns that aren't out in the open. If there's something you need to tell me that would hold you back from being with me, I want to hear it."

She cleared her throat, shaken by his earnestness. "Well, I'm not involved with another man, as I told you at the restaurant."

One brow lifted. "Not even Asa Harding?"

"Mr. Harding?"

His eyes danced. "Toly told me Asa has a crush on you."

"That's news to me. He's been in the store a couple of times, that's all."

"All it takes is seeing you once… Take it from a cowboy who knows."

Heat filled her cheeks. "He asked me to go a movie with him, but I told him I was busy that night."

"Were you?" he asked.

"No."

"The poor dude."

Brianna smiled. "He's nice, but—"

"But the spark wasn't there?"

She lowered her eyes. "Can we change the subject?"

"Gladly. I want to know your future plans."

So did she, but everything was a blur right now. "They're in flux."

"In other words they could change at any minute."

Brianna raised her head. "Maybe not that fast."

His eyes narrowed on her face. She saw no mirth in them. "In case you were wondering, my plans are fixed. Ranching's my life and the Sapphire Mountains are my home. If you have any intention of going back to California or getting a job somewhere else right away, I need to know so I won't be blindsided when it happens."

"*Eli*—"

"Eli, what?" he demanded. "You know what I'm saying."

She took a shaky breath. "I'm very happy living with my aunt and uncle."

"Until…"

He was driving her crazy. "Until, I don't know!"

Eli broke into laughter. "That answer will do for now. Tell me something. Does your uncle ever give you part of a day off?"

"If I ask, he tells me to take whatever time I need."

"That's a great boss. Could you plan for this coming Tuesday? Say two o'clock when I'm done with my ranching chores?"

"What do you have in mind?"

"Have you ever gone skiing?"

"Only when I'm here in winter. I have a pair of skis and boots at my aunt and uncle's. I've gone twice so far since I've been here."

"Terrific. I thought we'd go skiing at the Snowbowl outside Missoula. We ought to be able to get in a few hours and then have dinner. Sarah will be there for Libby so we won't have to worry if we get back late."

Skiing with Eli sounded wonderful. Doing *anything* with him sounded like Heaven. "I'd love to go skiing."

"Good. Then it's settled. Come on. I'll drive you home. Though I'd love to spend the entire evening with you, I want to be able to say good-night to Libby. Mom is watching her, but she's been a little needy since her hospital stay."

"I can understand that. She's lucky to have such a devoted father. Let's go."

Brianna decided he was a breed apart from most men. She still found it incredible that his ex-wife's condition was too severe for her to want a life with him. But tonight Eli had made it clear Tessa was a part of the past. At this point Brianna would have to operate on faith that she wasn't making a mistake by continuing to see him.

Eli saw her to the door.

"Thank you for a fantastic dinner." In the dim porch light she glimpsed banked fires in his eyes, but he still didn't try to kiss her. She wanted him to. Badly. So much for her deciding to take things slowly. *You're a mess, Brianna.*

He squeezed her arm. "See you on Tuesday afternoon. I can't promise I'll survive until then."

She laughed quietly but entered the house breathless. Much as she wanted to go straight to her room, she stopped by the den first where her aunt and uncle were watching television. Taffy limped over so she could rub her head.

"Hi! I'm home." Anticipating the next question, she said, "I had a wonderful time. Eli asked me to go skiing with him on Tuesday."

"That sounds fun," her aunt commented.

"I think so, too. Uncle Clark, would it be all right if I take off work at two?"

"Of course."

For once her uncle was unusually quiet, but maybe he was just too caught up in the movie they were watching to ask any more questions.

"Great. Well, I'm going to bed. See you in the morning."

"Good night, honey."

She went to her room not at all sure how she'd make it to Tuesday afternoon.

"Sarah? I'm back!"

After inspecting the cattle with Wymon and the stock workers, Eli hurried into the house at one o'clock on Tuesday to shower and change. He'd been living for today.

"Libby and I are building a castle!"

He found them in the nursery on the floor. "Dada!" Libby had blocks in both hands that she lifted to show him.

Eli hunkered down next to his daughter. "Well, look at you." He kissed the top of her head.

Sarah smiled. "She loves building things."

"Maybe I've got myself an engineer."

While Libby was busy building stuff, he got ready for his date and loaded his ski equipment into the back of the truck. Figuring it would be easier if Libby didn't know he was going, he left the house to pick up Brianna without saying good-bye. Sarah knew he'd be home late.

The best thing he'd done in a year was hire a nanny. He should have done it long before now, but he hadn't wanted to go into debt. Eli had worked hard to save money and now a new sense of freedom filled his being as he drove into town and pulled up in the Frosts' driveway.

The sight of Brianna in her black ski jacket and form-fitting ski pants nearly knocked him back on his behind. Her womanly shape filled his vision to the exclusion of all else.

"Bring your cowboy hat. You're going to need it later," he said.

"That's sounds interesting."

After she fetched it, he carried her ski equipment to the truck while she climbed inside the cab. Then they drove away. He put her hat in the backseat by his. Eli shot her a penetrating glance. "I feel eighteen again."

"Is that good or bad?" she teased.

"What do you think?"

"Was that a happy time for you?"

It seemed an odd question, or maybe not. "Let's put it this way. At that age I came to appreciate a fine-looking woman. But I can tell you right now there was no one like you around."

"I don't believe it."

"Just ask any of the guys who've been coming in

and out of the saddlery nonstop since you arrived in Stevensville."

"You're very good on a woman's ego. But when you see what a klutz I am on the slopes, you'll have to re-assess your thinking."

He raised an eyebrow. "Did I tell you I was once a bull rider, not a skier?"

"I'll reserve judgment until we call an ambulance for you."

"No, thank you. One hospital visit this month for any reason is enough."

She laughed gently. "I agree. How is Libby now?"

"Perfect. I left her constructing a castle out of blocks with Sarah."

"I've noticed she has an incredible attention span for her age."

He darted another glance at her. "I've noticed she's crazy about you. If you can prevail on your uncle to let you off work this coming Saturday, I want you to come to the house for part of the day. Libby will be ecstatic. I'll do the cooking and we'll roast marshmallows in the fireplace."

Eli knew he was getting ahead of himself, but being with Brianna felt so right, he couldn't stop thinking and planning. He was waiting for her answer.

"I'll arrange to do a split shift with him and leave after lunch. Mornings are the busiest time on Saturdays. He'll get a few customers in the afternoon, but we usu-ally close up early."

"Then it's settled." Eli reached over and grasped her hand for a few minutes.

The sky stayed overcast with more snow forecast to fall by evening. He'd buy them half-day passes and hopefully they'd get some skiing in before that happened. "If I ever had to go into another profession, I'd like it to be photography. I'd take pictures of Montana in winter," he mused.

"Everything does look like a Christmas card. It's so beautiful here."

"Don't you miss California, though?"

She was looking out the side window. "I haven't allowed myself to think much about it. At first I was in denial over my parents' deaths."

"And now?" he whispered.

"I miss them like crazy, but I've finally accepted that they're gone and life goes on. When I talk to my brother now, he accuses me of having forgotten him. That could never happen, of course."

"Has he been to visit your aunt and uncle since you came?"

"No. They've begged him. If you knew my brother, you'd realize he's such a responsible person that he's afraid to leave the farm, even for a short period of time. In some ways he reminds me of you and how dedicated you are. I've noticed how you keep watch over everything down at the ranch along with your brothers. He, too, has farm workers he's responsible for."

Her compliments warmed him. "You must miss him a lot."

"I do, but my aunt and uncle fill a big void. Clark and Dad are so much alike. As for Doug, he has his wife, Carol, so we're all doing better."

Yes, we are. I know I am.

They reached the crowded ski resort and got in line for the double chair lift. When they reached the top,

Brianna turned to him. "I'm a slow skier. If you want to go ahead, please don't let me stop you."

He shook his head. "I want to ski with you, so you set the pace. Are you ready?"

"Yes. But you'll be sorry." She lowered her goggles and started down the slope. He stayed near her side until they reached the bottom. "Forgive me for being so slow, Eli."

"Please don't apologize. You have excellent technique."

"Thank you. I love being out in nature with you. Let's go up again."

Halfway to the top, a cold wind kicked up. She smiled nervously at him. "I think the storm front is moving in faster than predicted."

"I agree. We'll make another run and see what happens."

After they'd made two more descents without incident, it started to snow. He saw that Brianna was anxious. "You ready to head into Missoula for dinner?"

She nodded, her relief obvious. When they reached the truck, he opened the passenger door for her. "Let me help you."

Needing to touch her, he grasped her around the waist. As her body brushed against his, a wave of desire spread through him. It was so strong that he pulled her close and her head fell back. The moment was magical. With the snow coming down, all he could see were her jewel-like blue eyes and sculpted mouth, a temptation he could no longer resist.

"I've been wanting to do this since the first time we met," he whispered fiercely before covering her mouth with his own. Her luscious warmth, combined with the cold air and snow, increased his desire. He forgot where they were as he deepened their kiss. She clung to him, causing his heart to race. In that instant he knew she wanted him just as badly and they kissed each other close to senselessness.

Having lost all track of time, he was eventually brought back to his senses when someone passing by let out a wolf whistle. With Brianna in his arms, he was in danger of being totally out of control. For a first kiss, they'd gone way beyond what was wise, let alone what was decent in a public place.

It was like the first night he'd laid eyes on her at the gem shop. The sight of her had stirred his senses to such a degree that he hadn't been the same since. All along he'd known that if he ever started kissing her, he wouldn't be able to stop. He'd never felt this way about any woman. His attraction to his ex-wife had grown slowly. The excitement Brianna whipped up inside him staggered him.

With sheer strength of will, he lifted his mouth from hers and could hear his own ragged breathing. "Up you go." This time he put her inside and shut the door before he could clasp her to him again.

Once behind the wheel, he shut the door and started the engine. She'd pulled off her headband. Her blond hair glowed with a life all its own. It was impossible to tear his eyes away from her.

"I feel like a good steak. How about you?"

"That sounds good." But her response told him she was miles away in the same world where he'd been moments ago. Eli needed to channel his energy in a different way and knew exactly the place to take her.

The snow continued to come down. She fixed her

makeup and brushed out her hair. Within a half hour they arrived at Rudy's, the best steak house in Missoula. He reached for their cowboy hats. Once they'd gotten out of the truck, they put them on and he grasped her arm to guide her inside.

"I hope you know how to line dance. If you don't, I'll teach you. They have a great band here." This way he could touch her but would have to control himself.

Her eyes lit up. "My aunt taught me. She and Uncle Clark go country dancing a lot. I love it."

The good news just kept coming.

They were shown to a table around the dance floor and removed their parkas. Every male in the place eyed her in her tight black cashmere sweater. He couldn't blame them, but thanked providence he'd gotten there first.

After being served some tapas for hors d'oeuvres, he led her out to the dance floor and they joined a dozen people sashaying to "Baby Likes to Rock It." Her aunt had taught her well. Dancing with Brianna excited him to no end.

They went back to the table to enjoy the main course and then returned to the floor and danced for close to an hour. Eli had forgotten he could be this happy. Her smiles let him know she was feeling the same way. But before long, he wanted her to himself and suggested they leave. He helped her put on her parka, loving the fragrant scent of her skin and hair.

Their stomachs filled with good food, the drive back to Stevensville in the snowstorm seemed just as magical as the rest of the night. Encased in the cab together, alone in the darkness, Eli felt he had everything he wanted.

"I guess I don't need to tell you how much this day has meant to me. There's only one problem."

After a brief silence, she said, "I don't think I want to know what it is."

"That's because you know what I'm going to say."

"Eli…"

"It's too soon to have the kind of feelings I have for you. I know it, and you know it. Tonight I want to take you home with me for good. You'd be lying if you told me you didn't feel the same way."

"I'll admit I'm overwhelmed with emotions right now."

"Whether you want to hear it or not, I've fallen in love with you." He detected a slight gasp. "I don't need to hear all the arguments floating in your head. I know them by heart and can just imagine what your brother would say.

"'It's too soon, Brianna. Eli Clayton has just come out of a marriage that couldn't work. He couldn't possibly know what he wants yet. He has a little daughter. You've never been married. You're still grieving the loss of our parents. You're a California girl and are only visiting our aunt and uncle for a season. You need to come home and deserve to meet a man with no baggage.'"

She straightened in the seat. "Everyone has baggage, Eli."

"Not like mine."

"Maybe not exactly. Why don't you tell me the whole truth and admit you'd be worried to take on a girl like me with no experience? You've been married and have a child. I'm sure I don't measure up to your expectations, not like—"

"Tessa?" he interrupted her. "You're right. You're not

at all like Tessa, who was afraid of her own shadow. I didn't know that at first. When she begged me never to go back to bull riding again, I thought that was a natural concern of some people. Later I took her skiing, but she couldn't bring herself to get on the lift, which surprised me.

"After we got married and moved in to my late grandparents' house, fear turned out to be her middle name. She liked to go dancing but not line dancing, where she felt like she was on display. It was clear Tessa needed to be home where she could be in control of her world and she begged for us to start a family. I'd wanted to wait, but I could see a baby would fulfill her."

"Oh, Eli... How hard."

"Her pregnancy made her so happy, despite her morning sickness, that I was overjoyed. We planned out the nursery and got everything ready. Little did I know Libby's arrival would bring completely new fears.

"If you have more questions about her, go ahead and ask. But you have to know I don't measure you against anyone else. You are a constant surprise in ways that make me thankful I've met you."

Eli pulled into the Frosts' snow-covered driveway.

"Meeting you has changed my world, too, Eli. So much that I don't know myself anymore."

Unable to stand it any longer, he got out of the truck and walked around to her side. After opening the door, he pulled her into his arms. "I need this again or I'll never make it until Saturday."

Once more he knew rapture as they gave each other kiss after kiss under falling snow that left their hair and clothing damp. But he wasn't aware of anything except the feel of the fabulous flesh-and-blood woman embracing him as if she would never let him go. To experience this kind of passion seemed nothing short of a miracle.

When she pulled away long enough to catch her breath, she cried, "You look like a snowman."

"To tell you the truth, with the heat we've created, I'm surprised the snow hasn't run off both of us." He covered her mouth once more before freeing her from his grip. "You'd better run to the porch while I'm still willing to let you go. I'll get your ski equipment."

After gathering it up, he put everything down on her porch and clasped her to him one more time. "I don't want to let you go, but I have to. Just be warned that on Saturday, things will be different. I'll expect you around one or one-thirty."

"I'll be there."

He gave her another swift kiss and walked back to the truck without turning around.

Chapter 7

Taffy was waiting when Brianna entered the house and removed her parka. Then her uncle came walking toward her. She didn't have to guess what he was thinking. Her disheveled hair, her flushed cheeks and swollen lips told him everything.

"I saw headlights in the driveway. I'll bring in your equipment. Why don't you go rest by the fire?"

Yup. He'd been waiting up for her. She sensed a talk coming on. Because she loved him so much, she didn't resent him behaving like a father, even if she was twenty-three.

While she waited for him, she took off her boots and stood in front of the hearth. The only parts of her body not burning up were her feet.

"Were you able to get in some skiing before the storm hit?"

She turned toward him. "Yes. We did four runs. Eli is such a good skier, I can't believe he wasn't an alpine champion."

"He was an even greater bull rider."

She nodded. "I'm sure of that, but he insists Toly is the true champion of the family. After we left the ski resort, we went to Rudy's for dinner and line dancing. I don't think there's anything the guy can't do. I had the time of my life."

Her uncle scrutinized her. "Your eyes are shining with a light I've never seen before. I dare say my niece is in love."

She took a steadying breath. "I *know* I am."

"Brianna—"

"Yes?"

He was unusually hesitant. "Nothing."

"Come on, Uncle Clark. You didn't wait up this late for nothing."

"I don't have the right."

"Yes, you do. What are you trying to tell me?"

"That your aunt and I love you and want you to be happy."

"I know you're concerned. You told me Eli was the complicated one of the Clayton boys. What did you mean by that?"

He shifted his weight. "It's something his father once said to me."

Brianna swallowed hard. "What was that?"

"Everything always came easily to Eli. For that reason his dad worried there'd come a time when he had to face something all his talents couldn't fix."

She folded her arms in front of her waist. "When did he tell you this? After Eli's marriage to Tessa?"

"No, before. He came into the store one day to buy some boots and mentioned that Eli was getting married."

"Wasn't he happy about it?"

"Not exactly. He felt uneasy because Eli and his fiancée hadn't known each other long and he thought they were rushing into it."

"You don't think that he was just a loving father who was worried about losing his son?"

"No. He had a real concern."

"In other words he felt Eli wasn't ready but didn't give you the exact reason why."

"I suppose that's it."

She thought of how wonderful Eli was with his daughter. "Who *is* truly ready when it comes to marriage?"

He took a deep breath. "I'm sure I don't know."

"It seems to me Eli did everything to try to make his marriage work and has proven himself to be a great dad. If his father were alive, I should think he'd be proud of him."

"Of course he would be. Honey?" His eyes looked at her with pleading. "Forgive me for saying anything."

Brianna gave him a big hug. "Thank you for caring so much. Good night."

She hurried to her room to get ready for bed. But no matter how hard she tried, she couldn't throw off her uncle's concern. Brianna believed he'd told her the whole truth as he knew it. So if she wanted to know the rest, she would have to ask Eli why his father had such reservations about his marriage that he'd even discussed them with her uncle.

For the remainder of the week her uncle kept mum

on the subject. Eli phoned her at work the next day to be certain she was still on for Saturday. He made another call on Friday while they were vaccinating the herd.

"When I left the house this morning, I told Libby you would be coming to our house tomorrow. It doesn't matter how much she understood—one thing was clear. She kept running around saying, 'Bree—Bree!' You've made a real impression on her. Neither one of us can wait."

"I'm looking forward to it, too," she said. "See you then."

After work that day, Brianna called Lindsay and they decided to go shopping for a present for Libby. Her pregnant friend was delighted by the idea and they met at one of the stores selling educational gifts.

They found a box of twelve different-colored moons. Six were full moons—pancake-sized and about a half-inch thick, while the other six were half moons in the same colors. All had adorable faces. Brianna knew Libby would love them. She also bought a coloring book of cartoon moon drawings and a pack of crayons.

Lindsay found a mobile of the solar system for the crib she and her husband had set up. Her friend's excitement made Brianna envious. To be expecting a baby with the man you loved sounded like the best thing in the world.

Brianna asked the clerk to gift wrap her presents. Afterward, they stopped for a hamburger before parting ways. She was so anxious for the next day that she didn't sleep very well.

Saturday turned out to be an especially busy day at the saddlery. At twelve thirty Brianna told her uncle she was leaving. He smiled and told her to have a great time. No more talks like the one they'd had Tuesday night.

After freshening up, she walked out to the truck with her gifts, aware of her heart thudding out of control. Under her parka she wore a pair of white jeans and a new, dark blue crepe blouse that buttoned up in front with a roll collar and pockets. The cuffed sleeves fastened below the elbow. She wanted to look beautiful for Eli.

Though it was close to freezing, no storms had been forecasted for the next three days. The sun was out today and the main highway was free of snow. Brianna turned in to the Clayton ranch and drove past the main house until she reached Eli's. His mother's Land Rover was parked in front, but there was no sign of his truck.

Surprised, she got out of her uncle's truck with the gifts and walked to the front porch. Before she had a chance to ring the bell, the door opened.

"Mrs. Clayton—"

"Hello, Brianna. I saw you pull up. Please come in."

She entered the house and closed the door behind her. "Is Libby sick again?"

"No, no. Luke, one of the stockmen, had a heart attack while they were all working this morning. He has no family in Montana so Eli drove him to the hospital and is staying with him until the foreman can get there to be with him. I'm sure Eli will be back as soon as he can."

"Of course. The poor man. I hope he got him there in time."

"We're all praying for that. As for Libby, she's had lunch and is taking her nap right now. Give me your parka." Brianna removed it so Eli's mother could hang it in the hall closet. "Why don't we go sit down in the living room?"

"Thank you."

"Have you had lunch?" Mrs. Clayton asked.

"Not yet, but I'm not hungry."

"Coffee, then?"

"No, thank you. I'll wait for Eli. If he doesn't get back soon, I'll fix myself something. Please feel free to go if you want."

"Well, if you're sure…"

Brianna nodded. "I'll stay here with Libby for as long as I'm needed. When she wakes up, I have a few things to give her."

Eli's mother looked at the gifts she'd put on the couch. "How exciting!"

"I hope she'll like them."

"That's very sweet of you."

Brianna smiled. "It's easy to want to spoil that child."

"Tell me about it." The older woman laughed.

"Eli has told me several times how grateful he is for you and how bad he feels you've had to do so much for him and Libby. Let me take over now so you can do whatever you want for the rest of the day."

"Solana and I do need to go grocery shopping…"

"Then go, enjoy and don't worry about us."

Mrs. Clayton walked out to the foyer and pulled her parka from the hall closet. After putting it on, she turned to Brianna. "I know my granddaughter is in the best of hands with you. She has said your name no fewer than a dozen times since I came over to help."

Those words thrilled Brianna. "I can't wait to play with her."

Eli's mother eyed her for a moment. "My son told

me what a great support you were when Libby was in the hospital."

"When I heard she had croup, I wanted to be there."

"Eli is very lucky to know you." She reached in her purse and pulled out a business card for the gem shop. "This has my cell phone number on it if you need me for any reason."

Brianna took it from her. "Thank you so much."

"I'll be back home in an hour. In the meantime, Libby has a sippy cup if you want to give her milk. Eli also has crackers and bananas on hand should you decide to put her in the high chair for a snack. There's baby food on the shelf."

"I'm sure he has everything. Libby and I will be fine."

"I have no doubt of it."

"Oh, and by the way, if I haven't told you before, my aunt adores her ring. I believe it has made her fall in love with my uncle all over again."

"How lovely," she said and smiled warmly. "I'll talk to you soon."

Brianna watched her walk to her Land Rover and drive off, then she went down the hallway to check on Libby and discovered the little monkey was awake. Through the gap in the doorway, she saw the toddler sitting up in her crib, playing with her polar bear. Her brown hair was in tangles, melting Brianna's heart.

Libby saw her and immediately got to her feet, clinging to the crib railing. "Bree—"

"Good afternoon, darling." She rushed over and picked her up. Those little arms were surprisingly strong as they wrapped around her neck. She gave Brianna a kiss on the cheek.

"Shall we change your diaper and put on one of your outfits?" She gave her kisses on both cheeks. "Then I have some treats for you."

Once she'd decked her out in a little brown-and-yellow cowboy outfit, she reached for Libby's hair brush and book from the dresser and carried her into the living room. To Brianna's delight, Eli's daughter spotted the brightly colored gifts on the couch at once and squirmed to get down.

"So, you love presents just like everyone else! Of course you do. Here you go." She handed her the box of moons. Libby sat down and started to tear the paper away. Brianna got down on her knees to watch and help her lift off the lid.

The moons spilled onto the carpet. She grabbed the yellow one.

Brianna tapped it. "Moon. Moon. See? These are all moons." She laid them out in a line. To help her understand, she put the *Goodnight Moon* book on the floor and opened it to the picture of the moon.

The little girl studied it and then looked at the moons before she reached for the white one and gazed up at Brianna. She was smart, just like her daddy. "Moo."

"Moon. That's right."

"Moo."

The *n* would have to come later. Libby picked out the dark blue half moon. "That is a moon, too," Brianna said. "Moon."

But Libby wasn't as interested in the half-moons. She started playing with the six pancake-like moons. Brianna took advantage of the moment to brush Libby's brown hair into curls. She really was a beautiful child.

The sound of the doorbell startled Brianna, but Libby was riveted with her new toy.

Who could it be?

Brianna put the brush down and got to her feet. She walked to the entrance and said, "Who is it?"

"Tessa Clayton. I'm here to see my daughter."

What?

Brianna's body went hot and then cold before she opened the door. Immediately she recognized the attractive woman standing there from the pictures Eli had placed around the nursery. Libby was the spitting image of her.

"Please. Come in."

"Thank you." She stepped inside the entrance hall.

"H-have you made arrangements with Mr. Clayton?" Brianna's voice faltered.

"No. He couldn't be reached, but I assure you I'm Libby's mother. Are you Sarah, her nanny?"

Good Heavens. "No. My name is Brianna Frost. I'm watching Libby right now." At this point Libby toddled into the foyer with a moon in both hands. Brianna bit her lip. "Perhaps you should check with Mrs. Clayton first?"

"I stopped at the ranch house, but no one was there."

Brianna couldn't believe this was happening. "Have you tried to reach Eli?"

"Not yet. I just want to see her. Eli came to see me a week ago and told me I could visit my daughter any time."

Think, Brianna. This is what Eli had been wanting all along. He'd gone to Thompson Falls to try one last time to work things out with his ex-wife. Now that she'd come all this way to see her little girl, who was Brianna to tell her she couldn't?

She pulled Libby into her arms. "Come in the living room, Mrs. Clayton."

Libby hid her head in Brianna's neck. This was a situation she couldn't have anticipated in a million years. She thought how strange it must be for Libby's mother to come back to this house where she'd lived with Eli, where she'd planned their baby's nursery. And now Brianna was inviting *her* in.

She carried Libby all the way in and set her down on the floor by her new toys, hoping they would distract her. Brianna sat down next to her. Tessa perched on the end of the couch by the two of them. She, too, was wearing jeans with a V-necked kelly green sweater.

Floundering for words, Brianna said, "I just brought her this present because she loves the book *Goodnight Moon*. It's her favorite."

"Eli and I bought it right before she was born."

Shock number two.

"If you'd like to hand her that unopened gift, she'll probably behave more naturally."

Tessa reached for it and handed it to her daughter. "Would you like to open this, Libby?"

At first Brianna didn't think Libby would accept it, but curiosity won her over. Libby started pulling the paper off to reveal the coloring book of moons. She opened the pages and pointed at the various moon faces. Brianna looked up at Tessa. In a low voice she said, "Why don't you get on the floor, too, and open the box of crayons for her? Show her what to do."

Tessa slid off the couch and moved down on the carpet. Brianna fought to control her breathing while

Tessa opened the crayon box and watched to see what would happen.

Tessa pulled out a red crayon and started coloring one of the faces in the opened book. "Do you want to color, too?" she asked Libby, handing her the box. Her little girl picked out the blue crayon, the same shade as one of the toy moons. The two of them sat there and colored. "That's a beautiful blue moon," she told her daughter.

Brianna's eyes blurred to see mother and daughter doing a project together. Since Libby's birth, this was what Eli had been wanting and praying for. "I'll be right back," she whispered. Reaching for her purse, Brianna disappeared from the living room and hurried through the house to the bathroom. She dug inside her bag for Eli's mother's business card and called her.

"Mrs. Clayton? This is urgent. Can you come to the house right now? Just walk in."

The older woman didn't ask any questions. She said she'd be right there. Brianna rejoined Tessa and Libby in the living room. The two of them were coloring more pages and seemed to be having a good time. A minute later, Eli's mother walked through the door into the living room. She hadn't even paused to put on her parka.

Brianna saw the shock on the older woman's face. And the love... "Tessa," she cried softly.

The woman's brown head lifted. "Mom Clayton?" There was affection in her voice.

"Don't get up, honey. Stay right there with Libby."

Brianna knew what this moment meant to the older woman, who'd been praying for this miracle, too.

But Libby had heard her grandmother's voice and

got to her feet to show her the crayon she'd been using. "Have you been coloring?"

"Moo," she said with great emotion.

"Ah." She walked over and hunkered down beside her granddaughter. "I can see the moon."

The three of them coloring together was a sight Brianna would never forget. If Eli could see this right now... Maybe he could. She pulled out her phone and took some pictures to show him.

While they were all engaged, Brianna tiptoed over to the foyer and got her parka out of the closet. This was one of those exits that didn't need to be explained. Instead of leaving by the front door, she hurried through the kitchen to the back porch. She had to traipse through six inches of snow, but it was worth it not to be detected.

After reaching her truck, Brianna prayed she wouldn't see Eli on her way out to the highway. Instead of turning left toward Stevensville, she made a right and drove the twenty-mile loop back to her uncle's house.

The miracle had happened.

Brianna didn't question what she did next. While en route, she stopped long enough to make a reservation for a flight to California that night. She followed that up with a call to her brother. When she told him she was coming home and would explain later, he said he'd meet her at the airport in Sacramento.

Her aunt and uncle weren't home when she arrived at the house. They'd thought she'd be gone until late, so maybe it was better this way. She called a taxi and made arrangements to be picked up ASAP for the trip to the Missoula airport. Then she hurriedly packed. Before the taxi arrived, she wrote a letter for her family to read when they got home.

Later on in the year she'd fly back to gather all her belongings. For the time being, she just needed to leave Montana. When Eli walked into his house, his whole world was going to change. Brianna didn't want to be there.

Tessa had obviously experienced a huge breakthrough. It appeared Eli's visit the week before had done something that no therapy could accomplish. He didn't need outside stress while he dealt with the fact that his ex-wife had come to see their daughter.

Brianna didn't want to jump to any conclusions yet. All she knew was that, after a whole year, Tessa had made an appearance. Who knew what would happen when he found her in their house, wanting to be with Libby? If all went well, their little girl would be getting her mother back.

Maybe Tessa's feelings for Eli had been rekindled by seeing him face-to-face, too. Nothing was impossible, but the thought of those two getting back together hurt more than anything. It was too painful for her to watch it happen.

Eli left the hospital and had just climbed into his truck when his mother called. He clicked on his cell phone. "Mom? Luke is going to be all right. They have to do tests, but after a few days they'll go in to repair a valve in his heart. Luis is with him until his girlfriend gets there, so I'm coming home right now."

"Well, that's great news, Eli. I'm relieved to hear you got him to the hospital in time. Now, there's something I've got to tell you. Tessa showed up at your house out of the blue this afternoon to see Libby."

He reeled. "She *what?*"

"I guess she decided to surprise you, too."

"With Brianna there?"

"Yes. Brianna let her in and called me to come over. While I was occupied with Tessa and Libby, Brianna left your house without telling me. I'm sure she went back to her aunt and uncle's because she knew how important this unexpected visit was."

His hand almost crushed the phone. He closed his eyes tightly. "Where is Tessa?"

"Carl and Diane drove her here. The three of them are staying at the Bitterroot Lodge in town. She just left the house and hopes to talk to you when you're free this evening. I took Libby home with me and will keep her overnight. Tessa's waiting for you to call her."

This was unbelievable.

But someone else was waiting for him, too. Someone who'd become so important to him that he needed to talk to her before he did anything else.

"What would I do without you, Mom? I'll be in touch soon."

He started the engine and headed straight for the Frost home. As he turned into the driveway, he had to put on his brakes. A taxi was getting ready to back out. That outfit ran a service to the Missoula airport.

Realizing what it meant, a pit formed in his gut. He left his truck blocking the driveway and got out. The driver honked, but Eli kept moving toward the taxi and opened the back door.

"Eli—" Brianna looked shaken.

"Yes. Where do you think you're going?"

"It's clear Tessa is back and wants to be a part of your and Libby's lives. Your world changed today. So did mine. You three deserve to be together." Her voice shook.

"Well, this is one trip you're not going to take." He went around to the driver and handed him forty dollars, half the amount to get her to the airport. "Thanks for coming, but she's changed her mind. I'll grab her luggage."

Eli opened the other rear door and pulled out her suitcase, and then he returned to where she was sitting. "Come and get in my truck so the man can back out. I'm not taking no for an answer."

He'd put her in a bad position, but he didn't care. She got out without making a scene and followed him to his truck. After helping her inside and putting her suitcase on the rear seat, he got behind the wheel and moved so the taxi could leave.

"Tessa and her parents drove here from Thompson Falls and are staying at the Bitterroot Lodge. I have to stop by and see them, and then you and I are going to have a long talk."

"Wait, Eli—if we're going to leave, I need to take my luggage back to my bedroom and get the letter I left for my aunt and uncle."

He groaned. She'd covered all her bases in such a big hurry that it astounded him he'd been able to catch her before she'd managed to sneak away. Eli took a swift breath and drove back into the driveway. He pulled the suitcase out and carried it to the door for her. Then he waited in the truck until she came out again.

"I'm going to have to cancel my flight and call my brother."

"You can do that while we're on our way over to the lodge. When we get there, we'll get something to eat in the coffee shop and I'll give their room a call."

After a silence she asked, "Have you seen her?"

"Not yet. As soon as Luis showed up at the hospital to be with Luke, I was able to leave. Mom phoned and explained what had gone on while I wasn't home. The second she told me you had disappeared, I drove straight here from the hospital. Another fifteen seconds and I would have been too late."

"You have to understand—" she began, but he didn't let her finish.

"I do. But you have to understand something, too. For now let's just take care of first things first, and then we'll talk. Agreed?"

"Yes," she whispered.

"As you know, one of our hands had a heart attack today. When I heard you'd slipped away from my house without saying good-bye, I almost had one myself. I recall a certain conversation where you promised me you'd give me fair warning."

She stirred restlessly. "All the rules changed this afternoon."

"They certainly did."

By the time he'd pulled into the parking lot of the lodge, she'd cancelled her flight and had left a message on her brother's voice mail.

In the coffee shop, the hostess showed them to a table and gave them menus before walking away. Eli didn't need to look at one. "If you'll order me steak and eggs and plenty of coffee, I'll be back soon."

"Eli?" she said as he stood up.

"What is it?"

Her heart was in those blue eyes that stared at him with such concern. "This *is* what you wanted."

"For Libby to have her mother's love—yes, it's what I've wanted. But not for you to disappear."

"I believe it's for the best."

"Not for me it isn't." Her unselfishness was a rare trait that meant more to him than she would ever know. He shook his head before leaning over to kiss her mouth. "I'll be right back."

The taste of her lips lingered on his as he walked to the front desk and called Tessa's room on the house phone.

"Eli?" It was Carl's voice.

"Yes. I'm at the front desk, but I've just come from the hospital and need to get home soon. If you're staying the night, I'd like to have a proper visit with all of you first thing in the morning at my house. We'll have breakfast with Libby. But if you have to leave tonight, I can come up to your room now."

"No, no. Tomorrow will be perfect. We all need sleep."

He could only imagine. "How did Tessa react to being with Libby?"

"She can't stop talking about how wonderful her baby is."

Eli's throat thickened. "Thank God." Major, major progress had been made.

"Bless you for coming to see her last week," Carl said with tears in his voice.

"See you in the morning," Eli told him.

He hung up, dazed by the events that had happened throughout the day. Brianna's plea not to give up on his wife had resulted in a turnaround of earthshaking proportions. This could potentially be the start of Libby's relationship with her mother.

When he returned to the coffee shop, he found Brianna eating an omelet and sipping on coffee. She looked up as he slid into the booth. Her searching eyes asked all the questions he attempted to answer.

"Tessa and her parents will be at my house in the morning to have breakfast with Libby. After they leave, you and I will enjoy the day we should have had today." He sat down to eat his meal.

"Don't worry about tomorrow because of what happened today." Brianna reached in her purse for her phone. "I want to show you something." She clicked on her photo gallery and found the pictures she'd taken earlier. "Take a look at these."

Eli took the phone from her. She saw him magnify the pictures. When he looked up, his eyes had gone suspiciously bright.

"I bought crayons and a coloring book of moon faces for Libby. I had Tessa give them to Libby after she arrived. At that point, I called your mother and she came over. Pretty soon the three of them were on the floor, coloring away. I couldn't resist taking some photos so you could see for yourself."

She heard his sharp intake of breath. "You're incredible, Brianna." He grasped her hand across the table. "I'm so indebted to you for turning their first meeting into something wonderful. I'm at a loss for words."

"It all happened very naturally. Perhaps because of the pictures of Tessa around Libby's room and your recent trip to go see her, Libby didn't act at all strange around her. But maybe that's because they were together for the first month of her life."

"Maybe. Whatever the reason, I know the encounter went well or Tessa wouldn't have wanted to stay over until tomorrow in order to talk to me."

Honesty forced Brianna to explain the rest. "But the truth is I almost didn't let her in, Eli."

"That doesn't matter." He gave her hand a squeeze before letting go. "She took us all by surprise. I did the same thing to her by showing up at her door unannounced. I'm sorry it put you in an awkward position."

"It's all right. At first she thought I had to be Sarah."

"What did you tell her?"

"That I was a friend looking after Libby. While they were all busy coloring, I decided the best thing to do was leave the three of them alone. I knew that without my presence, Tessa and your mother would be able to talk more freely until you got there."

He wiped his mouth with a napkin. "And, knowing how your mind works, I guess you decided to get as far away as you could in order to make it possible for me and Libby to reunite with Tessa and for us to get remarried. That's what you told your aunt and uncle in that letter you didn't want me to see, right? Don't bother to deny it."

She eyed him directly. "I won't."

Since she'd finished eating, Eli put some bills on the table and got to his feet. "Let's go."

Once more he walked her out to the truck where they could talk in total privacy. "Before I drive you home, let me make one thing clear. I'm not the same man I was a year ago. Even if I hadn't met you, I don't have the kinds of feelings for Tessa I once had. They're dead and can't be resurrected."

"How can you be so sure?"

"Let me ask you a question. When you were in your previous relationships and decided to break up with those guys, how could you be so sure you were making the right decision?"

It took her a while. "Though I felt love for them in different ways, I knew I wasn't *in* love with them."

"And you never wanted them back."

"No."

"I don't want to get back with Tessa and am positive she doesn't want to get back with me. Only time will tell if she wants a full relationship with Libby and we work out visitation."

He could hear her mind working.

"There's a question I want to ask you, Eli, but if you can't, or don't want to, answer it, that's fine."

"Put that way, I'm going to have to. Otherwise it will lurk in your mind and fester."

She let out a sad laugh. "This is about something your father told my uncle right before you got married."

"What did he say?"

"He was worried that you were rushing into your marriage."

Eli remembered that conversation very well. "And?" He knew there was an *and*.

"There's nothing else."

He didn't believe her.

Brianna shifted in the seat. "Why do you think your father said it?"

"Because he was right. We did get married too fast. No doubt your uncle passed on that bit of insight to you because he's afraid I'm getting ahead of myself again."

"I shouldn't have said anything," she murmured.

"I'm glad you did. No secrets between us, remember? So here's another truth. Tessa wanted to get married right away, but I didn't. I wished we'd waited another year so I could have earned more money on the circuit before working on the ranch again."

"Obviously she was in love and couldn't bear to wait."

He let out a sigh. "She made it clear that if we put it off, she wouldn't be around for me in a year's time. Though I didn't know it then, I now realize that she was in love with the idea of love and it made her impatient to get married. We had a serious problem because I wanted to stay on the circuit and get married a year later. That upset her and we didn't see each other for a month. While I was away at another rodeo, I learned from Wymon that she'd come down with the flu and was really sick. I went to see her and before I left the house, we set a date."

Brianna leaned closer. "Did your father know all that history?"

"No. That was my business. Toly always confided in Dad about everything. My older brothers did, too, from time to time, but I guess I was different in that regard."

"So because you kept quiet about the situation with Tessa, *that's* why my uncle called you complicated."

"Yes. Thank you for providing the other part of the *and*. I've been waiting to hear what you were holding back." Eli pulled her toward him. "Thank you for being so completely you. I adore you, Brianna," he cried softly and drew her into his arms, devouring her until some people got in the car parked next to them.

A male voice said, "Those two ought to get a room." The female voice laughed, breaking the trance that held them both.

Eli released the woman who'd become his whole world. "I'm going to get you home and we'll start over again tomorrow after Tessa and her family leave for Thompson Falls. I'll come by as soon as I can. Please tell me you'll be free. That's the only way I'm going to make it through tonight's separation."

"I'll be free, but I'll understand if something unavoidable comes up."

"It won't." Eli meant it and gave her a fierce kiss before letting her move to her side of the truck.

Chapter 8

After being kissed breathless outside on the porch, Brianna entered the house on unsteady legs. Her aunt and uncle were watching TV. Taffy lay in front of the fire. Brianna had hoped to go straight to her bedroom without being noticed, but no such luck. The dog got up and wandered over to her.

The TV went off. "Hi, honey. Did you have a good time with Libby and Eli?"

She removed her parka and sank down on one of the chairs. "You won't believe all the things that happened today, Aunt Joanne."

"Tell us. It has to be better than TV was tonight," her uncle teased.

"Well, for starters, Mrs. Clayton was at the house when I got there because one of the stockmen at the ranch had a heart attack and Eli had taken him to the hospital."

"Oh, no. That's terrible."

"I know. And then, after his mother left, I was playing with Libby when a surprise visitor showed up at the door."

"Who?"

"Tessa Clayton, Eli's ex-wife. Out of the blue, she decided to come see her daughter."

Both her aunt and uncle got to their feet, looking incredulous.

"I'm sure I looked just like you when I answered the door. At first she thought I was the nanny. I invited her in and we went into the living room where Libby had been playing with some toys I'd given her. I put Libby back down and Tessa joined her on the floor."

"And Libby was okay?" her aunt asked.

"Completely. I phoned Eli's mother to come over, and after she arrived, all three of them started coloring on the floor together. I took a picture. When you see it, you'll understand why my first instinct was to leave Eli's house right away. And that's only the beginning of what happened."

"Take your time. We've got all night," her uncle said.

Shock marred Uncle Clark's and Aunt Diane's features as Brianna told them how she'd almost flown to California, only to have Eli put a stop to that. "Tessa and her family are staying at the Bitterroot Lodge until tomorrow. They've arranged to go over to Eli's in the morning, but he wants to spend the rest of the day with me after they go back."

"Oh, honey." Her aunt put an arm around her. "I can't even imagine how you must be feeling right now."

"It's kind of like waking up from a strange dream. It's hard to tell what's real right now."

Her uncle studied her with concern. "I hope you told him you had other plans for tomorrow."

It could easily have been her father speaking. For once her aunt didn't interject. "Uncle Clark... I know what you're thinking, but Eli and I had a long talk tonight and I understand why his father said what he did about him not being ready for marriage. It's not what you think, but, to be honest, I'm exhausted and I'll tell you the rest in the morning."

She gave them each a hug. "Thank you both for being so wonderful to me. I'm very lucky you're my family. Good night."

Brianna hurried to her room, needing to process everything that had happened now that Eli's arms weren't around her. When he was kissing her, she couldn't think straight. Not two minutes after she'd climbed into bed and pulled the covers over her, her phone rang. She reached for it on the bedside table and saw the caller ID.

"*Eli—*"

"Thank you for answering. I couldn't go to bed without hearing your voice." She could relate. "Do your aunt and uncle know what happened today?"

"Yes."

"Everything?"

"Yes."

"Then I guess they don't want you spending the day with me tomorrow."

"It's my decision," she told him. "They would never interfere." Brianna rolled on her other side. "Is Libby at your mom's?"

"No. Mom stayed with her until I got here."

"She's a saint."

"Interestingly enough, that's what she said about you

today. I saw the painted moons you gave Libby. Your gifts were such a big hit. Mom said Libby went to sleep holding the big, dark blue moon. I found it in the crib and put it in the box with the others. We're going to have a lot of fun with those. How do I begin to thank you for everything?"

"Toys and children belong together."

"I'm talking about the way you handled the situation with my ex-wife. I don't know another woman who would have done what you did to help Tessa and Libby feel secure at the same time."

"She wanted to see her daughter."

"If they end up having a relationship, it will be because of you."

"That's not true."

"We'll argue about it later. Mom said the two of them seemed so comfortable with each other. That's *your* doing, Brianna. You urged me not to give up. If I hadn't gone to Thompson Falls last week, I'm certain this never would have happened." His voice had grown husky.

Her eyes teared up. "They belong together. Anyone could see that."

"I know another thing beyond any doubt. *We* belong together." She prayed he meant it. "I'll see you tomorrow. Sweet dreams."

Brianna hung up, clasping the phone to her heart. *I love you, Eli Clayton. I love you.*

"Come on, sweetie. Now that we've had breakfast, let's go get some toys." Eli lifted Libby out of the high chair and nodded to Tessa to follow him. They left her parents at the kitchen table and headed for the nursery.

After he put his daughter on the Hello Kitty area rug,

he found the little basket of blocks and dumped them on the floor in front of her. "Do you want to show your mommy how to build a castle?"

Tessa got down on the floor with her and the three of them started working together. This was his first chance to talk to his ex-wife alone. "I'm so glad you came, Tessa. How does it feel to be with her?"

"It means everything to me. After I saw her in your arms last weekend, something seemed to snap inside of me. Our daughter just looked so beautiful…and so familiar, too."

"How do you mean?"

"Well, I can see both our families in her. That face spoke to my heart. For the first time in a year I felt alive. After you left, I called the doctor. We talked about what had happened to me. He suggested that I come here this weekend and see if I felt the same way. I knew my feelings wouldn't have changed because her image has haunted me all week."

He wasn't thrilled that she hadn't phoned him first to let him know her plans. She had put Brianna in a terrible position, but there was nothing anyone could do about it now. Eli watched tears roll down Tessa's cheeks as she placed another block on top of the one Libby had just set down.

"I know I've been very sick and you have every right to tell me to stay away for good."

"You're her mother, Tessa, and she needs you. If you want to see her, we can work it out, easy. It's up to you."

She put a hand to her mouth. "You're such a good man. I don't deserve you."

"That isn't an issue. Libby's the light of my life. For her to be truly happy she needs both her parents. Agreed?"

Tessa nodded. "You didn't want to get married as soon as I did. Then, after I got sick, I pushed you away. I thought I didn't want to be married anymore and I'm so sorry about that, but I do want to take care of our daughter."

"Then we'll work it out. Talk to your doctor and ask him what he suggests. The next time you come, I'll introduce you to Sarah. We can take turns driving back and forth from Thompson Falls."

Fear entered her eyes. "Do you think it's too late for her to accept me?"

"She's playing blocks with you. That should tell you everything you want to know."

Tessa smiled. "She is, and she's doing a great job, too." She kissed her daughter's head.

They kept playing for a little while and then Libby suddenly got up. "Moo." She pointed to the box on the dresser. Eli got it for her. They sat down again and he removed the lid.

"What are these?" Tessa asked her. Eli's daughter emptied the box and began sorting the moons. "These are so cute. Where did you get them, Eli?"

"You met Brianna yesterday, right? She bought them for Libby."

"Bree—" his daughter said unexpectedly.

Tessa glanced at him. "When we met yesterday, she told me she was a friend."

"She's done business with Mom at the gem shop. You remember Frosts' Western Saddlery in town? Brianna works there for her uncle and helped him pick out a stone to give her aunt for their anniversary. She met Libby and played with her while mom mounted the stone for him. I started seeing her after that."

He knew Tessa was wrapping her mind around what he'd just told her and decided this was a good time to leave the nursery. "Tell you what. I'm going to slip into the living room for a few minutes. Let's see how you two get along alone."

"I don't know..."

"I think you'll be fine, but if you don't feel comfortable yet, that's all right."

"I'd rather you stayed."

It was hard to say no to Tessa. It always had been.

Eli tousled Libby's curls. "Do you want to show Mommy your push toy? It's over there in the corner."

Libby knew the word *push* and got up to find it. Pretty soon she was rolling the helicopter around the room while Tessa clapped and made excited sounds. All of a sudden Tessa got on her hands and knees and started chasing Libby. "I'm going to get you!" she said.

His daughter giggled and started running faster. Eli could hardly breathe. A week ago he couldn't have imagined this happening.

"Well, well. What's going on in here?" Carl and Diane had come into the nursery to see what all the excitement was about. Libby stopped running and came over to hug Eli.

Tessa rolled over on her back and smiled up at them. It was great to see her look that happy again. "Libby and I have been playing, but I think she's had enough for now." She got to her feet and turned to Eli. "We should go back, but I'll call you after I've talked to my doctor."

"Sounds good," Eli said and got to his feet. He carried Libby to the front of house. Tessa and her parents pulled on their parkas and he walked them to the front door.

"Bye, Libby," they all said. Tessa looked at their daughter with longing before kissing her good-bye.

Though Libby clutched him tightly, she did say bye. "Bye, Mommy," he encouraged his daughter to say, but she didn't.

When they'd left, he carried her back to the nursery and walked over to the larger picture of Tessa. "Mommy," he said the word several times, pointing to the photo. "Can you say *Mommy*?"

He waited, but she started to squirm and said, "Moo."

Eli smiled to himself. This was the best beginning he could have hoped for. He had to remember the old adage that Rome wasn't built in a day. Now it was time to phone Brianna. He checked his watch. It was noon. After putting Libby on the floor, he pulled out his cell phone.

Brianna answered on the second ring. "Hi!"

Just hearing her voice excited him. "Libby and I are on our way over to get you. Have you eaten lunch?"

"Not yet."

"Good. We'll stop somewhere and get hamburgers. Libby likes fries and soft ice cream."

"So do I. How fun."

"I thought after that maybe we could take a walk in the Lee Metcalf National Wildlife Refuge, and then bring her home for a nap."

"Perfect. I'll be ready."

Eating lunch at the restaurant and pushing Libby around in her stroller at the nature preserve, Brianna felt as if they were a true family. Only two of the walks were free of snow, but they were able to see a fox, geese, some swans and an osprey. They both took pictures with their phones before heading back to the truck.

Libby appeared oblivious to the cold, all bundled up in her snowsuit. The little girl had worked her way into Brianna's heart. As for her father...

When they got back to Eli's house, they entertained Libby until Eli put her down for a nap. Then he pulled Brianna into the living room. He threw some cushions down on the floor and they lay by the fire he'd made.

"This is the kind of day I'd planned for yesterday." He kissed the tips of her fingers.

She was dying to know his thoughts. "Tell me how things went with Tessa this morning," she said.

"Better than I could have hoped for," he admitted. "She said my visit last week broke down some barrier in her mind. She wants to be a mother after all."

Brianna's eyes filled with tears. "You must be overjoyed."

"I am. I told her to talk to her doctor and that we'd work things out as far as visitation and things go."

"I'm sure you have concerns."

He nodded. "What if this change of heart doesn't last and she decides she doesn't want to be a mom to Libby after all? For Libby to get to know her mother and then be rejected is too painful to think about, but it's something I have to consider."

"Maybe you should talk to her doctor about this."

His eyes studied her for a long moment. "That's exactly what I'm going to do with Tessa's permission. How did you get to be so wise?"

"TV."

"*Brianna*—" He pulled her close and started kissing her. She'd been aching for him.

"I want you," he whispered. "You have no idea how beautiful you are and how much I need you."

"I feel the same way," she confessed. The floodgates had been released. To be able to explore her feelings, knowing one of Eli's greatest concerns might be getting resolved, allowed her to open up to him completely. She couldn't get enough of him. No kiss was long enough or deep enough. Soon she found herself on top of him, their legs entwined. She could kiss every part of his ruggedly handsome face and hard, sinewy body. He was such a gorgeous man.

"Do you love me?" he demanded urgently after rolling them over so he could look down into her eyes.

"Oh, Eli—you *know* I do. I think I've loved you from the first time I saw you."

He kissed the corners of her mouth. "I've already told you I'm in love with you. I want to marry you as soon as possible."

Her breath caught. She cried his name, but he stifled any other sounds with a passion that swept her away to a place where she couldn't deny him anything. The words rang in her ears.

Eli wanted to *marry* her.

Those words brought joy to every last atom in her body. It was just as her mother had said she would feel when she met the right man.

When he finally came up for air, he said, "Don't tell me it's too soon to talk about becoming my wife. We both know our feelings run so deep there can be no doubt we're meant to be together, but I'm aware you might have reservations about becoming a stepmom."

She shook her head. "I already love Libby."

He caught her face between his hands. "Loving her and being a mother to her day and night for the rest of our lives are two different things. I'm positive that when you thought about getting married one day, it wasn't to a man who already had a child. It's too much to ask, yet I'm asking because I can't imagine my life without you."

Brianna sat all the way up, kissing his hand. "I love you so much it hurts. I want to be your wife. But now that Tessa has had a breakthrough, I'm wondering how she'll react to our getting married right away. Libby bonding with her mother is the most important thing."

"Our love is important, too, Brianna. I'll call her doctor first thing in the morning and tell him what's happened in case he doesn't already know. We'll go from there. But right now I want your answer. Will you marry me? We'll worry about the date later."

Brianna didn't have to think about it. "Yes! One hundred percent, yes!" She flung her arms around his neck. "You've made me the happiest woman alive, Eli Clayton."

On Monday morning, while Eli was at the barn talking with Wymon about Luke's pending heart surgery, his phone rang. It was Dr. Rutherford.

He clicked on. "Thanks for getting right back to me. I know how busy you must be."

"I had messages from both you and Tessa today. The news about her visit to see Libby is remarkable, but because you're contemplating marriage to someone else, I need to talk to you about it right away."

Eli tensed. "I'm available to talk at five today. Will that work for you?"

"Yes, that's fine."

"Good. We'll talk then."

After hanging up, he rode with Wymon to the range where the vet was meeting them to finish the cattle vaccinations. When they stopped for lunch, Eli called Brianna, but he got her voice mail. Undoubtedly she was having a busy morning. He told her he'd be talking to Tessa's doctor after work and would phone her at dinnertime.

At five minutes to five he walked into his house and scooped Libby up in his arms. The call came on time and Sarah took over while he went in his bedroom and closed the door.

"Dr. Rutherford?"

"I listened to your message and here's my concern," the doctor said. "This woman you're planning to marry—how long have you known her?"

"Brianna and I met a month ago." Eli had been ready for that question. To the doctor's credit, he didn't respond with shock or derision.

"How bonded is she to Libby?"

"We've spent enough time together that Libby loves being with Brianna and cries when she has to leave the house. Last week she was in the hospital with croup. When Brianna walked in the room, Libby couldn't have shown more excitement or affection. She acts as comfortable around her as she does with my mother."

"That sounds promising for the three of you. As for Tessa, her phone call was a revelation. I understand their first meeting over the weekend went very well."

"It was amazing."

"Have you set a wedding date yet?"

"No, but it will be soon."

"Whatever visitation you work out with Tessa, the next time you see her, I suggest you tell her you're planning to get married and give her the date. Tessa will need to factor that information into her thinking. By her reaction, I'll know how stable she is.

"The whole goal is for Libby to have a relationship with her mother. So may I caution you to move carefully where Tessa is concerned?"

Eli heard him loud and clear. Brianna's uncle would add the punctuation points to that advice. "Libby's bond with her mother comes first, Dr. Rutherford." Brianna had said as much earlier.

"Good."

"Bill me for this phone meeting."

"Don't worry about it, and don't hesitate to call me again," the man said.

He hung up, not able to imagine what the doctor must be thinking about Eli having met another woman who he wanted to marry this fast. But this was Eli's life and no one else's. Knowing Brianna's feelings were just as strong helped him to act on his dream to make her his own.

Just as he was about to call her, his cell phone rang again. This time Tessa's name showed up on the caller ID.

He clicked on. "Tessa?"

"Hi!" There was a time when he would have given anything to hear that voice. That had to be another lifetime ago. "I need to talk to you. Is that all right?"

"Of course." He sank down on the side of his bed. "What's on your mind?"

"I talked to the doctor today and told him I want to spend as much time with Libby as possible. Mom and I could drive to your house every day this week and spend time with her while you're at work, if that's okay. I know you have a nanny, but maybe we could work something out so I can be alone with her for part of the time? What do you think?"

Eli sucked in his breath. He could hear how nervous she was and wanted to reassure her. "I'm willing to work out anything so you can be with Libby. If you'd like to come every day, Sarah can disappear into her room while you're here. You and Libby can have the run of the rest of the house."

"You mean it?" Her cry rang right through the phone.

"Tessa, I always wanted you to be close to Libby. You're her mother."

"Thank you, Eli, from the bottom of my heart," his ex-wife said, her voice suffused with relief.

He got up and paced the floor for a minute. "There's one more thing we need to talk about before we hang up."

"Am I rushing you too much?"

"No. No, Tessa. This is about me, but it will affect you. As you know, I've been dating Brianna Frost since the last week of December. We're in love and want to get married in March." That was what he'd been planning in his mind. "When everything falls into place, it means there will be two women in Libby's life on a permanent basis."

Silence reigned. What she said next shook him to his foundation. "You must truly be in love to want to get married after only one month. I had to get sick in order for you to feel sorry enough for me to give in to my demands." She laughed as she said it, but he could tell the news upset her, and he couldn't blame her.

He frowned. "Don't compare the two situations."

"That's hard not to do. You weren't ready when we got married. This last year of therapy has taught me that I forced you into a marriage I wanted too much at the time and not for all the right reasons."

"I wouldn't have married you if I hadn't wanted to," he said.

"Even so, my guilt caught up to me after Libby was born. I was positive you hated me as much as I hated myself for preventing you from going out on the rodeo circuit another year. So I blocked you out. And I felt so worthless. I didn't believe I could be a good mother to Libby, so I blocked her out, too."

Eli marveled at the revelations pouring out of her. It was all starting to make sense.

"But when you brought her to the house two Saturdays ago, there she was, big as life and so beautiful. Eli—we have such a beautiful daughter."

He had to clear his throat. "Indeed we do."

"I want to prove that I can be a good mother. Tell me—is Brianna as in love with you as you are with her?"

"Yes." Thank Heaven. "We knew how deep we'd fallen for each other while Libby was recovering in the hospital."

"That's why I kept hearing Libby say the name *Bree* while she was playing with those toy moons. I had no idea another woman had become so important to you and her in such a short period of time."

"Just remember one thing, Tessa. She only has one mother. That's *you.*"

He heard her crying softly for a minute. "I can't believe you're giving me a second chance."

"That's because a part of me will always treasure the time we were married. Those memories will never be taken from me."

"I'll always love you, Eli, and our daughter means everything to me."

This was a conversation he'd never thought would happen. "Go ahead and make your plans to come tomorrow. I'll let Sarah know and we'll go from there."

"Mom and Dad are thrilled."

Yup. They would be. "We'll talk later, okay?"

The second he got off the phone with Tessa, he called Brianna and told her he was coming over. After they'd hung up, he went into the kitchen to talk to Sarah about what was going to happen for the rest of the week.

He got Libby prepared for bed and read her a story about an elephant, then took off for Stevensville. Tonight Tessa had sounded stable to Eli, even after he'd told her the news that he was in love again and planned to get married. As far as he was concerned, she appeared to have pulled a 180.

When he turned into the Frosts' driveway, Brianna came running outside and hopped into the truck. "You sounded so excited that I couldn't wait to hear your news."

Eli pulled her into his arms and kissed the daylights out of her. Nothing was holding him back now. "Not seeing you has made today feel like an eternity."

"Did you talk to Tessa's doctor?" she asked eagerly.

"Yes. There's so much to tell you that I don't know where to start, but I need to drive over to the hospital to see Luke before his operation in the morning. Then we'll have all night to talk. Don't you move one inch, all right?" He kissed her hungrily before backing out onto the street.

Two hours later, Eli drove Brianna back to her uncle's house. She'd been absorbing everything he told her.

Though the news about Tessa was absolutely wonderful for Libby, it was the doctor's warning to Eli that made her a trifle anxious.

May I caution you to move carefully where Tessa is concerned?

That advice sank deep inside her.

Carefully could mean a lot of things. Tessa planned to drive here every day to see her daughter and be a mother to her. It seemed the most natural thing in the world now that Eli had explained what had gone on in Tessa's mind throughout their marriage. Time had been lost and she was eager to catch up.

Eli turned to her. "You're being quiet all of a sudden. Come over here, please."

"I don't dare. The second you touch me, I catch on fire."

"That's why we need to get married ASAP. Let's make it the first or second Saturday in March."

She moistened her lips nervously. "I want it more than anything, but I'm worried."

"Tell me why."

"You know as well as I do that Dr. Rutherford sent us both a message. Move carefully, he said. What he means is we need to give Tessa the best chance possible to bond with Libby. So far your little girl has already had to adapt to a nanny, then me, and now her mother. Since you need Sarah to help you, she has to stay in the picture, but *I* don't."

"Brianna—"

"Hear me out, Eli. Please." She took a swift breath. "Libby shouldn't have to be confused. A huge dose of her mother is exactly what she needs. The more they see each other, the sooner Libby will be comfortable staying overnight with her mother and grandparents in Thompson Falls. Once Tessa becomes a fixture in Libby's life, then Libby will be able to see me as the woman in *your* life."

His head reared back.

"You know I'm right. If I'm always over at your house, or you're at my place with Libby, it will prevent her from making that attachment to her mother. She needs to see you and Tessa together often so she makes the necessary association. If this plan is going to work, I can't be there."

It was a long time before he spoke. "So what are you saying?"

"I love you so much, Eli, but we need to separate in order to help Tessa and Libby make it as mother and daughter. I'm going to go back to California, hopefully tomorrow."

"If you do that, I'm going to lose you." He sounded so bleak that it wounded her.

"If our love isn't strong enough to survive this, then it isn't strong enough to endure over a lifetime."

A groan came out of him. "I couldn't take you being gone for more than a week."

"I think it'll need to be at least three weeks for this to work."

"Brianna—"

"I know. I can't bear the thought of it, either."

"What will you do?"

"I'll help on the farm. Be with my brother and his wife."

He sucked in his breath. "How do you think your aunt and uncle are going to feel about this?"

"When they know why I'm leaving, they'll tell me it's the right thing to do."

"That's what I'm afraid of."

"Eli, you and Tessa brought Libby into this world. This is Libby's chance to learn to love her mother the way you love yours. I know in my heart you would never deny her that opportunity. You need to concentrate on helping them bond without any other distractions. Your little Libby is already on her way to getting close to her mother."

"Your good sense is killing me."

"If I don't go, we won't be able to stay away from each other. Do you have a better idea?"

"I wish I did. Brianna—I don't know how I'm going to be able to let you go. I don't think I can." He kissed her with such intensity she went weak in his arms.

After he finally let her go, she looked up at him. "You do understand, don't you?"

His eyes bore into her soul. "To be separated from you now…"

"I don't like it, either. Please, Eli—never forget how much I love you. We'll talk every day until you feel it's time for me to come back." Brianna raised her mouth to his one more time before she tore herself from his strong arms and got out of the truck.

He levered himself from the cab to walk her to the front door. After another passionate embrace, she let herself inside. While she stood against the closed door, trembling, she heard him barrel out of the driveway.

Taffy limped into the foyer. Brianna petted her before making her way to the bedroom. Her aunt must have heard her come in and followed her.

"Honey? What's wrong?"

She wheeled around. Her pain had gone beyond tears.

"I'm so sorry, but I have to go home tomorrow. Forgive me for leaving you in the lurch, but this is the only way."

"What do you mean?" her uncle said as he joined them.

"First of all, Eli has asked me to marry him and I've said yes."

"Oh, honey—you mean it?" Her aunt reached out to hug her, but her uncle stood there like a statue.

"The trouble is, when Eli spoke to Tessa's doctor today and told him about our plans to get married, he said to move carefully with her. Eli and I know what he meant. Tessa needs the chance to bond with Libby. The only way that's going to happen is for me to step out of the picture for a while."

"A very wise idea."

She'd expected her uncle to say that. "It seems Eli's surprise visit to their house last week proved to be the impetus that has brought Tessa around. She wants to be a mother to her daughter and will be coming here every day this week. The three of them need to work on this without me around. Do you understand?"

"You wonderful girl," her uncle said and wrapped his arms around her the way her father used to do.

No. She wasn't a wonderful girl. Dr. Rutherford was the one who'd pointed the way. If anyone was wonderful it was Eli, who was putting his daughter first, no matter how much he wanted Brianna with him. Talk about a man who matched these mountains...

Eli left the Clayton house with an idea he couldn't wait to present to Tessa. He had no intention of going longer than three weeks before he brought Brianna back from California.

En route to the ranch, he phoned his ex-wife, not caring how late it was.

"Eli?" Tessa sounded scared. "Have you changed your mind?"

"Of course not, but I have another idea. Why don't you ask your parents to drop you off here tomorrow and let you stay all week at the house? Sarah can go to Mom's and come over if she's needed."

"You'd let me do that? Be alone with her?" she almost squealed.

"Why not? If you're around Libby 24/7 for the whole week, you two should be able to bond more quickly. I'll drive you back home at the end of the week. Then we'll see if Libby wants to stay with you for a while. That is what you want, right?"

"You know it is." Her voice throbbed.

"Then let's do it. Call me when you get here and I'll come down from the range to help you get settled in."

If letting her live in his house would make this experiment work faster, then he could get the love of his life back sooner. Unfortunately, the fear that Tessa could suddenly develop inadequacy issues again haunted him. He didn't want to believe in another reversal, but Libby was her own little person and who knew what could happen.

There would probably be lots of anxious moments when Libby didn't turn to Tessa, which would prove difficult for her mom. Eli knew he was taking a risk and he would need to be patient. But it would all be worth it to marry Brianna once he knew Libby was secure in her mother's love.

Tomorrow he'd get up extra early and drive to the gem shop before work. He wanted another look at the dark blue sapphire, cut in the shape of a heart.

Blue sapphires with extremely high clarity were rare and very valuable. A three-carat stone of that quality was probably the most valuable of all the cut stones in his mother's collection.

Years ago she'd shown the stone to him and his brothers. She'd let them examine it with her handheld loupe. Their mom told them she was reserving it for just the right person. Most buyers wanted a round or princess cut. Not everyone wanted a heart-shaped stone. But whoever did would be getting a prize.

Not until he'd looked into Brianna's eyes for the first time and learned she was a Valentine baby did he think about that stone. For all he knew, his mother had sold it since then.

He would let himself inside the shop and open the safe to see if it was still there. Valentine's Day was coming up soon…

Chapter 9

Brianna came out of the shower to hear the one o'clock newscast. It predicted that Valentine's Day would be the warmest day in Marysville so far this year. Seventy degrees with only a few tufts of clouds. After the twenties and low thirties of Montana, it was positively balmy in California.

Three long, agonizing weeks had passed since she'd flown back home. Brianna was surprised she'd lasted this long without seeing Eli. Her decision to leave had been the right one. Eli had come to realize it, too. His nightly phone calls let her know Libby and her mother were connecting. The wonderful news helped Brianna to survive.

Today was her birthday. She'd been waiting to hear from him since morning, but his call hadn't come. She finished dressing in the black dress she'd worn with him to the French restaurant in Missoula a month before. It felt like a hundred years since then. Doug and Carol were taking her to the Napa Valley for her birthday dinner celebration. If their parents were alive, they'd all be going.

One thing about living in Montana with her aunt and uncle was that Brianna had done her grieving away. Now that she was back home, it wasn't as hard as she'd thought it would be to live around the memories. The farm was thriving and Doug was so much happier than when she'd first left. They were able to laugh and reminisce without going to pieces.

But by the time they arrived at the Beaulieu Vineyard and walked around the gardens, she'd grown a little despondent. Why hadn't Eli called?

They were shown to their reserved table on the terrace and given menus. The terrace had a gorgeous view of the vineyard with a trellis roof overhead covered in red bougainvillea.

Once they were seated, Brianna eyed her brother critically. "You've worn a permanent smile on your face ever since we got in the car. What aren't you telling me?"

"It's your birthday, remember?"

"How could I forget? But you're acting like you've got a huge secret. Do you want me to open my present now? Is that what this is all about?" Carol averted her eyes, letting Brianna know something was going on. "If you don't tell me soon, I'm going to explode with curiosity."

"Well, we can't have that." Doug winked. "Okay, then. A few days ago Carol went to the doctor—"

"Get out of here!" Brianna cried out, knowing exactly what her brother meant.

"We're expecting in September but wanted to wait until you were here to tell you."

"Carol—" Brianna jumped up from her chair and ran around the table to hug both of them. "This is the best birthday present I've ever gotten. I'm going to be an aunt!"

Her joy was so all-consuming that she didn't realize someone was approaching their table. When she looked up, she almost passed out when she spotted Eli standing there. In his tan suit and white shirt, he was easily the most gorgeous male in the restaurant. Their gazes collided.

"Happy Birthday, Brianna."

In the periphery she saw the waiter make another place at the table, but she was so spellbound she couldn't move.

He hurried to her side and put an arm around her waist to support her. "I flew into Sacramento and rented a car. Your brother and I got acquainted over the phone and he told me where to find you," he whispered against her neck, kissing the soft, scented skin. "Come and sit down next to me."

"Eli—" She sagged against him. "I can't believe you're here."

"I've been planning this for two weeks. You have no idea how much I've looked forward to your birthday." His eyes worshipped her. "You're my valentine."

Somehow she made it to her seat with his help. He sat next to her and pulled a small, dark blue, velvet box from his suit pocket. "Open it. I don't want to wait."

Her heart thundered in her chest. With trembling

hands, she opened the box and then gasped. Twilight had sneaked up on them. Light from the candle centerpiece lit up the facets of the large blue sapphire heart mounted in a white-gold setting.

"You already agreed to marry me. This makes it official." He took the ring out of the box and reached for her left hand, sliding it home on her ring finger.

The sapphire had to have come from the Clayton sapphire mine. She was thrilled out of her mind. "It's incredible."

"That's my heart. It's yours."

Tears ran down her cheeks. "This has to mean things are going well with Tessa and Libby. Oh, Eli—" Forgetting they had an audience, she threw her arms around his neck and clung to him.

"Brianna? The waiter is coming with our dinner."

Her brother's reminder forced her to let go of Eli. She knew her face was flushed.

"After we eat, we'll walk over to the other side of the restaurant where I can dance with my valentine," Eli whispered. "I've been dreaming about this moment for so long."

She tried to behave, but it was close to impossible to be seated next to him and not climb on his lap and kiss him nonstop. Brianna had ached for him during their separation.

Doug and Carol congratulated the two of them, and Brianna told Eli they were expecting a baby. That led to talk about being a new father. She could tell her brother liked Eli a lot. But, oh, how happy she was when he asked her to dance and they were able to excuse themselves.

With his arm around her waist, he walked them

through the restaurant to the dance floor, where a live band was playing. Dozens of red, pink and white heart-shaped balloons had been strung overhead. Eli pulled her against him and they moved as one to the music.

"I'm in Heaven right now," she murmured against his chest.

"You're not the only one. You look gorgeous tonight, by the way."

She was in an enchanted state when the lead singer announced that someone named Brianna was celebrating her birthday today. The band started to play "Happy Birthday" and everyone in the restaurant sang along.

"I can't believe you," she cried in surprise, hiding her face against Eli's shoulder.

"I gave him a tip before coming to join you."

Brianna finally lifted her head. "Eli? I'll never forget this night as long as I live."

"It's not over yet." He kissed her mouth and they danced until he said, "Let's go out to the rental car. I only have a half hour before I have to get back to the airport, and there are things we need to discuss in private."

What? "But you just got here—"

"I know. Wymon called the family together for some important ranching business we have to take care of tomorrow, so I have to get back to Missoula tonight. Even Toly is flying in from Reno after tonight's rodeo. Roce is going to meet us both at the airport and drive us to the ranch."

Eli said good-night to her brother and Carol, and they agreed to wait at the restaurant until Brianna got back. Then she and Eli headed out to the parking lot.

He slid behind the wheel of his rental car and pulled her into arms. They devoured each other before he finally pulled back and heaved a long sigh. "I have to go, Brianna," he said.

"I don't want you to leave. How am I going to let you go?" she asked.

He covered her face with kisses. "I want you to come back to Montana as soon as you can. Tomorrow if possible."

"That soon?" she cried with excitement. "Are you sure?"

"Positive. That ring is to remind you that we're going to be man and wife just as soon as we can find a date that works."

"Eli—" She tried to catch her breath. "While I can still think, tell me how it's really going with Tessa and Libby."

"The two of them are slowly making progress. I think letting Tessa sleep at the house for the first week was a good idea. We're all working on getting Libby to say *mama*, but it hasn't happened yet.

"Last week I drove Libby to Thompson Falls and stayed the night to see how she handled an overnight with Tessa and her family. She's been acquainted with her grandparents from the time she was born, but that night wasn't her best.

"They've set up a nursery, but she didn't want to be in there alone with Tessa unless she could see me. I ended up lying on the floor in a sleeping bag until she fell asleep. After breakfast we could tell she wasn't at ease, so Tessa went back with us and stayed all week.

"She's with her now and they seem very comfortable together at this point, but it's going to take time for Libby to get used to being away from the ranch with her."

"What about Sarah?"

"I'll continue paying her no matter what we work out. This week she's back home with her grandparents so Tessa and Libby can be completely alone in the house while I'm at work. Mom and Solana are nearby in case anything happens."

Brianna kissed his jaw. "I knew it wouldn't be easy, but it sounds like it's working."

"It is," he cried softly against her mouth. "That's why I want you back with me, Brianna—so we can make wedding plans. Call me after you've booked your flight, okay? I'll reimburse you after you're back."

She clung to him. The separation from him had only proved to her that, without Eli in her life, she couldn't imagine going on. Though people didn't die from a broken heart, they didn't fully live, either.

"I love you, Eli. I didn't know how much longer I could have lasted here without you."

"Don't you know I feel the same way? Soon we're going to be together forever."

Forever.

One more kiss and then she got out of the car and watched him drive away. All the way back to the patio where Doug and Carol were waiting, Brianna studied the spectacular engagement ring Eli had given her. To think he'd flown all this way just to give it to her on her birthday. The fact that he had to get right back for a family business meeting made it even more important to her.

Eli glanced around the ranch house living room. It had been a while since the whole Clayton clan had assembled. Wymon had indicated this meeting was important. He wore an expectant look after they'd all found a place to sit.

"As you know, our father took out a lawsuit against the BLM three years ago because they started increasing our taxes for the acid mine drainage coming from our mine and polluting the water. It's happening to many metal mine owners throughout the West. The problem is that there are so many abandoned mines in the country, yet the BLM has to find the revenue to clean those up, too, so they get their money by gouging active mine owners.

"One solution proposed to Dad was to implement a water treatment plan at our mine, but it's terribly expensive. Worse, we will be sued if the water still didn't meet federal standards. In other words, under the Clean Water Act, even if we tried to clean up the drainage, we would be liable for any pollution that continued to flow from it.

"Dad got together with our attorneys to work out a time frame with the BLM. But progress was slow and he feared a new tax would soon be levied against us. He tied up a lot of money to pay experts to come up with a different way to cut down on the contaminants, and we've been dealing with that problem ever since.

"Well, I'm here to tell you that our worries are over. The night before last, the lawyer told me the news that we've won the appeal. I'll read the history of the case for you.

"'Clark Fork is Montana's largest river and travels down from the Continental Divide. It threads its way between the Flint Creek, Sapphire and Garnet ranges that are filled with mines on its way to Missoula. In 1908, a flood washed tons of contaminated sediments from those mines into the river. Arsenic, copper, zinc, lead and cadmium contaminated millions of tons of sediment along 120 miles of the river's banks. The river's trout all but vanished.

"Montana is one of relatively few states that have active coal mining and one of still fewer allowed to use royalties from coal mines on non–coal mine reclamation. The state gets between three and four million dollars in Surface Mining Control and Reclamation Act royalties per year to deal with thousands of contaminated sites, not nearly enough to help its lands recover from over a century of mining.

"There are more environmental problems associated with abandoned mine lands than there will ever be funding to take care of them. If there was a federal royalty for the metal-mining industry, there could be a consistent source of funding revenue. Unlike oil, gas and coal industries, the metal-mining industry does not have to pay royalties to the federal government. This is due to the 1872 Mining Law, which hasn't been updated since it was first passed in an attempt to encourage the settlement of the West.

"In the case of the Sapphire Ranch versus the BLM, the Clayton Sapphire Mine is still active and taxes were levied against the mine because of the drainage coming from it. Acid mine drainage is a major problem in the West. Over half of impaired streams are contaminated by metals, many from draining mines like the Claytons'.

"Since the lawsuit, the Clayton Sapphire Mine has managed to implement two treatments that have brought the drainage into compliance with federal standards by making limestone sidings of the channel and spreading carbon over the forest area to reduce contaminants.

Therefore, there will be no more taxes levied against the Clayton Sapphire Mine for the foreseeable future.'"

While the rest of the family responded with a collective cheer, Eli quietly hugged his mom. He knew how much sleep she'd lost over the long-standing court case.

"I'm only sorry that Dad isn't here to celebrate with us," Wymon continued. "With the money we're going to save, we'll be able to buy more cattle and build some much-needed holding pens."

Roce got up and gave Wymon a bear hug. "You're the best, bro."

Their mother rose to her feet, as well. "This is the news our family has been waiting three years for. Wymon, I want to thank you from the bottom of my heart for doing a wonderful job of taking the reins at such a painful time and despite great personal sacrifice.

"And I want to thank all of my sons for working tirelessly alongside the stockmen and Luis to bring continued success to this ranch. I'm sure your father is rejoicing up in Heaven."

His heart brimming with emotion, Eli added his thoughts. "I, too, want to thank Wymon for his leadership and courage during a difficult period. I also want to thank all of you for helping me through a very dark time in my life. Libby couldn't have been born into a greater family. Mom has been a saint, and Solana has been right there with her this whole time, too."

Suddenly Toly spoke up. "Amen to everything Eli just said. And thanks to all of you for supporting my selfish ambition to make it to Las Vegas. If I get there, it will be my last attempt to win the gold buckle. After that, I'm coming home to ranch full-time again. I won't forget what you've all sacrificed for me."

"We're proud of you," Wymon added. "And now, Solana has prepared a feast. Let's head to the dining room, shall we?"

Luis joined them and they celebrated with a toast to the future. Once lunch was over, Eli was getting ready to leave for his house when his mother asked him to go upstairs with her.

Curious as to what she had to say, he followed her up to her room. She closed the bedroom door before facing him with a sober look in her eyes.

"Mom?" he asked, his heart rate picking up. "What's wrong?"

"Sit down for a minute."

He frowned but snagged a chair while she sat on the side of her bed. "Is this about Tessa and Libby?"

She sat straight with her hands on her knees. "Yes. We haven't talked since you left for California yesterday. No one knows you went. Did you give Brianna the ring?"

"Yes. If you could have seen her eyes…"

"I can imagine. Have you set a date yet?"

"We didn't have time, but she'll be flying in tomorrow evening and we'll discuss it then."

A deep sigh escaped her lips. "That's what I need to talk to you about."

"Why do I get the feeling I'm not going to like this?"

She got up from the bed. "I wish your father were here. This is the hardest thing I've ever had to do."

Eli didn't like hearing that. "You've never minced words, Mom. Don't do it now."

"After Tessa put Libby down yesterday, she asked me to come over to the house for a talk. I thought it had something to do with your daughter, but nothing could be further from the truth."

He waited.

"Tessa told me she wishes she was still married to you. She says she knows she made a mistake in divorcing you and insists her feelings for you have come back even stronger than before."

Eli shook his head. "No. That's her fear talking because she's still afraid to be alone with Libby. This insecurity will pass with time."

"Wait before you say anything else, honey. She asked me to intervene for her."

Anger built inside of him. "In what way?"

"She begged me to talk to you about breaking it off with Brianna."

He bristled.

"You told her yourself you've only known Brianna a month. Tessa doesn't believe your feelings for Brianna could be anything like your feelings for her when the two of you got married. She wants the chance for the three of you to be a real family again. Being with you these last three weeks has been a revelation to her and—"

"Mom?" he broke in on her. "Do you hear yourself?"

"I'm only repeating what she said to me. She wishes she hadn't gotten sick, but she swears she's all better now and she wants her life back. She wants her daughter *and* her husband."

Eli flew out of the chair. "I'm not that man anymore."

"Just finish hearing me out, son."

"There's nothing more to hear."

"Except this… Remember when she told you she didn't want to be married anymore and how much that hurt you? Well, think about it—a year later she's come out of her deep depression and now that she's in her right state of mind, she knows what it is she truly wants. And now it's *you* who's saying you don't want it. All I'm asking is that you think about this long and hard. I just want you to be sure you won't change your mind down the road and wish you'd kept your family together."

"I'm desperately in love with Brianna."

His mother cocked her head. "Isn't it interesting that Brianna was the one who urged you to try again with Tessa?"

"Which I did. Nothing's there, believe me."

"I hear you. All I'm doing is conveying the message that Tessa wanted me to give you."

"It's too late."

"Eli—"

"She shouldn't have asked you to interfere. It's not fair for her to fall back on your love for her to try to fix a problem that can't be fixed. I've been doing my best to help her bond with Libby, but that's as far as things go between us." He gave his mother a kiss and left the bedroom.

Instead of rejoining his brothers, he found his parka and left through the back door. The short walk to his house helped him get his emotions under some semblance of control.

Tessa was cleaning up the kitchen when he walked in. She darted a glance at him. "Libby had her lunch and I put her down for a nap."

"Good. That gives us the time to talk."

She acted nervous. "I…take it your mother said something to you."

"Yup." Eli removed his parka. "Let's go in the living room."

He perched on the arm of the couch while she started picking up toys off the floor and putting them into a basket. She finally met his gaze. "I can tell you're upset and I don't blame you, but I was afraid to approach you."

"None of that matters, Tessa. Our marriage is over and has been for a long time. Last night I flew to California and gave Brianna an engagement ring."

"*That's* where you went?"

He nodded, registering her shock. "We're planning to be married soon. She left three weeks ago in order to give you and Libby a better chance to bond, but she's coming back tomorrow. Once she and I have returned from our honeymoon, we'll work out visitation."

"But you and I were a family once." He heard tears in her voice.

Eli got to his feet. "A year ago we were in a totally different place. I can't tell you how thankful I am that you want to be a mother to Libby. But you and I have changed. One day you'll meet a great guy who will make you happy and whole again. Someone who will learn to love Libby as much as you do."

She got up from the floor. "So Brianna's the love of your life."

He eyed her frankly. "Yes."

"And you're ready to get married so soon after meeting her? Aren't you afraid it might not last?"

"No. What we feel for each other is deep and real. My only concern is that you and Libby continue to get comfortable so that she'll be fine staying overnight with you, without me being there. That's the goal, right?"

Tessa's cheeks grew flushed.

"As long as Libby is still asleep, I have an errand to run. I'll be back at dinner." Without waiting for a response from Tessa, he walked into the kitchen to retrieve his parka before leaving the house.

Once in the truck, he drove into town and pulled up in front of the saddlery to talk to Clark Frost. This was a visit he couldn't put off.

Brianna's uncle had two customers. Eli checked out some of the saddles on display. The minute the last person left the store, he walked over to the older man, who smiled at him.

"Eli! Haven't seen you in a while." They shook hands. "What brings you in here?"

That question told him Brianna hadn't told her uncle about their engagement yet. She probably planned to phone later that day after her aunt and uncle came home from work.

"I got here as soon as I could to tell you something important. Last evening, I flew to California and celebrated part of Brianna's birthday with her."

"You what?"

"It was a very short trip because I had to be back for a business meeting at the ranch this morning. To get straight to the point, Brianna and I are now officially engaged. I know how much she loves you so I came right away to tell you. Besides my mother and ex-wife, you and her brother and his wife are the only other people to know yet."

"You got engaged…" Clark repeated it as if he was talking to himself. His reaction wasn't reassuring.

While the older man stood there, visibly stunned by the news, a couple came into the store. Eli would have to make this quick.

"I adore your niece and I gave her a ring with a blue sapphire from the mine. We're hoping to plan our wedding soon. But you're busy now and I have to get back to Libby. We'll talk again later after Brianna calls you with the news. Give my best to your wife."

Eli walked out of there, realizing he'd dropped a bombshell.

Her family knew why Brianna had gone to Marysville. No doubt they had ideas that, after Eli spent time alone with his ex-wife and daughter, the three of them might end up a family again, leaving Brianna on her own.

The more he thought about it, the more he realized that the people closest to him were probably thinking, maybe even hoping, that that would happen. He couldn't blame them. A year ago, he would have given anything for Tessa to recover and come back home.

But not anymore. His heart was with someone else.

He got in his truck and headed to a drive-through to get a coffee. After finding a parking space around back, he phoned Brianna, needing to hear her voice.

She picked up on the third ring. "Eli?"

"Sweetheart?"

"I'm so glad you called," she said softly. "I'll be coming in on the five-thirty evening flight."

"I'll be there to pick you up. But first you need to know I just dropped by the saddlery to tell your uncle we're engaged. I'd assumed he already knew, but I was mistaken."

He heard a slight gasp. "I was waiting to tell them tonight when I phoned to let them know I'll be home tomorrow." Brianna knew her uncle wouldn't be thrilled about the news.

"I'm glad he knows," Eli said.

"You're right that he had to be told. Oh, Eli, do you really think it will be okay for me to come home now?"

"I *know* it will be," he assured her. They'd followed the doctor's advice for these past three weeks. But the game plan had changed because Eli hadn't expected that Tessa would start to get ideas about rekindling their marriage.

"Is Libby acting like a daughter around Tessa?"

"To some degree."

"That's good news."

"The good news is that you're coming home. I can't live without you any longer."

"Same here. As soon as we get off the phone I'll call my aunt and uncle and let them know I'm coming."

"I love you," Eli said in a husky voice. "We need to start working on those wedding plans."

"I'm way ahead of you."

His heart leaped. "Phone me later. I'm heading back to the ranch now. I'll be listening for your call."

"You're my whole world, Eli."

"Oh, Brianna." He sighed. "You don't know how good it feels to hear you say that."

Chapter 10

Later that afternoon, Brianna grabbed her suitcase off the carousel and hurried out the main doors of the Missoula airport into the freezing cold air.

She spotted Eli's truck right away and headed in its direction. The tall, gorgeous rancher saw her coming and stepped out onto the sidewalk. Her heart thudded out of control.

"You're home!" he cried, picking her up and swinging her around. In front of all the other cars, he kissed her long and hard.

"I've been living for this," she whispered against his cheek.

"Come on." He reached for her suitcase and walked her to the truck with his arm around her shoulders. "Someone's waiting to see you."

"You brought Libby?"

He opened the rear door and there sat his adorable daughter all bundled up in her car seat. The second she saw who it was she cried out, *"Bree! Bree!"*

The joy in her voice warmed Brianna's heart. She hadn't forgotten her. "Darling girl. It's so wonderful to see you!" She leaned in and kissed her on both cheeks.

Libby wanted to get out and held up her arms for someone to pick her up, but Eli intervened. "You have to stay where you are until we take Brianna home." He kissed her brown curls. After putting the suitcase on the other side of the seat, he closed the door and helped Brianna into the truck, kissing her again before starting the engine.

He clasped her hand all the way to the Frosts' house. Meanwhile, Libby had a meltdown in the backseat.

"I'm right here, Libby. Oh, Eli. She's so upset."

"She'll get over it in a hurry as soon as we reach your aunt and uncle's house. I want them to realize the three of us are going to be a family. Libby adores you, and I want them to see that."

Between Libby's crying and Taffy's barking, the reunion with the Frosts was noisy and chaotic until Brianna finally picked Libby up. Then her tears magically disappeared.

Everyone gathered in the living room in front of the fire. Brianna removed Libby's parka and sat down in the easy chair with her. The dog crept closer to sniff and lick both of them, causing Libby to giggle. Then the little girl caught sight of the sapphire ring and grabbed Brianna's hand.

"This is something new, huh, Libby? Your daddy gave it to me. That big blue heart came from your family's sapphire mine." Libby looked up at her. "It's my ring. Can you say *ring*?"

"Reen."

Brianna's gaze collided with Eli's. He said, "That's the seventh word to come out of her mouth. She can say *ring* now. And notice how she's pronouncing the *n*?"

"That's right! Good job, sweetie." She kissed her again. "Ring. Do you want to hold it?" Brianna slipped it off her finger and let Eli's daughter examine it. Libby kept trying to put it on her own fingers with no luck. Everyone laughed. "It's too big. We'll have to get you your own ring one of these days."

Her aunt Joanne walked over and hugged the two of them. "Congratulations on your engagement. You too, Eli." He was sitting on the chair next to them and she hugged him, as well. "We couldn't be happier with the news, right, Clark?"

"Absolutely. By marrying Eli, we're going to have our niece living close by for the rest of our lives. There could be no greater blessing. Welcome to the family, Eli." Brianna was overjoyed that her uncle was taking the announcement so well.

"Thank you. Libby and I have been waiting for this day from the first time the three of us met. It was love at first sight. I intend to love your niece for the rest of her days and make her as happy as she makes me."

"Have you two set a date?" her uncle asked.

"Not yet, Uncle Clark." She put the ring back on her finger. "We'll have to look at a time that's good for everyone on both sides of our families."

"We want it to be soon," Eli added.

Brianna let Libby get down off her lap so she could pet the dog. "I told Doug we'd probably get married at the church here in town and have a reception. He and Carol offered to hold an open house later in the year for our friends in Marysville, but nothing's been decided for sure." She looked at her uncle. "Will you give me away, Uncle Clark?"

His eyes misted over. "It will be a great honor."

"Can I offer your daughter a cookie, Eli?" Aunt Joanne asked.

His smile turned Brianna's heart over. "She'd love it."

"Okay, let me just run to the kitchen. Be right back."

Her aunt returned quickly and knelt next to Libby, who was patting Taffy. Clearly the dog loved the attention. "Would you like a treat?" The sound of that word caused the dog to lift her head.

Libby studied the sugar cookie before taking it from her. After biting into it, she broke off a piece to feed the dog. Then she took another bite and the whole process began again.

Eli chuckled. "I'm afraid she thinks eating is a game. I take a bite and she takes a bite. We do it all the time."

"She's precious," Brianna's aunt murmured.

"Guess what, Aunt Joanne? Libby has spotted your pink sapphire ring and can't take her eyes off it."

Her aunt put her right hand in front of Libby, who touched the stone. "Do you like my ring?"

"Reen," Libby said again.

"It came from your family's sapphire mine, too." She smiled at Brianna. "We're two lucky women."

"You can say that again." Brianna was so happy that she felt as if she could burst.

By now Libby was toddling around the living room inspecting everything. The dog followed close behind, causing them to chuckle. Eli's little girl had won her family over to the fact that a wedding was going to take place. Eli's decision to bring her to the house had been the perfect way to break the ice with her uncle.

When Libby started removing magazines from the basket in which they were housed, Eli scooped her up in his arms. "I think my little cowgirl has had enough excitement for one day and needs to go home for dinner and bed."

Brianna's heart fell. She didn't want the evening to end, but she knew this was one time she had no choice. She was acutely aware of the fact that Tessa would be waiting at home for them. Reaching for Libby's miniature parka, she helped Eli put it on his daughter.

Eli said good-night to her aunt and uncle and then Brianna walked him to the foyer with Taffy at her side. He kissed her, but it didn't last nearly long enough. "I'll phone you in the morning and we'll make plans for tomorrow."

"It's getting harder and harder to say good-night." She half moaned the words.

"I know. It's close to impossible," he ground out. "We need to pick a date tomorrow. I'm crazy in love with you."

"That's how I feel, exactly." She kissed him again and then Libby, but she didn't say good-bye in the hope that his daughter wouldn't cry because they had to leave.

No such luck. The second he opened the door and walked outside into the cold, Libby protested and cried all the way to his truck.

Brianna's heart couldn't take much more. Their wedding day couldn't come soon enough.

Eli sang one song after another to entertain his daughter on the drive home. When they arrived at the ranch, he carried her into the house and discovered that Tessa was still awake. She got up from the couch, where she'd been watching TV.

"Hi. You're back kind of late."

"Yeah, sorry. She's ready for dinner. Then it's bedtime right away."

Tessa reached for her, but Libby hid her face in Eli's neck. It was the first time Libby hadn't gone to her since Tessa had started staying the night. He carried his daughter into the kitchen and put her in her high chair. Tessa got out the jars of baby food and fed her without a problem.

When Libby had finished eating, they walked through the house to the nursery.

Together they got her changed and tucked her into the crib with the new stuffed bunny Tessa had given her. To his relief Libby hugged it. The action had to please her mother.

Eli left the room first and went to the kitchen to make some coffee. "Would you like some?" he asked as Tessa walked in.

"No, thank you, but I'd like to talk to you."

"Go ahead."

"I smelled perfume on Libby's outfit. Just how close is our daughter to Brianna?"

The question had been inevitable. He chose his words carefully. "In her own way Libby loves her, and vice versa."

"That explains why she wouldn't hug me when you arrived back here."

"Tessa—she'll never be Libby's mother and could never take your place. But I'm glad they're getting close. That way Libby will always be happy whether she's with me or with you."

"How soon are you getting married?"

"We're going to discuss that tomorrow evening."

"So you won't be home again until late?"

"Probably not."

She leaned against the counter. "You must have some idea of a date."

"Hopefully mid-March. Maybe sooner depending on everyone's schedules."

"Is she going to continue working at the saddlery?"

He looked at her over the rim of the mug. "I don't know, but whatever we end up doing, nothing's going to interfere with the visitation schedule we set up."

"I've been thinking about that. It's not going to work if we have to drive back and forth from Thompson Falls all the time. It's too long a trip. After talking it over with Mom and Dad, I've decided to move to Stevensville and get a condo."

Eli hadn't seen that coming.

"They'll finance it until I get a job and they're buying me a car, too. That way I can have Libby several times a week and every other weekend or one overnight every weekend. My doctor thinks it's a good idea, but only if I'm ready. I *know* I am."

Something fundamental had happened for Tessa to consider stepping out of her comfort zone, away from her family, and he had to admit the idea made a lot of sense.

"That's a big change for you. I agree it'll be a lot easier on both of us."

"So, you wouldn't mind if I moved here?"

"No, Tessa. I just want all of us to be happy."

"You don't think my living in town will bother Brianna?"

"No, I don't. I think she'll be relieved we don't have to make the long trip to Thompson Falls so often. But even if you don't find a condo you like right away, be assured that we'll do whatever it takes to make this work." He got up from the table and rinsed out his mug. "I have to be up at the crack of dawn, so I'm going to bed. Good night."

"Good night," she whispered.

Eighteen hours later, Eli sat in the Frosts' living room while he and Brianna discussed wedding plans with her family after dinner. Because of a conflict with Toly's rodeo schedule, they chose March 18 as the date so everyone they loved could make it. The minister said the church in town would be available that Saturday and they were able to book the Stevensville Hotel for the reception.

Eli's first marriage and reception had taken place in Thompson Falls. Another reception had followed the next evening at the Clayton ranch house. His marriage to Brianna would be different and exactly the way she wanted it.

Still needing to settle some details, they left her family to talk things over with Eli's mother. But when Eli got Brianna into his truck, he didn't start it up right away. Instead, he pulled her over so she was half sitting on his lap. They kissed with a hunger that was growing out of control. He finally lifted his head. "Now that our plans are made, there's something important I have to tell you."

"If you're worried that we're not going to have a long honeymoon because of Libby, don't be. I don't care about that as long as I'm your wife. There'll be time for a trip later on in the year when she feels totally secure being away from you."

"You're one amazing woman, Brianna Frost. But this is about something else. Last night Tessa wanted to talk after we put Libby to bed."

Her blue eyes searched his. "You sound concerned."

"She's planning to move here and get a condo in town."

Hearing those words, Brianna sat up and turned to him. "I can understand why she wants to do it. Don't you?"

"Yes, and it makes sense. During our marriage she made friends here, so it won't be as if she feels completely isolated. What's bothering me is that she's now in competition with you for Libby's affection. Last night our daughter didn't go to Tessa when we walked in the house." He hadn't told Brianna that Tessa wanted to get remarried to him. No way did he intend to tell her that.

Brianna groaned. "I suppose that was inevitable."

"I'm convinced that no matter how long you stayed away, Tessa would still feel threatened. It's something we have to deal with and not let it impact our plans."

"I agree. But I feel sorry for Tessa. She's lost a whole year."

"I know. Let's just be thankful she has her doctor, who's going to continue to work with her. In the meantime, all we can do is go on with our plans and do what has to be done. I only told you this so you'll be aware of her feelings."

"I think her feelings are normal and I'd probably be just as threatened if our positions were reversed. I'll be as careful and sensitive as I can."

"You think I don't know that?" He clasped her to

him, burying his face in her hair. "Let's change the subject. I thought this coming weekend we'd start tearing the house apart and paint it throughout with a color scheme we both want. Nothing's been done to the house, except for the nursey, since my grandparents lived there for the last twenty-five years of their lives."

"You're kidding."

"Nope. I'm letting Sarah go after the wedding and sending her a check for three months' wages. I hope that will leave her with enough money so she won't worry until she finds a new job.

"The rest of the money I set aside for a nanny can now go to transforming this house into *our* house. Tessa and I got married fast with zero money to our names and were grateful the family let us move in here just as it was. But that's in the past.

"I want us to buy new furniture, art we both love, new windows and window coverings and carpeting—the works! I'd like you to design the master bedroom. I'm sure there are things your parents left you. Use them any way you want throughout the house. All the old things we'll put in storage at the ranch house for any family member who might need them in the future."

For her response, she hugged him so hard around the neck that she practically cut off his breathing. "When I went to bed last night, my aunt hinted that they were going to buy us a car for a wedding present. She told me to think about the kind we wanted that would be best for Libby."

Eli sent up a silent thanks for Clark's wife, who was in their corner. Eli had a hunch it was going to take longer to win Clark over completely. Clark and Eli's father had shared confidences over the years. Unfortunately

Clark hadn't been fed the right information about the circumstances surrounding Eli's first marriage. One of these days he'd pull him aside and tell him the truth.

"Come on. I'd better get you home. Do you know how great it's going to be when we get to go home together? Give me one more kiss so I can make it through tonight." Since Brianna had come into his life, he couldn't imagine having to live much longer without her.

On Saturday Eli had asked Wymon to help him move the furniture out of the master bedroom. Brianna did her part, dressed in an old T-shirt and a torn pair of jeans. They loaded two trucks to the brim and drove them to the ranch house. Until their new California king–size bed arrived the next Saturday, Eli would be sleeping in the guest room.

"We'll be gone until after lunch," Eli said to Brianna.

"Take your time. I've got a ton of work to do here."

He swept her into his arms, kissing her breathless before leaving the house. After he left, she freshened up in the bathroom and removed her ring. Now she was ready to start painting and walked into the master bedroom to get started. She tuned the radio to a soft rock station and spread some drop sheets on the floor. Some cans of primer sat in one corner.

After sorting through dozens of paint samples, they'd settled on lemon white for the master bedroom walls.

Gone were the old curtains. The new bedroom furniture would be coming in a mellow cream color. She and her aunt had picked out the most gorgeous quilt in a Western motif. Talk about the room being transformed!

She poured paint in the tray and dipped the roller in it, and then she began applying the first coat to the walls. Eli had already filled all the nail holes and sanded them.

When the first wall was finished, she took a break and went down the hall to the bathroom. When she came out again, she saw Tessa standing at the end of the hall with a pile of folded clothes in her arms. Brianna stopped in her tracks.

"Oh—you surprised me!"

"Hi, Tessa. I didn't realize you were here." Eli had told her his ex-wife was staying at the ranch house with Libby and his mom for the weekend, but there was no sign of their little girl with her.

"I just thought I'd come over and finish the wash while Eli's mom is watching Libby. Maybe Eli told you Sarah isn't working for him anymore, so I've taken over the household duties. I was just about to put Libby's clean clothes in her drawers."

Brianna blinked. She was pretty certain Eli hadn't expected her to come over here today while they were working on the house, but Brianna didn't want to make her feel unwelcome.

"No problem," she told her. "Go ahead and do what you need to do."

Trying not to let Tessa's presence bother her, Brianna went to the bedroom and started painting the next wall. She'd barely gotten started when Tessa appeared in the doorway.

"You've gotten busy in a hurry."

Brianna was surprised at the comment but chose not to let it get to her. "The wedding isn't that far off. We're planning to paint all the rooms."

"I wanted to transform the house. This room was always so dark. But after I got pregnant, I had terrible morning sickness and couldn't be around paint so we had to let that project go."

Brianna thought she knew where Tessa was going with this but blathered on nervously. "My friend had morning sickness for a while. I know it can be bad."

"You have no idea." Tessa paused a moment and then asked, "As long as I'm here, do you mind if I talk to you?"

"Sure," she said and turned off the radio she'd placed on the stepladder. As she did so, Tessa said, "I understand he's given you a sapphire from the mine."

"Yes. He surprised me with it when he flew to California for my birthday."

"A heart for an engagement ring. How unusual."

"I was born on Valentine's Day."

"You're kidding."

Brianna took a quick breath. "Tessa, I'm sure you're anxious to talk to me about the visitation schedule for Libby. I'm willing to work out anything you want, as far as that goes."

"I appreciate that, but there's something else I have to say. Brianna... I still love Eli."

She knew it.

"My illness caused a chemical reaction in me, but when he brought Libby to see me, it was like I'd awakened from a deep sleep."

With those words, Brianna put the roller down, her hand shaking too much to paint. "Why don't we go in the living room," she said and walked into the hall. Tessa followed her.

"Eli didn't want the divorce."

"I know. He's told me everything."

"No doubt. I don't blame him for dating you. I told

him our marriage was over, and he finally took me at my word. But I've recovered from my illness now. I never dreamed I'd be stricken by the kind of depression I had, but it's over and I want my family back."

Brianna sank down in one of the living room chairs.

Tessa stood in front of her, her whole body pleading. "As one woman to another, I'm begging you to call off your engagement so Eli and I can have a real chance to put our marriage back together. He says he loves you and I believe him, but I know deep down he still cares for me. Otherwise he wouldn't have let me live here with him while you were away.

"Let me ask you a question. If you were in my shoes, would you give up on your marriage so easily after knowing that your illness made you say and do things that you wouldn't normally do? Wouldn't you fight for Eli with every breath in your body before it was too late?"

Yes, she would.

"That's what I'm doing now. Did Eli tell you I spoke to him about getting remarried? We talked the other night and I begged him to reconsider what he's doing. If he didn't tell you about our talk yet, that means he's thinking hard about it."

Brianna didn't know. He hadn't said anything to her.

"Both our families want to see us back together. That hasn't changed. It's the reason I've come to you. Please consider carefully everything I've said. You don't have a daughter. Your life isn't on the line in the same way.

"It was as if a miracle happened when he came to my door that day. At first I sent him away, but that was because I was in shock. As the day wore on, I felt like I'd been let out of prison and was free to be myself for the first time in a year."

Brianna feared that if she was forced to listen to any more it would kill her. She got up from her chair and stared out the window. Her words from a few weeks ago came back to torture her. *Don't give up on winning your wife back. The chemistry in the brain can change. Good-bye, Eli Clayton. You're the best.*

Taking a fortifying breath, she turned to Tessa. "I wouldn't wish the experience you've been through this last year on anyone. I promise I'll think about everything you said."

"Thank you for listening to me. I'd better go."

She put on her parka and left the house. Brianna watched through the window until Tessa was out of sight. Then she went back to the bedroom to finish painting the rest of the wall. When it was done, she put the lid on the can and washed out the roller and tray in the kitchen sink.

Eli still hadn't returned. It gave her time to freshen up and put her ring back on. After slipping on her coat, she left the house and got in the truck to head back to Stevensville.

When she looked down, the light from outside had captured the facets of the sapphire on her ring.

That's my heart, he'd said.

But did he truly mean it?

Chapter 11

There was one person Brianna had to talk to and she needed to be alone to do it, where Eli couldn't walk in on her. When she reached her uncle's house, she hurried to her bedroom. To her relief her family had gone to visit friends and had taken Taffy with them.

Beyond tears, she phoned her brother.

Pick up, pick up.

"Brianna?"

"I'm so glad you answered."

"What's wrong?"

"Oh, Doug—everything is so horribly wrong, I don't know if I can marry Eli."

Silence prevailed before he said, "Are you thinking of calling off the wedding?"

Her pain had reached its zenith. "Is that what you think I should do, too?"

"Too? What are you talking about?"

"Eli's ex-wife wants her husband back. She came to the house earlier to ask me to walk away and give them a chance. She said both families are hoping for the same thing. If you'd heard the pain in her voice, you'd understand why I'm in such agony."

"Was she cruel to you?"

"Not cruel. Deep down I know she's hurt that Eli has found someone else. I know she's anxious. All she did was plead for her life back with Eli. Let's be honest. She couldn't help the depression that changed her. But it's gone now and she wants them to be a family again. At least she was honest with me. How can I stand in the way of that?"

"I'm sorry her illness changed their lives. But now Eli loves *you,* Brianna. Carol and I can see it and feel it."

"But he loved her first and married her. Now that she's not ill anymore, she wants to honor the vows she made to him and keep their family intact. Libby needs her parents."

"She has them and always will, no matter the situation. Does Eli know about today's conversation?"

"Not unless she's already told him."

"Where are you?"

"I left Eli's house and came home. Uncle Clark and Aunt Joanne aren't here right now."

"Do yourself a favor and don't tell anyone about this until you talk to Eli. He deserves to know everything. I like the guy a lot. So does Carol."

"I'm so glad, but apparently Tessa did talk to him about how she feels and he chose not to tell me. What does that say about him?"

"Tessa has put him in a difficult position, but you're

the woman he's planning to marry. Get on the phone to him as soon as we hang up and straighten this out before it causes real trouble," her brother said.

She gripped the phone tighter. "I'm scared, Doug."

"About what? Surely you don't doubt that he loves you."

"No. It's actually something I said to Eli weeks ago after telling him I wouldn't go out with him anymore."

"What was that?"

"I—I told him to fight for his marriage," she stammered. "I told him a miracle could happen. And now it *has*. She wants him back. If I don't step away, then—"

"Then you've deduced that you're a terrible person for interfering with the miracle. I know how your mind works. Don't take on guilt and do this to yourself. Eli loves you. Brianna? Are you listening to me? If you run away now, then you're not the strong woman he adores or the strong sister I know you to be."

"But if you could have heard her."

"I swear if you don't call Eli right now, I'll call him myself and then get on the next plane for Missoula if necessary. Do you hear what I'm saying?"

It took her the longest time before she could respond. "I'll do it."

"Don't make a promise you can't keep."

He always said that.

"I promise. I love you, Doug." Tears pooled in her eyes and started running down her cheeks.

Before she lost her nerve, she hung up and phoned Eli. He answered on the third ring. "Hi, my love. I know I'm late, but we had to rearrange the storage room before we could fit all the new stuff inside. It took forever, but now it's done. I'll be at the house in a few minutes."

She held her breath. "Eli? I'm not there. I left and drove to my uncle's for a clean change of clothes. I had an accident and got paint on my blouse and jeans. But I'm leaving now and will meet you there ASAP."

"Okay, hurry!" he said.

She clicked off and sat with her head in her hands for a minute. Then she went to her closet and swapped out her clothes before walking back to the truck, resigned to meeting her fate.

After dropping Wymon at his place, Eli drove to his own house. When he walked inside, he discovered Brianna had painted two of the four bedroom walls with the primer before she'd had her accident.

He turned on the radio and decided to put on the first coat of paint over the dried primer while he waited for her. His heart raced when she walked in a few minutes later wearing a white T-shirt and jeans, her outfit hugging her curves in all the right places.

She came right over and kissed him on the neck. "I'm so glad you're back. I missed you this morning."

"I didn't mean to be so long. You've done a great job on these walls."

"Thanks. I would have painted all of them, but I had a visitor." She poured more primer into the pan and reached for the other roller.

"Who was that?"

"Tessa."

Eli kept the roller moving evenly. "Did she come to get some of Libby's toys?"

"No. She was finishing up the laundry and put some clothes away in Libby's room."

He frowned and looked over at her. "She shouldn't have been here at all. Was Libby with her?"

"No. She said your mom was watching her. I could tell that doing the laundry was an excuse for her to talk to me."

When she knew he wouldn't be there.

Bristling with an anger he'd never felt before, Eli finished the wall he'd been working on and put the roller down. "Brianna?"

"Yes?" She'd started painting as if nothing was wrong, but he knew differently.

"Hell," he swore softly. "My hope that Tessa wouldn't be brazen enough to approach you on your own went up in smoke today, didn't it?"

"I'll admit I was surprised she'd come in the house. Why didn't you tell me she's already told you that she wants you back?"

He expelled his breath. "Because I don't care what she wants and told her as much. I'm sorry, Brianna. She knew Wymon and I were busy, and she no doubt saw this as her last chance to get me back. She probably told Mom she wanted to talk to you about visitation and my mother agreed to stay with Libby until she got back."

"I can tell your mom loves her very much."

"She does and always will, but I'm sure Mom had no idea of her true intentions today. Tessa's tendency to push the envelope hasn't changed, despite her illness. If anything, she's shown an incredible amount of willfulness. You and I have been over this before, but I'm going to tell you a few things I didn't tell you the first time."

"About what? She only wants what any woman would want after what she's been through."

"Both parties have to want the same thing, Brianna.

When Tessa and I were dating, she demanded that I marry her right away or I would lose her. I saw a selfishness in her that surprised me. She wasn't willing to wait a year, even though we needed the money my time on the circuit would provide. Her ultimatum disturbed me and I needed time to think about it.

"Here's the part you *don't* know. When I came back to find her ill with the flu, she implied that if I hadn't left, she probably wouldn't have gotten so sick. Looking back now, I realize she wanted me to feel guilty so I would cave and agree to get married. Do you hear what I'm saying?"

She was slow to nod, hopefully a sign that he was getting through to her.

"Tessa asked me to break off my engagement to you," she said.

"What did you say to her?"

"I told her I'd talk to you."

He shook his head. "When she came out of that depression, what she hadn't counted on was the fact that my feelings for her had died during the hellish year we'd lived through. I'm sorry it happened, but her illness changed everything.

"And there's still one trait about Tessa that hasn't changed—she wants what she wants when she wants it. I see a little bit of that in Libby. We'll have to work on it with her. This time, however, Tessa can't have everything she wants and she will have to make a new life with someone else if she wants to get married again."

"She's a good person."

"I agree, and she'll always have a piece of my heart. But that was another world and another time. *You're* the woman I'm in love with. Together we'll keep each other happy and have more babies. Libby's going to need a brother or sister. We'll shower her with love. Tessa will give her the love she needs from her mom. It will work out, all of it."

Brianna finished painting the wall and put the roller down, looking haunted.

"What is it?"

"You make it sound so easy, but she said both families wanted the two of you to get back together."

"Of course they did in the beginning. Her condition was a tragedy that shouldn't have happened, but it did. Now I'm going to tell you something my mother told me when I bought the heart sapphire right after you left for California. She said she'd decided never to sell it but changed her mind when she saw the way we looked at each other. She said it was as if two pairs of blue eyes glowed like flames. She knew at that moment that what we had was magical."

Brianna's face lit up. "She really told you that?"

"Cross my heart, you beautiful creature. Do you honestly believe she would have said those words, or let me give you that ring, if she didn't want you to be her new daughter-in-law? I'll tell you something else. She gave us that stone as her wedding present to us."

Taking advantage of Brianna being at a loss for words, he reached for her. "So now you've got two choices. You can get on a plane with me tonight. We'll fly to Las Vegas and get married. That's my personal choice."

He heard a moan before Brianna started to cover his face with kisses. "What's my other choice?"

"To go ahead with our plans for a March wedding and make everyone happy. At least they will be, after I have a little chat with your uncle."

Her heart was in her eyes. "I'm glad you're going to tell him the whole truth. Uncle Clark takes his job as my protector seriously."

"Don't I know it. Your aunt had to provoke him into congratulating us."

"No, she didn't," Brianna said, but her words came out muffled against his neck.

He laughed. "He's about as subtle as a mounted bull rider ready to slaughter the competition. I have a feeling he left dead bodies all over the arena when he used to compete. Was your father the same way?"

She cupped his jaw with her hand. "The two of them were pretty equal in the tough dude department, but Dad had a bit of a softer side. Doug and I ruined him."

"Well, we've got Libby, who's going to turn your family's house upside down. No doubt Grandpa Frost will morph into such a marshmallow that we won't recognize him."

A giggle burst out of her, the happy kind he'd wondered if he'd ever hear again when they'd first started talking.

"Come on. The rest of the painting can wait for another day. You drive back to your uncle's. I'll be there after I've cleaned up the paint and showered. Once I've talked to Clark and put his mind at rest, there'll be nothing stopping us. What do you say?"

She pressed her mouth to his. "I'm praying for March to get here *fast*."

"You don't know the half of it."

Twenty minutes later, he pulled up to the ranch house and went in search of Tessa. He found her upstairs in the guest bedroom. She saw him out in the hall and got off the phone. Eli was glad his daughter wasn't with her.

"I'm glad you're free for a minute. We need to talk."

"Uh-oh. I can tell you're upset with me for talking to Brianna."

"Not upset. Let's go to the study where we can have privacy."

They made it downstairs without Libby spotting them. He imagined she was in the kitchen with his mother and Solana.

"After you," he said waving Tessa inside his father's den and shutting the door behind them. "Go ahead and sit down."

He perched on the end of the couch while she sat in one of the overstuffed leather chairs. "You told her you still love me. I don't doubt that you care, but it's not love. In fact, I'm not sure it ever was, not in the deepest sense of the word. You wanted to get married. Your friends were getting married. It seemed the exciting thing to do. Am I right?"

She stared at him for a long time before nodding.

"I didn't want to lose you, so we got married. But our year apart changed everything, except our love for Libby."

"I know, but I've been confused since you brought her to see me. Forgive me for what I said today."

"You were being honest, so there's nothing to forgive, Tessa. More importantly, there's something vital you should know. Brianna urged me to try and reconnect with you so you and Libby could have a relationship. *She's* the reason I went to see you in Thompson Falls in the first place."

At that revelation Tessa's complexion paled.

"Her parents were killed in a car crash almost a year ago. She has cried to me over her loss so many times.

Brianna and her mother were very close and she'll miss her every day for the rest of her life. When she begged me to go see you and take Libby, it was because she knew what it would mean to our daughter one day to have a loving mother, the kind Brianna had. The kind *you* have. The kind *I* have.

"The woman I'm engaged to has always put you and Libby first. You'll never have to worry about her trying to undermine you. I'd like to think that the woman I was once married to will respect Brianna for the big part she'll play in Libby's life. Our daughter is going to need all of us to pull together."

Tears glimmered in Tessa's eyes. "You really are in love. I can feel it. I'm so sorry for approaching her today. I'll apologize to her. Brianna Frost is a very lucky woman."

"She says the same thing about you because Libby is your little girl and Brianna adores her. Libby's the best part of both of us, Tessa."

She rose to her feet. "I know." Her voice trembled. "I'm going to go find Libby right now. God bless you and Brianna, Eli."

He followed her out of the study but left the house through the front door and raced to his truck. In his heart Eli knew there'd be no more trouble with Tessa. His biggest concern was to get Clark Frost on his side.

Chapter 12

It was almost Eli's wedding day! He came down from the range Friday after work, jubilant that this would be his last night alone. Tomorrow Brianna would become his wife.

His clunky truck creaked and groaned as he made the turns. It was on its last legs but had served him well. He'd bought it used on his sixteenth birthday with his own money. One of these days he'd invest in a new one, but he and Brianna would work it into the budget later in the year. He was thankful her aunt and uncle had bought her a new car.

For the moment, he and Brianna were using his money to finish up the rest of the changes to the house. He loved Brianna's taste. Already, the house looked like a completely different place. Halfway home he received a text from Roce:

Hey, bro. TGIF party in the barn. You'd better show up pronto because you're already ten minutes late!

He let out a bark of laughter. His brothers were throwing him a bachelor party in the barn tonight? Trust them to keep him in the dark. His excitement over the wedding caused him to drive too fast. When he pulled up to the barn, he had to apply the brakes before he drove right through the closed doors. Their squeal resounded in the cold night air.

No one seemed to be around. What was going on in there? He parked the car over by the corral fence and then jumped down from the cab and rushed to open the doors.

"*Surprise!*"

To his shock, he saw all three of his brothers standing in the bed of a brand-new Silverado 1500 full-size four-door black truck parked at an angle inside the entrance. If he didn't know better, he would think he was face-to-face with a giant dealership ad.

He took a step back. "That's a lot of manhood I'm looking at."

Toly grinned. "You're supposed to be looking at the truck!"

"It's yours, bro." This from Roce.

Eli's heart almost failed him.

His big brother, Wymon, flashed him a rare smile. "No one has worked harder than you this year to earn it. Climb in and show us what it can do. The key is in the ignition. Let's be sure it can take you and that gorgeous bride-to-be of yours on your honeymoon without a problem."

This gift was totally unexpected. Eli was so humbled by their generosity that he couldn't talk for a minute. "I can't accept it."

"The hell you can't!" they said in unison.

Luis suddenly appeared at the entrance. "You'd better do as they say. Your brothers mean business."

"So you were in on this, too."

"I just do what I'm told. For what it's worth, no one deserves this more than you. Luke says the same thing. That's the highest praise coming from him. Go on. I'll shut the doors after you leave."

With a whoop, Eli leaped into the cab. The smell of a brand-new truck was like nothing else on earth. So was the feel of so much power as he drove them up the mountain. When there was too much snow to go any farther, he parked the truck and got out.

As his brothers jumped down, he hugged each one. Together they looked out at the magnificent Sapphire Mountain range silhouetted against the night sky.

"I don't know how to thank you guys," he said in a husky voice. "I'll never forget it."

"Don't worry. We won't let you," Roce teased him.

They all laughed, but this time his brothers climbed into the cab for the drive back. Eli suddenly realized it was freezing out. But he was so on fire for Brianna that he'd been oblivious. Tomorrow was almost here. He could hardly breathe.

Brianna's aunt and uncle had lived and worked in Stevensville for years. Between all their friends and those of the Claytons, the church didn't even have standing room by the time the three o'clock ceremony was set to begin. Brianna was stunned at the overflow. She couldn't see Eli for all the people.

The organist had begun playing as Brianna's uncle helped her inside the foyer with her bouquet of yellow and white roses. She wore a white silk wedding dress she and her aunt had bought after a quick trip to Missoula. It was a princess design with short sleeves and a scooped neck. A shoulder-length lace veil partially covered her hair.

"Don't be nervous," her uncle whispered. "I can see Eli and Wymon at the altar waiting for you."

She knew Eli had wanted his older brother to stand up for him. Brianna had asked Carol and Lindsay to be her bridesmaids. They were both pregnant and looked lovely in pale yellow chiffon, but Lindsay was the only one showing.

Doug and Eli's other brothers acted as ushers. Libby was too little to come to the ceremony, but Eli's mother would bring her to the hotel for the dinner afterward.

"It's time, honey. Pretend I'm your dad."

She squeezed his arm. "No. You've been my other dad since the day I came to stay with you. You and Joanne are the greatest blessings in my life."

"And you're the daughter we never had. Shall we go and get you married now? If we don't start down the aisle, Eli's going to come striding back here to find out the reason for the hold up."

Brianna smiled up at him. Eli and her uncle had become good friends since the night Eli confided in him about his first marriage. Their talk had helped her uncle understand the truth about why Eli hadn't felt ready to get married the first time.

Once her bridesmaids began to make their way down the aisle, Brianna entered the chapel with her uncle and started her journey toward the ruggedly handsome cowboy she'd loved from day one. He stood tall in a formal, navy blue suit and white shirt with a yellow rose in his lapel.

His dark blue eyes lit up as she drew closer to him. He grasped her hand and mouthed, *I love you*, before he walked her the rest of the way to where the minister waited for them. She stared at Eli and mouthed the same words back, feeling the warmth of his hand travel through her trembling body.

"Dearly beloved, what a glorious day for this man and woman to come together to become one in the sight of God and these witnesses."

Brianna heard the minister speaking, but so many thoughts were spinning in her head that she couldn't absorb them all until she heard him say, "I now pronounce you man and wife."

A gold wedding band had now joined her engagement ring. She'd given Eli a gold wedding band inlaid with small blue sapphires. Brianna had picked it out with his mother's help.

Before the minister could tell Eli to kiss his bride, Eli was already fulfilling that part of the ceremony. It was a husband's kiss he was giving her, so full of desire Brianna had to cling to him so she wouldn't fall.

The minister finally cleared his throat, and Eli took his time before releasing her mouth. "If you'll please turn to face your family and friends... May I present Mr. and Mrs. Eli Hartman Clayton! You may congratulate them in the foyer."

The length of their kiss had brought heat rushing to her cheeks and Brianna knew her face looked flushed as she smiled at her aunt and Eli's mother. It appeared that the whole congregation was smiling back. Eli gripped her waist. "I wish we could skip the reception," he whispered.

She noticed his brothers grinning as if they knew exactly what he'd just said.

"If we don't make an appearance, we'll miss seeing Libby," Brianna said.

"I spent all morning with her, but I wouldn't keep her from seeing you in that exquisite wedding dress. She'll think you're a princess come to life. My princess bride. I thank God for you, Brianna," he said, his voice shaking, before they worked their way down the aisle to the foyer.

Later at the hotel, Alberta walked Libby over to the head table. She wore a little yellow dress trimmed in eyelet and a yellow bow in her hair. Brianna saw her coming and turned to greet her.

Eli's little girl stared at her for the longest time. "Don't you know me? Maybe this will help." She carefully removed her veil and Eli took it from her. That did the trick.

"*Bree!*"

"Yes, darling. Come here." She pulled her on her lap. Libby reached out to touch her pearl earrings. "You like those?"

Libby kissed her and they hugged before Eli plucked his daughter away and handed her back to his mother. Libby didn't like that and started to protest.

"It's time for us to go, Brianna."

Her heart thudded because she'd seen the burning look of desire in his eyes.

"I'm ready."

Eli led her out of the room and they left the hotel through a side exit near their new truck. He helped her inside and drove them to a motel on the outskirts of town where there were individual chalet-style cabins nestled in the woods. He'd stopped by ahead of time to pick up the key and had dropped off food and snacks for them as well as their luggage.

Tomorrow they'd take a short trip to Helena for a few days, but tonight they weren't going anywhere. The fifty-degree temperature had melted the snow, making it easy to get around.

"I've been waiting for this for so long," he said as he helped her out of the truck. Then he scooped her up in his arms and carried her over the threshold of their cabin. Once the door was closed, he found her mouth and kissed her long after he'd put her down on the bed.

"We need to get you out of this divine wedding dress, but I don't want you to move."

"How about I just turn on my side and you can undo the buttons without either of us having to get up?"

"But I need to get up, if you follow my meaning."

"If you're talking about protection, I don't want to use any, but it's up to you. The last thing I want is for you to feel rushed into anything."

He kissed her neck. "Brianna…" She saw his tie and suit jacket fly through the air. That gave her his answer.

Somehow he managed to undo her dress. Before she knew it, they were entwined on the bed and her cowboy husband was loving her with a hunger she hadn't even imagined in her dreams. It was after midnight when he allowed her to breathe for a minute. "It's shocking how much I love you…how much I love making love with you, Eli."

"This is only the beginning, sweetheart. We've got the rest of our lives."

"The minister said this was a glorious day, but he didn't know how glorious."

He kissed a special spot. "So you like being married to me already."

"What if we'd never met?" she cried softly. "I can't imagine…"

"You don't have to, because we *did* meet, thanks to Roce. One of these days we'll do something nice for him, but right now all I want to do is make love to you for the rest of the night. You're the most gorgeous sight I have ever seen."

"You're my whole life, Eli. I can't believe I'm lucky enough to be your wife. You just don't know how happy I am. When I was in California I was so worried that something might go wrong. I don't know how I would have handled it if you'd decided to put off our marriage until Tessa was ready to deal with it."

He rolled her over on top of him. "Brianna—let's never talk about it again. She belongs in my past."

"I know."

"I'm going to work on making sure that you do. Give me your mouth again. It's life to me, don't you know that?"

If she didn't then, he managed to convince her so thoroughly that by late morning she truly felt they had become one flesh. She'd never really understood the term until now.

"Brianna? Do you think you want to drive to Helena today?" he whispered against her neck.

"You want the truth?"

He kissed the corners of her mouth. "Always."

"I don't want to go anywhere. I don't want to move from this bed."

He groaned. "How did I get so lucky to have you for my wife?"

"Let's just stay here until we have to go home."

"Mrs. Clayton, have you no shame?" he teased, nibbling on her lower lip.

"None. That's what you've done to me."

"I'm afraid I might have done something else to you."

"There's nothing I'd love more, but are you now wishing we'd used protection?"

"Of course not. I want a baby with you and hopefully more down the road. We haven't talked about it a lot, but I think it's important we give Libby a brother or sister soon. She's so used to being the center of attention that it will be good for her to be surrounded by siblings and have to learn to share."

"I agree. It's not only important, but siblings can be best friends. I'll always be thankful I grew up with a brother."

"You and me both."

She ran a finger over his compelling mouth. "If I do get pregnant right away, are you going to worry I might suffer postpartum depression after the delivery?"

"Not really. What happened to Tessa is quite rare. I refuse to let fear dominate our lives. I believe in us and our love."

Her eyes glazed over. "You're very brave. It's the quality that made you such a good bull rider. There isn't anything you can't do, is there? I love you so much."

"*You're* the one who's brave. Not every woman would have taken me on. Not every woman would have sacrificed her own needs and urged me to fight for my happiness and Libby's. Yet you hung in there."

"That's because you told me we have to operate on faith that everything is going to be all right. We're in this forever."

"Forever. I love you. Come here to me, sweetheart."

* * * * *

With stints as an innkeeper and radio talk show host, **Heidi Hormel** settled into her true calling as a writer by spending years as a reporter (covering the story of the rampaging elephants Debbie and Tina) and as a PR flunky (staying calm in the face of Cookiegate). Now she is happiest penning romances with a wink and a wiggle.

A small-town girl from the Snack Food Capital of the World, Heidi has trotted over a good portion of the globe, from Tombstone in Arizona to Loch Ness in Scotland to the depths of Death Valley. She draws on all of these experiences for her books, but especially her annual visits to the Grand Canyon state for her Angel Crossing, Arizona series.

Heidi is on the web at heidihormel.net, as well as socially out there at Facebook.com/authorheidihormel, Twitter.com/heidihormel and Pinterest.com/hhormel.

Books by Heidi Hormel

Harlequin American Romance

The Surgeon and the Cowgirl
The Convenient Cowboy
The Accidental Cowboy
The Kentucky Cowboy's Baby

Visit the Author Profile page at
Harlequin.com for more titles.

THE KENTUCKY
COWBOY'S BABY

Heidi Hormel

Thanks to my editors who don't say no when I suggest llamas, alpacas, or cowgirls and cowboys who don't fit the mold.

Chapter 1

EllaJayne was gone. The car seat in the back of the battered king-cab pickup was empty, the door hanging open. Even flat-as-a-pancake Oggie, her toy doggie, had vanished. AJ had been right there, fixing the loose hose while his daughter slept in her safest-for-its-price-tag car seat. He'd been standing *right there*. He hadn't heard a damned thing. He should have a loyal dog so no one could sneak up and— *Call the cops*, his mind snapped.

He pulled out his phone as he scanned the dusty lot stretching behind a stuccoed cement-block building. Empty, except for a purple SUV. He ran, his well-worn boots kicking up whirls of bleached-out grit. No Ella-Jayne in or behind the small SUV. How could he have forgotten she was Houdini in a diaper? No sign of her in the dirt-and-gravel parking lot baking in the Arizona high-noon sun. The emergency operator picked up as he raced back to his grimy truck for one more check in every nook, cranny and crevice.

"What's your emergency?" the operator asked.

"My daughter's gone." He ran for the short alley that ran along the building and onto the main street. "Shit," he said.

"Excuse me, sir?"

He kept moving. "Get the police out here. She might have gone onto the road."

"I'll need your location, please."

Her voice was too calm. He wanted to reach through the phone and tell her that his baby girl had disappeared. Instead, as he panted for breath against the heat and the pain in his hip, he said, "I'm in Angel Crossing. I only stopped for a minute to check the truck before I went to find Gene's—" He stopped the rush of words. None of that mattered. "My daughter is sixteen months old. She has dark hair and eyes."

"What's she wearing, sir?"

"Purple shirt with sparkles."

"A little more information, then the police will contact you. I'll need your full name, place of—"

He hung up. He couldn't run and talk. They should be sending police, the K-9 unit, not asking him stupid questions. He stared up and down the uneven, broken sidewalk that stretched in front of the bright-colored facades of empty buildings. Had someone driven in and stolen his daughter while he'd had his head under the hood? A wailing, escalating cry drifted to him. He squinted without his hat brim to shade his McCreary-gray eyes, hoping to catch a glimpse of his sturdy toddler daughter, with hair as dark as his own, its straight-as-a-preacher silkiness direct from her out-of-the-picture mama. He took off, ignoring the sharp bite of pain in his hip and back.

Was the crying closer? The familiar piercing sob was one he'd come to dread, his daughter letting him know he had no business calling himself her daddy.

"EllaJayne. Where are you, baby?" He kept moving as he yelled, not caring that his Kentucky twang had thickened. The cries stopped. He stopped. Where the hell was she? Dear Lord, he'd been so sure he was better than any foster parent or her mama could be. Now he'd lost his baby girl.

After searching another five minutes without hearing her voice again, AJ turned back the way he'd come, moving as fast as he could down the uneven concrete. Where the heck was she? He stepped into a hole where there should have been sidewalk and sharp pain shot down his leg. He hobbled two more steps until the sign for the police department and town hall sprang up like an oasis in the desert. He raced toward it and yanked open the door into a narrow lobby with plastic signs lining the walls. He scanned them looking for…on the right, a small sign in red declared: POLICE. He hurried to the door. Beyond it, a battered metal desk with neat in and out trays stood empty. He didn't hear anything.

"I want to report a missing child." He raised his voice, needing to talk with someone, right now, or he'd—

"What the hell's going on?" asked a tall, blond, unexpectedly familiar man. "AJ? What are you doing here?"

"My daughter." He pulled in as deep a breath as he could with his heart pounding enough to hurt his ribs. "Are you a cop now? I need a search party."

"Not a cop. Mayor. So you're the daddy."

"Where is my daughter?" he asked slowly, with menace. He wasn't playing here. No matter this was Danny Leigh, his old partner in crime. The big blond angel—fitting that he was mayor of a place called Angel Crossing—to AJ's dark-haired and black-hatted devil.

"Pepper said she found the baby walking around by herself."

"Where is she?"

"I don't mean to tell you your business, but—"

AJ had been right there under the hood while Baby Girl slept after hours of crying. He'd been right there. "I'm getting my daughter." AJ turned from Danny, whom he'd last seen at a rodeo in Tulsa. Now it seemed neither of them was following the money on the back of a bull.

AJ listened for his daughter's cries, but the blood roared so loudly in his ears he wouldn't have been able to hear a jet take off.

"Let me get the chief," Danny said, his hand on AJ's arm. Tight. AJ hadn't lost an ounce of muscle since "retiring." He used it to throw off his friend. Danny let go but stayed beside AJ, saying, "I heard them talking about calling Child Services."

Every one of AJ's straining muscles tightened until his back sent a shooting pain down into his still-aching hip. Even if he'd been able to speak, he wouldn't have known what to say to such crap, except a lot of four-letter words, which he tried not to use anymore because of EllaJayne. Everything he did now was to protect her. He'd quit riding bulls and wrangling for the rodeo.

No one was taking his daughter. He'd rescued her once. He'd do it again. AJ moved past Danny to the doorway beyond the desk. Finally, he heard voices and—"EllaJayne," he shouted, except he felt like he'd been gut-punched and only had enough air for the shout to be a strained whisper.

Danny moved past him in the narrow hallway, through an open archway on the left and said, "She belongs to my buddy. He's one hell of a bull rider."

AJ followed him into the room with a fridge and microwave. There she was. Baby Girl in the arms of a woman wearing scrubs, her hair in a no-nonsense golden-brown ponytail. The disapproving line of the woman's mouth couldn't mar its soft pink charm. He held out his arms for his daughter. EllaJayne lifted her head from the woman's shoulder, tear tracks silvery bright on her rounded cheeks where strands of her McCreary raven-black hair lay in a sticky mess. His heart hurt. His baby girl had been crying…again. He sucked at this father stuff.

"She was wandering around on her own. She could have ended up getting hit by a car or kidnapped," said the woman's voice, firm and soft at the same time.

"My daughter," AJ said as he continued to hold out his now shaking hands. The woman glared at him.

"Absolutely not," she said, clutching the girl tighter to her.

He dropped his arms. "I was fixing a hose. She was asleep."

"You should have been paying more attention," whispered the woman as she patted the little girl's back, soothing her into laying down her head. "I found her wandering and brought her to the police. I could probably report you for neglect. I'm a physician's assistant and we're obligated by law to—"

"Neglect?" AJ didn't try to keep his voice down and

Baby Girl's head popped up. He moved closer to snatch EllaJayne away.

A large man stepped in front of him. Where had this guy come from? "Now, sir, I'm Chief Rudy and we need to have a talk before I can release your daughter to you."

The man, just shy of AJ's six feet two inches with close-cropped, cop-style graying brown hair, took AJ by the shoulder with a big hand and steered him out of the break room and down the hall. He directed him into a cramped office. "Sit." The chief pointed to a chair across from a wooden desk that nearly filled the room, his steel-blue gaze clearly telling AJ he was taking the situation seriously. "Seems like you know our mayor, but I still want details and information so I can check your background." The man pushed a paper across the desk.

AJ felt a yawning chasm of fear and despair opening at his feet. The same one that had been showing up in his nightmares as he and his daughter worked their way across the country, and before that, when he'd learned he had a daughter in foster care. He'd hooked up with her mother during a stint in Kentucky when he'd been drinking more than he should. When he'd first seen EllaJayne... He couldn't think about that now. The police chief wasn't fooling around, no matter this town wasn't much more than a wide place in the road. Then there was the woman, who didn't look old enough to be such a...stick in the mud. Why hadn't she just found him and chewed him out instead of going to the authorities? He focused again on the paper asking for his vital details. He filled it out quickly and handed it to the uniformed chief.

"Stay here while I run this."

AJ stood and paced in what space there was in the room. What the hell would he do if they didn't give him back his daughter? He didn't have money for an attorney. Nothing like this had been covered on any of the parenting sites he'd been reading every night. Other parents didn't lose their kids.

He'd had to fix the truck and she'd been sleeping after screaming at the top of her tiny lungs on their trip into Angel Crossing. He'd only stopped here to pay his respects at Gene's memorial, then they'd head to California, where an old rodeo buddy had promised him work and regular hours. He wasn't going back to Kentucky no matter what.

When he'd found out about EllaJayne less than three months ago, he'd vowed he'd be a better father than any of the long line of McCreary men had been. He'd ditched life on the road and promised himself no women who would come into and out of the little girl's life. She'd already had more knocks than any child deserved.

"Mr. McCreary," the police chief said. "Your record looks clean, other than two drunk and disorderlies. Mayor Leigh said those were 'misunderstandings.'"

AJ relaxed by a millimeter. "I'll take my daughter and be on my way."

"Before you do that, I'd like you to talk with Miss Pepper. I know a little one can be tough to keep track of—you're not the first daddy I've had in here. But... Miss Pepper's heart and her worries are in the right place. Plus, being a medical professional, she's got to be extra careful about these kinds of situations."

AJ stayed silent, following the chief back to the break room. The Pepper woman was seated at a table, holding his daughter. EllaJayne didn't even turn to him when he said her name. That hurt.

"The little darling's daddy checks out. He's here to take her back." The officer hovered just behind AJ.

"Did you hear that? Daddy's here," Pepper said, turning her head, pinning AJ with a glare of condemnation from her autumn-brown eyes.

"Baby Girl," he said, walking to the woman, holding out his hands for his daughter. Contrary as any McCreary, she pulled away and buried her face in the stranger's shoulder.

Pepper Bourne held tight to the little girl. No matter what this tall man with his worn jeans and boots said now, he couldn't be much of a father if he hadn't even known his child had wandered off. She'd seen plenty of cowboys like him over the years, especially friends of Daddy Gene's. Just thinking that name still hurt. She snuggled the toddler closer.

"Hand her over," said Chief Rudy. "Kids wander off. It's happened to every parent."

"Are you sure? Her diaper was dirty."

"That happens to all kids, too," the cowboy said swiftly. "I was right there. Under the hood."

"And that worked so well, didn't it? She didn't even have a hat or shoes. What are you doing in town?" Not that it was really her business.

"Come to pay my respects to Gene Daniels. Got word he'd passed, and there was a memorial."

Pepper squeezed the little girl who squeaked in protest. Daddy Gene had been gone for a month. Tears filled her eyes and she couldn't choke out the words. A tiny hand patted her cheek. Pepper feared she would burst into ugly sobs.

"How did you know him?" she asked to distract herself.

"Barely kissin' cousins and the rodeo," the man answered. "Now, if I can have my daughter, I'll be going."

"Chief, I don't know that I'm comfortable with the situation." She stared hard at the toddler's daddy, while ignoring the muscled strength and length of him. "Where's your wife? Your daughter's mother."

"None of that's your business, lady. The police chief here says I'm good to go," he snapped back, his storm-cloud-gray eyes locked on hers.

"That may be but as a health care professional, I have a duty to ensure that any child is not being abused or neglected." She made sure her tone let this cowboy know that he wasn't fit to care for a chicken, let alone a precious little human being.

"Mama," the toddler whimpered and rubbed her forehead into the crook of Pepper's neck.

"Chief, you've got to let me examine her. Who knows how long she was in the sun?"

"Fine. Come on, Mr. McCreary, let's get this settled," Rudy said.

Pepper hesitated for a second. McCreary. That last name struck a chord. She needed to focus on the little girl. Her daddy didn't look like a bad guy. He had dark hair like his daughter's, though his had an unruly curl around his nape and ears. But the little girl hadn't gotten her mink-brown eyes from him. He didn't look or act like an abuser. An outlaw, maybe, a bad-boy rodeo cowboy. Still, it was her duty to make sure the toddler was being cared for properly. She had to give the girl a good once-over.

Followed by the chief and the cowboy holding his

daughter's stuffed animal, Pepper carried EllaJayne on her hip, coming out of the building that housed the town hall, the police station, a real estate office, and a law office. The clinic was half a block down on the right, across from the Angel Crossing Emporium of Wonders. The sign, with its painted roadrunner and mountain lion, always made her smile, even though the emporium had closed long ago. The mayor was trying to get a grant to hire artists to paint the plywood and "re-fresh" the sign to make the town look less abandoned.

The facades along the main road, which was pictur-esquely called Miners Gulch, had been added in the 1970s to entice tourists to the town, as the nearby mine and the county's biggest employer started to close its operations. Tourists hadn't been lured in, but the towns-folk had come to love the signs that gave the vibe of a Spaghetti Western set. Or a bona fide ghost town. The problem was a ghost town was a dead town. With no good jobs, Angel Crossing was edging toward that as the younger residents scattered to the wind. Pepper was the exception, rather than the rule. Although techni-cally, she wasn't local, not having moved to town until she was seven.

Today wasn't the day to worry about Angel Cross-ing. She had a little darling in her arms who needed her attention. Like the old-timey facades, her clinic had the feeling of a bygone era. It served residents well enough, even if it housed more than one piece of equipment that should have been in a museum. She did what she could for her patients, many of them retired and living on minuscule pensions and Social Security. She regularly had to beg, borrow and nearly steal supplies, especially free samples. She knew of more than one patient who skimped on medications to pay for food. That's why the garden would make such a difference.

"Oggie," EllaJayne said into Pepper's ear, reaching out with her hand and flexing her fingers. Pepper followed her gesture and saw the girl's cowboy daddy, still holding onto the flattened stuffed animal she'd given him. The man had a hitch in his step that didn't keep her from noticing his rodeo swagger. He needed a hat. What cowboy didn't have a hat? It would have shaded his handsome face. Pepper knew trouble and she didn't need anyone to tell her this guy was that plus more. She also didn't need anyone to tell her that his kind of trouble could give a woman memories to warm up her nights.

Pepper focused on the bundle in her arms as she walked into Angel Crossing Medical Clinic. "I'm going to Exam One," she said to Claudette, her right-hand woman at the reception desk.

"Who is this?" asked Claudette, her short dark hair streaked with highlights and spiked to fit her warrior-woman attitude in a grandmother's body.

"We'll give you everything as soon as I'm done with the exam." The ring of boot heels followed Pepper. An uneven sound. She glanced back and caught the man grimacing. No time to worry about that.

"Okay, little darling, let's just see how your 'daddy' was caring for you." She ignored the snort from the cowboy.

She put him and everything else out of her mind, concentrating on the girl and the exam. She didn't want to miss anything. But other than the dirty diaper—which Pepper changed from her own supplies—and a little diaper rash, the toddler was fine.

"So?" he asked when she finished with the final tug of the girl's T-shirt.

"What about her vaccinations?"

"I... I... Of course she's had them. I have papers in the truck."

He didn't know. "Allergies?"

He stood feet planted and long fingers tapping against his leg. "It's all in her records. She's fine. You just said so."

She'd been working with patients ever since she'd started as an EMT in her teens, and read annoyance in the tightness of his mouth. She also saw fear in the tilt of his head. What to do? The child looked fine.

"You're good to go, then, but little ones are quicker than their parents think and can easily get into things they shouldn't. Let's go see if Claudette can't find cream for the rash." Pepper scooped up the girl and walked out. The exam room as they'd stood there had suddenly gotten smaller. She'd started to think trouble might be what she needed in her life. Because trouble had started to look a lot like a good time, which she hadn't had since... forever. Then smart Pepper reminded not-so-smart Pepper he was a patient's father...and a cowboy. The kind of man she'd long ago figured out wasn't for her. They might look pretty, but the shine wore off quickly.

She kept her gaze on Claudette and glanced at Chief Rudy, who had an odd look on his face as he stared down at his phone.

"What?" she asked because it was obvious that something had just popped up on the screen.

"I ran his name, but, well, I didn't connect it... Hell—"

This was bad. The chief didn't swear. It was a contest

in town to see who could make him curse when they got pulled over or visited the station. The man just didn't get provoked, and if he did, he didn't say bad words. So that meant whatever he'd just discovered was horrible.

"His name is Arthur John McCreary."

"Everybody calls me AJ," the cowboy said irritably.

"You're Daddy Gene's cousin." The words popped out of her mouth in shock as the connection fell into place.

"Yeah, Gene is…was my cousin. I told you that." His voice had thickened with true emotion.

"Welcome to Angel Crossing," Rudy said. "Sorry the circumstances aren't better. Gene was a good man and a good friend."

"Thanks," AJ said and added, "I should have known. How many Peppers could there be in Angel Crossing?" He rubbed his hand over the back of his neck. "Gene talked about you and your mama. Please accept my condolences."

She nodded. Now she remembered him. He rode bulls and had dragged Daddy Gene from the ring when the animals had nearly stomped him to death. The one or two pictures she'd seen of AJ, his black hat had nearly covered his face.

"I guess I should take you to the ranch. Faye would never forgive me if I didn't bring you out to say hello. Daddy Gene hoped you'd come for a visit one day, but I don't think this is how he imagined it."

Chapter 2

Pepper's directions to Gene's ranch had included exact mileages, road names and landmarks. Even in the sameness of the rocky terrain, dotted with gray-green bushes and low trees, he'd easily found the turnoff that wound through a short downhill drive. Flatlands opened up for a distance before moving into another set of foothills that rolled into mountains. The ranch included a low house, outbuildings and corrals. The animals milling around ranged in color from white to shadows-at-noon black. But they weren't cattle or horses or even goats.

He checked his rearview mirror to see his daughter, who was eerily quiet. Her head swiveled back and forth as she looked out the windows, staring wide-eyed, her lost-all-its-stuffing dog clutched tight in her fist.

Contrary as any McCreary, after days on the road wishing she'd quiet down, he wanted noise from his daughter now so he could stop thinking about Pepper. She somehow made scrubs look as good as painted-on jeans and a tight cowgirl shirt. She actually looked better than the buckle bunnies who'd been the honey to his bee for years. EllaJayne's mama had been Miss Kentucky Rodeo two years before he'd met her.

He stopped the truck in front of the house that had a lumpy outline of clearly unplanned additions. It had been Gene's home. He'd talked of the ranch with a lot of pride. Gene had retired from the rodeo circuit after a string of bad wrecks. Both Danny and AJ had tried to talk him out of it because he was the best at reading the animals. They'd been young and hadn't understood what it meant to have a body that had been battered and broken again and again.

AJ knew he couldn't stall any longer. Though he hated to intrude, his nearly maxed-out credit card and flat wallet told him otherwise. He had to swallow that pride and ask—beg for—their hospitality. He'd stay for the memorial, then move on. He'd come west for a brand-new start where no one had heard of the Mc-Crearys of Pinetown, Kentucky.

He held EllaJayne firmly in his arms when he knocked on the weathered door. Up close, the ranch house looked like a cross between a trailer and a cabin.

"There you are," said the woman who opened the door. "Come in." Obviously, this was Faye, just as Gene had described her: "Stevie Nicks who bought her duds at Sheplers and her jewelry at swap meets." She stepped back, pushing a drape of gray-streaked hair with strips of color like her daughter's out of her watchful green eyes.

"Thank you, ma'am," he said, finally remembering

the manners that had been knocked into him with a spatula and fly swatter.

"Oh, my," she said as tears filled her eyes. "Don't you have the look of Gene? It's just like he's here. And those nice manners."

"Yes, ma'am." He and Gene looked nothing alike.

"And who is the gorgeous baby? Yours. Look at that hair, that skin. Oh, my, but she'll be a beauty. Come here, sweetheart," Faye said and held her hands out to his daughter. The little girl went right to her. "I bet I have a cookie you'd like. You can call me Grana. I always wanted someone to call me that. I'm in the Crone phase of my womanhood. The most powerful. You are in the Baby phase, still finding your power. But don't worry. It's there."

He followed her closely in the wake of the deep scent of incense and sharp desert herbs. "Ma'am," he tried, "I'm here to—"

"Have you eaten? No. I can see you haven't. Sit."

"Thank you, ma'am. I know that I should have called as soon as Gene…passed. But I'm here to pay my respects and attend the memorial."

She waved a thin, elegant hand covered in silver and turquoise. "Gene understood. He spoke of you often. Now, I'll fix you a plate and give this little one a cookie."

"Ma'am," AJ interrupted. "I don't want to put you out at a time like this."

"A time like what?"

Jeez. Gene had told him that his wife and he…well, actually not his legally wed wife. They had never married. AJ said gently, "A sad time like this."

"Sad?" She laughed brightly and his daughter joined

in. "We're celebrating Gene's life. That can never be sad." Faye walked through a listing doorway into a kitchen filled with brightly painted cabinets and mismatched appliances.

"Now," she went on, "you're a Taurus and you've been traveling, so I think you need scrambled tofu, with sprouted bread, yogurt…no, not yogurt…kefir. Then I'll move in with Pepper so you can have my room."

"Please, I couldn't ask you to do that."

"Of course, you'll stay here. It's what Gene would have wanted."

"I couldn't do that," he protested politely, even though he'd planned to ask for such hospitality.

"I couldn't let Gene's family stay anywhere else." Tears filled her voice and she squeezed EllaJayne closer to her.

AJ couldn't afford to protest too strongly. "If you insist, ma'am."

"Perfect. This food will balance you, and then you'll have a wonderful night's sleep. Here. Hold your daughter while I finish." She plopped the little girl into his arms and magically produced a chunky cookie that EllaJayne immediately started gnawing.

"What's in there?" he asked. This cookie looked like it might have all kinds of things that were bad for babies. Except what were those things? Chocolate? No, that was dogs. What had the website said?

Faye crossed to the stove. "Wheat germ, oats… You ride bulls, Gene said, and you're a Taurus. Isn't it wonderful the way the universe makes things like that work?"

"Used to ride bulls."

"Oh, no, I don't think the universe will like that."

She turned to him and a frown marred her surprisingly smooth brow.

"I don't think the universe is very happy with me right now." EllaJayne looked up at him, the cookie in one hand.

"No," she said clearly. The one word she said regularly and loudly. Her brow wrinkled. *Uh-oh.* He knew that look. That was the look that meant something smelly was going to come out of one end or the other. *Really, Universe, what have I ever done to you?*

Pepper expected to see Daddy Gene come around the side of the house and onto the patio, to greet everyone with a big shout and a laugh, then smooth his handlebar mustache into place before announcing that it was time to get the party started. Except that wouldn't be happening. Faye had tried to make it festive with lights strung around the patio and a table laden with food. Of course, everyone knew the kinds of dishes Faye cooked so a number of pies, casseroles and platters had magically appeared, too.

Pepper saw the mayor chatting with Gene's cousin AJ. The man and his daughter had stayed with them last night at Faye's insistence. Pepper had been so busy between work and getting everything set for the memorial that she'd only been home to sleep. Pepper turned away, not sure exactly what she was feeling. Today was a celebration, she reminded herself, but the weight of responsibility made her shoulders ache. Daddy Gene had been a part of her life since he'd shown up at the commune. Pepper had only been five years old, but she'd known he was the kind of man they both could count on. Now what?

"It's time," Faye announced. "We're here to celebrate

the life of my lover, companion and soul mate." Then she started singing "Witchy Woman" while the silence got increasingly uncomfortable.

Dear Lord. Angel Crossing had more or less accepted Faye...they'd loved Daddy Gene and he and Faye were a package deal. Alone, Faye might be just a little too filled with hippie hokum.

Danny stepped up to Faye and stopped her swaying, off-key rendition mercifully short. "That was one of Gene's favorites. You know, he was my mentor... AJ and I wouldn't have stayed on any bull without Gene. He could read those animals like most men read the want ads." Nods rippled through the crowd. Faye smiled at Danny. It might just work out okay. "I'll miss Gene, just like all of us will. But I know he wanted us to have a good time tonight. Drink a little beer—his favorite, Lone Star—jaw a bit and eat good food...and I see the tables are filled. To Gene." Danny lifted his beer bottle and everyone joined in.

Pepper turned away to pull herself together. A celebration, she told herself again. She could do this for Daddy Gene. This one last thing for him. The man who'd been her father and the one person she could count on no matter what. "Love you, Daddy Gene," she said quietly, looking out toward the mountains dark against the brilliant pinks, purples and reds of the sunset. "Thanks for the show." She smiled and then wiped away the tears. Time to honor a life well lived. She wouldn't remember those last days of illness and pain. She'd remember him laughing. That was her favorite Daddy Gene.

"Faye asked me to do the reading of the will tonight."

Pepper stared at Bobby Ames, Angel Crossing's attorney and part-time taxidermist.

He went on, "Everyone grab a seat. This won't take long."

They were in the living room of the ranch house, sitting on an assortment of chairs salvaged from roadside garbage piles or built by Faye's friends.

"Come along, Pepper Moonbeam," Faye said, formal and stiff. She'd been holding back her sadness tonight so they could "rejoice in" Daddy Gene's life, not mourn his death. Pepper knew how tough that was as she'd worked over and over to hold her own tears in check. He'd been gone for just a month. They'd scattered his ashes weeks ago, but today was the real goodbye and much more painful than the one at his bedside. She didn't understand what the lawyer was doing. Gene had left the ranch to Faye, what else could the will say? My god, he'd named the place for her: Santa Faye Ranch.

Pepper sat and waited for the attorney to speak again, a moment out of a soap opera or a telenovela. Bobby Ames finally started to read the will. Daddy Gene named a couple of friends and gave them his riding gear and two of his trophies. Then Bobby Ames did the strangest thing. He put the will down, sucked in a breath and spoke in a voice that Pepper was sure he'd learned from *Law and Order*. "I want to let you know that if Gene had come to me... I'll just read this, then you can ask questions."

What had Daddy Gene done? Put the rest of the will in verse? Or maybe he'd set up a scavenger hunt for the remaining items, like his bear-claw necklace. That would be like him. He'd been just a big kid at heart.

"The ranch goes to my cousin and savior, Arthur John McCreary."

Pepper's breath clogged her lungs as she ran over the words again in her head. They didn't make any sense.

"He left me the ranch?" AJ asked. He didn't sound like a man who'd just hit the jackpot.

"You've got the wrong will," Pepper told the attorney. Well, maybe more like accused him of gross incompetence.

"Now…" Chief Rudy started.

"It's wrong," she said. *It's got to be.* She'd used the inheritance she'd been sure she and her mother would get on the grant application to get the Angel Crossing Community Garden Project started. "Daddy Gene always said… I used the property—"

"How could I have forgotten," Faye said with something like regret and worry, two emotions she rarely acknowledged. "You told that agency you would use the value of the ranch as the matching money."

"You did what?" AJ's storm-gray gaze locked on her. No chance that she couldn't figure out what he was thinking. "There's a lien on the property?"

"Not exactly," she said.

He hitched up his sleeping daughter so her head fit more firmly on his shoulder. "You. Me. The attorney. We need to talk now."

"What are you, a caveman? I already told you there's some mistake." She moved closer to whisper what needed to be said so no one—especially not her mother—could hear. "You didn't even visit. When he was…when the doctors said that he…you didn't visit. Why would he leave this to you? Did you call him? Talk to the attorney?"

"Are you saying that I scammed Gene? My God,

he was kin. He watched out for me when I first started riding bulls."

"What other reason could there be?"

Bobby Ames pretended to clear his throat.

Pepper moved around the room restlessly as the silence stretched. Not only was her plan on the line, her mother's future was, too. The ranch would have been plenty to keep Faye in yogurt and tofu. One good thing about her mother was that she didn't need a lot of cash to get along. That's why Pepper had been so sure the community garden plan would work.

"Now, we need to discuss this frankly," Bobby Ames said, still using his TV-attorney voice. "There'll be no more talk about this will not being legal. It is. Faye and the chief looked everywhere for another one. There was nothing at the house. I called around to other attorneys and there was nothing. This is his will."

Pepper wanted to say no. She wanted to scream no, but she was nothing if not a realist. She left the dreaming to her mother.

"Why me?" AJ asked.

Yeah, she wanted to know that, too.

Bobby Ames adjusted his glasses. "Could be that it's an old will and you were his cousin? Or maybe because you saved his life."

"I'm not sure I saved him," AJ said, moving his daughter to his other shoulder.

"The way Gene told it was that if you hadn't run into the arena and grabbed him, he'd have been stomped to death. He said the clowns had gotten tangled up with a loose calf and you were the first one to him. He said you took a good kick to the ribs." AJ's hand went to his side. "I believe you nearly lost your spleen."

"He thanked me plenty," AJ said. "I never expected—"

"You don't need to make any decisions today," Bobby Ames said, "except this thing with Pepper and the grant. What did Faye mean?"

Pepper searched for a way to understand the new lay of the land. She'd never imagined Daddy Gene wouldn't leave the ranch to Faye. She'd never asked him about it in those last weeks. They'd all known he was dying but they'd still tried to deny it until the very end.

No one spoke and the silence stretched out long enough that she could hear the deep breathing of the baby. *Come clean, girlie girl,* Daddy Gene's voice said in her head. Dear Lord. What would they do? What would the state office where she'd filed her paperwork say?

Pepper said, "Daddy Gene loved Faye, you all know that. You know what he would do." Her voice squeaked to a stop. Her chest hurt from holding back the tears. She had to get through this next bit, then she could fall to pieces. She needed to protect Faye's future and her own plans for the garden, her patients and the town. Pepper breathed deeply as she'd seen her mother do before a big announcement. "I'm planning the Angel Crossing Community Garden here at the ranch and we needed a grant for the equipment. Faye agreed I could use the value of the ranch's land and outbuildings to match the money the state would grant us. It was the only way to get the money, so I put that on my application. I've already set up the greenhouse using my own savings and promised loans to my farmers. I told you all about it, chief. Remember? There would be fresh food for those who worked the ground and plots where others could grow specialty plants that they'd then sell and pay me land rent. It would be run by a nonprofit and support small businesses as well as senior and children's health. The mayor even agreed it was a good idea."

"It is a good idea," Chief Rudy said, cutting off AJ when he started to protest, "but you didn't tell any of us that you basically were promising money you don't have or that the plan had been put together with a spit and a prayer."

Finally, AJ spoke, his voice low but no less angry. "So you've used my ranch and now there's a lien and I won't be able to sell."

"It seems that you've gone awfully quick from 'I can't believe this is mine' to ordering us all around because you inherited some land," Pepper said, facing him and forcing her voice to be steady. "There isn't a lien on the property. I've only just put in the paperwork. I'm sure I can explain things and rescind the application…if I have to, which I'm not convinced I'll have to."

"It's the Spring Equinox right now," Faye said out of nowhere, as she sometimes did. "This was always Gene's favorite time of year. He said spring was when anything was possible."

Chapter 3

Butch, the Australian shepherd, sat happily in the front seat of Pepper's small SUV. The one her mother had insisted Daddy Gene buy and then paint an eye-searing purple. On the plus side, Pepper was easily recognizable. It meant when she went to homes up in the mountains, her patients immediately recognized her. Faye may have known what she was doing. Maybe. Pepper pushed away the panic and flexed her hands on the steering wheel. "Butch, we're in a lot of trouble, and I don't mean because you sat in Dr. Cortez's chair. I used a ranch I didn't own to try and get money from the government. It's not like they gave me any money or that I lied. I really, really thought the ranch was ours. It was just two weeks after Daddy Gene died. I might not have been at my best, but there was a deadline." The black, brown and white dog with mismatched eyes turned and gave her one of his smiles. Butch had been picked out of a litter of wriggling puppies to herd Faye's Beauties—her alpacas and llamas. She'd talked Daddy Gene into getting the animals about a year ago, about the same time as the ranch that had rented most of Santa Faye Ranch had closed its gates and broken its lease. Faye insisted the fleece from the animals, which she planned to spin and weave, would make up for the lost revenue. Not long after the animals arrived, Daddy Gene had gotten very sick again. Faye had been more worried about him than about making her spinning and weaving venture profitable, even though she loved her Beauties. Butch, who acted like a poodle in a hairy shepherd body, had worked hard with her to earn his good citizen certificate and therapy training. He visited the office on the days it was just her and Claudette. Dr. Cortez, who came to the clinic twice a week, didn't like Butch or believe any animal could help calm patients. Butch actually did a good job with people facing needles—kids and adults alike.

Only two minutes from the ranch, Pepper needed to come up with her talking points fast. She'd avoided AJ and Faye this morning. She had, however, called an attorney—not Bobby Ames—for advice that wasn't free. He'd said she might have a case for overturning the will, and he didn't think she'd end up in jail, probably, for using the ranch to try to get the grant. He'd advised withdrawing the application immediately, but not explaining why unless she was forced to. The goal was to not look like a liar and a cheat to the agency. Pepper understood what he wasn't saying. If she ever wanted Angel Crossing or herself to get another grant from the state or anyone else, she had to clear up this problem quickly and quietly. She'd already started and so far so good.

Pepper parked next to AJ's king-cab pickup, dusty and dented. "Come on, Butch," she said unnecessarily. The dog was already at the front door waiting for her. She gripped her tote tighter and went in.

Butch raced from her side, yipping with excitement. He disappeared into the kitchen. Pepper took papers to review later that night out of her tote, then hung the bag on its hook. She toed off her clogs and slipped her feet into sandals. A place for everything and everything in its place. One of those sayings from kindergarten that had more than a little ring of truth.

Butch ran back to her, his doggy smile stretching across his face. *No more stalling, Pepper.* Butch sprinted ahead of her again. She strained to hear voices.

"Faye, I'm home." That was stupid. Of course she was home. Silence.

Butch trotted into the kitchen and then looked over his shoulder at her. That was his open-the-back-door look. That must be where they were. Pepper sniffed the air. Someone had been cooking. She almost felt sorry for AJ because she knew that smell. Faye had made scrambled tofu, which was okay, but she'd added kimchi, fish sauce and...dear Lord. She smelled the cheese Faye insisted on making—the kind that tasted like dirty socks. Maybe Faye's cooking would convince AJ to move along, except no one would walk away from a ranch.

Butch sat on her foot and leaned against her leg. He really was a remarkable therapy dog. He always knew when anyone was in distress. She patted his warm furry head before making herself a little taller than her five feet seven so she could more easily face the people on the patio. Specifically, the tall, lean AJ.

Faye in Earth Mother mode held EllaJayne as she danced her around the patio. Pepper didn't see AJ, though.

"Faye, where's that child's father? Did you kill him with the kimchi?" Faye's Korean-style sauerkraut had peppers hot enough to singe nose hairs. Pepper didn't eat the kimchi or anything else with peppers—hot or sweet. One of life's little ironies.

"EllaJayne and I are enjoying the rebirth of the world since it's spring. Aren't we? You're an old soul, aren't you, little one?"

"Faye," Pepper said with patience.

"You're thirsty. I can hear it in your voice. Go get a drink." Her mother danced another three steps. "This will all work out for the best."

"Good to know."

"No need for sarcasm, that's the work of a small soul."

"Sorry. It's just that today has been—"

"I know, dear," Faye said, taking the little girl's arm and waving. "There's your daddy."

AJ was a cowboy, from his hip-rolling walk to his well-used boots and frayed-at-the-seams jeans. Pepper couldn't read what he might be thinking. She could guess, though. *Don't borrow from the bank of trouble,* she heard Daddy Gene's voice in her ear. She wanted to snap back at him that she wouldn't need to borrow if he'd just left the ranch to Faye. But he wasn't here. She needed to leave that go.

"You and I need to talk," AJ said in a soft drawling voice that didn't have a hint of friendly.

"Absolutely," Pepper said. Acting confident—even when she wasn't—convinced people that she knew what she was doing. "We can talk in my office."

"No, darling," Faye said. "You should take advantage of the energy of spring and the outdoors." Her mother took the child and walked inside.

"I made some calls," AJ said.

"Okay." She would let him talk so she could figure out what he knew and wanted. She watched him pace around the patio. He definitely was handsome—she had to be honest.

"I spoke with Danny Leigh."

Did he think being the mayor's friend was a big deal? Like she should be impressed? Everybody knew the mayor. This was a small town.

"Telling a state agency you owned land you didn't could end up getting you and the town—including Danny and others who signed the papers—into a lot of trouble."

"Daddy Gene meant for Faye to have the ranch. Everyone in town knew that was his plan." She plowed on, pushing back the tears. "Faye agreed with me about the garden because it would provide food and a chance to earn extra money for anyone who needs help in Angel Crossing. How can you take that from them?"

"This is about what's legal and fair."

"Fair? I'll tell you what's fair. Giving my patients a fighting chance to get healthy with fresh fruits and vegetables. Helping kids understand where what's on their plate comes from and what real food is. What about the entrepreneurs? Liddy already has her name in for a loan to make soaps and salves from the herbs she'll grow. With that money, she can go to the community college, get a degree and earn enough so she can rent a bigger place and be allowed to have her kids back."

"It's the law. The will is clear. The ranch goes to me." He turned his back to her and his shoulders—his wide and muscled shoulders—lifted with a deep breath. "I have plans, too, and they all have to do with giving my little girl the best. Bobby Ames said that it will take months to settle the estate and that's if there are no challenges or issues." He turned and glared at her. "I was going to go to California but it seems that we have a place here. Plus, I need to make sure you don't do anything else with the property that will make it less attractive to a buyer."

She whispered, because that was all the air she had, "You're selling the ranch?"

Looking at Pepper's horrified face nearly made him take back the truth.

"I can fix this so you don't have to sell. Or—" Her voice trailed off as her shoulders drooped.

He couldn't weaken now. Not only did his future ride on this ranch but his daughter's did, too. For the first time in his life, he had something to lose. "Promises won't put food in me and my daughter's bellies." Good Lord, he heard his daddy in those hard words. He couldn't stop now even if he really believed that he could make this work out for all of them…somehow. "And what will keep me out of trouble if the state doesn't like that you lied on the grant, huh?"

Her gaze dropped. "I've already started withdrawing the application. You don't need to worry."

Good thing for him she'd given in. He'd had about another ten seconds of meanness before he'd have caved. "My original plan had been to stop to pay my respects before heading to California to work on a dude ranch for a buddy of mine. Since the estate might not be settled for months—and it looks like there are a few things to take care of in preparation for a sale and to make sure you don't try anything else with the property—that means EllaJayne and I will need to stay on here, in what's technically my house...or will be. I mean, Bobby Ames explained that until everything is settled, you and Faye don't *have* to let me stay. But hotels get mighty expensive, and there's the attorney to pay, as well as food and diapers and such for Ella-Jayne. Faye already agreed and you wouldn't put out a little girl. Also, I'll have to look for work, which leads to my next problem. I need someone to look after El-laJayne, from time to time. She likes your mama and since you're a nurse—"

"Physician's assistant," she corrected.

He'd better hurry because she was recovering her spit and vinegar. "Physician's assistant. Danny Leigh vouched for you, too. You and your mama could do in a pinch, but I need to have something steadier, more permanent. So, here's the deal. In addition to staying here, I need your help in tracking down someone to care for my daughter. You've got to know who's good at that sort of thing. Does Angel Crossing have a day care? Either way. I want good care at a reasonable price."

"I'm sure I can give you care recommendations. But I'm a little confused as to why I should be helping *you*? What do I get out of the deal?"

He worked to not admire her backbone. Up against a wall and she wasn't afraid to negotiate. "What's your counteroffer?"

"Since Faye said you can stay, then you should care for Faye's Beauties."

"Her Beauties?"

"The llamas and alpacas. Faye does most of the work but she needs help."

"Seems fair."

Her face had relaxed into a smile. He liked that smile. It shouldn't matter if he liked it or not. His only goal here was getting the ranch free and clear, selling it and moving on. He'd considered staying but he couldn't do that and raise a daughter. Plus he'd never even worked on a ranch. He'd helped with animals at the rodeo but that wasn't the same thing.

"I could write everything up in a contract," he went on, "but I'd like to think we could do this on a shake of the hand?" Despite her hippie mama and using a ranch she didn't own, Pepper was practical and trustworthy, he thought. He'd gotten that impression, anyway, from everything Danny and Bobby Ames had said to him.

Her stiff shoulders and etched-in-stone chin told him she wasn't giving up or giving in without a little more fight. She might have been down, but she wasn't out. "Since you already settled the housing with Faye, I don't see that I can take issue with that. I'm sure I can find your daughter care. She's a sweet baby. I need some assurance you won't sell out from under me *and* I want a chance to buy Santa Faye Ranch before it goes on the market."

"If that's legal, sure, why not." He didn't care who bought the property. He just needed the money. "When everything's settled and I'm ready to sell, I'll let you know."

"Wow. So kind of you to tell me when you plan to sell my home."

He almost laughed at her snarky comment. He might appreciate her backbone and the way she filled out her scrubs… Jeez…what was his problem? "Promise." Her gaze stayed on him. He couldn't look away. "Cross my heart, hope to die, stick a needle in my eye." Now, what had made him say something that juvenile and stupid?

She laughed. "You know, Daddy Gene said that same thing." Suddenly, she stopped smiling.

Her face settled into lines of pain, her eyes darkening. He knew that pain. He was feeling it, too. Missing Gene. The man who'd helped him become…a man, with his rough-and-tumble advice and affection. AJ reached out and dragged her into a hug, pulling her against him to stop the pain, for both of them. "I'm so sorry. I know how much Gene loved you and your mama."

She didn't move and he stared out over her head and into the expanse of scrubby desert and mountains around them. He'd never been in mountains with so little vegetation. In Kentucky, the only time a mountain looked this bad was after mining. Here it was the natural order of things. The lack of green wore on his eyes.

"I miss him. I miss him so much," Pepper said in a hoarse whisper.

AJ wasn't good at this sort of thing, never had been. But he couldn't walk away from her sadness and tears. "I know, honey," he said. He looked down at her, where she'd buried her face into his shoulder. Her hair was pulled back from a center part to a loose and messy bun at the back of her head. It had streaks of golden red in the light brown. The lush fullness surprised him. She appeared so tightly wound except for the softness of her hair, and her brightly colored toenails. No way should he be spending so much time determining the exact color of her hair or noticing that she had daisies painted on her toenails. He relaxed his hold a little, needing some space between them. She clutched at him.

"Not yet," she whispered as a breath shuddered from her.

He brushed his cheek against her temple and he nearly kissed her, wanting to soothe her distress and let her know she wasn't alone. Instead, he held her loosely against him. He could guess what her curves would feel like and what they might do to him if he pulled her closer. He wasn't that much of a dog.

Her scent of spice and citrus filled his head, such a sweet fresh smell. It reminded him of the time between spring and summer, full of promise.

"Did Daddy Gene really talk about us when he was still riding bulls?" she asked, not moving her face from his shoulder.

"Sure." This topic was much safer than where his mind had gone when his hand encountered the sexy deep curve of her waist. He'd just stopped himself from testing the swell of her hip. He kept his eye on a large cactus in the near distance. "He said that Faye loved turquoise and pepitas. Pumpkin seeds." Pepper nodded so he went on. "He said you refused to let him get you another horse when yours died from colic." Crap. Why had he brought up that story? He could feel the sadness course through her as she burrowed into his shoulder again, like she could hide there forever. Surprisingly, he would have let her if it would have helped.

"Toni," she said, her voice muffled. "Her name was Antonia. I didn't think I'd ever not be sad again. For a while, I wanted to be a vet, but then when Daddy Gene got sick the first time, I realized medicine—human medicine—was for me." She relaxed against him.

He wrapped his arms more fully around her, wanting to...he wasn't sure what, other than make her feel better, to lessen the sadness he felt in her every muscle and heard in her voice. She hadn't asked for this any more than he had. They both needed to weather the situation as best they could. He could guess at her sorrow now. It was an echo of his own. He missed Gene. He'd been someone AJ knew he could count on if anything went wrong. He hadn't kept in close touch during the years after Gene left the rodeo, but he'd known his cousin would be there if he needed him. "I'm sorry I didn't get here earlier, before Gene passed, but...there was EllaJayne and her mama."

Pepper stiffened and not from sorrow. Crap. His smooth tongue had deserted him. He usually wasn't so clueless with women.

She pulled away and turned her head but he saw her wipe at her eyes. "I'm good now," she said with taut determination. "What do we do? Shake hands?"

Chapter 4

Pepper thrust out her hand and stepped away from AJ's heat. Shake hands and move on. That was what she needed to do. Forget she'd broken down in his arms and had liked—way too much—the warm strength of him. He took her hand in his and lingered for a second. She didn't change her grip, making her gaze stay on him. How had she not seen the tiny white scar that stretched up from the corner of his upper lip and another on the outside of his dark brow? His face told her what she needed to know. A rodeo cowboy. They didn't stick around.

"Okay?" he asked with soft gruffness.

She shifted her eyes to a place over his shoulder where she could see the mountains that surrounded Angel Crossing. "I'll get you sitters' names." She could do this. She had to do this for herself, for Faye and for Angel Crossing. They were all counting on her.

As for the other part of this debacle, that he and Ella-Jayne remain at the ranch? That would be all right, too. No matter there would be months and months of sharing a bathroom, a kitchen. It would be very intimate. No. Cramped. And she'd already gotten a good view of a fit-for-bull-riding cowboy walking around in a towel.

Faye danced onto the patio, bouncing EllaJayne on her hip. "We're going to breathe in the colors."

"Grana," the toddler agreed as they danced off.

Pepper gritted her teeth and glanced at AJ to gauge his reaction. Until she was a teen, Pepper had stayed at the ranch, with Faye homeschooling her. Then she'd gone to public school, where a cowboy wearing anything but Wranglers was cause for comment, and her mother's unusual view of the world after years of living in a commune had mortified Pepper. Now, some days she could appreciate how growing up with Faye had taught her compassion and patience. Angel Crossing needed both. The residents were stubborn about changing anything, even things that would make them healthier.

"All done," Faye said, snuggling her nose against the toddler's. "The blue sky smelled like Aqua Velva and the white clouds made us both think sheets dried outside." The little girl giggled.

"I'll take her now," AJ said, holding his arms out for his daughter.

"Wait," Pepper said. Suddenly, the whole day felt too huge, like something had shifted in the world. Dear Lord, she was starting to sound like Faye. She dug deep for the calm and unemotional Pepper who took over during emergencies. "I want to make sure that we're clear on our responsibilities." AJ nodded. She went through the list, while she kept a professional eye on him. She needed to use her PA Spidey Senses. She could ferret out a lie at twenty paces—at least that's what she told patients. She just wanted to be certain that he would stick by the agreement.

She looked at him hard. It didn't take a medical degree to interpret his bloodshot eyes or the dark circles underneath. He was exhausted. Why hadn't she noticed that before? She wanted to tell AJ to go get some sleep and she'd take care of everything. But he wasn't her responsibility. She didn't have to care for him. She needed her attorney to straighten out the will. *Where you goin' to find the dinero for that?* Daddy Gene's voice rang in her head. She'd find it because everyone she cared about—which didn't include AJ and his daughter—was counting on her.

Pepper quietly closed the door to the bedroom she now shared with her mother. AJ and his little girl had been given Faye's room. Faye hadn't minded—she hadn't been spending much time there since Daddy Gene had died. Pepper could only imagine how long tomorrow would feel because last night she hadn't gotten much more than an hour of sleep. Good thing Tuesday was a Dr. Cortez day. It meant her patient load was reasonable.

Pepper headed to the kitchen, not needing to turn on any lights because Faye, as always, had left the house well-lit. Her mother, despite her love of the moon and staying up late, did not like the dark.

Having grown up in a commune, more or less, before Daddy Gene had showed up, Pepper had a high tolerance for sharing space. But sharing the house with AJ made it feel really, really small. Like right now, she could've sworn she smelled his scent of dusty leather, baby powder and…bubble gum? That last was new. It smelled like the flavoring in children's medicine. She moved a little faster. Was EllaJayne sick?

AJ stood in the kitchen shirtless, the top button of his jeans undone so she could see the band of his tighty-whites. *Stop looking,* she told herself firmly as she stood in the shadows. She made her gaze move to his hand and the small white bottle he held.

"Is EllaJayne okay?"

"What?" He jerked around, the bottle dropping from his hand, pink syrup spraying everywhere. "Damn it."

"Sorry. Didn't mean to startle you," she mumbled as the syrup dripped down his chest. His well-muscled chest. She had to stop noticing things like that right now. She rushed to the sink for a dishcloth and the cleaning supplies underneath.

"This stuff is sticky. What are you doing awake?" he whispered. She glanced over her shoulder to see him rubbing at the pink drops.

"Here," she said, taking the cloth and wiping at his chest, using her best professional voice and touch. She concentrated on the pink syrup that had caught in the light furring of hair on his chest and the arrow…she looked back up. His pupils had enlarged so that his storm-gray eyes looked black. "Umm…maybe you can do that while I clean up the floor." His hand covered hers. She didn't feel threatened. Instead she felt his warmth and strength, and that was dangerous. Much more than dangerous. That kind of heat could make her…had made her…do stupid things. His mouth softened and the ends curled just a little as his gaze moved over her. She scrutinized his well-defined jaw, hollowed cheeks and the strong column of his neck before fo-

cusing on the small white scar that looked doubly pale
against his dark skin in the shadows made by the night
lights in the kitchen. She wanted to use the tip of her
tongue to trace that little ridge of skin and then listen
to his breathing catch and his skin pebble and shiver
with excitement.

He cleared his throat and the spell of near darkness,
his heat and her own addled brain startled her back to
reality. She stepped back quickly, not even cringing
when she felt the sticky syrup on her sole.

"If you need a refill for EllaJayne, stop by the clinic
tomorrow." She turned slowly, refusing to run from the
kitchen, even though that's what she should do. "I think
you can clean up the rest of the spill."

"It's been years since anyone bathed me, but I think
I might like it."

She swung around. He was a macho, jerk bull rider.
They were the worst of the worst, Daddy Gene had
told her, and he should know since he'd been one of
them for a while. Crazy enough to climb on the back of
three-quarters of a ton of testosterone-pumped muscle
again and again. She needed to remember that about
AJ. He was not the man who awkwardly tried to care
for his daughter, making her heart go "aww" and her
hands itch to smooth the daughter and father's similarly frowning faces.

"Good night," she finally said when he wouldn't stop
looking at her.

"You know, your mother told me that she'd seen my
arrival—something to do with your sign and a chart."

Pepper pulled in a breath and let it out slowly through
her nose. Why couldn't her mother say normal moth-
erly things, like stay away from my daughter, you no-

good rodeo bum? Because that sort of comment had been Daddy Gene's job and he wasn't here. "Faye also believes that a bit of bacon and the water drawn from a well on the new moon cures ingrown toenails." She walked away from him, like a woman who knew where she was going, not one running away from herself.

AJ stared at the unfamiliar ceiling, wishing he were in an anonymous hotel room in an anonymous town. His daughter's cranky whimpers would soon be a full-throated I'm-up-and-I-want-attention yell. From his short time as a dad, he'd learned he had another forty-five seconds of peace. He'd take those measly seconds to remind himself he'd climbed on bulls bent on killing him. Dealing with the constant worry and anxiety Baby Girl'd brought into his world was a cake walk, with a huge wobbly cake.

His daughter's cry stopped his thoughts. He had the morning routine down: diaper, T-shirt, socks and then into the car seat so he could use the bathroom without her wandering off. Not that it had worked so well when he'd been fixing the truck. Maybe bungee cords would hold her in the seat? Even he knew that was a bad idea.

He got both of them cleaned up without running into any of the women. Not surprising since EllaJayne liked to wake before the sun. On the bright side, she'd allow him twenty minutes of uninterrupted peace for his first cup of coffee while she sat in his lap sipping her morning milk. It was a part of the day that he could feel almost competent at this fathering thing.

He took both of them out onto the patio to enjoy the cool breeze with EllaJayne wrapped in a little sparkly pony sweatshirt in eye-searing green. He enjoyed the first dark hit of his coffee and Baby Girl's warm head against his shoulder as he watched the pink rays of sun warm the horizon. For those suspended-in-time moments, all was right in the world.

"Oh, you're out here," Pepper said accusingly.

AJ jerked, spilling coffee on himself with a few drops landing on EllaJayne's thick sweatshirt. The little girl squalled. "Shit," he said as he checked her for burns. The hot liquid had splashed across her sweatshirt, which meant he needed to change her. For a toddler who had bad aim with a spoon, Baby Girl was particular about her clothing.

"Did you burn her?"

"No thanks to you," he shot back as he stood with his daughter, who had pitched her sippy cup to the ground where it popped open and spilled. His own jeans were stained with coffee, too, and he knew he'd have a nice red welt. "I'll clean up out here after I change Ella-Jayne...again."

Pepper opened her mouth to say something then closed it. Her gaze moving from his face downward, skimming quickly over his crotch. "Umm...you okay?" she asked grudgingly.

"Are you going to examine me?" he asked. Her head snapped up and their eyes met. The heat that had filled the space between them last night was back, searing and unexpected. His daughter's head thumped his chest as she wiped her tear-streaked face against his once-clean shirt. Back to reality. "Next time warn me."

He made a strategic retreat. Inside, her dog gave him a cocked-head stare that said: Don't mess with her, buddy.

After he'd redressed himself and his daughter, he returned to the kitchen to make breakfast. He needed to talk to Danny about where to find work. He'd turned down Pepper's half-hearted offer to help him look. His guess was that she hoped if he didn't have a job, he'd move along.

AJ heard the shower running and worked really, really hard to not imagine Pepper in there, naked, wet and soapy. Dear Lord, what was his problem? He heard Baby Girl in her high chair starting to wind up for another good cry. Just as he turned to deal with her, Faye entered the kitchen with a vague smile on her face.

"I dreamed good things for you, Arthur John."

"AJ," he corrected as he pulled out the last container of yogurt for his daughter. His coffee would have to be enough until he could find a grocery store. All the food from the memorial had been eaten over the weekend or was in the freezer. He didn't recognize anything in the fridge. He'd learned already to be very, very wary when Faye offered him a meal.

"I have goat yogurt. Much better than store-bought," she said.

"We're good," AJ said as he offered a spoon of the pink goop. His daughter quickly made her way through the yogurt.

"Neither of you were burned. Good," Pepper said as she walked into the kitchen, giving him a professional once-over glance. Silence filled the room. Both Faye and EllaJayne remained quiet as he and Pepper stared at each other. He couldn't turn his head. Her honey-brown hair lay on her shoulders in damp whirls. The scrubs, shapeless on anyone else, highlighted her curves and showed off the length of her thigh. His gaze landed on her toes, the nails with their cheery flowers and neon color.

He'd promised himself that he'd mend his cowboy ways now that he was a daddy. No more women, at least until he got the hang of being a father, which meant his next date would be around the time EllaJayne left for college.

"Do you want me to make you breakfast?" Faye asked Pepper. Finally, AJ could look away.

"I can't be late today. Dr. Cortez is in."

"Oh, my," Faye said and turned to dig in the refrigerator. "Okay. I'll make breakfast for Arthur John."

He'd rather face Tornado the bull again. "I'm good, ma'am."

He quickly got himself and EllaJayne into the truck. He'd stop somewhere for food, maybe take donuts for Danny as payment for his advice. In town, he drove by the Angel Crossing Medical Clinic. Why couldn't he have met Pepper six months ago, before Baby Girl, before his life had gone from fun to grinding responsibility? Six months ago, he'd have taken her out for dancing and drinks and then back to his room. Well, maybe. If he was honest with himself, those anonymous hotel rooms and buckle bunnies had lost their allure. He'd just not figured out what else to do with himself. Now he had a new life, whether he wanted it or not. No use crying over spilled moonshine because he had EllaJayne to care for and was stuck at Santa Faye Ranch. Once he sold the property, he'd have the cash to make sure Baby Girl stayed with him permanently. Of course, until that happened he needed to make money. He didn't care how, really, just so long as it put bills in his pocket and it was legal. *Okay, cowboy*, he told himself. *Saddle up and get to work.*

Chapter 5

Pepper got into her purple SUV to look in on a patient before hitting the clinic. Many of her patients had a standoffish attitude toward her, but she didn't let that stop her from trying to win them over. It was better than when she'd started at the clinic three years ago. From the beginning Daddy Gene had been embraced by Angel Crossing, maybe because he'd leased parts of the property to local ranchers or because he'd been known on the rodeo circuit. She and Faye had never quite fit in, starting with Faye homeschooling her, then sending her to high school with lunches filled with tofu and homemade wheat bread. Between being an EMT after high school and now treating the town, the attitude had been changing. More slowly than she'd like, of course.

After checking her patient, she had plenty of time to get to the clinic, which meant plenty of time to mull over her situation. She figured what she had to work on next was finding day care for AJ's daughter. Could Faye watch the little girl? Probably, except her mother's idea of child rearing and AJ's didn't seem to be in the same universe. Could Pepper watch EllaJayne? Exactly how would she explain that to the doctor who came to the clinic two times a week? It wouldn't come to that. She'd find him a list of women to choose from.

A caregiver by nature, she knew she'd have to make sure she didn't allow herself to get drawn into AJ and his daughter's troubles. And there was trouble there. A cowboy like him didn't set off across country on his own with a toddler if there wasn't some sad story. She'd become a PA to help people. It was why she'd put up the ranch for the grant to start the community garden in the first place.

Even after withdrawing her application, in another three weeks, she'd have her first crop from the greenhouse and cold boxes. She already had plans on how to get the word out and who would get the first veggies. So many of her patients should be on assistance but were too proud. With fresh veggies and eventually fruit, everyone would win. She wanted chickens for eggs, too. First the garden…no, first was getting the ranch into her hands. Daddy Gene had meant for it to go to her and her mother. He'd told them that. His time had just been shorter than they'd all wished and he'd never changed his will. She had to believe he wouldn't have been upset that she was going to fight AJ for the ranch.

Could she just threaten to go to court? Her attorney seemed like a go-getter. AJ, with his drawl and cowboy swagger, wouldn't know what hit him.

"Knock, knock," a woman's voice said as the door opened. "I know you're not officially open but…"

"Not a problem. Come in, Lavonda."

"I wouldn't be here for myself, but I live with a big stubborn Scot who is about to die from coughing. I think you saw him, didn't you?"

"Yes. And I told him if the cough didn't clear up to come in."

"Silly you." Lavonda Leigh Kincaid laughed. "I would think that you've dealt with enough cowboys to know the routine."

Lavonda was Mayor Danny Leigh's sister, and newly wed to Professor of Archeology Jones Kincaid. She'd also taken over a company that provided guided tours of the Arizona desert. She'd been friendly with Pepper, explaining that women under the age of sixty in this town needed to bond together since there were so few of them.

"The routine being that unless he can't lift his head from where it hit the ground after he fell down, he's fine?"

"Something like that. Really, if you could just give me something strong enough to knock him out, he'd get better. He just needs to sleep for a couple of days."

"Let me write a prescription for cough syrup. It's not fancy but it'll work and better yet, it should make him drowsy. Keep him from driving, operating machinery, and so on while he's taking this."

"Bless you." Lavonda watched Pepper write up the prescription. "How are you doing?"

"I didn't catch whatever the professor has."

"That's not what I meant. The memorial. The relative who inherited the ranch."

Pepper reminded herself that she really did love Angel Crossing even if the gossip mill would give the

NSA a run for its money. "It's been tough. But having the service… I don't know. It…it gets better every day."

"And the situation with the ranch?"

That Pepper really didn't want to talk about.

Lavonda went on, "Your community garden would make such a difference. Of course, it would give people food, but I also think that it could be a way to get and keep the under-sixty crowd living here. I did a little research and community gardens are a thing."

Not surprising Lavonda had done research. Before moving to Angel Crossing, she'd been a PR mogul… or something like that. "I really think it's more about feeding people and giving others a chance to create businesses."

"I agree. Is there a way to work with Gene's…cousin, right? Maybe he'd give you a chance to pay for the ranch over time? Or something like that?"

Pepper handed over the prescription and shrugged. "I'm working on it."

"You know, my sister's brother-in-law is an attorney in Tucson, if you need a legal opinion."

"Already got that but thanks."

"I want to help. The garden is a good idea."

"I thought so, but it's causing nothing but headaches. Would you believe that I've got to find day care now? And on the cheap and top-notch."

"Everybody wants something for nothing."

Lavonda's gaze immediately went to Pepper's waistline. "Not for me. Good God, no. That's just what I'd need." Another reason to stay away from AJ. He apparently easily made babies. "It's Daddy Gene's cousin." That sentence was harder to say than she'd imagined. "He's—"

"The ranch stealer."

Lavonda went up three notches in Pepper's book. "He will be the new owner and he's got a little girl who needs looking after."

"I saw them at the memorial. If you can't find anyone, let me know. I can probably squeeze in a few hours here and there. Why isn't he looking?"

"He's out on the job search and I said I'd help." Lavonda didn't need to know any secrets that weren't general knowledge.

"Nice of you, considering."

Pepper just nodded.

"I'd better get going so I can dose up my cowboy, but seriously, call me either for the attorney or the babysitting."

"I will," Pepper said and meant it. Angel Crossing had changed. She needed to let go of some of the snubs and name-calling. That had been so long ago. Look how people had come out to the memorial and brought food. Plus, she thought she and Lavonda just might become friends. That would be nice.

"Going to court is the wrong path," Faye said later that night when they were cleaning up the dishes. "It will only lead to disaster."

Her mother didn't think AJ inheriting their ranch was a disaster and yet for her, Pepper calling an attorney was a problem. "You need some Windex to clean up your window into the future, Faye. I'm protecting you, me and Angel Crossing."

"It's still the wrong way. Karma will get you."

"You always say that."

"She always says what?" AJ asked as he came into the kitchen.

"Nothing," Pepper answered, giving her mother "the

look"—the one Pepper had perfected for recalcitrant patients.

"I should have a job by the end of the week. Do you have caregivers for me to check out?"

"You know, this really should be your job. I work full time plus." She wanted to be sure that he understood what he'd asked of her.

"Do you have a list?" His storm-gray gaze stayed glued to her face.

"I have better things to do with my time." That was true, except she had Lavonda and a couple of other leads. Why was she being such a pain about this? She opened her mouth to give him the names.

"We shook on it."

It wasn't the words. It was the self-righteous tone. "Only until this entire situation gets overturned by the courts." Damn it. She hadn't meant to tip her hand. Why did he get her so mad? She was the calm one. Faye was the one who let things slip out. Faye was the one ruled by emotion.

"The will is legal."

"And you know that how? Seems like you fell one too many times on your head."

"Children, children," Faye said, drifting into the space between them. "You mustn't use your energies on arguments."

"Faye's right," AJ said, crossing his arms over his chest. "You'd be wasting your time and energy, fighting the will. It's airtight. Gene left me the ranch."

AJ didn't raise his voice. He didn't need to. She read his anger in every solid inch of him. None of it stopped her from saying, "So says the man who is the will's beneficiary."

Faye waved her hand, making her bracelets clink. "We are all beneficiaries. Gene always thought of others." Her mother paused and cocked her head. "I can almost hear him saying: 'Pepper, face the facts and don't hire a snake-oil attorney.'"

Pepper could feel AJ's gaze and knew that it would have pity and maybe a little bit of smugness. Faye brought that out in others. Early on and even after Daddy Gene entered their lives, Pepper knew it was up to her to make sure that the practicalities of daily life got taken care of. Like now, if she didn't fight the will, Faye and Pepper would be homeless, abandoning Faye's Beauties and living on a rural PA's meager salary.

"So are you going to listen to your mother?" AJ asked.

She searched his face and found something there that might have been laughter or... "I always listen to my mother, but I'm also a grown woman and know our rights. We have a right to this ranch and my town has a right to good, healthy food. You aren't going to stop me from getting both of those things. No matter what karma I have to defy."

"Karaoke?" AJ asked as he read the flyer behind the bar.

"Country-western karaoke," Danny said, lifting two fingers for the bartender to refill their beers.

AJ considered telling Danny no and going home to Baby Girl, but today had sucked big-time. He'd driven to the mine two towns over and stopped at four ranches. No work for a former bull rider and sometime-wrangler. Everyone had been nice and polite, but that didn't pay the bills.

"You think they need help?" he asked Danny, lifting his shoulder to the bar. He was only half kidding.

"Woman-run and woman-owned." The mugs of beer were set in front of them, and they sipped in quiet for a few moments. "There's a prize for the best karaoke singer."

"The hell you say."

"Come on. You're the one who said you needed to make money."

"At a job, not making a fool of myself singin' 'Crazy' or 'Friends in Low Places.'"

"Just trying to help. How's everything else going? Settling in okay?"

"As long as I don't let Faye cook for me, everything's good. Still don't know why Gene didn't change his will."

Danny shrugged. "He was your cousin, right? And you did save him at that rodeo. When was that? Eight? Nine years ago?"

"I was just at the right place, that's all. My God, I didn't even make it out here to see him after he got so sick."

"You called. He understood. It wasn't like you didn't come because you were shacked up with some buckle bunny. You were fighting to get your daughter. Don't look a gift ranch in the mouth."

"I'm not, just wondering." They sipped their beers in silence again. "Since she's watching my daughter tonight, guess I should ask what Pepper's story is?"

"I wondered how long it'd be until you asked about her." Danny grinned knowingly.

AJ wanted to take back the question and walk out of the bar. He went cowboy-quiet.

"I haven't been here that long but I understand Faye and Gene came drifting into town when Pepper was six." Danny paused, took a gulp of beer and went on. "You know that she and Gene hooked up at the commune where Faye grew up, free love and all that. Pepper was born there. No one knows who Pepper's biological father is. Why Faye and Gene came to Angel Crossing is a mystery. She insists there are vortexes here like up in Sedona. If there are, it hasn't brought us the tourists and the money like that place."

This explained a lot. "Pepper wants to start a commune at the ranch?"

"Nah. Just a community garden. She wants to grow fresh veggies to give or sell at low cost and then expand to rent plots for residents to grow their own for themselves or to sell. That's how she'll have a bit of income beyond grants and donations. There are a lot of older folks and proud poor ones who need just a little help. It's not such a bad idea."

AJ couldn't feel guilty for putting that plan in jeopardy. He had his daughter to worry about. Tonight he didn't want to talk about the ranch or any of the responsibilities that went with it. He wanted to be a cowboy, here to enjoy his beer, the music and maybe a cowgirl or two. AJ looked around the bar. Not many people, but then, it was a weeknight.

"If you're looking for work, I keep in touch with the guys from the circuit. I'm sure I could find some place that needs a wrangler or a rider."

AJ shook his head. He didn't want to go on the road and leave his daughter. That's why he'd given up the only job he'd ever wanted. He'd not been in the big money but he'd made a living. There was an ache in his back and hip, but that was to be expected and it hadn't been enough to keep him off a bull. "Can't leave my daughter."

Danny nodded his head. "You miss it?"

AJ could tell there was something in his friend's voice that made it more than a casual question. "I'm responsible for my daughter. She's got to come first."

"Seems like everyone is getting hitched and having babies."

AJ couldn't imagine his friend pining for the settled life. On the other hand, he had come to Angel Crossing and become mayor. AJ couldn't have imagined that when the two of them were rippin' it up in every honky-tonk from San Antonio to Laramie. "We're all getting older," AJ said lamely.

"Not that old. Let's do a shot," Danny said and motioned to the bartender again.

AJ shook his head. "I've got to get going, man." He stood up and for just a moment he longed again for the days when he would have stayed until the bartender kicked him out, maybe leaving with a woman who was soft and willing. Had that really just been last year? He clapped Danny on the shoulder. "Drink one for me and we'll go out another night to celebrate when I get my new job."

Darn. Lights were still on in the ranch house. He didn't want to talk with anyone. He wanted to crawl into bed and hope tomorrow was better. His back and hip ached after being forced to change a tire on the pickup along the side of the dark road. All of it was a reminder that his life was quickly sliding toward crap. Could he hold out until the ranch was his? He had to.

He stopped inside the door, listening. He didn't hear a TV, the baby, Faye or Pepper—who'd convinced him she could deal with his daughter's bedtime. He pulled off his boots and snuck to the kitchen. He'd get a glass of water, take an aspirin so he could sleep until the Baby Girl pre-dawn alarm clock went off.

He slowly opened the door to his room so he'd not disturb EllaJayne. Shi...crap...da...darn. There on his bed was Pepper herself with a wide-awake EllaJayne in her arms. The baby was contenting herself with playing at opening and closing the snaps on Pepper's cowgirl shirt. When she wasn't in scrubs, Pepper wore the cowgirl uniform well. He'd noticed that before, especially her second-skin jeans.

He could pick up the little girl without seeing or touching anything on Pepper he shouldn't. He tiptoed toward the bed. EllaJayne's eyes narrowed. Of course, his daughter wasn't thrilled to see Daddy. She'd rather hug Oggie than him. Where was the stuffed animal? He looked around and then saw it squashed between Pepper's arm and breast. Lucky dog.

"Come on, EllaJayne," he whispered as he reached out his hands slowly. "Time for night-night." He held his breath as the little girl shook her head. If he grabbed her quick enough, she'd be in his arms before she could make a noise. He reached forward, thinking that he'd ease Oggie out before swooping in for his daughter. He leaned over, breathing slowly and calmly, like he was working with a skittish horse. He caught a scent of baby powder mixed with lemon and clove. He leaned in farther, his hand hovering just over the dog. EllaJayne stared at him without blinking. He touched Oggie. She grasped the toy and yelled. Pepper's eyes popped open, just as his hand got squashed between her breast and the stuffed animal.

"What are you doing?" she asked as she sat up, pulled away and grasped his squawking daughter to her.

"Putting EllaJayne to bed," he said, keeping a wary eye on the suddenly quiet girl.

Pepper stood, her lush mouth transformed into a straight, thin line. She handed over the girl and walked out.

His daughter cooperated and went into her bed without a peep. AJ wanted or maybe needed to apologize to Pepper. "EllaJayne is down for the night," he said when he found her in the kitchen where she was putting away dishes. "Thanks again for watching her." She didn't look any less strained or annoyed. "And, well, sorry...about earlier."

She nodded. She didn't move. He didn't move. The tension in the kitchen neared the twanging tightness of a guitar string. He had to break it somehow. "So," he said. "I'm going to have a snack."

She still didn't move from the drain board. He dug into the back of the cupboard and pulled out a box of Fiddle Faddle.

"Where did you get that?" she asked.

"I bought it."

"I know you bought it. How did you hide it? Faye always finds my stash."

"Your stash?"

"She always finds my Cadbury fruit-and-nut bars. No matter where I hide them. It's like she's got radar. Daddy Gene always hid Devil Dogs."

"I didn't know I had to hide stuff."

"Share and I won't rat you out," she said and held out her hand.

He offered the open box to her. "There's a place near to home that makes better caramel corn than this but a beggar can't be a complainer."

"If you say so. This is pretty darned good." She popped a piece of caramel-covered popcorn in her mouth and chewed in obvious bliss.

He would have laughed if that picture didn't make him think of the brief flash of heat he'd felt when his hand had cupped her breast as he'd worked to get Oggie. He wasn't proud of it, but there it was. He may have, possibly without conscious thought, copped a feel.

"You can't distract me anymore," she said as she walked to the sink and turned on the tap. "We need to talk about—" She stopped, gazing out the window over the sink, then she turned and ran out the back door.

What the hell? He looked out the window and saw flames. Crap. He followed her, yelling, "Pepper, don't."

"My plants," she yelled. He was nearly to her.

"I'm calling 9-1-1, then we'll get the hose."

She stopped and turned to him, her face eerily illuminated by the flames. "The plants…the greenhouse…"

"I know. Go get the hose. I'll call." She started toward the greenhouse and its attached shed, but the flames were higher than the nearby barn. He grabbed her arm to stop her. She seemed to be in a trance. "You don't want the barn to catch fire. The greenhouse is gone."

"Oh, my God, Faye was right. Karma doesn't like attorneys."

Chapter 6

Pepper concentrated on watching the volunteer fire-fighters roll up their hoses. It had taken them less than ten minutes to put out the fire. In all, the greenhouse and shed couldn't have been burning for more than twenty minutes and it was all gone. The flames had been hot enough to twist the metal and burn up all the tubes and the electronic control system.

"Sorry," the fire chief said, followed by nods from the other volunteers, most of whom had been treated at the clinic.

"Thanks for trying to save it." She'd known from the moment she and AJ had run outside that the greenhouse was a goner. She looked around for him. He stood with a small cluster of men. She moved her gaze away from AJ, where it had been landing far too often. He'd pitched in as the firefighters had sprayed the greenhouse, then used rakes and long poles to poke at the charred remains so they were sure no spark or ember was left.

"We'll be out of here soon. Chief Rudy will be by tomorrow to check, but it doesn't look like arson to me. I'd say electrical or maybe from compost. You'd be amazed how quickly that stuff can catch fire."

Pepper stared at the charred remains of her dreams. She sounded a lot more like Faye than herself, which gave her an idea of how crazy upset she was. She'd face it all tomorrow—including the insurance company—when she wasn't exhausted. Then she'd come up with a way to salvage her garden and her plan for Angel Crossing and her mother.

"At least the barn didn't catch fire," AJ said, his drawl thick and his words soft.

"Yeah, at least."

"It was just plants and they weren't even that big." He stood beside her, both of them looking over the ashes, white-green in the weak light from the old dusk-to-dawn lamp crookedly attached to the barn.

"You'd think that, you…cowboy jerk." She wanted to punch him, too, but this wasn't elementary school. *Cowboy jerk*? Really, that was the best insult she could come up with?

"I'll ignore that," he said easily.

Why was he being nice? She couldn't keep up a good head of anger if he was nice to her. If he didn't stop it, she'd be crying. He pulled her without warning into a one-armed hug. She stiffened. She wouldn't be coddled or humored. She was an adult, as much a tough-as-horseshoes cowgirl as anyone else. Daddy Gene had told her she had to be the one to live in the real world, make sure the bills were paid because Faye was… Faye.

Pepper had done it whenever Gene was on the road or had gone off to find work. She'd made the same promise when he knew his disease had come roaring back and he was dying.

AJ's words drifted over her head, making the hair move. "I *can* be a jerk, just ask around. But not tonight."

She relaxed into his embrace, feeling surrounded not only by his warmth but something more, a comfort that surprised her. She wanted to lean into him, let him take on her fear, disappointment and anger. Just for ten seconds. Yes, for ten seconds, she could be defeated and let someone else take on her responsibilities. She reached her arm around him, pressing her face into his shoulder, into the muscled solidity of him. Substantial and safe.

She counted off the seconds in her head but somewhere around six her brain just stopped and she only felt. He held her more tightly against him. She didn't pull away. She wanted to melt into him.

"Pepper?"

She glanced up at him. His gaze roamed over her face. She tipped up her chin, offering herself to him.

No. She needed to step away. She needed to—

His mouth came down on hers, feather-light in its touch. Testing and tasting her. She tasted back, then opened her mouth on a deep inhale of need and desire that ran through her, racing from the notch at the base of her throat south, settling hotly between her thighs. She should pull away. That would be smart. Instead, she turned into his one-armed embrace, reaching up and around his wide, solid shoulders, digging her fingers into the bunching muscles, enjoying the strength and resilience of his flesh. His arms wrapped around her. They fit just right, everything aligning as it should, as if they had been a couple for decades with every curve and hollow matched to make something that was greater than just the two of them.

His hands moved under her ponytail to pull her mouth more firmly against his, urging her to open to him further. She did and the explosion of taste, feeling and heat went straight to her knees, which wobbled with the unexpected but not unwelcome rush of lust. Lordy be. She reveled for long moments in the heat and want of that dance of their tongues but finally made herself pull her head away. She didn't move out of his loose embrace, though, slowing her breathing even as she enjoyed the hot scent of him. His gaze didn't leave her face, searching but not demanding. At last, she stepped out of his arms.

"Thanks. Good night." She walked with purpose back into the house, where the bright lights and Faye's questions would wipe away the kiss. Just part of the shock of the fire, she told herself in her best medical-professional voice. Nothing was going on between her and the cowboy. Nothing. He and his little girl were not her future. She would have a community garden and settle down with a man who held the same values as she did and understood how important it was to sacrifice for the community. Someone sort of like Danny Leigh. He'd given up a lot to become mayor. Yeah, that was the kind of man for her. Not AJ McCreary, a broken-down bull rider who'd sell off her ranch.

"AJ has Aries rising, a fire sign," Faye said to Pepper when she came into the kitchen.

"Are you saying the fire was his fault?"

"Of course not. He would never do anything like that. I meant that he is a good complement to your air sign. You'll feed his fire."

Pepper stared at her mother. The woman must have seen the kiss. "AJ is an unemployed cowboy with a baby and an attitude, who will soon be stealing our ranch."

Faye reached out her hands with her palms toward Pepper, reading her aura, something her mother insisted she could do. "Don't think too much, sweetie. Allow your heart, not your stethoscope, to make your decision. Have a cup of the yam root tea and then go to bed. Everything will work out." Faye drifted out of the kitchen. Pepper couldn't go to bed yet, not with the fire department still working.

I would've told you that the idiots in Angel Crossing can take care of themselves. Your job was to settle down and give me grandbabies. A voice drifted through her mind sounding a lot like Daddy Gene at his most exasperated. She was going to put that down to stress. Tomorrow she'd come up with a plan that would save her garden and Faye's future. Daddy Gene had been right to expect Pepper to care for her mother. That was the way it worked between the two of them, which meant she had to get rid of the cowboy and his claim.

AJ used Baby Girl as a shield when he walked into the kitchen the morning after the fire. He wasn't sure exactly what to expect from Pepper. He certainly didn't believe she'd want a repeat of the kiss. He had enough experience with women to know that. He also thought he might need to apologize, which he would do if he had to—even though he hadn't done anything she hadn't wanted to.

No one was in the kitchen, despite EllaJayne allowing him to sleep in until a time when other humans usually got up. Everything was neat and clean, not one coffee-mug ring. His daughter wriggled in his arms, letting him know that her patience had worn thin. She was hungry and he'd better insert food quickly. He went through the morning routine and still not one of the Bourne women appeared. Finally, both he and EllaJayne had eaten, and he'd drank two cups of strong coffee.

He walked outside with Baby Girl on his hip. Pepper stood by the heap of ashes that had been the greenhouse. His daughter flapped her arms, holding out Oggie, babbling and pointing at Pepper. She seemed to be more enthused seeing the stranger than she was to see him. That could be because he washed her face, and made her do things like eat eggs and sit in her high chair.

He heard the bark just before he felt the solid weight of Butch landing against his legs. At least one living being on this ranch appreciated him. The dog danced around his feet as AJ moved toward Pepper. The woman looked determined—no sign of the vulnerable person she'd been last night. Phone to her ear, she paced through the ashes. Butch brought AJ a rock to throw. AJ sent it sailing and the dog raced after it. EllaJayne jabbered loudly in his ear as she pointed at Pepper, who continued to pace. He understood about every tenth word his daughter said, so he knew enough to take her to Pepper. He set EllaJayne on the ground, putting out his hand so she could totter around while continuing to wave Oggie to Pepper, who gave them a quick nod. Butch came back with a new rock. He waited, sitting on his haunches until he caught sight of the moving stuffed animal. AJ saw the direction of his gaze and moved to grab it before the dog lunged. Too late. Butch nabbed Oggie and raced away. EllaJayne screamed. AJ closed his eyes as a sharp pain radiated from his back to his brain. The stupid reach for the toy had tweaked his back. He hadn't been doing his physical therapy exercises, the ones meant to loosen his muscles and keep them from knotting up. When his back acted up, his hip would start throbbing and soon his shoulder would join in. Darn it. He finally opened his eyes as the sharp pain dialed back.

Now the pain moved to his heart as he saw the shiny tracks on EllaJayne's face, her eyes swimming with tears and her brow scrunched in hurt. He whistled sharply for the dog who came trotting back to Pepper instead of him. She stuck the phone in her pocket and then pointed to the ground. Butch dropped Oggie a good twenty feet from AJ.

"Look, baby," he said to his daughter. "Butch brought back Oggie. He's fine. Let's go get him." He didn't know if he could pick her up right now. She wasn't heavy, but pain shot from his back and down his leg. His daughter toddled, then collapsed, pulling on AJ's arm, and his back chose that moment to freeze into a sheet of pain that sent him to his knees beside EllaJayne.

"Oggie," his daughter screamed, her little arm shooting out toward Pepper and the stuffed animal. AJ worked to get his breath and stand up. If he was lucky, the muscles would unclench without him having to lie flat out on his back on the ground.

"He's fine, EllaJayne. Butch didn't hurt him," Pepper said in soothing tones as she approached the two of them. AJ's back muscles clamped down again, his breath stopping for a second. When the spasm loosened, he made himself look at her and even smiled.

"Thanks." Another thirty seconds and he'd move, he assured himself.

Pepper looked at him intently, her eyes scanning up and down his body, before turning to EllaJayne. She handed over the stuffed animal. "See. He's fine." The little girl clasped the pile of balding fur to her chest, then gave a dark-eyed glare at Butch. If AJ had had the breath, he would have laughed because that glare was pure Nanny McCreary, his great-grandmother, who'd been the terror of the clan. No one crossed that woman. She'd kept the family fed and on its land through the Great Depression with willpower and a shotgun.

"Oggie," EllaJayne finally said, still hugging her toy. "Bad Butch." At least that was what AJ thought she said. With the throbbing pain now settling into his back, it was tough to think about much more than getting to the house and finding a flat surface to stretch out on and a bottle of pills to take. Only he couldn't knock himself out because he had EllaJayne and calls to make. He took a deep breath and levered himself slowly and painfully to his feet, keeping his gaze on the ground. He didn't want to see anything like pity in Pepper's eyes. "I'll need the names of the sitters and directions," he said, to give himself something else to focus on.

"I've got the insurance to deal with today but come with me into the clinic and let me check you out. It's obvious you're in pain."

"Just an old injury. It's nothing. It'll only take you a minute to get me the names," he said tightly, feeling the hot wave of clenching pain starting again at his hips. He needed to relax or it would never unknot. He needed to get horizontal, too. Crap. That one small thought had him remembering their kiss and the promise of the heat they would have generated if they'd gotten horizontal together. At least imagining that made him forget about his back for a moment or two. He straightened a fraction of an inch and the stiffness eased. "I plan to go out on interviews tomorrow. I need the sitter hired today." He looked at his daughter happily sitting on her once-clean bottom in the dusty yard, sifting gravel and dirt over her legs. Leaning over the tub to wash her again wasn't going to happen. He'd figure something out because he and EllaJayne needed to make a good impression on the sitter. "Come on, Baby Girl," he said to her. His daughter looked up, her face marred by the now dirty streaks of her earlier tears.

"Up," she said, lifting her arms. "Want up."

No way could he do that. "Not now. You walk. Get Oggie and come." He saw her lip start to stick out, ready for a long pout. "You can play horsey," he promised. His daughter loved sitting on his saddle that had a place in the corner of the room until AJ could clean out the barn enough for his equipment. Finally, EllaJayne pushed herself to her feet and started to walk like a drunken sailor toward the house. "I want to leave for town as soon as I have the names," he said to Pepper before walking away.

Twenty-five minutes later, EllaJayne was as clean as a wet washcloth could make her. His back had settled into a dull throb that he might keep under control with double doses of aspirin and stretches. He'd ridden with worse.

"Pepper," he called, Ella Jayne toddling beside him into the kitchen. She was there, the morning sun highlighting the golden red in her hair and making her eyes glow. Dear Lord, her earthy beauty knocked the breath out of him, but in the good way, like a beautiful sunset or a first kiss. "Baby Girl is cleaned up, aren't you?"

he asked his daughter so he had to turn from Pepper. He needed to get some distance. "We're ready to go find a sitter."

"I didn't have much time..."

Her voice drifted off but he resisted checking out what had shut her up. He stared at the top of his daughter's dark head. "As soon as you get me the names, we'll be out of your hair."

AJ had the two measly names she'd finally given him and his daughter strapped in her seat when a semi pulled up with pallets of plants on its trailer. What the heck? This must be for her garden, but what had she been thinking? She'd ordered enough plants to feed the entire state. Not his business, he reminded himself. He walked over to talk with the driver who jumped out of the cab.

"You order a thousand King Kale plants?"

"That wouldn't be me. Could it be Pepper Bourne?"

The guy looked at the paperwork. "Angel Crossing Community Garden."

Butch raced over barking, and AJ heard the llamas and alpacas calling out. He couldn't bend to catch the dog's collar, so he clicked his fingers and pointed to his side. Butch circled him once, then plopped his hairy butt in the dirt.

"What's going on... My plants?" Pepper was ten feet away. He saw her eyes go wide. "I didn't order—"

"You Angel Crossing Community Garden?" the driver asked, approaching her with the clipboard as Butch continued to race around again, barking like a maniac.

"Butch, hush," Pepper said ineffectually, and then to the man with the clipboard, "I ordered kale but—"

"One thousand King Kale, five hundred Queen Mustard and another thousand Marquis Artichokes."

"I only ordered a dozen of each plant."

"Nope. See here?" He tried to show her the clipboard.

AJ joined them. "Is there a problem with the order?"

Pepper said tightly. "I never ordered that amount. That would be enough to feed the city of Phoenix."

"I have the invoice," the man said just as Butch's barking went from loud to shrill. The sound of hooves pounded nearby. They all turned to see the herd of alpacas and llamas stampeding to the low trailer of plants. The animals nearly trampled each other getting to the greenery.

Pepper turned, waving her arms at the creatures to shoo them away. Not one furry beast paid attention. "Get out," she shouted. The man with the clipboard stood frozen to the spot as Butch raced around, deciding he really was a herding dog. He barked and nipped at the llamas and alpacas.

Pepper yelled, "Faye, get your animals. Now."

AJ moved as quickly as he could when he saw that the creatures weren't going to be moved along. He was stopped short and sent to the ground by a muscle spasm that froze his legs and took away their strength. The truck driver continued to stand with his mouth open.

"Oh, dear," Faye said, "My Beauties are being bad today."

"Lady," the driver yelled over the racket. "Get them out of there or I'm calling the cops. They're going to ruin my other deliveries."

"You shouldn't have tempted them," Faye chided.

AJ caught his breath between the muscle spasms

and said, "Get in the truck and drive away before they eat everything."

The driver took the advice. The truck started up. Startled, the animals scattered and stampeded off into the desert with Butch and Pepper racing after them.

Faye stood quietly. "I tried to warn her about the attorney. She always did have to figure out things the hard way."

Chapter 7

Worrying over her patients at the clinic, working on a way to get AJ to come in for an exam on his back and hip as well as finally getting to making a longer list of child care alternatives for EllaJayne were preferable mental exercises to going over the disasters Pepper'd had at the ranch, culminating with the destroyed plants last week. She shoveled in her yogurt to make up for the missed lunch, which she'd spent talking with the insurance company…again. The greenhouse and damaged plants weren't covered. Every day got her deeper in debt with no end in sight. Maybe she should have listened more seriously to Faye and her predictions on how the universe viewed their situation and Pepper's calls to the attorney. It didn't seem fair or right since she'd only called in the law to look out for everyone's best interests—except AJ's.

"Mrs. Carmichael is here. Need you in Exam Two," Claudette said and looked almost sorry for interrupting Pepper's furtive meal.

No rest for the wicked or those who went against the universe. She threw away the yogurt and focused on her next patient. She'd take care of everything else later. Although…perhaps Mrs. Carmichael might be a good choice as a caregiver for EllaJayne. By working out a deal with the grandmotherly Mrs. Carmichael, like a couple of free appointments and insulin samples, Pepper might get on the universe's and AJ's good side.

Pepper watched EllaJayne babbling to Oggie from her car seat in the back of the purple SUV. AJ, desperate and harried, had called her early in the day asking her to pick up the little girl from the high-priced day care near to Tucson. Lucky for him, they'd had an extra car seat for her to borrow. She hadn't even had a chance to tell him about Mrs. Carmichael, who already looked after her own grandchildren and was happy to take on another little one—and at a bargain-basement price. She was perfect. Pepper loved when things worked out. She'd bask in the glow of this success before tackling the will and the damage at the ranch. "Right, EllaJayne," she said to the little girl.

"Oggie," she yelled in agreement, shaking her stuffed animal.

Pepper smiled. "Oggie and you will love Mrs. Carmichael. She makes the best cookies, which might be why she can't keep her blood sugar under control. I should look for low sugar recipes for her. Good idea, EllaJayne." It was kind of nice to have another person in the car, even if the toddler's conversation was limited.

"I wonder what Faye's making for dinner. It doesn't matter. I have a secret stash of sausages in the back of the freezer that I'm going to cook to celebrate." She thought her triumphant solution deserved a special dinner. Faye would fuss about the meat for ten minutes tops, Pepper predicted. Her mother tried to be a good vegetarian, but she rarely turned down pork—and pork in the form of sausages was irresistible to Faye.

As she lifted EllaJayne from the car seat, Pepper glared at the jerk-face llamas and alpacas placidly hanging out in the corral. Her mother still insisted on calling them her Beauties, despite the destruction they'd caused with their stampede. Pepper would be paying off that stunt for who knew how long and how far back it would set her plans for the garden. She'd play Scarlett O'Hara on that—tomorrow was another day. Tonight she'd celebrate her one victory. Mrs. Carmichael would get her points with AJ, which had nothing to do with what had happened after the fire and everything to do with the agreement they had.

"Down. Want down," EllaJayne insisted, drumming her feet against Pepper's thigh. She wasn't falling for that. If she put the toddler down, she'd be off and into something. She knew only too well now how AJ could have lost track of the little girl on that first day they'd met. "Boot," the little girl insisted and pointed. Pepper followed her finger. Butch was racing toward them, panting happily. He barked and ran in circles around Pepper as she tried to walk inside. He didn't quiet until EllaJayne was on the ground and he'd sniffed her over, licked her face and then knocked her down with his enthusiasm. Pepper waited for the little girl to cry. Instead, she giggled and shouted, "Boot, Boot, Boot." Apparently that was toddler for *Butch*.

"You look much better," Faye said as she walked calmly into the chaos on the porch.

"I'm cooking dinner, and we're having sausages on the grill." Her mother protested for eight minutes and then agreed it was probably for the best since AJ needed extra protein. Pepper didn't ask why. When Faye made those kinds of pronouncements, it was always better to not know why. She made her way to the kitchen listening to the dog, her mother and the little girl play in the living room.

When the food was ready, EllaJayne pounded a spoon against the table, giggling at the barking Butch. Finally, twenty minutes after the sausages came off the grill and with no call from AJ, Pepper said, "Let's eat," putting a cheery lilt into her voice for the little girl. She'd only agreed to the day care pickup. AJ shouldn't assume that because she and her mother were female, they were built-in babysitters. She focused on dinner. It had been a long time since they'd had such a treat. She'd been given the sausages by a patient, who used a secret family recipe to make them. They were nearly as precious as gold in the Angel Crossing bartering system that was used for everything from an office visit to a bag of coffee at the general store. They were bliss on her tongue. She glanced over at the suddenly quiet EllaJayne who was trying to give Butch her sausage.

"No, you don't," Pepper said, swooping in to snatch the meat and clear off the little girl's plate. She immediately started to wail, until Pepper plunked down a bowl of yogurt—not Faye's but handmade at a small dairy that had started up in the next town—along with fresh fruit. Pepper began feeding her. EllaJayne didn't have the coordination to use the spoon fast enough for her yogurt greed.

"You loved yogurt, too," Faye said, "although cheese curds were your favorite. There was a dairy woman from Wisconsin who lived at Dove's Paradise."

Pepper remembered quite a bit about Dove's Paradise, the commune that she'd lived in with her mother and her mother's parents.

"You know," Faye started, "the universe had a plan when Gene's truck broke down at our door that day."

Pepper had heard this story, but there was a comfort in listening again to how Daddy Gene's radiator had leaked, he'd stopped for water and her mother had been there. Faye insisted their water signs had immediately recognized each other. Daddy Gene had said all he'd noticed was her halter top and Daisy Duke shorts. They'd gotten together then, but Daddy Gene had been on the road nearly all the time. It had been two more years before he bought the place outside Angel Crossing and invited Faye to join him, telling her that he'd already named the ranch for her, so she had to agree. Pepper felt tears gathering. She couldn't believe he was gone.

"Daddy," EllaJayne yelled.

Pepper started, spilling yogurt. She looked but didn't see AJ. "Not yet, baby," Pepper said, offering another spoonful. The little girl shook her head and Butch barked.

"They must hear something," Faye said serenely. "I'll make AJ a plate so it's ready for him. I feel he needs a little pampering."

Pepper wondered if something in the air was turning everyone—except her—into a nutcase. "Are you done?" she asked EllaJayne.

"Want Daddy. More yogurt." The toddler smacked the table. Butch went into another frenzy of barking.

Pepper lifted the wriggling child from her chair and carried her back to the tub for a wash down. Both yogurt and potato salad decorated her hair. Butch joined them despite the fact he hated the tub as much as he hated getting his feet wet—lucky for her and him that they lived in the desert.

She'd only gotten EllaJayne's shoes and socks off before her mother called for her. Something in her voice caught Pepper's attention. She picked up EllaJayne and went to the kitchen.

"What, Faye?" she asked.

"Daddy," EllaJayne screamed in her ear. The little girl was right this time. AJ was standing beside Faye. Then he turned around slowly, painfully and she knew why Faye had sounded odd.

AJ's aching cheek and back stopped him from smiling at his little girl—who for the first time seemed happy to see him. He noted the concern and something more in Pepper's eyes before her gaze traveled over him like a doctor. He opened his mouth, but she beat him to it.

"Don't move until I can check you over. Faye, take EllaJayne." She handed off his daughter, who snuggled into Faye with her thumb in her mouth.

"I'm fine."

"That's a lie." She stared hard at his face, then turned to her mother. "Get EllaJayne ready for *b-e-d*."

Every creature at the ranch knew his little girl hated

the word *bed*. AJ allowed the homey smells of food and baby powder to waft over him, erasing a fraction of the day's disasters. Still, he had a job, even if it was temporary.

"Sit," Pepper said.

"I just need aspirin, a beer and dinner."

"Sit first. I want to look at that cheek and where else? Your back?"

He nodded carefully because the muscles in his neck were the consistency of concrete. Soon he'd be frozen in place from the tip of his head to his heels. He hadn't had spasms like this since he'd tweaked his back two years ago. Of course, he hadn't been regularly hauling hay and feed or helping a reluctant heifer give birth— her bucking and twisting had ended with him flat on his back, a bruise on his cheek. Although when she'd first smacked him with her thrashing head, he'd thought she'd broken his entire face.

Pepper's touch, strong but light, quickly traveled over his body. Professional but not without sympathy. When he'd gone to the ER or hospital before, they'd treated him like an inanimate object who periodically made noise.

"When did you injure your back?"

"While ago," he hissed out as she touched a particularly sore spot. It might have been where he'd landed during the birthing fiasco.

"Do you have muscle relaxants?" She didn't stop moving her hands over him as she talked.

"A beer?" He'd prefer that right now to any pills. He'd seen too many guys sliding into relying on them to get out of bed every day.

"Not the same thing. I don't have anything here." Her

voice trailed off as she slowly, thoroughly and painfully poked at his cheek. "You didn't break anything, but you should have tended to this immediately. We'll get ice for your cheek and back after I check your vitals, then I'll help you to bed. Do you need to use the bathroom?"

He blushed, darn it. No man wanted a woman asking him if he needed help in that department. "I'm good."

"I've been a nurse and an EMT. I've seen it all."

Could be, but he'd had enough humiliation today. He didn't need much in the way of dignity but he wasn't giving this up.

"I'm getting my bag out of the car. Don't move until I'm back to help you."

She went off. He gathered himself to stand, which would be a long, slow, painful process. He was getting that beer. Then he'd get EllaJayne ready for bed so they both could hit the sack. Tomorrow would be bad but he'd have to keep moving. The job only paid well if he showed up, no matter what had happened today.

His arms still worked, thank the Lord, which allowed him to lever himself to a crouched-over stand. He couldn't straighten just yet. He shuffled to the fridge, stopping twice for a cramp to release his leg muscles.

He took two long chugs of beer and toddled with a gait less steady than EllaJayne's toward the bedroom.

"Stop," Pepper said. "You're going to fall." She wedged herself against him. He wished he could appreciate her fragrant softness. She smelled of spicy sausage. His stomach growled despite the pain. He couldn't be too bad if he was hungry.

"Got extra-strength aspirin in my gear."

"That's a good idea. I'll get you settled in bed with ice, then food, then aspirin. No beer." She held onto his bottle and had him moving down the hall before he could say boo.

Fortunately, the bed sat well off the ground and he could fall onto its pillowy top. She tried to strip him, but he fended off her attempts, allowing her to only pull off his boots and socks. She efficiently rolled him onto his stomach, left with the beer bottle and came back with ice packs for his spine and face.

"I'll be back in twenty minutes to move those and you."

Was that a threat or a promise? He'd wanted to say that but hadn't had enough breath. Damn it, he hurt. Just falling onto the bed had put his back into spasms again. By the time he counted to forty-two, the ice had numbed the muscles. How long until she returned to torture him? He closed his eyes and waited for the cold to finish numbing his face.

"Boot, Boot. Come," EllaJayne yelled as the dog's toenails scrabbled on the plank floors of the bedroom.

AJ cracked open his eye and saw his naked toddler and the useless shepherd racing around the room. This would not end well. It never did. He took a second to allow himself to imagine ignoring it. Then he moved his arm to push himself up in bed.

Faye's voice floated into the room. "Children, come." Magically, the dog and little girl raced from the room.

He relaxed back into the bed's downy embrace. Could he be selfish until morning and ask the women to care for EllaJayne? He did allow himself to close his eyes. He'd lay here for another five minutes, tops. Then, he'd get up, get the aspirin and find his girl. He'd give her a final snack, settle her into her bed and read her to sleep if she needed it. He'd need to set a double alarm for the morning. He couldn't be late to the ranch.

"Time to take off the ice." The packets of numbness were whisked away before he could protest or even snatch them back. "I'll work on your back. Then we'll sit you up so you can have dinner, then ice again, then sleep."

He tried to break in, explain that EllaJayne would need him—until Pepper tried to sit him up. Obviously, the numbness wasn't muscle deep.

"Relax. Tensing your muscles only makes it worse. We'll wait ten minutes and ice you again. Will you be okay here on your own while I refill the packs?" By the time she came back he wanted to lie down again. Honestly, it had never been this bad before. Instead of helping him lie flat, she put ice behind his back and on his cheek as she eased him back on the pillow. Then she handed him a mug of soup. It was mainly broth. He didn't care. His finally loosening muscles were making him drowsy.

"Thanks," he managed just as she handed him the aspirin.

"All in a day's work."

"EllaJayne—"

"Faye is taking care of her. She'll sleep in our room tonight. It's no bother. You wouldn't be able to get up if she needed something."

"I'm good."

"I don't think so. I'm the professional. I say tonight, we'll take care of that little girl. You'll be with her all day tomorrow."

"I'll be at work."

"There's no way you can work tomorrow. The swelling in your face should be minimal, but your back is another matter. Turn over again. You need another round of ice."

He resisted. "I don't have a choice here. This is the best job I've found so far. This problem with my back isn't new. I'll be okay in the morning. If I dose myself with aspirin, I'll be good to go. I thank you and Faye for watching Baby Girl so I can get sleep."

The ice packs landed on his back, his face pressed into the pillows. "I'll be back in twenty minutes to take these off. Then I'll help you to the bathroom."

He didn't respond but she would not be helping him. When he heard her and Faye in the kitchen, he pushed the ice off and gathered himself. He could stand. He could walk.

Pepper was outside the bathroom door when he opened it. "I told you I'd help you."

"Didn't need help." He held himself in the perfect position where his back only ached. The stabbing pain was gone. He stepped forward and his leg buckled, so he reached out to grab at anything to stop his fall. Pepper's surprisingly strong arm and shoulder propped him up.

"Nope. You didn't need any help. I can see that. Do you want to add severe concussion or a broken limb to the mess you've made of yourself?"

"Slow down." He wrenched the words out. God. He didn't want to admit that standing had been about all he'd been capable of. He pulled in a breath, blew it out and readied himself. He could do this because tomorrow he'd have to be fit enough to do ranch work. "I'm ready now."

The two of them shuffled to his room. She got him

into bed without another word. She even worked on his back again. When she replaced the ice packs, she asked, "Which ranch are you working at?"

"Why?" He couldn't imagine she cared.

"I know almost everyone within one hundred and fifty miles of Angel Crossing."

Too tired to argue from the brain-sapping pain, he said, "The Double Cottonwood."

"That's a long drive from here. The staff only come to Angel Crossing once in a while."

"The money is good."

"Of course it is. No one wants to work that far from civilization. Let me make a call."

He pushed himself up and held back a moan as his back clenched. "Who are you going to call?"

"The ranch manager. He and Daddy Gene were friends. I'll explain the situation."

"I'm going to work."

"You're not. Don't worry, though, he'll keep the job open until you're ready to go back day after tomorrow at the earliest."

AJ pushed himself up a little farther, wanting to show her that he could do this. "I'm a bull rider. This is nothing."

"Tell it to someone who'll listen. I'm the medical professional here and I say no." He'd get out of this blasted bed. "Look," she went on, ignoring his struggles. "I've helped him out on more than one occasion. He certainly owes me."

"I didn't ask you to call. I don't—"

"I offered. You're staying in bed tomorrow. I'm calling so you don't get fired."

He wouldn't argue with her anymore. He'd just get up early and sneak out.

"By the way, Daddy Gene taught me how to fix trucks and tractors. I know where the distributor cap is. Or maybe I'll take off the spark plug wires. In case you're thinking of sneaking away. And, right now, I can run a whole lot faster than you."

Her smile of triumph should have irked him. Instead, he wanted to grin at her...well, to say it not so politely, he wanted to grin at her cajones.

Chapter 8

Mrs. Carmichael, or Grammy Marie as she insisted Pepper and EllaJayne call her, looked so happy to see the little girl. She beamed, showing off perfectly polished false teeth and folds of good living that nearly hid her button-black eyes—something like Oggie's. Over her comfortably plump body, she wore stretch slacks and one of the many sweaters she had that were decorated for each season. The woman looked just like a grandmother should.

AJ had been skeptical when Pepper had suggested Mrs. Carmichael, but over the last two days, Pepper had talked up the older woman's stellar childcare skills. AJ agreed that she was worth a try, but it meant that Pepper had to be the a.m. transportation since Grammy Marie's home was in the opposite direction of AJ's job, which he left for long before dawn. Today was AJ's first day back to work after being off a total of two days. It was also the first day of this new schedule. Pepper would have preferred him to stay at home for at least two more days. His answer had been he'd sleep in his truck so she couldn't tamper with it.

"You and Oggie be good," Pepper said as she hugged EllaJayne. The little girl's eyes widened.

"Peep?" she asked, her lower lip trembling.

"You and Grammy Marie are going to play today." Pepper worked to make her voice chipper and positive. She didn't want the girl to cry.

"Home. Boot."

"Not today. You'll play with Grammy Marie."

"Home," EllaJayne said stubbornly.

"Later. First, you and Grammy Marie and her friends will play, then Daddy will pick you up and you'll go home."

The girl tried to glare like AJ did. Pepper had to keep herself from laughing. Then a sly look came over EllaJayne's round-cheeked face. Uh-oh. Pepper knew that there would be bargaining. How had she already learned that? "Peez. Pity peeze."

"Grammy Marie is very sad you don't want to stay." Pepper tried a new tack and gave a nod to Mrs. Carmichael. The grandmotherly woman smiled.

"Home."

Pepper had run out of ideas. At the ranch, she usually invoked playing with Butch to get EllaJayne to comply. Finally, Grammy Marie spoke, "Come on, EllaJayne, there's a baby doll just waiting for you."

"Baby?"

Grammy Marie held out her hand and EllaJayne toddled away with her. The older woman waved at Pepper, dismissing her. She waited for more wails, cries or an escape attempt. Nothing. Pepper walked to her SUV, wondering why she didn't feel happier that EllaJayne had given in relatively easily. Coffee. That was it. Pepper needed more caffeine, plus the car could use a fill-up. She drove to the nearest station. It was owned by a patient and the gas was a few cents more. She stopped, though, because it just seemed right. She pumped her gas, then went inside to pay and get coffee. Pepper checked her watch. She'd better get a move on. Being late on the doctor-is-in day could get her fired. Dr. Cortez was a great boss that way.

"And I got gas, too," she said to her patient—high blood pressure and dry eyes. Pepper swiped her card when the sale was totaled. It didn't go through. She tried two more times before Mr. McCarthy took the card and tried for her. His gaze wouldn't meet hers.

"Seems there's a problem."

"What?"

"The card is declined."

Pepper stood frozen. "It can't be."

"You're over your limit."

She couldn't be. Could she? Without the grant, she'd been using her credit card for the garden at the ranch as well as to pay the attorney looking at the will. Her bank account wasn't in much better shape. She had enough—barely—to pay for her gas and coffee. She handed over the bank card, trying to not feel embarrassed.

Mr. McCarthy smiled as the sale went through. "Don't worry. Happens to everyone."

She took her receipt and hurried away. What was she going to do?

At 7 p.m., Pepper was on her way home and still trying to come up with a plan to find more money. She missed having EllaJayne in the backseat "talking" to Oggie. She needed to remember the little girl was a temporary fixture in her life. She and AJ would be moving on. Daddy Gene had taught Pepper that. Not that he'd moved on, but he'd told her all about watching out for rodeo cowboys. He said he'd stuck around because he'd ridden himself to ground, like they did to unruly stallions. "Just let 'em run till they can't run no more, then run them again. Takes the fight right out of 'em, then the barn looks danged good. That's what I done." She could so clearly hear him and see her mother's knowing smile.

This had nothing to do with the little seed of a fantasy of her, AJ and EllaJayne living at the ranch, growing food and even keeping the spitting llamas. She could see a circle of women making the fleece into yarn and then the beautiful scarves and sweaters they made sold to bring in much-needed money to their families.

Regardless of the lawsuit—which she might have to drop with her credit maxed out—she'd talk with Faye about using the fleece from the Beauties to help the local women. Instead of a quilting bee, they could do a spinning and knitting bee. Pepper could see that as another way for Angel Crossing to help itself. Hadn't she read about a small town somewhere in Arizona or maybe New Mexico setting up an art cooperative? She'd research that and add it to her ever-changing plan. She could already imagine people feeling better about their town, getting healthier with the food from the community gardens and then finding new ways to earn cash. She had become a PA to help people. This was just another way to do that.

"Hello," she called, as she walked to the kitchen. Not

a sound. Even Butch was missing, making her worry. Had something happened to EllaJayne? Had AJ hurt himself again? She went out to the patio. No one. No noises except the brush of a hoof from the Beauties. Then she caught the light in the small barn they used to store weed-killing chemicals and the sharp blades for cutting down brush. She pulled her phone from her pocket, ready to call for help. She didn't know why but a dark weight of disaster had landed on her chest. Her brain ran through all the possible horrors she might see when she walked into the barn.

Filling the middle of the space was Pepper's first greenhouse. Before she could ask any questions, Butch barked and EllaJayne squealed, "Peep." Pepper was not an easy name for a toddler to say.

"Look what we found. You can get back in the growing business," Faye said, her enthusiasm genuine.

AJ didn't turn but stood at the greenhouse, fussing... yes, the big bad sexy cowboy was fussing with the ties that held the plastic in place.

Pepper asked the obvious. "Where did you find this? I thought it'd been thrown away." Then she added because Faye was involved, "Exactly what are you planting?"

"Always so suspicious," Faye said. "It's beans. That's a good crop, right? We were going to do the broccoli next but Butch ate the seeds."

"Boot like bockalee," EllaJayne screeched and hugged the dog, who looked pleased with the world.

"How much did you help, AJ? You didn't overwork your back, did you? Did you eat?"

Finally, he turned and his face was blank. "I just put things together. This was all Faye's idea. We ate."

"What do you think? It will help, right?" Faye asked hopefully.

Her mother might live in a world that paralleled the real one at times, but she really did love her daughter. Pepper never doubted that…or now that she was an adult woman never doubted it. As a teen that had been a different matter. "It'll definitely help. We'll get the seedlings started and then we can transplant them when they're big enough. By then, we should have things plowed and ready. It looks like you're done and I'm starved."

In the bustle of corralling the dog and the child as well as putting away the gardening equipment, Pepper hadn't noticed AJ had wandered off. She couldn't worry about that now. He looked okay and he was fully capable of caring for himself, except…he was a cowboy. Of course, if she hadn't insisted, he would've gone to work even though he could barely move. She needed fuel, then she'd track him down to make sure he hadn't done more damage.

Pepper and EllaJayne sat at the kitchen table while Faye brewed a special tea. The little girl played with her plate full of Oaty O's, stacking them and knocking them down. Pepper didn't even care that Faye had added kimchi to her sandwich, she was so hungry.

Faye turned from her tea and stared at Pepper. "You'll call the attorney tomorrow and tell him that you're done." Her mother didn't smile, didn't show any of her usual compassion.

"The lawsuit isn't just about the garden and my plan. It'll help you, too."

"I don't want it."

"I'm sure Daddy Gene meant to change his will. He wouldn't have wanted to leave you in such a position."

"I'll be fine."

"Faye," Pepper started. "I loved Daddy Gene. I talked with him a lot, especially after he got so sick, and I know what he wanted."

"He wanted you to be happy. Now, you must call the lawyer tomorrow and tell him you've changed your mind." Faye sat a cup of steaming tea in front of Pepper. "I can see something happened today. You know that's because you're putting negative energy out into the universe with this suit, right?"

"My credit card is over the limit." There was no use not telling Faye because she'd find out eventually. The gossip-vine was too good in Angel Crossing.

Faye went pale and her voice dipped. "Pepper, don't you see you've got to stop fighting the will?"

"'Top," EllaJayne mimicked.

"I'm doing this for Angel Crossing and even for you," Pepper insisted. Her long-range plan was for the ranch to bring in enough from renting lots for an income for Faye.

"It's not. It's for you and your ego." Faye suddenly stiffened, then said with more conviction than Pepper had ever heard, "I won't accept the ranch, and if you keep fighting the will, I'll leave. I'll take my Beauties and go. Dove's Paradise could use the fleece."

Pepper would have laughed off the threat but Faye's core of steel was showing. "It doesn't make—"

"I won't accept it. I should have stopped you sooner."

Pepper stared into her mother's green eyes, so different from her own. The one thing Faye had passed to her was a stubbornness that had gotten them both through a lot. Her mother would walk away if Pepper continued to try to overturn the will. "I'll call the attorney tomorrow," Pepper said, and AJ came into the kitchen.

"What's happened now?" His gaze ping-ponged between the women.

Faye answered, "Pepper is listening to the universe. She's dropping the lawsuit."

"AJ?" Pepper asked as she tapped on the door to his bedroom.

He rushed to stop her from rapping again so EllaJayne didn't hear her second favorite person in the world—right behind Butch. "Shh. I just got her down," he said, sidling out. Dang it. He'd closed himself up in his room to stay out of Pepper's way.

They went to the kitchen and she rooted through a cabinet before holding up a bottle of whiskey. "Would you like a drink?"

"Sure."

She poured the liquor and sat with him at the table. After a small sip, she said, "I do actually plan to tell the attorney to drop the suit."

Drinking the entire of bottle couldn't have made him feel any more off kilter. "You will?"

"Not because of Faye and the 'universe.' The lawyer said we didn't have much of a case and… I'm not sure how I'll pay the bill I've already racked up. I'd wanted to talk with you about buying the ranch on a payment plan, but I can't even do that now. So… I've talked with Danny about moving the garden idea onto vacant lots in town, which might work even better. I'll talk with my patients about finding homes for the Beauties. I can make it work even without Santa Faye Ranch."

"If you do raised beds in town, you should double your yield."

"I thought you were a cowboy."

"I've done some reading." He stared hard at the whiskey. He didn't want to see whatever was in her voice reflected in her eyes.

"You know, Angel Crossing could be on the cutting edge with in-town community gardens. I've been reading more and more that urban farming can be a revitalization technique. There are even gardens in New York City like that. Wouldn't it be great?"

He couldn't resist her enthusiasm. "I saw the article you printed out. Angel Crossing would be lucky to have you helping them to create that. The town. Well, you know what it's like."

"When the mine closed, most of the businesses left. We only got reliable internet access two years ago. We don't even have a full-time doctor."

"My hometown is kind of the same."

They both stared at their glasses, until she finally broke the silence. "The work at Double Cottonwood going okay?"

"Not bad." He wouldn't think about whether he'd be there in another month. If he did a good job, maybe they'd keep him on as a cowhand, at least until the inheritance was settled. *If* it didn't work out, he could go back to the rodeo, except there was EllaJayne and the ranch and—

He'd always been, like his buddy Danny, good at shootin' the breeze with anyone from buckle bunnies to old-timers to fellow competitors. Now words just jammed up in his mouth. Every one either sounded backwoods stupid or more flowery than a Sunday morning TV preacher.

"I guess I'd better—" Pepper said just as he unjammed his tongue to say, "Why don't you show me—" They each laughed in the nervous way of two human beings acting like circling dogs, not sure of the welcome and ready to tuck tail and run.

AJ took the conversational bull by the horns. "I'm all healed up so why don't you show me what you want tilled. It's the least I can do for you, after you took care of my back and EllaJayne. What about manure? You got anything from those yarn balls with four legs? I can work that in. There's some ancient horse manure, too, isn't there? Wish I could have brought Benny with me. But I wasn't sure where I'd land and if there'd be a place for him."

Pepper looked at him with her autumn-brown gaze quickly warmed to something like interest and maybe a tinge of happiness. "I'll get a sweater and meet you at the field."

The unnaturally bright lights on the two barns and the pole by the house illuminated her field and the milling Beauties. Still, shadows made parts of the yard darkly secretive. He wanted to pull her into that shadow and kiss her. Half a year ago, he'd have done that. "This area you have marked off, right?"

They walked around the sections she'd staked off, each a neat rectangle with paths between to make access for weeding and harvest possible.

"I want the folks who'll benefit from the crops to be able to help. Most of them have probably done this at some point in their lives, but we've forgotten where food comes from and how different it tastes when it comes out of the ground and goes right on the table. Plus, I've already tried to get vouchers for food and no one would take them. They don't want a handout. If they put in the work, then they'll get the food. I've already come up with a formula: one hour in the garden equals five pounds of vegetables. Or they can deliver produce."

He never could have imagined he would get hot under the collar listening to a woman talk about how she was helping her neighbors. He'd always said the only woman he wanted was one with long legs and a short fuse. Now, here he was wondering how he could get Pepper into his arms so he could kiss her until she... what?

"Angel Crossing is lucky to have you." He and El-laJayne were lucky, too.

"It's just my job. I can't treat my patients if they don't have the food they need."

"Maybe. But I don't see your doctor doing this."

"He doesn't live here." She stood, feet planted and looking out over the patch of ground. She didn't wear a hat or boots most of the time, but she was more of a cowgirl than any of the women he'd ever known.

"That's not it. You care. You see what needs to be done and you do it." He stepped closer and caught the lemon and clove he'd come to know as Pepper. The hint of her scent made him want to bury his face into the hollow of her collarbone. Right there, he was sure her skin was soft and so fragrant that he'd—

"I've always done what was needed. Faye doesn't always have both feet on the ground."

"Or her taste buds wrapped around real food."

Pepper laughed with her whole body. "I smelled her famous 'Energy Casserole.'"

"Is that what that was? I just closed my eyes, held my nose and hoped for the best."

"When she made that, I always said I'd had a snack and wasn't hungry. Daddy Gene would sneak me banana and peanut butter sandwiches before I went to bed."

"I'm out of Fiddle Faddle, too."

She'd turned and even in the unnatural light, he caught her smile and the transformation of her face. Could he taste that joy? He stepped up to her, lowered his head and pressed his lips softly to her smiling ones before he could think.

"Oh." She breathed out and he didn't resist, slipping his tongue into her tantalizing mouth. He cupped her jaw, his fingers sensitive to the vibrations of pleasure racing along the tender edge. Her own hands rested lightly at his waist, everywhere they touched warmed with sensation.

"Mmm. Better than caramel corn," he whispered against her lips. He pulled her against him slowly, giving her a chance to her to slip away as he hoped and prayed she wouldn't.

Chapter 9

Pepper should not have been surprised by the hard strength of AJ's shoulders and waist when she'd held on as he kissed her mouth, her neck and then the hollow of her throat. Even now, weeks later, her breath came a little faster. The man might not know much about living in a house of women or even about growing veggies—except what he'd read on the internet—but he did know how to kiss. He hadn't learned that on Kiss.com. Unfortunately, she had a good idea how he'd come by that knowledge. Daddy Gene had warned her that what brains hadn't rattled out of bull riders' skulls settled between their—

"Pretty plants." AJ broke into her thoughts. "Pat them nice, Baby Girl."

Had she come out here again knowing AJ would show up? He and EllaJayne had been spending every evening in the greenhouse. As summer approached, the days were getting longer and she enjoyed checking the garden, weeding and picking off bugs. For some it might have been more work after a long day. But Pepper loved it and she lo—enjoyed AJ and EllaJayne coming out to keep her company. Although yesterday the toddler had pulled out half a row of plants before they'd figured out what she'd been up to.

"Peep," EllaJayne said, and Pepper turned to smile at the little girl and motion her closer. Butch was there, too, sniffing between the rows. He might not herd the Beauties but he watched out for EllaJayne.

"See," she said to the little girl, ignoring the man who stood not far away. "Soon it'll have a flower. We won't pick them, right?" EllaJayne shook her head vigorously, her straight fall of hair swinging wildly. Pepper looked up. AJ's own similarly dark hair curled at the sides and in messy tangles along his nape. "You both need haircuts. I'll do it this weekend." She startled herself with her own pronouncement.

"You're a barber, too? You've got no end to talents," AJ said.

"I think I can handle the two of you before you begin to look like you've been living at Dove's Paradise."

"I can return the favor if you want. I was good at trimming up Benny's mane and tail."

"No way. I go to Tucson for a day of beauty every six weeks or so."

"You do it so you can go to Taco Gino's and get a Philly Cheesesteak Chimi."

"Never." She couldn't stop the grin. One night talking in the kitchen about the garden, he'd pried out of her the guiltiest of her pleasures—a hole-in-the-wall taco place in Tucson near the university. Faye would have a fit and cleanse Pepper with a nasty tea or herbal potion if she knew her daughter had eaten a deep-fried tube of steak oozing processed cheese food. She also didn't let her medical professional side tell her how bad the taste-bud nirvana was for her.

"Next time you're taking me," AJ declared.

"We'll see. Maybe. *If* you let me cut your hair and EllaJayne's. I can't be seen hanging out with a shaggy cowboy."

"Otherwise you'd like to be seen with me?"

"Why not? You were a big-time bull rider, right? Isn't that what every cowgirl wants?" She hoped a little snark would add back the distance she'd lost. Why had she said she'd cut his hair? Dear Lord. She'd be so close. She'd be touching him again and again.

"I'm not a bull rider anymore. Just a cowboy with a little girl and a living to earn. Although at the rate I'm going, I'll run out of places to draw a wage before EllaJayne has her next birthday."

"Oh, no. Double Cottonwood is letting you go?"

"I knew it was temporary when I was hired on."

"You want me to ask around?" This conversation was where she wanted to be with him. Friends. Her providing expertise and help, like she did as a PA. Then she would only see him as a patient, like any of the other local men she treated at the clinic.

"If you don't mind," he said and turned away. "Baby Girl, are you petting the plants nice?"

The toddler looked up, her nearly black eyes guileless in her chubby face. "Pretty." EllaJayne patted a plant almost flat.

"Why don't you help me get the straw?" Pepper

asked as she walked over and scooped the little girl up. "We'll spread it around to keep down the weeds. We don't want any of those yucky old weeds."

"Yucky weeds," EllaJayne echoed. Pepper didn't want the intimacy that had been wrapping around her and AJ. The two of them were roommates at best and not for much longer. The court system, now that she wasn't making noises about contesting the will, was slowly grinding forward.

"You two ladies take care of that," AJ shouted. "I'll settle the Beauties."

Pepper smiled. AJ, who'd been less than enthused with the llamas and alpacas, had come to a détente with the little herd. They stampeded Pepper given a chance, and Faye would rather let them roam the desert to find their inner animal. AJ had them disciplined now, and he'd even talked about asking around for someone to take care of their fleeces. He said that they should be able to get decent money for them. He'd done internet research. She wondered how he'd known she'd been planning the same thing.

"Boot," EllaJayne said over Pepper's shoulder, her arm thrust out and waving at her buddy. "Boot." The dog obediently followed them.

Pepper filled the wheelbarrow as Butch and Ella-Jayne solemnly watched, then the girl "helped" Pepper wheel the pile to the rows of beans.

EllaJayne, with Butch's help, scattered more hay than spread, but they stayed entertained. When Pepper finished, she stood with EllaJayne on her hip looking out over her patch of garden and could see, really see, what it could look like if she stayed or if she could afford to buy the ranch. They'd have acres of vegetables and then she'd put in fruit trees and maybe strawberries. Since finding that kind of money was beyond anything she could manage, she'd call the mayor tomorrow about the empty lots in town. She could transform those into gardens that would provide the same sort of produce she'd imagined at Santa Faye Ranch. Or maybe she should approach AJ with something she'd thought about. A rent-to-own situation. She'd pay him so much per month to stay on the ranch. The trouble was the amount she could afford per installment. She'd put that idea on the far-back burner.

"Peep," EllaJayne said sleepily before her head thunked down on Pepper's shoulder. Darn it. The little one's bedtime had come and gone. AJ must still be dealing with the Beauties. While she and Faye often helped entertain EllaJayne in the evenings, AJ always put her to bed and usually stayed in the room, watching the small TV he'd found with a pile of trash. It worked, he said, and was the best price: free.

She'd take EllaJayne inside and get her ready for bed while he wrangled the herd. She could do this for them. Since he was caring for the Beauties, it was only fair.

Pepper lay on the couch watching TV with a sweet-smelling and sleeping EllaJayne stretched across her chest. Her own eyes drooped, and she wondered how much longer she should wait for AJ to make his way inside. She didn't feel right about entering their bedroom anymore to lay the little girl down. He had another fifteen minutes, then she would go out to look for him. She set her internal clock and closed her eyes, confident that she'd wake up. She always did, a trick she'd learned as a kid.

"Pepper," said a deep voice. "I'll take EllaJayne."

She cracked open her eyes. AJ's face was on level with hers. She started back. "What?"

"Whoa." His hand shot out and covered hers where it lay on the girl's back. "Didn't mean to startle you."

His rough-palmed hand fit easily over top of Pepper's. "What time is it? Where were you?" Pepper struggled to sit up and AJ let go of her. EllaJayne whined and wriggled. Pepper stopped, not wanting to wake her.

AJ's voice fell to a soft whisper. "One of those cotton balls got out. It took time to get her back with the others. I know I need to get EllaJayne to bed but could you watch her for another ten minutes? I want to get cleaned up."

Pepper nodded. She watched his cowboy swagger, not taking her eyes from him for medical reasons only. After all, she had to check to make sure his back problem hadn't flared up again. Clinical interest. That's all she had.

EllaJayne had fallen back into a limp-limbed sleep, so Pepper carefully sat up, ready to stop if she made any movement. She nuzzled a little closer. Pepper stared at the TV, wondering when the smell of baby powder had gotten so soothing. That was dangerous, though. EllaJayne wasn't hers and neither was her daddy. Both of them were visitors in her life. AJ had made clear that as soon as he could sell the ranch, he would. Maybe she shouldn't give up on the idea of buying it. There had to be a grant or an organization that would help. Her plan had so much—

"I can take her now." AJ reappeared and leaned close. Pepper pulled away instinctively, then relaxed her shoulders so she could lift the girl away and toward AJ.

"Here she is." Pepper released EllaJayne to her daddy and immediately wanted her sleep-warm weight back.

"Thanks." AJ didn't move. Pepper looked at him, the muscles of his arms bunching and shifting as he adjusted the little girl onto his shoulder. She stood, abruptly wanting…needing to be far away from him. She was not the kind of woman who went for cowboys, especially of the rodeo variety.

Pepper kept her voice level. "I'll ask around about work." AJ nodded and she got up and slipped past him without touching. Faye had taught her to respect her body's needs. Not this time. AJ would be as bad for her as a Philly Cheesesteak Chimi.

AJ watched the dark strands of his daughter's hair slide to the kitchen floor with every snip of Pepper's scissors. He couldn't decide if he liked the way it made her look less like a baby and more like a little girl. Dear Lord. He had a daughter who'd date cowboys. He reminded himself that was years from now. He would be better at this daddy thing by then. He'd better be, because right now his skills were only marginally better than his own parents'.

"Boot," EllaJayne squealed pulling away from Pepper and reaching toward the dog.

"Darn it," Pepper said.

"What?" he asked as his eyes scanned over his daughter, looking for blood.

"Her bangs. I'm so sorry. She moved just as I was doing the center."

His daughter's bangs were not a nice even line. A large chunk was missing from the middle of the dark fringe of hair. He laughed.

Pepper stared at him, her face starting to relax. "I really am sorry."

"It's hair. It'll grow back. I think we're done. Maybe later you can try to even it out." He had to raise his voice as EllaJayne squirmed and screeched for the dog. Pepper nodded and quickly swept off the towel they'd used to keep hair out of her clothes. He lifted her from the chair and put her on the ground with Butch. The two of them immediately ran around the table, scattering hair.

"Out. AJ, get them out," Pepper said. He lifted his now-kicking daughter and carried her back to the bathroom for her nighttime scrub down. Less than thirty minutes later, his Baby Girl and Butch were asleep. He'd tried to chase Butch from the bedroom. The dog wouldn't budge. He could have carried him out, but it hadn't seemed worth the effort. Today had been another long one. He wasn't complaining, though. It was work. If he was lucky, he'd have another week, maybe two. So far Pepper hadn't turned up any leads, and he hadn't either, at least not anything in reasonable driving distance. Going back to the rodeo was beginning to look more like a certainty.

"Your turn," Pepper said, pointing him to the makeshift barber chair as he stood in the kitchen's archway.

"You don't need to do me."

Pepper grinned. "Good to know, but I was just going to cut your hair. Ever consider a beard to go with the mountain man look?"

"In the winter in Kentucky, I had one…sometimes. Keeps your face warm when you go out to take care of animals."

"Scarves do the same thing."

He grunted because he really didn't want to talk

about Kentucky. He had an idea that having her cut his hair wasn't a good idea and not because of the missing chunk in his daughter's bangs.

"Over to the sink," Pepper said. "I can't cut that mop when it's dry. Sit on the stool there. You can lay back in the sink. Just like a salon."

He hesitated. Now, wasn't this a kick in the head. He was scared. Afraid of Pepper and her nearness. Ridiculous. He could do this. She'd trim up his hair, probably a good thing since he was on the hunt for a new job. He sat and leaned back.

Water ran in the sink and then Pepper leaned over him and her breast brushed his shoulder. How could he not have anticipated what would happen? He was a bull rider, he should have been able to predict the next corkscrew twist. Pepper shifted and her breast moved as she reached over him. Now, she was nearly pressed chest to chest with him. Was she doing that deliberately?

"Hope you don't mind baby shampoo," she said as her fingers dug into his scalp, massaging in the soap.

He waited for his leg to start twitching like Butch's did when AJ found the perfect place to scratch. When her fingers found a spot at his nape, he moaned.

"Did I hurt you?" Pepper asked and her fingers stilled.

He stifled another moan. He didn't want her to stop. The pleasure-pain of her massage had released the tension all over his body. "No," he said, his voice hoarse. "You a professional?"

"We lived without a shower or tub for a while." Her fingers went back to their magic work and every one of his muscles melted, just like butter on a stack of pancakes. Behind his closed lids, the stack of pancakes disappeared and instead he saw Pepper leaning over him, her lovely pink-as-a-carnation lips soft and ready—

"All done," said the real Pepper.

He cracked open his eyes, giving himself a few seconds to gather what was left of his wits. He stood, staying hunched to hide the part of him behind his zipper that had been obviously paying attention and shuffled to the chair. His body hummed with the touch of her fingers, her breasts and the scent of her skin.

"You want me to go short or just trim it up?"

She distracted him from the words with her fingers moving through the wet strands and skimming along his skull. He turned his moan into a hum of agreement.

"Okey dokey, then." The scissors snipped close to his ear, jerking him from his pleasurable haze. "Careful. I don't want to nick you."

He stilled. "I don't need anything fancy."

"Don't worry. You won't get anything fancy. This is strictly an I-don't-want-to-go-to-the-barbershop cut."

"I didn't know there was such a thing."

"I gave Daddy Gene that kind of cut a lot. Faye, too. Now, be quiet and I'll get this done."

He shut up and closed his eyes. He didn't want to have his vision filled with her chest because then he could imagine—nothing. He didn't have a towel or anything else to hide his interest if he let his thoughts run wild, like Pepper in the cowgirl seat above him, naked, sweaty and ready—

"Did you say something?" Pepper with the scissors asked. He needed to remember that Pepper.

"Just, umm…" He shifted in the seat to distract himself.

"Watch it. You're wrigglier than EllaJayne." Her

hand squeezed his shoulder. That touch shuddered through him. She stilled. "I see that…well, okay—"

His hand reached up and lay over hers. She didn't pull away. He picked up the magical hand and kissed the palm. He heard her intake of breath and rubbed his nose into her wrist, a place soft and fragrant with shampoo and the fresh lemon that clung to her. The rich scent made him imagine darkened rooms. He kissed her wrist, her forearm, then she was in his lap and her mouth was on his, the carnation pink lips as soft as he remembered.

He didn't start the kiss softly. He couldn't. A storm had started low in his gut. His mouth devoured hers as she opened to him, her fingers finding that magical spot at his nape. He pulled her closer but not close enough. He stood, lifting her easily, and her mouth nuzzled into the space at the top of his open shirt. He had to have her laid out where he could taste and touch. Not his bedroom and not hers. She stilled. He knew that he had to move. He couldn't let the spell of heat and sex blow away. Not now. He rushed out to the patio and the lounge with its thick cushion. He got her settled with another long kiss, the chair just big enough for the two of them—if they stayed close. He threw his leg over her hip. Through their clothes, her yearning heat warmed him from chest to groin. Closer. He needed to be closer. He didn't even know he'd said that out loud until Pepper answered, "Yes," as her hands worked at all his buttons at once.

His own hands yanked at her jeans and her shirt until he met her buttery soft skin. Taste. He had to taste. Half-dressed he slipped from the lounge so he could bury his mouth into the softness of her belly and then upward to her straining breasts. Her hands clutched at the back of his head.

"Arthur John, you are a devil," she moaned out as she arched under his lips, tongue and teeth.

"Then you're a witch," he whispered, laying himself out on top of her so he could return to her sweet carnation mouth. She opened to him, her legs wrapping around him, holding him tight to her so that their bodies aligned. So that there was no question what they each wanted.

Chapter 10

Pepper's breath caught again in her throat as AJ's hands and mouth made love to her. Sweetly, hotly and with expertise. She gasped over and over. Except it wasn't enough. She wanted them skin to skin, nothing between them.

"Pepper, honey," he whispered into her ear, his slow Kentucky drawl thick and dark, like molasses and whiskey. "I can't wait. I need you now, darlin'."

He didn't move though and she wanted him to, like she'd never wanted another man. "Why are you talking?"

"I need you to be sure," he said, hushed and serious. His lips at the lobe of her ear as his words brushed along her face.

"I'm sure. I want you, now, AJ McCreary, and if you don't—"

He moved enough that together they quickly stripped

her of her shirt and pants. He slowed her hands on the clasp of her bra, watching with wide eyes as it came off, while he slid his hands under her panties and pulled down. His fingers drifted over her before he turned away for a condom packet, then he was back to her ready, eager, but so in control she wanted to scream.

"If I do anything you don't like, you just tell me, ya hear."

She held his face as he braced himself above her, and she shivered in delight at the moon-silvered strength of him. "I'm a woman, not a girl. I will always tell you what I 'like.' Right now, I'd like you to stop stalling." A devilish smile to match his pirate-dark hair made her vibrate with anticipation. Then she no longer thought but only felt his heat and hers building and building until she cried out.

He whispered in a hoarse voice, "Let's see if we can't make you 'like' it again."

Pepper couldn't read the stars to know what time it was or how long they'd been spooned together on the narrow lounge. She enjoyed the press of their flesh. Neither of them had said a single word since they'd used the last of AJ's condoms. Not that he had a huge stack. The haze was lifting, and Pepper's brain was re-engaging. She refused to regret what she'd done, but she knew it needed to be a one-of.

"Boot!" a crackling, amplified little-girl voice broke the silence. Pepper jerked.

AJ jumped from the lounge, impressively and explosively fast as he went to his jeans. EllaJayne called the name one more time, then silence. He pulled on his clothes. With his back to her, in what Pepper assumed was a gentlemanly way to allow her to dress in privacy, he finally said, "The new baby monitor has an app for my phone."

"Oh," Pepper said, looking for her socks, after pulling her top over her head. "That's convenient."

"Much better than carrying around the walkie-talkie thingy."

So this was the way it was going to be. They'd pretend that what had happened hadn't? "Sounds like she went back to sleep."

"She does that. She talks a lot. At least she doesn't go sleep-walking. Had an uncle who did that."

They were both dressed and facing each other. Pepper kept her gaze somewhere over his right shoulder. Even though the now shadowed darkness of the patio wouldn't have let him see her face, she didn't want to take the chance, not sure what she feared exactly.

"Somnambulism can be a problem and a sign of sleep apnea or even heart trouble."

"Huh."

She interpreted that as a marginally interested noise. He stepped toward the house and froze, going stiff before taking another careful step. "Stop. Did you hurt your back again?" She went to his side, her hand tracing over his lower spine to feel what was going on. He skidded from her touch. "Did that hurt?" What had their... Had they damaged his back somehow?

"I'm fine. I don't need you poking at me."

"I could see your back is giving you trouble." She used her firm clinic voice.

"I'm not a flippin' patient." His words came out on a rush of air as his gaze kept steady on her face.

She pulled back immediately. "I'm sorry. I just saw your back hurt and—"

"Jeez. What man wants to…after we…jeez. I'm a *g.d.* guy. Give me a little dignity, okay? I want you to at least remember what I…jeez." He rubbed at his neck. "I'd rather face Tornado," he mumbled.

Lordy be. Men could be so dumb. Or maybe not. Would she want him to treat her like something less than a woman after what they had just done? On impulse she stepped up and pulled his head down for a kiss. His arms wrapped around her, and he stepped into the lip-lock that caused explosions through her body. How could she want more? But she did. That one thought had her pulling away slowly…but still moving away. "I know you're all man, sweetie." She gave him what she hoped was a saucy smile. The trembling wasn't in her lady parts. It was her heart, scaring and exciting her at the same time.

AJ didn't grab Pepper again, even though that was what he wanted to do. Bad idea. The two of them had just had amazing…sex. He had to remember that's all it was. She'd tried to take his ranch. She'd made it clear she thought rodeo cowboys were only one small step up from puppy kickers. Plus, he had his daughter to think about. He'd be selling out and moving on. California might still work out. He'd always wanted to live where the sun shone every day. Arizona had that, an annoying voice said, and what about asking Pepper if she was interested in paying him to use the property for the garden, once she reimbursed her attorney? That was a pipe dream.

The lingering scent of clove and lemon snapped him

from his thoughts. They'd had a damned…moment. Yep. That's what it was. A little craziness for both of them but no reason to change any plans. He stepped toward the house and stopped as pain shot down into his hip again. Taking a deep breath, he looked into the house. The kitchen was empty. He could get a beer and an aspirin. The two would settle his back and his mind. He had to be up early—as always. He also needed to be using his time and energy on finding a new job. He was already behind on his truck payment and his daughter needed new clothes. She'd outgrown nearly everything she'd had when they'd landed at Santa Faye Ranch more than two months ago.

As he sipped his beer in the bedroom, he ran through what he'd need to do the next day, and it overwhelmed him. He already knew the next evening, Pepper wouldn't be waiting for him in the garden, ready to talk about their days, figure out their schedules and just hang while they did the relaxing work of caring for the fields and animals.

Darn it. He knew sex messed things up. Maybe not this time? He snorted. Sex would more than mess it up this time. Pepper wasn't a buckle bunny or a woman looking for a honky-tonk good time. She was a woman who cared—deeply—and wouldn't take what they'd done lightly. What he wanted to do again and what he deep-in-his-gut feared would be difficult to forget.

AJ hated being right. Their night…not even a night… on the lounge a week ago had messed with whatever had been happening between him and Pepper. If he accidentally brushed up against her now, she jumped away like she'd touched a boiling pot. He hadn't known how much he'd liked those casual touches and how much he'd miss the evenings in the field together with Ella-Jayne. It was all wrecked now.

"Yeah, sorry about that, son," he said out loud to the face in the mirror as he shaved. Baby Girl yelled for Boot from the floor of the bathroom. He'd had to give up on her car seat as a corral. She'd figured out the extra tie he'd put over the buckle she'd Houdini-ed her way out of when he'd been under the hood on that first day in Angel Crossing. He tried to keep her in his peripheral vision because she'd figure out the bathroom lock soon enough, then she'd roam freely. She made a pitiful cry for Butch again. Another five minutes and she could be reunited with the useless dog. Yesterday while AJ had been moving the Beauties, Butch had raced through the herd, scattering them. Two hours later, AJ had finished rounding them up—with Butch locked away in the house. Good thing the llamas and alpacas had a weakness for black licorice.

Now, his daughter happily played with her toes, then picked up Oggie, talking to the flattened toy. "What am I going to do?" he asked her. She stopped chattering and held out the dog to him. A big compliment. "Thank you, honey. You keep Oggie." When had he gotten so soft that tears sprang into his eyes because his daughter offered him her darned toy?

Since he was facing the fact he might just have to leave her.

He'd looked everywhere for work. Everywhere that paid a decent wage with decent hours. Then, of course, the rodeo had come a-callin'. One stock contractor he'd worked for was looking for a replacement wrangler and was willing to pay top dollar. It meant AJ would need to hit the road. It would mean…what? Could he take Baby Girl? Yeah, right. Exactly how would that work? He could leave her here, couldn't he? EllaJayne liked the Bourne women much better than she did him most days. After all, he was the one who made her go to *b-e-d*.

Leaving Baby Girl wasn't forever, not like her mama had. It was just until he could get caught up on the truck payments and other bills. Until the ranch was his. Bobby Ames kept saying it wouldn't be much longer, but that man's idea of long and AJ's weren't exactly the same.

"I'm going to have to do it, EllaJayne. I'll miss you," he choked out. He stared at his face in the mirror again, hardening everything like he did before a ride. He wouldn't think about the possible pain. He'd focus on what he had to do to make it through the next eight seconds. He'd track Pepper down and sweet-talk her into listening to his plan. If that didn't work, could he ask Faye to convince Pepper to care for the little girl with Grammy Marie's help? Faye more often than not acted like a flake but she was more together than her gypsy skirts and herbal remedies had led him and everyone else to believe. He'd begun to understand what Gene had seen in the woman, and how she'd helped raise a daughter like Pepper. The two of them were caregivers, just from different roads.

As he'd hoped…sort of… Pepper was in the kitchen finishing up her breakfast when he and EllaJayne were done with their morning bathroom routine. Now what should he do?

"Good morning, EllaJayne. How is Oggie today?" Pepper asked his daughter. The girl squealed in delight.

"I need to talk with you," AJ said. Pepper's eyes

widened, before shifting to the doorway. "It won't take long."

She looked down at his daughter who had raced over to sit at her feet, talking again with Oggie. "She needs her breakfast."

"I can take care of that while we talk." He went to the fridge, stopping to get himself a cup of coffee. He needed the shot of caffeine. He plopped his daughter down in her chair.

"Here's the thing," he said as he helped her spoon yogurt into her mouth. "I've been looking for work."

Pepper nodded, standing as far away from him as the kitchen would allow. Dang. She looked cute in her oversize shirt and ratty shorts that she'd obviously slept in. He didn't want to think about her, warm and soft in the morning light in a big bed with nothing on but—
"There isn't anything around here. I've looked."

"I thought Danny had leads for you. I can try again with people I know."

He started on his daughter's cereal, focusing on each spoonful. "I've run out of time and my old boss called. I'm going back on the road with the rodeo. For two months, maybe a little longer. I'll make more there than I could anywhere here."

"What are you thinking? You have a daughter."

"I know I have a daughter. That's why I'm doing this."

"You'll drag her with you and leave her with strangers?" Pepper turned away.

"I'm not—" He cleared his throat. How could he leave his daughter if he couldn't even say the words? He would because without the work, neither of them would be okay. "That's why I needed to speak with you. I'm hoping I can count on you…and Faye to look after EllaJayne."

"Look after her? She's not a puppy. Plus, we're talking months. I know I've dropped her off at Grammy Marie's but that's not the same as being solely responsible…that's a lot to ask."

"I know it is, but it's temporary, and I'll get home as often as I can. We should be in Vegas or nearby for part of the time."

"You're telling me there's nothing that you could find—"

"It's not just the wrangling, though that pays well. My boss said he'd stake me for rides. If I end up in the money, I'll be back sooner, rather than later."

"What?" she shouted. "You're going to crawl onto the back of a bull with your…knowing that your daughter… No. I won't do it."

"What do you mean no?" What had he seen before she turned from him again? Fear? Anger?

"I would think even your addled brains could figure that out. *N-O*. I'm not doing it."

"Peep?" EllaJayne asked in a quavering voice, reaching out her hands.

Pepper dashed across the kitchen and snatched up his daughter, obviously forgetting for a moment about the belt that held the little girl in place. AJ fumbled with the buckle along with Pepper's hands. She was close enough for him to see the fear in her usually warm brown gaze.

"It'll be fine," he said gently, like he would to a skittish horse. "It's what I've done for most of my life."

"And look what it's done to you? Your back? Your hip? Do you want to be in a wheelchair? Do you want to have surgery after surgery?" She had Baby Girl in her arms now and buried her face in that sweet baby-smelling spot in the crook of EllaJayne's neck.

"First, that ain't happenin'," he said with the bravado he needed to get through the next few months. "Second, it won't be for long."

"As your…your medical professional, I'm saying you're not fit."

"I can give you money to care for EllaJayne. I wouldn't expect you to do it for free. You could use the money for the garden." His hope had been she'd offer to watch the little girl and not expect cash, but if he had to pay for her as well as Grammy Marie, he would. It wasn't a perfect solution, but it could work until the ranch was his.

"What's wrong?" Faye asked, startling him. AJ hadn't heard her come into the kitchen, his focus on Pepper.

Pepper answered for him. "He's being a cowboy. He wants to go back to the rodeo and expects us to be good little women and watch his child."

"Oh," Faye said. "He's a Taurus."

As usual, exactly what Faye meant eluded him, but he thought she was supporting his decision. "I can't find work locally and I've got bills." That really was it in a nutshell. "I might even have a chance at a few purses. It wouldn't be for long. I told Pepper I'd get back here as often as I can."

"And you need us to watch out for the precious little one? Of course we will. That's what we do for family."

"Family?" Pepper spat out. "He's not family. He's the kind of cowboy Daddy Gene—"

"That's not true," Faye said. "Gene loved Arthur John. Why else would he leave him the ranch? Although maybe he had a bigger plan in mind, but that's not for now. We have a chance to have this wonderful soul all to ourselves. What a great time we'll have. Arthur John has to do this."

"Thanks, Faye." He still needed Pepper to agree. He trusted her—when had that happened? Over the two months they'd been here, it had crept up on him. Or maybe it was that night on the lounge? How could he not trust a woman he'd been…well, been with. "Pepper, what do you say? It'll be best for everyone."

"Except you," she muttered and glared at Faye and him.

"Outside," Faye said, pushing them out the back door and onto the patio. "I'll get EllaJayne ready for her glorious day."

The snick of the lock on the back door worried AJ but not as much as what Pepper wanted to do to his plan.

"I'm a PA. I know what you've done to your body and what more rides could do to it."

She'd come out swinging. He would've admired that tenacity if it hadn't been aimed at him. "It's my body and my decision."

"I'm your doctor."

"You're not and even if you were, I'd still be going out. I've got bills and—" He wouldn't go into the pile of debts he had, having to do with his own misspent youth, paying off EllaJayne's kin. And of course there was his truck and care for Benny back in Kentucky.

"We've all got bills. But you've also got a little girl."

He stepped up to her, wanting to make her understand he had no choice. He was down to the best of the bad choices. "Pepper." He put his hand gently on her arm. Mistake. Big Mistake. "Pepper, I have to." He pulled her into an embrace, speaking softly into her hair. "Honey, I've got to do this. There's no other way until I can sell the ranch." For a second, such a brief moment, she relaxed into him and her arms reached around him. He leaned back enough to take her chin, gave her a chance to pull away, then kissed her. Kissed her for the weeks, months he wouldn't be around to see her, touch her and be with her. Oh, God, she was so spicy sweet. How could he leave her? Sheep tails!

Chapter 11

Pepper pulled AJ even closer as his mouth explored hers gently, insistently. The shift of muscle under his shirt took her right back to the lounge. Him. Over her, under her. No. She pulled away, and it felt like tearing a bandage off a wound. He could…would hurt her so badly if she allowed it.

She stepped farther away, feeling the loss of his warmth even under the morning sun that was quickly heating up the patio. She made sure her gaze didn't land on the lounge.

His hand went to his nape and rubbed hard. "I've got to go. I've got no choice. All I need from you is to watch over EllaJayne. If you won't…then I'll take her along. I'll figure something out. I always do."

So he'd use blackmail? He knew she wouldn't allow him to drag that baby over hill and dale, staying with who knew who. The man didn't have the sense God gave…a…a damned llama. "You're fighting dirty and you know it." His jaw tightened and his eyes darkened to rainstorm-gray. Good. He knew she knew what he was doing. "I can't let you bring that toddler on the road. I'll take care of her." She straightened her shoulders because she wouldn't be walked over. "But I have rules."

"Of course you do."

She ignored the snide tone. She needed these concessions. "You will call every day to speak with Ella-Jayne. You'll give me a schedule of when you expect to visit the ranch. Finally, I must be listed on any forms as your emergency contact and as the person medical information can be released to."

"Why would I do that?"

"Because I want to make sure you're okay for Ella-Jayne." Yep, that and he was a patient.

"That's it? I do that and you'll look after her, you and Faye and Grammy Marie?"

What was she agreeing to? To do what had to be done. He was going no matter what she said. She'd come to care for EllaJayne. Her decision was the only one that made sense. "We'll do it as long as you agree to my conditions. When do you leave?" She needed to stay all business and not think about ending up back in his arms.

"Ten days. I'll catch up with Dave in New Mexico." He stood on the patio looking…she didn't know exactly like what, except she had to turn away to keep herself from kissing him again, telling him he shouldn't go and that she'd miss him.

Before her brain fully engaged and made her shut up, she said, "It would take me a little time—I need to pay off my attorney and some other bills—but remember me saying that I could pay you for the house and some acreage over time, like rent to own? You'd still have plenty of land to sell and you'd be getting money while you waited for a buyer. What would be left is better for running cattle anyway." It was the land Daddy Gene had rented out to the next ranch, until they'd closed up shop.

He shook his head and rubbed his nape again. "I can't wait. It's for EllaJayne," he said, raking his fingers through his hair.

The night she'd played barber came back to her, in every nerve ending. Focus on EllaJayne. "It won't be that long, and you might even end up with more money."

"You don't get it. Faye acts like...well, Faye, but she loves you like any other mama. She would never abandon you."

Pepper couldn't understand exactly where the conversation was headed now. She stayed quiet.

"You know that EllaJayne's mama allowed her to go to foster care," he said and paced away from Pepper, hands clenched at his sides. "A little baby. She just dumped her. I don't know why...it doesn't matter why or why she didn't tell me I had a daughter. When I agreed to take Baby Girl...there was paperwork and Suzy, EllaJayne's mama, said she wanted money. For enough cash, she agreed to sign away her rights, that EllaJayne would be all mine. The next payment is due and if I default, Baby Girl goes back to Suzy, which means she'll end up who knows where until I can get to court and prove I'm the daddy and sue for full custody."

Dear Lord, that poor little girl. And AJ. What a burden. She'd made it worse with her insistence on fighting the will, drawing out the settling of the estate. Why hadn't he said anything before? Maybe because she'd been such a pain in his behind. Right now, she needed to act like the adult she was. "AJ," she said as she approached him. "I had no idea. Of course you've got to get the money. If I had any, I would give it to you."

He turned, his eyes so dark with pain and fear, her heart stopped for a second. "I know you would. That's the only reason I feel right about leaving EllaJayne."

Pepper didn't know why but that simple statement made her chest tighten. He trusted her. Really trusted her. Not because she had letters after her name or because it made things convenient for him, but for her, for what she'd said and done. She took his hand, calloused and rough, but so solidly male and dependable. He might be a rootless bull rider, but he did what he could to protect those he loved. He hadn't walked away from his daughter. He stepped in and stepped up.

"Thank you," she said to him as she gave his hand, the one that had touched her so gently, a squeeze. "I... just thank you for trusting me with your daughter. We care about her and want her to be safe and happy."

"That's all I want. Just that. It's not too much to ask, is it? But the darned universe wants to mess it all up." He squeezed her hand back as the frustration made his voice deeper and cloudier.

"You know what Daddy Gene used to say? The universe can go take a flying leap." He stared at her. "He usually said that to Faye."

"Sounds like Gene. What do you think he'd say about the situation now?"

Talking about Daddy Gene didn't hurt so much with him. "He'd say 'Pepper-dew, a cowboy's gotta do what a cowboy's gotta do.'"

"What does that even mean?" His eyes cleared a

little, but he didn't drop her hand. Her gaze stayed on him, taking in the soft curve of his lips, the straight shoulders and suntanned skin.

"How would I know? I'm not a cowboy." She smiled when she saw his lips curve and his shoulders relax.

"If I could stay, I would." AJ gripped her hand and his mouth straightened into a firm line.

"I know. Maybe you really aren't a cowboy. Aren't you supposed to be a tumblin' tumbleweed?"

"Not Kentucky cowboys. We're the kind who stick around."

What was he saying? She searched his face, his eyes…something flashed there right before he lowered his head and took her mouth with his. How could this feel so right when he was leaving, no matter what he said about Kentucky cowboys. His arm wrapped around her and pulled her flush to him. She couldn't stop herself from stroking the rigid nape of his neck with her free hand, massaging at the tightness and the vibrating strength of him. She lifted herself onto her toes to put her mouth more solidly on his. He hummed his approval just before unsealing her lips to taste her fully, to make her understand exactly what a cowboy had to do.

When the patio came back into focus, Pepper's hands held onto his arms not sure whether she wanted him closer or farther away. The kiss had been unexpected. She had to be honest with herself, though. It hadn't been unwanted. What did she want, then? Hell. She wanted AJ, a rodeo cowboy with a baby, a debt and more integrity than sense, to be *her* cowboy.

For the week since AJ had told Pepper he'd be hitting the road, he'd been preparing himself and EllaJayne.

That hadn't been as odd or as difficult as dealing with the population of Angel Crossing. When he'd gone to town to pick up this and that at the small, convenience home-improvement-feed store, he'd gotten unsolicited advice that all suggested he'd better keep his zipper up and locked while on the road. Grammy Marie had been the bluntest. She'd said: "AJ, you know we all know how to skin a rabbit and shoot a buck. Don't make us test out our aim and sharpen our knives."

Even Faye had said something about his trip. Her warning was cloaked in astrological signs, but he'd known what she meant: keep it in his jeans.

He'd wanted to confront Pepper to find out what she'd been saying to their neighbors, but his house-mate had been coming in late and leaving early. She might be avoiding him. He was leaving day after to-morrow and the final errands and chores would fill up all those hours.

Today he and Danny were having lunch at the town's one sad diner. AJ pushed his way into the Devil's Food. The red-vinyl-topped chrome stools at the long For-mica counter were full and the booths with the same red vinyl seats and worn tabletops were mostly occu-pied. The diners' choices leaned toward coffee and pie.

He saw Danny in a far booth and two oldsters stand-ing and wagging fingers at him. This place was just like Pinetown without the pine trees and slag heaps. The one diner in his hometown was always on the edge of killing patrons with the sameness of the fare and filled with seniors with more opinions than sense. Danny looked relieved when AJ walked up and slid into the booth. The couple were one of those weather-beaten twosomes whose clothing, while not matching exactly, looked alike. AJ smiled at them.

"Don't grin like an idiot," the woman said. "You're leaving Pepper with your baby."

The man chimed in before AJ could gather his wits. "Marie said she's been watching the little one and you seemed like an okay daddy. Now you're just up and running off."

AJ tried to figure out if there was a question in there. "I've got a job with the rodeo."

The two shook their heads. "Heard that," the woman said. "Just like Gene when he first came to town. Think you can be a family man and chase around the country."

"No, ma'am," AJ said. "Just trying to make a little money until I—"

"Thanks, Loretta," Danny broke in. "I appreciate that you and Irvin are only looking out for the little girl. I'll keep an eye on the situation. AJ and I go way back."

The couple glared hard at AJ before making their goodbyes.

"Don't worry," Danny said. "It's just the Angel Crossing grapevine. Not much goes on, so whatever happens at the clinic or anywhere else in town gets passed around quickly. Marie might be a good kid sitter, but she likes to visit with friends here in the back room and I'm sure you and your daughter have been a hot topic."

"I thought Pinetown was bad. It's got nothing on this."

"We're tight. Have to be so far from much of anything, even the Angel Crossing community college campus is a thirty-minute drive."

AJ decided to move the conversation along. "What should I order?"

"So you've heard about the diner. It's fine. Whatever problems they had were months ago. A bad cook. There's a new one and he's getting things ship-shape. I'm going to have the Cowboy Casserole, nice spicy chili and corn chips with plenty of cheese. Can't go wrong with that combo."

"Sounds good."

"So what do you need from me?"

"Why would you think I need something?"

"Other than that one drink, I haven't heard from you."

"Been busy." Danny's gaze called BS on that comment. "Things have gotten complicated."

"What I heard. So you're getting extra friendly with our Pepper? Damn it, AJ."

"No one's business."

"This is Angel Crossing. It's everyone's business."

"So everyone's concerned now, huh?"

"It's not just Pepper but that little girl of yours Marie dotes on."

"Good thing, then, that I'm talking with the mayor about looking after all of them."

"What do you mean 'looking after all of them'?" Danny's normally smiling face darkened into a frown.

"Run out to the ranch a few times a week to help with the Beauties—"

"Beauties?"

A woman's voice cut in, "So, mayor, what you up to now? Getting a beauty pageant started? I'll sign up for that."

"Marlena, that just wouldn't be fair." Danny grinned at the frizzle-haired waitress, who wore blue jeans hacked off at the knee and a plaid cowgirl shirt that had had scissors taken to its sleeves, too. Her lined face fell comfortably into a grin.

"You got that right. Now, whadya have?" She took their order and poked fun at Danny, glared at AJ before insulting another customer on her way behind the counter where she pushed their order through a long rectangular window that gave a glimpse into the kitchen.

"Back to these Beauties," Danny said.

"Faye's alpacas and llamas. They don't need a lot of work and Pepper will help if she has the time. And speaking of the lady, her garden will need work, too. She takes care of the weeding and such. I usually haul out the fertilizer, otherwise known as manure, and move the irrigation and portable greenhouses. She has a list. She's really good at those."

"So you're a farmer now."

"I live on Santa Faye Ranch. I help out where I can."

"Uh-huh."

"It's what a normal human being does." Danny was really starting to annoy him. "Finally, I need to ask you to be backup transport for EllaJayne. She'll still be going to Grammy Marie's, but sometimes Pepper can't pick her up or drop her off, and you know Faye can't drive."

"What do you mean she can't drive? Everybody drives."

"Not Faye. She talked about putting a baby seat on her bicycle. We talked her out of that. Maybe with Gene…gone and Pepper so busy, she'll reconsider learning to drive. So… Pepper or Faye can call you?"

"I guess. But I don't have a kid seat or anything."

"I'll leave mine." AJ had to fight to not choke up. What the hell?

"Are you going to cry like a—"

"I rode Killer Storm." No need to say more. He'd broken bones and not complained. Nothing was going to leak out of his eyes now. Thank God and little green apples, Marlena showed up with big bowls of Cowboy Casserole. He and Danny ate and talked about men they'd known in the rodeo. They also talked about which bulls AJ should consider riding to put him in the money. They both turned down the pie that seemed popular, although AJ nearly took a piece for later. He thought better of it when he realized he'd have to hide it. Boxes of candy were easy. Pie, not so much.

"I still have to wonder why you're here. I mean, you're selling the ranch, right?"

"Easier than other options."

"Could be. But you never really said what might be going on between you and Pepper. Claudette said—"

"We're housemates. My God, she and her mother are sharing a room. Me being on the road will be a good thing."

"As you well know, Faye lived in a commune. Her idea of what's right and proper isn't quite the same as most folks around here." Danny gave him a level stare, his blue eyes boring into AJ's brain.

"No one's business."

"You dog. I knew there was another reason you were hanging around."

"I told you why I'm here."

"Yep. You said it was easy." Danny actually waggled his eyebrows. AJ wanted to reach across the faded Formica tabletop and strangle him. What went on between him and Pepper was private.

"Nothing is going on," he said evenly, hoping to shut Danny up.

"That's not the AJ I know."

"That AJ is long gone. Disappeared as soon as I found out I had a daughter."

"Not so sure. After all, there's you and—"

This time he didn't stop himself. His hand shot across the table and snatched at Danny's collar, twisting it. "I told you it's none of your business, if there was anything going on. And there isn't. Do you understand?"

"Boys," Marlena said. "What's that sign say? Take it outside."

AJ let go, stood and stared hard at Danny. "I expect you to answer your phone. And I expect you to treat Pepper with respect."

Danny somehow looked unruffled but a knowing smile stretched his lips just before he said, "Hot damn. Lavonda is going to owe me fifty dollars."

Chapter 12

"Did you ask the mayor to call me?" Pepper inquired as she and AJ made a final tour of the crops. EllaJayne was settled for the night with Butch curled up on the floor near her playpen that doubled as a make-shift crib. Faye was in the living room watching a movie. The ranch felt strangely quiet. Expectant. AJ left tomorrow. Her feelings about that were complex.

"I talked with him about being on call if you needed anything."

"This was about the garden and a grant that would allow me to rehab lots in town. I've been asking him about the town gardens for weeks."

"Nope. Didn't say anything about any of that."

Could something finally be going her way? Something other than AJ leaving. And she only cared about that because it meant she had another responsibility to add to the teetering stack. The little sting right around her heart had nothing to do with anything. They stopped at the end of the row. Now what?

"Dave said I could swing by in two weeks." She nodded. "I'll try to call every night but on show nights, it might not happen. I don't know what I'll be up against. He's only had temp wranglers, and I got the feeling things are a mess. On a couple of venues, he'll be the producer, too." She nodded again. "I wouldn't be doing this unless I had to."

"You love the rodeo. I understand." Her brain understood. Other parts of her didn't get why he needed to leave, especially why he had to risk everything to crawl onto the back of an angry bull.

"I loved the rodeo. It got me out of Pinetown. I was good at it. Not the best but darned good. Danny was better. I made it into the money, though. I was really good with the stock and…it doesn't matter. Once I found out about EllaJayne, I couldn't be on the road. I had to look after her."

"Yet, here you are going out again."

"Only because I know you and Grammy Marie and Faye will keep her safe. I would never go if I didn't have you all."

She shouldn't feel so proud of herself. He'd say anything to get her to care for his daughter so he could go play the cowboy. Except she knew that wasn't true. He wasn't a liar. Just like Daddy Gene. He'd always been honest, even when she hadn't wanted to hear it.

"I'll check on the herd one more time, then I'd better hit the hay. I've got a long day tomorrow." He didn't move.

She didn't want him to leave. She didn't want to be the

one stuck at home worrying about him. She didn't want to care. "They'll miss you. Butch, too, and EllaJayne."

"I'll miss them, too," he said gruffly.

Pepper took in the final rays of the spectacular sunset. The Arizona skies regularly put on a show of magentas, oranges and purples. Tonight's seemed particularly vivid. The colors highlighted AJ's strong nose and cheekbones and the softness of his lips. His eyes were no longer on the faraway herd or the crop. They were on her, his stormy gray gaze searching her face for…what?

"I might even miss you," he said quietly, touching her face slowly and gently. She could have moved, stepped away. She didn't. She wanted the rough softness of his touch on her. She hadn't allowed herself that until this moment. She moved into his embrace. Opening to him and to his kiss.

Lordy be, this cowboy could kiss, warming her from the tips of her toes to the ends of her hair. She melted into the heat of his tongue. His hands roamed her back and down to her butt, yanking her hard against him, just where she wanted to be.

"I might miss you, too," she whispered against his ear when she could finally pull away enough to catch her breath. "I won't miss you hogging the bathroom in the morning, though." She squeezed him hard, not wanting to let go even as she tried to give herself space to breathe. To keep her heart and her head together. "I won't miss hiding your stash of Spam from Faye. No one actually wants to eat that." She felt giddy from the lack of oxygen and the heat of his hands on her back and hips. How could he surround her with warmth that was so different from the lingering heat of the summer day?

"Spam is cowboy ambrosia. I noticed at least one of

my cans was missing," he whispered against her temple. "I should've reported you to Chief Rudy. Maybe I'll just take it out in trade." His mouth nuzzled down her neck and his hand traced up her waist until it landed on her breast. "Tit for tat."

She laughed out loud—freely, happily. "What are you—" She couldn't say more because his hands and lips stole her breath and her reason...again. "Oh," she whispered when she realized that her shirt was open and his hand was inside her bra. When had that happened?

"Pepper, I have to... Come with me." He clasped her hand and dragged her toward his truck. He'd bought a second-hand capper to transform the bed of the pickup into a Hillbilly RV. She hesitated for a moment, not sure she wanted another memory of them together, skin to skin and heart to heart.

"AJ. Wait."

"What's wrong?" He turned his storm-cloud gaze on hers, edgy with desire and want. Was that enough? Was that what she wanted?

"You're leaving."

"I'm just traveling."

"I know. You'll be back when you can." What did that mean for her? For the ache that filled her chest?

"Pepper, honey," he said, pulling her to him, chest to chest. Not one millimeter of air seeped between them. He kissed her again and just like that everything fell into place. She needed and wanted him tonight. Tomorrow would take care of itself.

"I've never been in a Hillbilly RV," she whispered against his mouth. "But I hope you put oil on those shocks."

"Really?" he said as he kissed the side of her face

with gentle fun. "You expectin' to give them a work-out, honey?"

"Maybe. I plan to see if a bull rider is as good at being ridden."

He yanked her against him so she knew that he was ready, more than ready to meet every one of her demands. No, not demands. What she needed and what she wanted to give to him. And only him.

AJ had never laughed, teased and enjoyed the lead-up to getting horizontal so much. Pepper made it so easy—and so hard. He laughed at himself, then she used her hand to remind him what they would be doing in…he didn't care how soon or how long from now because every moment took forever and that was just fine with him.

"Into the RV you go," he said, helping her into the bed of the pickup that had been transformed into something like living quarters. Well, a place to sleep on the road. He laid her back on the nest of blankets and pillows, looking like a woman ready for him to love. Damn.

"What are you waiting for?" she said with a saucy smile as she arched her back and took off her bra.

In the dimness lit only by the glow of the barn light, he caught glimpses of Pepper. He lowered his head to her breast, nuzzling there as his hand moved to the waistband of her jeans. "Oh, darlin', I was just waitin' for you," he said, his drawl thickening his words as his finger delved between her thighs and found her more than ready. Dear Lord. She writhed as his fingers discovered that place he knew could set her off. He'd found it on the lounge and had dreamed about making her—

"Not yet," she gasped holding his hand still. "I told you I'm going to test your mettle."

"My mettle?" His brain fogged with the smell and feel of her.

She sat up and pushed him back. He didn't protest. He kept his grip tight on her, though. He didn't want her to be more than inches from him. Her clever hands and mouth made time speed up and slow down all at once. Finally, she stopped, found his condoms, then said, "You know cowgirls go for more than eight seconds."

"Really?"

"Really." She lifted herself up and over him. Settling down as he thrust up. "Giddy up," she gasped as she moved her hips.

Afterward, he held Pepper close, her limp body sprawled over his. He didn't want to break whatever spell had landed on them. For the first time in his life, his heart fluttered not with the thought of doing what they'd just done again...though they'd be doing that. Hell, yes. He'd pictured clearly, him on the phone talking to her—not dirty talk. Just everyday talk like they'd had in the evenings in the garden. It wasn't sexy, but it still made his heart thud. What the hell was that about? Then he heard Gene. The Gene he'd known as a teenager when he'd first hit the rodeo circuit. "You know how you know you're hitched to the right woman?" he'd counseled AJ after an ugly split with a barrel racer. "You want to talk with her. Not the kind of talk that'll get you between the sheets. It'll be the woman who makes the everyday extraordinary. That's when you'll know."

Sheep tails. Pepper made the everyday extraordinary. Why else did he want to go out into the garden with her every night? Why else did he share his Spam? Did he love her?

* * *

Pepper glued her gaze to the folder balanced on her knees while she listened to her patient. So far only one person this morning was not a member of the AJ fan club. Most of the town watched him whenever he rode and had adopted him as one of their own. Her current patient went over twist by turn every second of AJ's soon-to-be famous ride. What she and none of the others talked about was how he'd limped out of the arena. What had he done to himself? Not that it was Pepper's business. The rodeo had doctors. Three more days until he came back to Santa Faye Ranch.

"Shame it wasn't a big money ride."

Shame, indeed. "Wilma, I don't like these reports."

The middle-aged woman had a more than comfortable roll of spare weight around her waist and swollen ankles. It wasn't just her name that had an old-fashioned flair. She had the blood test numbers of the octogenarian her name reminded Pepper of—

"Just give me a pill."

"Instead of a pill, you need to eat better."

"Uh-huh." She agreed. "When did you say AJ's coming back?"

"I didn't. I know things are tight. I have a crop coming in and I'd love to give you some—"

"Harold doesn't like it."

"You don't even know what I'm going to say."

"He won't like it. You know how it is. If it doesn't come in a can or box or had a hoof before it was packed in Styrofoam, he ain't got no interest."

"I understand, but maybe just one part of the meal?"

"We don't need the help," the woman said stubbornly, even though Pepper knew that she shopped at the food bank in the next town and the dented-can aisle at the big grocery outlet. Gossip didn't just run to AJ and his bull riding.

"Maybe you could come out and help next week? We'll be picking beans, and Faye—" here Pepper paused for strength "—is shearing her herd and wants some help spinning."

"Spinning? This is the 21st century. If I want yarn, I go to the Mountain of Crafts. I like making baby blankets for the children over in Siberia." There was a group of women who got together to knit and crochet and sometimes even quilt.

"Would your Angel Bee like the yarn?"

"Maybe," Wilma said slowly. "I'll ask. It's just that the other yarn is so bright and pretty."

"I understand."

"I'll ask and I'll be out to help pick beans. It's been dogs' years since I did that. We had a garden in Iowa when I was a kid. I hated weeding so I never wanted to have one after I got married. Harold feels the same way."

"It is a little bit of work. But the mayor and I are looking at a garden in town, with raised beds that wouldn't have weeds. It would be close to home and you could grow whatever you wanted."

Wilma didn't say no. Pepper figured that was a victory. She gave the woman some free samples of a new blood pressure medicine she hoped would help. If Wilma and Harold didn't change their diet, the pills wouldn't make much of a long-term difference. Pepper made a mental note to work on the woman when she came out to help at the ranch.

Today the closed clinic was as quiet as it could be with a toddler and dog racing around the waiting room.

Pepper had stopped in for just a minute to pick up a file. "EllaJayne. Butch. Stop running, please." She looked through her desk, the file wasn't where it should be. She couldn't leave the dog and girl alone very long. The destruction they could wreak in seconds was awesome in its breadth and depth. When she finally found what she was looking for, tucked inside another unrelated folder, Pepper's gut told her something was wrong. The clinic was quiet. Too quiet for a dog and a girl to not be getting in any trouble.

"EllaJayne," she said as she walked toward the waiting area. It was empty…except for the toppled basket of magazines and a small ficus tree on its side spilling dirt everywhere. The front door was open. Crap. How could she have forgotten the girl's magician abilities?

"EllaJayne. Butch," Pepper yelled, trying not to sound mad. She didn't want them to hide or run from her because they feared punishment. At this point, she wasn't sure what she'd do when she found them. She looked up and down the street and still didn't see them. "Think, Pepper. Think." The diner? Pepper had braved the place for a treat for the little girl the few times they'd come into town during the six weeks her daddy had been gone. Pepper raced down the sidewalk sweeping her gaze around the town, hoping to catch a glimpse of the girl. What had she been wearing? That was the first thing the police always asked.

"Whoa," Danny said as he caught her arm, half a block from the town hall. "Didn't you hear me call your name?"

"EllaJayne," she gasped. "I can't find her."

"She's at the office," Danny said with a gentle voice. "Her and that useless dog. He tried to bite me."

She didn't wait for him to say more but raced to the town hall, wrenching open the door and moving toward the sound of the girl's sobs. "EllaJayne." Had she'd been hurt? The sobs' volume turned to eleven and Butch yipped anxiously before he growled with menace.

"Pepper Moonbeam, get in here and calm down your danged dog," Chief Rudy's deep voice boomed out.

She ran through mud and molasses as she tried to reach Baby Girl. "EllaJayne."

"Peep," a watery sob came back.

Almost there. She moved as fast as her uncooperative legs allowed her through the police department's door. There was EllaJayne behind the reception desk with Butch guarding her.

"Peep," EllaJayne squealed and ran toward her, the sobs rising in volume again, along with Butch's now ecstatic yips.

Pepper dropped to her knees and opened her arms. The little girl threw herself against her, her body quivering with her cries. Butch licked her ear. "It's okay. I've got you, baby," Pepper whispered to EllaJayne, cupping her head into the hollow of her shoulder rocking the two of them. "Shh, sweetie. It's all right. You're safe." Pepper buried her own face into the top of the girl's head to calm her own racing heart.

"The mayor found them ready to cross the street," Chief Rudy said sternly.

Pepper's heart clenched. Oh, God. She could see the disasters. A car hitting them, hurling them into the air. She clutched EllaJayne closer to her. "She opened the door at the clinic. I was just in the—" Her words dribbled to a stop. She sounded just like AJ when she'd first met him. The little girl really was a quick-escape artist.

She understood better his fear, frustration and defeat. Pepper slowly released EllaJayne to stand.

"Déjà vu all over again, huh?" Danny said.

Pepper nodded her head, looking down at the two escapees. Now, her fear was transforming into something not quite so pretty. She wanted to shake both of them. EllaJayne's tear-streaked face hurt Pepper's heart. Butch turned his head to the side, looking ashamed. Those faces. How could she do anything but hold them tight? She sighed deeply.

Chief Rudy said, "Maybe a bell on them?"

A laugh burbled up from her churning insides. "Or one of those things that's supposed to help you find your keys?"

Danny smiled. "I think Lem's store has them. That better be your next stop."

EllaJayne giggled along with the adults, and Butch waggled his butt in excitement. "Thanks, Danny. I don't know what… Thanks." She looked again at EllaJayne. The toddler who'd wriggled her way into Pepper's heart. Darn it. This was not the way her life was supposed to go. Pepper shook her head. Time to go home and focus on what would matter when the girl and her father left Pepper. The garden, the community. Those would fill up that hole.

"Peep. Wuv you."

Pepper gulped back a sob of her own.

Chapter 13

AJ leaned back on the pillows in his Hillbilly RV, enjoying the scent of bee balm Faye insisted would strengthen his Taurus tendencies. He didn't think the scent or the special tea she'd sent with him had changed the outcome of any of his rides. Still, he didn't throw it away. Just knowing someone thought about him and cared enough to help did something for him. He shook his head to get rid of those stupid notions. He'd soon be selling and moving on. Then his "real" life would begin with EllaJayne and a job that didn't batter his already hurting body.

He checked the time. Two minutes until he could videochat on his phone with his daughter. He could see in the month and more he'd been away that she'd changed. She could point at objects in the room and tell him what they were. He'd also swear she'd gotten inches taller. He rubbed at his sore shoulder—yanked by a reluctant bull—and wondered if the bruise on his cheek had turned a darker color. Pepper would notice. She always noticed. Time to call and not think about what Pepper's attention meant to him.

"Daddy," EllaJayne said when their videochat started. While he still didn't think he was her absolute favorite person, she seemed genuinely excited to see and speak with him. The picture disappeared as she said, "Boo-boo." He guessed she was patting the bruise she saw on his face.

Well, that answered his question about the bruise. "It's okay, baby," he said, seeing her frown.

"Peep. Boo-boo."

"Daddy's boo-boo is fine. Did you pet Boot today?" he asked. His daughter nodded her head, pointing and telling him what she saw, the growing skill with language something he'd missed being a part of, except through a phone screen.

"We need to tell Daddy about you running away today? Right?" Pepper finally said.

"What?" AJ's heart lurched.

Pepper picked up EllaJayne and sat down with her so the two of them could talk with him. "She and Boot went exploring. But I told her the rules. No going off on her own." His daughter shook her head no, the dark fall of hair swinging. "Next time you'll wait for Pepper or Grana or Daddy. Right?" EllaJayne nodded vigorously along with Pepper.

AJ wanted to find out more about what had happened but he knew getting the full story from the little girl wouldn't happen. He listened for another few minutes, then too soon, Pepper said, "Kiss Daddy good-night.

Butch is ready to go lie down." That was the new routine he was missing for getting his daughter to *b-e-d*.

"Night, Daddy," she said as she leaned forward so only the top of her head showed. He heard the loud juicy kiss. He smiled feeling the virtual touch deep in his heart.

"Night, Baby Girl." EllaJayne ran off yelling for Boot. Pepper's face appeared on the screen both concerned and a little fearful.

"You probably guessed that we had an adventure today?"

He nodded, waiting for her to explain.

"I took EllaJayne and Butch with me to the clinic. I needed to pick up a folder. I was in my office—for thirty seconds tops—and she opened the front door and got out." Pepper said all that in a rush full of fear and self-reproach.

"Of anyone, I know what a magician that kid is with doors," he said, almost feeling pride in his daughter's scary talent.

"She and Butch were ready to cross the street when they were caught. She wanted to see the animals from the picture over the Emporium. That took me a while to figure out." Pepper sealed her lips, obviously trying to not cry. "I was so scared. I could imagine everything that could have happened."

"Oh, Pepper, baby," he whispered. He ached to pull her into his arms. "You did everything you could to keep her safe."

"Don't be so nice. You should be yelling at me," she accused wetly.

He touched his fingers to the screen, trying to reach

through the danged phone. "Don't cry, please. I can't stand seeing you cry," he whispered.

"I'm sorry. It's just—" she swallowed another sob.

"I know, honey," he said softly. God, he couldn't stand this being away from the ranch and from his girls. He was in deep. "Hush, now. It's all right."

"I know I'm being stupid," she said fiercely, wiping at her face. "And don't think I didn't notice that bruise. Did you put ice on it?"

Now, she sounded more like the Pepper he knew. "Not yet." He wouldn't tell her that his plan was to hold a cold beer against it. He had one left in his cooler.

"How's the back and hip?"

"Well enough. How are the Beauties?" He wanted to distract her from her interrogation.

"Still not apologizing for spitting at Danny."

He laughed a little. "They don't seem like the kind of critters who feel regret."

"They will when we shear them and all of the other animals laugh at them being naked."

Great. She'd said naked and he wasn't picturing alpacas or llamas. He was long past being a teenager so why did she make him feel that way? "No one would laugh at you."

"We weren't talking about me," she said sternly, then her face softened and her eyes heated. "Plus, I don't think you've entirely seen me like that."

"Could be. Should we solve that problem now?"

She pulled in a breath. "I don't... How can you make me go from crying to—"

"To hot—"

"No," she said on an embarrassed laugh. "Time to

say good-night. Put ice on that cheek and maybe use some on your little bronc, too."

"My little bronc? That's just cruel, woman." They both laughed. It felt good to enjoy a little sexy teasing, almost like they were a couple. Except they weren't. He sobered instantly. "Well, then, good night."

"Good night," she agreed. "We'll talk tomorrow." She switched off the chat.

Two more weeks until he was back at Santa Faye Ranch. By then, he needed to get himself in control and remember that their...whatever it was had a sell-by date. She understood that, and he was happy that she wasn't holding him to anything more than short-term fun, right? He needed his beer and not just to ice his face.

Pepper couldn't believe all the "helpers" who'd come out today. The small field was filled with people picking beans and weeding and even planting the next crop. More amazing was the crew helping with shearing the Beauties. The cluster of ladies outside the corral eyed the beasts with greed. Apparently, Wilma's Angel Bee had connections to a co-op of spinners and weavers who would, for a percentage of the fleece, take care of spinning the fiber. Then they'd show the Angel Bee ladies how to dye it so they could use if for their own projects.

Faye, for maybe the first time since they had moved to the town two decades ago, was fitting in comfortably. People didn't even roll their eyes at her tofu snacks. Of course, that might be because they were outnumbered by a covered dish spread rivaling the one from a Fourth of July fifty years ago that was so legendary oldsters still drooled when they talked about it.

What Pepper was thinking about, though, was AJ's return. His late return. He'd stayed longer on the road than he'd initially promised. Today, she'd been asked a dozen times when he was expected. A second successful ride had moved him to hero-of-Angel-Crossing status. He'd called almost every evening as promised and spoken with EllaJayne. Of course, a toddler couldn't answer the phone or say much. Usually, Pepper filled in the conversational gaps. Sometimes he called very late, after EllaJayne was asleep, so they talked. Sometimes they even had what Pepper had been calling in her head "adult" talks. Ones that left her hot and bothered. Worse, they usually led to steamy dreams featuring AJ without a shirt and saying silly things like he loved her. She even said that she loved him back. Good thing she didn't believe her dreams meant anything more than she'd been speaking with him before she fell asleep.

What a disaster. She barely had time for her career and the farm. How would she squeeze in a boyfriend? Could a man with a child even be a boyfriend? How did that work? Besides, she had to remember that he was going to sell the ranch.

Butch dashed by, followed by an overly excited EllaJayne. Pepper chuckled and went back to sorting the beans and other produce that had been donated by a nearby grocery store. She wasn't calling any of it a donation, though. These were samples and giveaways.

Butch barked furiously, running to the barn and back, with EllaJayne trying to catch up. Pepper could see the disaster coming. The little girl would soon be crying or screaming.

"Butch," she called as she walked toward the duo.

The dog listened as well as he usually did, which was not at all. "EllaJayne, sweetie, come here."

The girl turned, frowned, pointed and said, "Boot. Daddy."

While Pepper's grasp of the toddler's vocabulary had gotten better, she didn't get all the nuances. Had AJ been gone so long EllaJayne thought the dog was her father? Butch galloped up, sat, barked and raced away. The girl tried to follow, but Pepper took hold of her because the dog had started down the drive.

Butch raced back and sat panting at her feet. Ella-Jayne hugged him, repeating, "Daddy. Daddy." What was wrong with them? Then she heard it. A pickup truck. It could be one of a hundred trucks from around the area. Not everyone from town had come out to the ranch, even if it looked that way.

She refused to think or let her heart leap at the idea it might be AJ. She was better than a toddler and certainly smarter than a cattle dog who thought he was a poodle. Except it was AJ and her heart did a fluttery leap and she couldn't make it stop.

AJ cursed long and foul. He'd need to break that habit…again. This was not the homecoming he'd imagined. He'd pictured saying hello to Pepper and Ella-Jayne. Then Baby Girl and Faye would be picked up by Danny so they could go on a road trip for a few hours, while he and Pepper finished what they'd started during their phone calls. Instead the ranch was filled with people. It looked like the entire town was there. He parked his pickup in a line of six others.

He got his bag from the king cab and sucked in a long breath to stop the roil of nerves from his chest to his gut. He settled his hat and adjusted his sunglasses. None of it mattered when Butch hit him, quickly followed by EllaJayne, who launched herself at him, wrapping her arms and legs boa-constrictor style around his torso when he bent to her. She squeezed him hard and repeated with a shrill excitement: "Daddy."

"She and Butch heard you before anyone else," Pepper said when she strolled up. "Let Daddy breathe, honey," she coaxed, then went on, "Your drive was okay?"

He didn't want to be disappointed she hadn't greeted him as enthusiastically as his daughter. They weren't an item, and the entire town, including her patients, clustered nearby. "Trip was good," he said. "What's all of this?" He motioned with his head toward the garden and the corral. Why hadn't she said anything?

"The first harvest in the garden and the Great Fleecing—that's what Faye is calling it. We found a use for all of that fuzz. I didn't tell you because I didn't want you to feel like you had to come home for any of it."

"I wish you would have told me," he said, his gaze locking back onto her. He'd forgotten the warm richness of her hair and the invitation in every curve of her body.

She shrugged. "Everyone insisted on bringing food. You hungry?"

"Nah. Better put away my gear, then I'll help." EllaJayne pulled hard on the thumb in her mouth, her head heavy on his shoulder. He couldn't stop gazing at Pepper.

"AJ," Danny shouted from ten feet away, breaking his concentration. "Saw your last ride. Nice. Made it into the money."

He had and now it didn't matter because he'd—

"I'm Harold and I just want to say that we're proud to have you here in Angel Crossing. I mean the mayor was famous and all but that was years ago. Now, we've got ourselves a real live bull rider."

AJ's shoulder smarted from the back slaps that went with the congratulations he'd gotten as he'd helped with the Beauties. He followed up that excitement with spreading manure and preparing another field. This one for "fall" crops—peas and broccoli. Not his favorites. Now, if they were prepping for a Fiddle Faddle field or a Spam tree, he'd think it was time well spent. But he knew what Pepper was doing would make a difference for Angel Crossing. The fresh produce was important. He was *not* that big an idiot. He could also see having everyone out here helping was just as important. The little town, like his own in Kentucky, was struggling not only with providing jobs but also with losing its heart. Angel Crossing still had a chance. Not that he'd be here to see that or see Pepper's vision become reality. He hadn't said it, but he hoped she knew she and Faye could live here and farm the land until the place sold.

"Arthur John," Faye called from a long stretch of food. "Marla made Spam salad just for you."

He wished Faye would stop calling him by his full name. He wasn't that man. Never had been. He was AJ, hell-raiser and bull rider. He saw EllaJayne in Pepper's arms. The two looked natural together and Baby Girl could have been hers, theirs. Damn. No more swearing. He blanked out his thoughts and focused on right here and now by enjoying the food, the beer and even the congratulations, but none of it would last.

* * *

"Faye found her tribe," Pepper said as they watched her mother wave to the crew of women who had helped turn some of the Beauties' fleece into yarn. They'd made plans for a dye-in and spin-a-thon in a couple of weeks.

"Could be," he said. His back had started to ache an hour ago and his ribs burned from where they'd been bruised by a shove from a bull who hadn't wanted to co-operate. He'd had fantasies of taking Pepper to bed—a big soft bed—not a tiny lounge or in the back of his pickup.

"What?" Pepper asked.

"Nothing. Just a long day. Not just for me, either. Time for—" he stopped before he said the most dreaded word in EllaJayne's world, which directly led to long tantrums and negotiating.

"I'll take care of that. You haven't even had a chance to unpack."

Pepper left him alone, looking out over the land that was his now. He'd gotten word from Bobby Ames that the estate was settled. He could put it on the market and then move on. California. Maybe Oregon. Both places could use cowboys, and he already had friends there. *Just like in Angel Crossing.* Gene's voice filled his mind. Dang, that was creepy.

"So good to have you back, Arthur John."

"It's AJ," he told Faye again. Butch had followed her over and sat on his foot. The dog had been trying to stick as close as he could, between the temptation of dropped food from the buffet and the pull of a passel of kids willing to rub his belly and throw a toy.

"We missed you. Your male energy is important to the ranch."

"I'm happy to be here." For how long was the question. AJ hadn't even told his boss Dave about his change in fortune. Why not? He should be shouting all this from the top of the pickup that the ranch was *his*. Finally, luck or his sign or whatever was going his way.

"You know Gene had a plan."

"Yes, ma'am."

"When he got sick again—" she choked off the words, her eyes glistening with tears. Butch moved from AJ's foot to lean against Faye. "He knew. We knew his time wasn't long. We talked. We laughed. We even made love." Tears rolled down her cheeks and AJ wasn't sure what to do. He'd never known what to do when women cried, but he stepped forward and pulled her into a one-armed hug. Faye was stiff and went on, "I've got to get the rest of this out. Pepper's making this work. She's found her place here. She's finally accepted that people wanted her, not just her skills, and didn't judge her…well, not too much…for how we lived. I knew it would be difficult for her, but I knew it would make her both tough and compassionate."

My God, Faye sounded almost like a normal mother. "She's definitely both. Look what she did today." His gaze took in the harvested and prepped fields. He smiled at the shorn llamas and alpacas, looking slightly embarrassed by their new haircuts.

"Did she tell you that our little one is starting to use her crayons and markers? I think she may be an artist. She's an old soul. You know that, right?"

The Faye he knew was back. "So you've said."

"She'll be sleeping with me tonight."

"Pardon?" he said because what else could he say?

"I think EllaJayne needs some Grana time." She

cocked her head to the side, looking a lot like Pepper when she was trying to find an argument to get her own way. "And because I've been told it's icky, I'm not saying anything else, especially not about you and Pepper."

"Jeez."

"Everyone knows you're a couple. We all expected to find you'd gone missing at some point during the party."

"What do you mean everyone knows?" The entire town knew he and Pepper had done...crap. This was a horror fest.

"You can't hide that kind of thing. Everyone approves by the way." She patted Butch's head as she pulled away from AJ, her expression calm and the tears dried. "Gene approves, too, in his own way. Pepper is his daughter, after all." Faye walked away, her long skirts swirling. Butch stared at AJ, yipped, then ran after Faye.

He cursed long and foul again. He'd mend his ways tomorrow. What the hell did he do now?

Chapter 14

Pepper stood in the living room staring at the crooked bookcase, her brain working really hard to get her body and her heart in line. Faye had taken EllaJayne to the bedroom for a slumber party and "a little Grana time." Why couldn't Faye be a disapproving, you-won't-have-sex-until-you're-married kind of mom? Because then she wouldn't be Faye.

"So, Faye and EllaJayne are having a party?" AJ's voice came from the other side of the couch, close enough that she could smell his unique cowboy mix of dust and leather.

"They just went into *b-e-d*."

"You don't have to spell it out for me." His mouth curved in a half smile, but his eyes were a grim gray. He took a step and stiffened abruptly.

"Your back? Hip?" she asked. His apparent pain

putting her back on familiar and comfortable territory. Physician's Assistant Pepper to the rescue. She'd take care of this and that would put the distance back between them.

"It's nothing. I just need to get to bed. Long day. Long week." He didn't move and his posture stayed stiff.

"How about a little ice? Then I'll get the heating pad. Daddy Gene used it for his back, too."

AJ frowned. "I'd rather go with aspirin and beer."

"You know what I think of that home remedy. Lie down on the couch and I'll get the—"

"I'm not your patient. If I need to doctor my back, I'll do it myself."

"I know where your daughter gets her 'me do it' gene." She stared at him with her most intimidating PA glare. He glared right back. "Fine. I've got things to take care of, then I'm going to bed." She swallowed and plowed on. "If you can't wake Faye, let me know, and I'll get EllaJayne for you."

"She said everyone thinks we're a couple."

Pepper gave a half shrug. "Faye also decides when to grocery-shop based on her horoscope."

"She didn't seem surprised or upset."

Pepper closed her eyes so she wouldn't see the ridicule in AJ's eyes. Then his scent and his heat were beside her. How had he moved so quickly?

Without touching her, he whispered in her ear, "I might not understand astrology, but I do understand I want you. I've wanted you every night."

Her breath caught in her throat on the hunger in his voice, on the yearning racing through her body. "I want... I need...what we had when we talked."

"Nothing shameful in that," he said across the suddenly sensitive skin of her cheek.

"Nothing," she agreed. "An adult woman chooses her own partner when and where she wants."

"Absolutely." He pulled her close for a deep kiss, wringing a moan from her. "Only this time we're not doing it on patio furniture or in the back of my truck. We're using a bed…and I refuse to feel weird about it."

She laughed. Nervous and turned-on. "A bed. I can do that. I want to do that." He pulled her to him without another word and kissed her again until she couldn't breathe. Then she pushed back enough to say, "I just want you to know that I understand it doesn't mean—"

"We're not talking anymore. We've talked enough." She couldn't argue with that.

Pepper had learned in high school you couldn't die from embarrassment—even if it felt that way. She reminded herself of that as she made her way to the kitchen for coffee. She'd woken on her own and hoped it was late enough that everyone had gone to do something that meant she wouldn't have to face them until later. She heard the whole household including Butch. She could do this. Whatever she and AJ had done last night wasn't wrong. They were adults. They were free and single. They were responsible. She really needed coffee.

"Peep, mine," EllaJayne said as she held out a handful of Oaty-O's from her high chair. The little girl only got the meaning of "mine" about half of the time.

"Thanks," Pepper said, taking an O and munching it with grinning pleasure. EllaJayne squeaked out her delight and Butch pressed against Pepper's leg. She refused to look at the two other people in the room. She made herself walk without rushing to the coffeepot.

"Sweetie, fire and earth signs bond strongly and securely," Faye said out of the blue. Pepper glanced over to AJ now feeding his daughter and ignoring everything but the spoon of yogurt. "You know, those signs make good couples or partners, whether friends or lovers. Now, Pepper, you should have juice and yogurt to rebalance your chemistry. I've already told Arthur John he needs to eat double protein to replenish—"

"Faye," both she and AJ said with an equal amount of dismay.

EllaJayne frowned and looked fiercely at Faye. "Bad Grana," she added.

"What?" Faye asked with her own brand of innocence and hurt.

"We don't… It's none of your business," Pepper finally settled on. She glanced at AJ and caught him watching her, a look on his face that made her heart flutter in a way that made her think of forever.

"I was going to say to replenish the muscles he injured on the road." Faye stood regally. "EllaJayne, Butch and I will go outside since you two refuse to talk with us here. You need to iron out the evening and then Pepper, sweetie, you need to tell Arthur John about the mayor's plan." Faye gathered up the baby and the dog and went swishing out of the house.

AJ got up slowly to put his daughter's dishes in the sink and refill his coffee.

"I can write you a prescription for muscle relaxants."

"I told you before aspirin is enough. It's just that I… We… God, this is awkward."

"Welcome back to my world. You've already met

Faye." She kept her gaze on the milky brown swirl of coffee.

"So what are we doing here?" he asked his voice belligerent.

"I assume you mean besides having morning-after coffee?"

"This isn't our first morning after, so why is it so awkward?"

"Faye. She has that talent."

He shook his head. "It's us. I think we both knew what would happen when I got back here. We wouldn't have talked on the phone like that otherwise."

There was that. "Faye knows. Butch knows. Even EllaJayne knows something's up."

"According to your mama, everyone knew what was going on before I even rolled into the ranch."

"Maybe." She thought there was something else. Something he wanted her to pull out of him.

He opened the fridge and kept his head inside as he said, "I'm home for three days, then back on the road for three weeks." She waited for him to say whatever he was building up to. What if he wasn't looking for a repeat of what they'd done in the bed? What if he'd found someone else? Why would he have—

"I got a call from Bobby Ames."

The ranch. This was about the ranch. "You did?" she said, trying for nonchalance. "He didn't say anything when I saw him in town."

"He's a lawyer. There are rules." She waited again. He stood with a loaf of bread in one hand. "The estate has settled, and I'm putting the ranch on the market. The whole ranch."

He'd known that last night. While he'd made love to

her, he'd known he would be breaking her heart today. No matter she knew this day would come. She'd hoped he'd change his mind about at least giving her a chance to buy the house and the acreage around it. Not because they'd slept together but because it was only fair.

"That's okay. Danny helped me find a grant to create the gardens we need in town. He and I have been working on a plan."

"You and Danny, huh?"

"He understands how important this is to me and to Angel Crossing."

"Good to know." AJ said as he crushed the loaf of bread. "I need to check my equipment."

So much for Faye's prediction about their signs and compatibility.

AJ had hit the road a day early and ended up with nothing more than an aching back and a hangover. Pepper and Santa Faye Ranch weren't his future and it was good he'd figured that out. He still owed his ex her money. The rides hadn't netted him as much as he'd expected. He'd thought he might get away with splitting up the ranch, but he needed to sell it quickly. He'd been told that would be easier if he kept the acreage intact. Once he sold the ranch he'd give Suzy the final payout, go to court and get full custody with no strings attached. Then he'd be done with her and Kentucky. His step after that was still hazy. He had a lead on at least one job, but maybe he should buy land of his own. But if he was going to buy land, why not just stay in Angel Crossing? He could sell off a portion of the ranch, just like Pepper had asked, even if it took a little longer to sell the rest of it. Except he wouldn't have enough to pay off Suzy.

If he stayed to raise cattle and horses—once he learned how—and…marry Pepper. Yeah, right, like that was happening. So they'd done the midnight do-si-do? Didn't mean anything. He'd done that particular dance with plenty of other women, except the other women hadn't made him want to settle his butt down. To come home to the same person, to wake to the same face on the pillow. When they'd woken in bed together—the first for them—for a second he'd seen the mornings stretched out before them and he hadn't wanted to run away. It had looked like the best future he could imagine. Why not? Maybe because he'd be taking Pepper's ranch and her dreams from her. Since selling just a portion of the ranch wouldn't be enough to pay off Suzy and get him started on a new life, with a little nest egg for EllaJayne's future, he couldn't go down the path with Pepper toward something permanent. Even if that had begun to look mighty nice.

He checked his phone. Two more hours until he said he'd call home. Sheep tails. He couldn't think of Santa Faye Ranch as home. It wasn't. It was the cash cow, the top bull that would guarantee him his daughter and a fresh start. His lead on a ranch manager job was at a big place up in Oregon where they raised rodeo animals and ran a rodeo school. It seemed best to keep as far away from Kentucky as he could, not only because of Suzy. There were also the McCrearys. If they found out he had money, they'd be right there with their hands out.

Dang. His thumb ached from the crushing it had taken. He hoped he wouldn't lose the nail. Faye would have a remedy. Probably having to do with the rising moon and mouse feet.

The producer of this event had gotten a cheap block of rooms, and AJ had "splurged," actually renting one of them. He couldn't face two more nights in the Hillbilly RV. His back and hip wouldn't take it. This near the end of the trip, he ached all over. Getting home... not home, but getting back to Arizona, meant being able to rest up a little as he put the ranch on the market and decided on his next job. His current contract was up at the end of the week. The work in Oregon was looking less shiny, too. No living quarters were included, and the place was more than fifty miles from the nearest town. Exactly how would he find someone to care for Baby Girl?

If it hadn't been thirty minutes until his nightly call to EllaJayne, he'd have headed to the honky-tonk across the parking lot for shots and a little uncomplicated company. Yep. It was the call keeping him from seeking out a good time.

He paced around the room and pushed his duffel back into the closet. His pocket vibrated. Crap, it would probably be a stock problem. The bull who'd been acting up earlier? He pulled out the phone and saw Pepper's name. That thud in his heart was not excitement.

"AJ?" she said.

"Who else?"

"I'm not telling him to find out the birth dates of the bulls, Faye." That comment had not been meant for him.

"Pepper, what's wrong?"

She went on, "We had a visitor today."

Faye's voice came through the phone, "Tell him our

visitor has to be a Capricorn. He has all the signs of the goat and a rising—"

"I heard that. Who was there? Danny?"

"Why would you think Danny? He's been a big help."

Not much of a friend if he was swooping in to "solve" Pepper's problems. "Danny is a selfish—"

"It's not Danny. It's your family."

He stopped pacing. "My family? Gene had kids?"

"Your family from Kentucky. A cousin. Your father's step-brother's... I can't remember all of it. But he said that Suzy told him about the money you were paying her. Then he said if you didn't show your face and start ponying up, he was calling child services because your paperwork wasn't legal and you'd left your child with strangers."

Nevin. It had to be Nevin. He'd been after Suzy, too. The man had never worked a day in his life. He'd been using all his brain power since they were teens on schemes to get rich. Hell. This was bad. "He's there? At the ranch?"

"He's staying by the interstate. He came out today and—"

"He made EllaJayne cry and Butch tried to bite him. Good boy," Faye said loudly and the dog added a yip.

"Did he leave a number?"

"Yes, but why would he do this? I don't understand." Pepper sounded truly confused.

"Too complicated to explain. I'll call and straighten him out." She wouldn't understand. Even with the challenges of Faye as a mother and Daddy Gene being her sort-of step-daddy, Pepper had had more love and support from them than he'd had in his whole blasted extended family. Pepper seemed to want to say more. Instead she put EllaJayne on the line.

He knew what he had to do as soon as this call was over. Call his cousin and figure out his price. His and Suzy's. They had to be in this together. He nearly had enough for this installment. The ranch couldn't sell fast enough so he'd be done with her and now Nevin.

He didn't have the right to drag Pepper into this mess. He'd take care of it on his own. He'd been doing that for a long time.

"Nevin," AJ said when his cousin picked up. "What the hell are you doing in Arizona?"

"Good, cuz, they did call you. Wasn't sure that hippie would remember."

"Just tell me what you want." AJ paced the tiny worn-out motel room.

"Seems Cousin Gene forgot he's got more family than you."

AJ didn't speak.

"You know us McCrearys. Share and share alike. Doesn't seem right he left everything to you."

"Get to the point, Nevin."

"Then there's your daughter. You took her from her mama without even telling her about the ranch. That's her daughter's inheritance. She wants to make sure her baby isn't cheated like Gene done to me and the rest of us."

The two of them had drawn a line through the dots even faster than he would have thought possible. "Suzy signed the paper."

"She did but then she didn't know about the ranch or that you were leaving her precious baby with strangers."

They wanted money, obviously, but how much? All of it? He couldn't do that. "I didn't leave my daughter with strangers. The ladies were Gene's family, and we've been staying with them."

"You're not here now and haven't been here much for months. Doesn't seem much like the way a daddy should act, according to the courts and all."

AJ couldn't really argue with that, except the only reason he wasn't there was for his daughter. "Just tell me what the hell you want." He kept his voice low and even, clenching his fists and kicking the dresser.

"Obvious, ain't it? Suzy deserves at least half of the ranch, on top of what you already said you'd pay her, or she's going to the authorities and telling them how you kidnapped her baby. Her new lawyer said your agreement wouldn't hold up because she was under 'duress' when she signed it."

"Half the ranch. What else?"

"She don't like that agreement you made her sign. I know that ain't legal. Coercion. Read all about it on the internet. So she's not giving up her rights. She'll expect child support for being EllaJayne's mama, so that'll mean visits from the baby. You'll be moving back to Kentucky."

"She never wanted EllaJayne." His chest hurt from holding back the roar of words.

"Now, that ain't true. Post-whatever what not. Read about that, too, on the internet. We clear, cuz?"

"Clear as Kentucky moonshine."

"That woman said you have another week on the road. Guess that will be fine. I'll be here. Oh, now I remember the other thing. Since the ranch is yours, I think those women should be more hospitable-like. You know, open their home so I don't have to stay in this motel."

"Keep the hell away."

"That's not very friendly. Tell them I'll be by tomorrow."

AJ hung up and threw the phone across the room. He had to get to Arizona now. He picked up his duffel, shoved in his crap and left. If he drove all night, he'd be there by late morning. Maybe by then, he'd figure out what he could do to save his daughter and keep Nevin away from the ranch. He feared it meant ruining what he was only beginning to see he wanted his life to be.

Chapter 15

Pepper dialed AJ again and got his voice mail. Her texts hadn't been answered, either. She wanted to talk with him about the yahoo who'd stopped by making threats. Luckily, she'd taken two days off and had been working in the garden when he'd shown up. Despite the visit, it'd been good to get outside and dig in the dirt. She'd be spending another day outside, too. The cooler temperatures of the approaching fall made the work pleasant, even though she'd spent a good part of the morning keeping EllaJayne out of trouble and fending off sloppy kisses from Butch.

The garden was doing well. Better, since Danny had all but promised the funding to move the project into town. He'd even suggested she add a flock of hens to eat bugs off the plants and to provide fresh eggs as part of her latest round of applications. The downside was that there was no way she could help turn the hens into fried chicken. She'd have to think on this longer. She pulled out her phone, hoping that AJ had called her back. Nothing.

"Daddy," EllaJayne yelled and Butch barked.

"Don't I wish," Pepper said softly, then told the little girl, "Pick the pretty flowers right here." EllaJayne grinned widely. Pepper had sat her down in a patch of desert dandelion that had sprouted up between the rows. She figured that would keep the toddler busy for a little bit of time. Pepper went to work fast on the weeds among her plants. In less than a month, they'd have a crop of peas, garlic and peanuts. She needed to look on the internet for recipes. She should check with— Darn it. Someone was coming. Probably that Kentucky cousin. She gathered up EllaJayne and started herding Butch to the house. The little girl drummed her feet against Pepper's thighs yelling for her daddy. She could be as stubborn as one of the llamas.

"Daddy's at the rodeo, remember?" Pepper said in a reasonable voice. Like the toddler would respond to that.

Butch ran away. EllaJayne screamed for the dog.

"Lordy be, you two." She would take the toddler inside and then chase down the useless dog.

"I told you he'd come home," Faye said as she came out the front door and held out her arms for EllaJayne. "Go welcome him home."

Pepper turned. AJ stood by the truck, patting the dog, then strolled toward her. Oh, my, that was one fine man. Even if he was a cowboy like any other. The kind of man who didn't stick around.

Except she'd called and here he was. Yeah, well, he wouldn't have needed to be there if it hadn't been for his relatives. Of course he should have hightailed it home. The man was his problem.

"Nevin been back?" he asked when he was near.

She shook her head and looked him over. Exhausted and sore was her professional opinion. "Wait. You were in Idaho? You couldn't have gotten here driving."

"Since that's where I was and I'm here now, guess I could have driven."

"You were on the road all night? That's dangerous. Why would you do that?" Pepper didn't know whether to be mad or wrap him in a hug. He did look rode hard and put away wet. And still he looked good. Not fair.

"I need coffee." He hesitated for a second by her, sighed deeply, then turned to Faye, who placed Ella-Jayne in his arms.

"I have breakfast ready for you. You'll eat, then sleep," Faye said, surprising Pepper by the firmness of her voice.

"Yes, ma'am. But I've got phone calls to make."

"Food, then you can call. That cousin of yours was definitely born under a troubled sign."

"Trouble sign," EllaJayne agreed and patted AJ's face. His eyes closed for a brief moment as he pulled her tighter to him.

Pepper had made herself stay out in the garden for an hour. When she'd finally come in, AJ looked even worse—dark circles under his eyes and his face gray-white instead of the usual healthy tan. Faye had already told her that he'd eaten nothing, but drunk a full pot of coffee and been on the phone non-stop.

"What's up?" she asked casually when she came into the kitchen.

"This is how it is," he started, staring hard at his inky cup of coffee. "EllaJayne's mama has two good legs to stand on for what she and Nevin are saying, according to my attorney from back home. He helped me come up with the agreement, which isn't worth the paper it's written on, apparently. Guess he wasn't much of an attorney." He took a slug of coffee. "He told me to not fight her about custody until I pay her off, then get the papers signed, sealed and delivered."

"You can't turn that little girl over to a woman who'd…sell her," Pepper said, keeping her voice low. Faye had EllaJayne in the living room, playing with the plastic ranch kit AJ had brought with him.

"No choice. This is short-term pain for long-term gain."

"This is a child we're talking about."

"I know that." He stood abruptly, the chair skittering away. Butch moved quickly, aware as Pepper was that AJ was volatile, and could lose it at any second. She wasn't afraid of him. She was afraid *for* him.

"Let me call Lavonda's brother-in-law. He's an Arizona attorney. We're in Arizona. Or what about Chief Rudy? He'd send your cousin and that woman—" she couldn't believe how angry she was at AJ's ex "—scurrying back under their rock."

"If I get the law involved, it might not just be my custody that we'd lose."

We? What did he mean? "What more can there be than custody? The money?"

AJ rubbed again at his nape.

"What else is there?" she whispered to him.

He pulled away and kept his back to her, like he couldn't face her.

"The shyster attorney Nevin got for Suzy says if I don't hand over Baby Girl—" his voice wavered just enough that she could hear his heart breaking "—they'll...have me arrested for kidnapping. They're saying I didn't have custody, so I had no right to take her from Kentucky."

"He's your cousin... She didn't want—"

He turned to her and his storm-gray eyes were flat and dark. She wanted to pull him back into her arms.

"I'll get this place on the market. Bobby Ames will take care of that. I'll go back to Kentucky and fight it there, but I have to let them take EllaJayne."

"You can't."

"I'll get her back. I'll be right there. I'll move in with Suzy."

"What?"

"It's simple. I'll go with my baby's mama until I can get the money. That's all they want. The money."

"AJ, we can fight this."

"There is no we."

"But you just said—" she stopped herself. They'd knocked boots, but they hadn't made any promises. They certainly hadn't said the L word. *Words don't matter much when the heart's involved*, Daddy Gene's voice echoed in her head. She couldn't let AJ walk away like this. "Of course there's a we. We've been living together and caring for your daughter. You've been helping me make the Angel Crossing Community Garden a reality. We've been sharing a bed."

"We shared a bed once, and I was stuck here until the estate settled."

"You could have stayed with Danny. You could have done a hundred other things."

"This was easy," he said. His mouth had pulled into a grim line. "I'm leaving. I was always leaving. I don't know what kind of fantasy life you've built for us. I was never staying."

"Maybe that was true before—"

"I slept with you? You were here. I'm a man. That's all it was."

"Go. Go now." Her voice barely pushed past the knot of pain in her throat. How could she not have seen that he didn't care, that it was all about the sex? She was a grown woman, not a girl. Dear Lord, this hurt.

"That's what I've been saying."

Finally, he walked away, his cowboy stroll less confident, more hesitant. She didn't care if he'd hurt himself again. Why would she care?

"You're not taking that baby with you," she shouted after him. He didn't stop. She watched him walk away from her and understood that today was officially the worst day of her life.

"You're just going to let your ass of a cousin take your kid and your ranch?" Danny asked AJ while they sipped beer at his apartment.

"I'm regrouping." AJ really wished he could get drunk. Wasn't happening, though, because just a sip of beer was trying to crawl back up his throat.

"That's what it looks like. Your daughter is out at Santa Faye Ranch. You're here and your slimy cousin is staying at the motor court."

AJ slammed down the beer bottle. Didn't anyone in Angel Crossing understand? None of this was what he wanted to do. It was this or put the final nail into Pepper's life. He'd inherited her ranch, and now his cousin was threatening her career. He'd refused to say anything to her earlier. He couldn't add that to her burdens. He'd take care of it by going back to Kentucky, paying the money and getting all this straightened out. Then he'd stay far away from Arizona because he'd guess after all this, Pepper would never want to see him again. He got up from his chair and paced around the small apartment.

Danny squinted at AJ as he sipped his own beer. "Finally got your mad on. Thought you were going to spend the whole night moping."

"I'm not moping."

"Coulda fooled me."

"I gave Nevin two days to produce the paperwork. Then I'm going back home to fight it out there. Pepper and her job will be safe." AJ shut up. He'd not meant to say anything about Pepper.

"What about her job?" Danny's blue eyes were cold and fierce.

"Well, hell." AJ picked up the beer again to have something to do with his hands.

"Tell me now. Or I'm getting the chief involved. I'll tell him that your cousin threatened Pepper, which it sounds like he did?"

"He's making noise that he and Suzy will tell the authorities Pepper knew that I had my daughter illegally and she didn't report it to the authorities. It could mean her losing her license to practice medicine."

"Shit, man," Danny said. "Why didn't you tell me? I *will* call Rudy and have him go out and arrest that piss-ant."

"I'm taking care of it by going back to Kentucky and selling the ranch, then no one will need to deal with me again."

"Not the way it works in Angel Crossing."

"What do you mean?"

"Your cousin threatened not only your daughter but also Pepper. I've already told you that's not allowed."

"What are you talking about? This is my problem."

"This is Angel Crossing."

"I know where I am."

"Sit down and let me tell you what's going to happen. What's already happening." Danny pointed to the hard wooden kitchen chair. AJ dropped into it, suddenly exhausted.

"Everyone knows it's BS what your cousin is saying about 'kidnapping' your daughter, then 'abandoning' her. You know how family is. Well, maybe you don't, but in a family, you can say anything about your siblings or your crazy great-aunt. The minute someone not family says a word, you close ranks and are ready to kick butt and take names."

"What does that have to do with Angel Crossing? They want me to kick Nevin's ass?"

"Maybe. What I meant was that Angel Crossing might say things about Faye and Pepper but they're family. No one else can say things about them."

"Makes no sense."

Danny held up his beer bottle in salute. "Welcome to town, son."

AJ sort of followed what Danny was saying, but it didn't matter. He feared Nevin might actually have the law on his side.

Danny tried again, "I see you're still confused. Bobby Ames was working on the attorneys in Kentucky before he went to his Stuff and Display Conference. Chief Rudy's already talking to the law. Claudette at the clinic is making calls and sending emails. Apparently, the twins at Jim's refused to serve Nevin, said that he was 'visibly intoxicated' when he walked into the bar."

"Was he?"

"Nah. They were just messing with him because he messed with Faye and Pepper."

"It's my problem. My daughter. My ex."

"You've been adopted. Gene vouched for you even before he died. Leaving you the ranch means that you're a stand-up cowboy. Pillar-of-the-community kind of guy. Who'da thought it, huh? Considering us, back in the day."

"Jeez. This is crazy. I can't stay. Nevin isn't smart but he's clever. He's not kidding that he'll try to get Pepper's license revoked. It'll be better for her if I go back to Kentucky. Nevin will follow me. I don't even need to be here to sell the ranch. I can do all of that remotely."

"What about your daughter?"

"I'm doing this for her as much as for Pepper." Right now, she was with the Bourne family, including Butch—her favorite people. AJ had made his way onto her list, but taking her back to Kentucky... He didn't have a choice if the papers said what Nevin insisted they did. He'd do what the order said. Breaking the law and him getting thrown in jail wouldn't protect Baby Girl. He was fighting for her no matter what Danny or anyone else thought. And what did Pepper think? He was a coward? That really hurt. He took a slug of beer. Everything had been so easy before he'd met his daughter. He wouldn't change it, though. Life without her... he couldn't imagine it. Then he'd met Pepper and everything— "Sheep tails," he said out loud.

"What finally made it through that thick skull? That I'm right?"

He wasn't sure he could say it. His tongue had gone numb as the truth smacked him between the eyes, ringing his bell as hard as Twister II, the high-money bull of the 2010 season. "I love Pepper," he said thickly, his tongue too big for his mouth.

"Of course you do, you idiot. Everyone knows that. That's the real reason they like you."

"Claudette, who's next?" Pepper asked, hoping for a long, complicated case with a crotchety old cowboy. She wanted a distraction and someone to vent her annoyance on, no matter if that was unfair.

"*You're* next, missy," her assistant said. "We've organized an intervention."

"Very funny. I know I've been hitting the Fiddle Faddle pretty hard, but I don't think I've gotten to intervention level."

"We're done with appointments for today and Devil's Food reserved us the meeting room. Lavonda wanted to call it the war room. Faye said no."

Pepper froze. What exactly was going on? She'd assumed Claudette had been speaking figuratively. "Faye? Lavonda?"

"Yes. Grammy Marie, too. EllaJayne is going to be hanging with Chief Rudy. He's hankering for grandkids, so he wants a dry run. We're out of here." Claudette shooed Pepper down the sidewalk and into Devil's Food.

As Pepper walked through the diner, she got looks of sympathy and a couple of encouraging nods. Danny waved to her from his stool. "He's not here," he told her. "I'm working on it, though."

What did that mean? Pepper tried to stop her momentum. Claudette gave her a poke. Pepper jumped forward through the door to a small side room with one large table, which was used as a meeting room.

Faye drifted out of her seat and enveloped Pepper. The patchouli and baby powder scent comforted her for a moment. Then Pepper looked at the filled chairs and the determined looks on all the women's faces. It really was an intervention.

"Sit," her mother said as she directed Pepper to the head of the long table. "We need to re-align your—"

"It's an intervention. We decided," Grammy Marie said.

Lavonda with her sleek hair and large dark eyes stood and immediately commanded the room. "Whatever we call it doesn't matter. What matters is saving that precious little girl and getting Pepper her—"

"Her destiny," Faye said.

Lavonda just smiled. "Again, the labels are less important than the actions, and we've got a lot of actions to organize. Danny said AJ will get his paperwork from Nevin tomorrow, which doesn't give us much time to straighten everything out, including making sure that Kentucky yahoo doesn't get your license taken away."

"What?" Pepper breathed.

"Now, don't get mad at AJ," Grammy Marie said. "Nevin threatened to go to the authorities about you to get your license pulled."

"Why didn't he say anything to me? Nevin couldn't do that—" Pepper stopped, knowing Nevin might have been able to get her in trouble. But could she think about AJ's silence?

Faye said, "Gene was the same way. He'd think I was

too delicate to face the ugly parts of life. But I wasn't. We're not." She smiled at her daughter.

"Of course she's not," Lavonda said. "Danny told us and I added that to the list of items that Spence, my lawyer brother-in-law, and the chief needed to address. Nevin had some hopped-up charge that you should have reported EllaJayne as kidnapped. Danny's getting a copy of the document so we have all the details. Spence said he'd check it out. We'd have asked Bobby Ames, but he's at a taxidermy conference in Oregon. But I called him and he said Spence would have been his choice if we'd asked him."

Pepper wasn't certain exactly what was going on. AJ had been protecting her even as he planned to leave her and take his daughter with him. She needed to stay focused on what was important: AJ getting custody of his daughter. Knowing he needed the money for that had made her less hurt that Daddy Gene had left the ranch to him. It had all worked out for the best.

"I see you thinking through this," Faye said. "Don't use your brain. Use your heart. You're so good at that. That's why you work at the clinic and why you're starting the gardens. You've got such a huge heart." Faye's voice had a tender edge to it.

"I'm just confused what we're doing here," Pepper said. "If it's to help EllaJayne and you need me to sign something for the attorney, Lavonda, just let me know. Otherwise—"

"Later. We may need that signature," Lavonda said. "But that's not what this is about."

Pepper looked at the women. Some were patients and all were friends.

Grammy Marie stared right at Pepper and said,

"You're in love with EllaJayne, because who wouldn't be, but more importantly, you're in love with AJ."

"I don't think so," Pepper said but with the words hanging in the air, her answer wasn't as sure as she would have liked.

"Grammy Marie, we decided that wasn't what we were doing today," Lavonda said patiently.

"She's right," Faye said. "Marie's right, I mean. It's as obvious as the nose on my face. Pepper has to come to that conclusion on her own. We shouldn't be pushing her."

The room erupted, the women talking over each other in their enthusiasm. The passionate faces around the table made Pepper warm and fuzzy inside, just like when she got a hug from a patient. Not like her and AJ. That was volcano and silk. She certainly wanted him. So what? She wanted a lot of things in life that she couldn't have. Plus, she had more than enough with her patients and the garden project. Then she remembered her and AJ together. It wasn't just burning up the sheets that came to mind. She also felt in her heart the nights they spent in the garden together with Butch and Ella-Jayne, even the meals with Faye.

"Lordy be," Pepper said. The room got silent.

"She figured it out," Faye said. "Good girl. I knew you could do it on your own. I told them."

"AJ's made it clear he's moving along, and I'm not leaving Angel Crossing. This is my home."

"Of course you're not leaving Angel Crossing or Santa Faye Ranch," her mother said.

"We can't stay at the ranch and AJ...that's clear, too. I'm in infatuation."

"No. You're not, plus it can work," Lavonda said.

"My sister did a long-distance thing. And look at Jones and me. He wasn't going to stay in Arizona, but here we are. The good thing about life is that it changes."

Grammy Marie chimed in, "Love conquers all."

Faye fluttered over to Pepper and took her hands while the room quieted again. "You know what to do. That's one of your gifts. You can see clearly the path that you need to take, even if it's tough. You do it with compassion and caring, but you always know. So what do you know about AJ? That you love him. He loves you. He has to clear up his past and you'll help him with that. What else do you need to know?"

"How exactly this can work? And how exactly I can be sure that AJ cares for me? Or even that I really care for him?"

"That's easy, sweetie. You love him because he loves your dog, my Beauties, his daughter and Santa Faye Ranch. Of course he loves you. Why else would a cowboy take up farming and herding walking yarn balls?"

Chapter 16

"What did you want, Danny?" AJ asked as he walked into his friend's office. He stopped when he saw Pepper sitting there. His breath got gummed up in his throat. He reached out his hand before he could stop himself but let it drop without touching her. Didn't matter if he loved her. His life was crap right now and he couldn't drag her into that. "Pepper," he said, nodding to her and pulling off his hat. He didn't take the chair next to her. He'd be too close.

"Good," Danny said. "Sit."

"No. You're busy—"

"We were waiting for you."

AJ looked hard at his friend, trying to understand what he wanted and why he was involving him. The plan was already in motion. He'd meet Nevin, see the papers, then go back to Kentucky with EllaJayne.

"AJ, sit. This might take a little while," Pepper said. He couldn't look at her because he might just break down. He kept his gaze on Danny and sat.

"What did you two want?" AJ asked.

Danny gave a politician's smile. It looked as genuine as Dolly Parton's...hair. "Pepper and I spoke with Spencer...my sister's brother-in-law. He's a good attorney. He and Lavonda actually came up with this. I hate to say that my sister had a good idea, but there it is."

"You going to get to the point sometime this century?" Sitting this close to Pepper had AJ thinking about those few precious nights together and how giving up on ever being with her like that again was like breathing underwater. Impossible.

"I want you to understand that this isn't an off-the-cuff idea, you blockhead. We only had two days, but we've made it work. So when you go see Nevin this afternoon... yes, everyone knows you're meeting with him...you can present him with this, and the chief will go with you. Yes. He will because he doesn't want any trouble. And I know you, AJ. There could be trouble when your Kentucky cousins are involved. They're like a pack of jackals."

"Get to the point, Danforth," AJ said, glaring at the man who used to be his pal. The lemon and clove scent of Pepper surrounded him, weaving its way through his scrambled brain.

"Danforth?" Pepper asked. "Really?"

"Family name," Danny said with another politician's smile. "I want to make sure you understand, AJ. All of Angel Crossing helped with this plan and will benefit from it, including Pepper and Faye. We take this very seriously. You understand?"

Did he? He didn't really believe that the town had

adopted him. He'd never felt like that before. He'd lived in Pinetown his entire life and people wouldn't spit on him if he were on fire.

"I'll take the silence as understanding," Danny said. "We have a grant from the state that is earmarked for the Angel Crossing Community Garden Project."

AJ finally turned to Pepper. "You got the money. Why didn't you tell me?"

"You're leaving."

That about said it all. She didn't look like she cared for him. Danny had been wrong. "Congratulations."

"Yeah, yeah, yeah. Hooray," Danny said. "What that means is that we have money, which Angel Crossing never has."

None of this mattered. AJ was leaving. He had to clear up things in Kentucky, which he guessed, knowing his luck, would go as smoothly as concrete through a straw. It was just he'd changed so much in such a short time, it was hard to remember that AJ. Knowing about his little girl and then seeing her for the first time…he'd known right then life would never be the same. Exactly like when he'd seen Pepper in the flesh.

"Put us both out of our misery," she said. AJ turned to her and saw the pain on her face. He wanted to pull her into his arms. He stood up and leaned across Danny's desk.

"Stop beating around the damned bush and just tell us."

"Sit down, AJ. I'm getting there. I'm not dragging this out. I really need both of you to understand what's at stake."

"Are you saying there's a chance that the grant will go away?" Pepper asked. "What's that got to do with AJ?"

"Fine. I spent at least fifteen minutes on my speech

but you two are ruining it. The council and I met. Then the ladies from Devil's Food talked with me. You know who I mean, Pepper." AJ was surprised when she blushed. "We believe the best use for the grant is not to buy equipment and the empty lots in town. The grant will be a down payment, along with the collection that came together from Angel Crossing, to buy Santa Faye Ranch from AJ."

AJ looked at Pepper to gauge her reaction to her grant being hijacked by him and his problems. She looked...happy. She smiled at him, tears shining in her eyes and her smile wobbly at the corners. "Why didn't they tell me? This is a great solution."

"Good thing you think so because it's a done deal. We didn't want to wait. Afraid if Nevin got wind of this, he'd find some way to mess it up. He's smart like a fox."

AJ wasn't listening to Danny. His gaze hadn't left Pepper's face. Dear Lord. She *did* love him. He could see it in her eyes. He pulled her from the chair and into his embrace. "Thank you. Thank you. I didn't think I could love you more than I did, but now I do."

"You love me?" she asked with wonder, leaning back enough to look directly into his eyes. "Thank God. You love me. I love you, too. I love you enough to...well, I would have let you go if that was the best thing. You know that whole 'if you love something, leave it go' nonsense."

He pulled her close again and said into her ear. "I'm never leaving you go."

"But you don't want to stay in Arizona. You said that—"

He kissed her and she kissed him back with her whole heart.

* * *

"You're thinking too loudly," AJ said as he squeezed Pepper's hand where it lay between them on the bench seat of his pickup. "It will all work out."

"Later I want to talk with you about what Nevin threatened me with and you not telling me. Right now, I'm just trying to take in the fact that you aren't on your way out of town. I had prepared myself for that. Instead we're… What are we?"

"Not sure. Not worried."

He was right. What did it matter? They knew they loved each other. They'd said it right there in the mayor's office. About as official as you could get. Now, they were going to save AJ and his little girl. And then what?

"You're doing it again. We'll worry about tomorrow, tomorrow."

"That sounds like something from a fortune cookie. What if this—" she waved her hand at them "—is just physical?"

"You really believe that?" he glanced away from the road and smiled that special cowboy grin.

"It could be."

"I don't think so. I pulled weeds for you. I haven't done that since my mama threatened me with no dinner."

"You were just trying to get me horizontal by impressing me with your green thumb."

"Could be. But I want to stay here and keep pulling weeds and plowing and growing good food for good people."

Her chest tightened and her eyes stung. He got it. Got her. "I love you."

"Well, duh," he said and laughed, before pulling

her hand to his mouth and gently kissing the knuckles. "Now, stop distracting me. You don't want me to drive into a ditch."

She allowed herself to float in the sparkly bright love. The next few hours wouldn't be so sparkly bright. She was going to enjoy this little bit of time alone. They were driving to the ranch to meet up with Nevin, as well as Danny, half of the town council, and half of the women from the Devil's Food Diner Back Room Mafia—a name invented by Chief Rudy. Faye said that once everyone heard what would be happening between AJ and his cousin, they insisted on coming out as witnesses, moral support or muscle, in the case of one or two of her cowboy patients. They were going to get Nevin to sign the paper or else. Taking care of people didn't mean she had to do it all herself. When had she thought it was her exclusive job to save the world? And when had she become so arrogant she thought she could?

"You're doing it again. Tell me what you want to plant and what kind of chickens you fancy?"

She pulled in a breath and turned her brain to the question, allowing herself to think about the new life that would be hers. Not exactly the one she'd planned, but that was good, too. She wouldn't be alone to face her problems. There was everyone from Angel Crossing and even Faye. She turned to smile at AJ. He'd be there today, and she was pretty sure that might be all she needed for the rest of her life.

"What the hell is this?" AJ's cousin Nevin asked after strolling potbelly first from his pickup with Kentucky plates and twenty years of dirt and rust. "Do they know what you done?"

AJ moved forward, and Pepper stayed glued to his side. Chief Rudy stepped in. "This is Angel Crossing, and we look after our own. These are our own."

Nevin's washed-out blue eyes were nearly hidden by bangs of thinning dirty-blond hair. "I'm here to settle personal business with my cousin."

The chief spoke before Pepper or AJ could open their mouths. "Whatever business you have to transact with AJ, you'll do here in the open."

"Fine. Then you can all hear what kind of man he is, stealing that there baby from its mama."

"He did not," Pepper said, surprising herself with her own vehemence. "He saved that baby. He sacrificed—"

"Nevin," AJ broke in and walked around the chief to stand squarely in front of his cousin. There was no resemblance at all, even with both of them in jeans, boots and T-shirts. "You and Suzy want money. I've got money. You just need to sign this." AJ whipped out the paperwork and the assistant for the police department came forward. She would notarize the document on the spot. They weren't leaving anything to chance. There was at least one smartphone filming the entire exchange.

Nevin looked down at the papers. "That's not enough. I talked to people who know what our cousin Gene left you."

"This is all you and Suzy will get. I think the courts frown on blackmail. Don't they, chief?" AJ didn't take his eyes from Nevin.

"That's right. We take threats like that very seriously."

"Do ya now?" Nevin asked, looking around the crowd before his nasty gaze landed on Pepper. "You're his piece, huh?"

AJ reached forward and grabbed the front of his cousin's Hell Raiser, Hay Maker T-shirt, bunching it in his fist. "Shut up and sign the paper."

She waited for Chief Rudy to step forward and stop AJ. When the chief didn't move a muscle, Pepper started toward the men. Her mother held tight to her, whispering in her ear, "You've got to let your man be a man."

What did that mean? She couldn't let him get beat up, not for her, not for the ranch. Except this wasn't her fight. This was AJ's. This was about his baby. For EllaJayne she would do the same thing. She didn't struggle, carefully sizing up Nevin. AJ could definitely take him in a fair fight but fair didn't seem to be in his cousin's vocabulary.

"Don't you see what he's doing?" Nevin squealed. "Arrest him."

Chief Rudy turned away.

"Sign the damned paper," AJ said again, his voice low and menacing.

"It's not enough, cuz. We've got expenses."

"Sign the paper. What's in there—that's all you're ever getting from me." AJ's fist tightened in the thin T-shirt material while sweat beaded Nevin's pasty face.

In the silence, Nevin's breathing rasped. Heat beat down on Pepper's head. No one moved. Every eye was on the men.

"Boot," EllaJayne yelled from the house as the dog bolted across the yard and into the crowd. The toddler followed on his heels, snatched up by Faye. Butch stopped at AJ's side and growled at Nevin, hackles raised. Pepper gaped at her poodle of a shepherd. She'd never heard that noise before, low and threatening.

"Get that dog away," Nevin said, kicking out his foot and hitting Butch squarely on the nose, knocking him to the ground where the dog lay stunned. Pepper raced forward and saw Nevin's feet leave the ground as the crowd yelled.

"That's it," Chief Rudy said. "We've given you a chance to be a man about this, but kicking a dog...what kind of man does that? No man at all. Let him go, AJ, he's under arrest for animal cruelty."

A murmur of approval went through the group as Nevin protested and Butch stood, shaking his head a little in confusion. His butt started wagging and he took three steps and sat on AJ's feet.

Pepper looked at her cowboy, his face stiff with disgust and anger. His storm-gray gaze stayed on his cousin and his grip didn't loosen. She went to him.

"You can release him now. The chief will arrest him, and Butch is fine. We're fine. He'll sign. We're giving them money, and it's more than they deserve. How can he and Suzy refuse? They should just take the money and run." She turned to Nevin using the same stare she used on cowboys when they came to the clinic. "He knows what the score is. It's like the sheriff said: Angel Crossing looks after its own, and we're its own."

"He and Suzy don't deserve a dime," AJ ground out.

"Maybe not, but if it makes sure EllaJayne is yours forever, without strings and without a mama who only sees dollar signs, then it's money more than well spent. Plus, you don't have a choice," she said and then rose on her toes to speak directly in his ear, "We all decided to spend our money this way. If you don't sign, what will that mean to Angel Crossing Community Garden?"

He turned and his face relaxed a tiny bit. "I should have known this was about your veggies." His hand loosened. "He's all yours, chief."

Pepper pulled AJ into her arms and the cluster of friends and neighbors clapped as she kissed him hard on the mouth.

AJ just stopped himself from pulling Pepper closer by the butt. "I love you," he said, not feeling silly or scared. It all felt right. He could barely remember the cowboy he'd been, the one who'd gone from woman to woman looking for…well, for what he had now. Family. Friends. Home. Lordy be, as Pepper said. His eyes burned with tears.

"Boot, Boot," EllaJayne yelled. He and Pepper broke apart. He scooped up Baby Girl. His finally. No more Suzy. The mother who didn't want this gorgeous human. A part of him was sad for that. Another selfish part was grateful because it meant that she was all his. No. Not just his. His and Pepper's. His chest started to burn along with his eyes. Lordy be.

He pulled Pepper back to him, squashing his daughter between them and loving all of it, even the scrabbling of Butch's claws on his leg and his daughter's screams for her favorite playmate. His little girl needed a brother or a sister…whoa, cowboy. He'd barely gotten a grasp on being a daddy and on knowing he loved Pepper. Now he was imagining new babies. He pulled them all closer before letting them go enough so Pepper could stand beside him as they faced the small crowd. How did he thank this town that had accepted him as one of their own?

"Wait," Faye said before he could open his mouth. "Gene would be so proud. So happy." The tears in her voice were clear, but she smiled.

AJ tightened his grip on Pepper, knowing mention of Gene would make her a little sad. The wound of his passing, the only father she'd known, had not completely healed.

"He certainly would be," AJ said when Faye didn't continue. "I know he loved this town. I know that because he told me. Gene was the greatest cowboy I knew. Not because he won buckles or was in the money. He was the best because he shared his knowledge and his six-pack, when needed, for purely medicinal purposes, of course." He paused for the knowing laughter, then went on, "I'm not certain why he left me his ranch, but I will be forever grateful because it got me my daughter and—" He stopped himself, uncertain he was ready to share exactly what he felt for Pepper.

"Oh, man, just kiss her again," Danny said.

The crowd shouted and he did kiss her again. A light promise of more to come.

"This is just what Gene wanted," Faye said when things quieted.

"What do you mean?" Pepper asked, stepping away from AJ and staring down her mother.

"Sweetie, you know Gene loved you, and he knew he wouldn't be on this earth forever." Faye hesitated and her voice quavered when she went on. "He was so sure AJ was the cowboy for you."

Now, AJ wondered what exactly Faye was getting at.

Faye said, "We discussed it. So, Gene decided… sweetie, he just wanted you to be happy. And when I saw AJ and his baby, I knew Gene had been right."

"You're saying he set us up?" Pepper asked sounding as gut-punched shocked as AJ.

"Why else wouldn't he leave the ranch to us?"

"Faye, he didn't do that. He left it to AJ because he saved Daddy Gene from that bull."

"He certainly was grateful but that debt was paid to AJ in the hundreds of ways he helped him over the years at the rodeo and by checking in with him even after he left. This was about you, sweetie. He wanted to make sure you were cared for."

AJ could think of a lot of reasons that had nothing to do with matchmaking. The sparks of heat from Pepper told AJ she might be ready to explode with all that anger directed at her mother, which would lead to a lot of words Pepper couldn't take back and would regret for a long time. "Faye," he said loudly, catching everyone's attention. "Gene knew his stuff. But," he said emphatically because this was important to him, "Pepper can take care of herself and does it with empathy and style. She's cared for you and for this town because that's what she does. She didn't need Gene to find anyone to care for her. But I'm grateful he did because I can't imagine my life without her." He finally looked at Pepper and had to look away so the burning in his eyes didn't turn into tears. "I'm grateful he brought me to Angel Crossing because there's no place on this earth I'd rather be. Or where there are better folks."

Chapter 17

AJ stood with his dusty booted foot on the lowest rung of the corral. Another time in his life, there would have been bulls or horses on the other side of the fence. Not in his new life. No. Here was a milling herd of furballs. Alpacas and llamas. He shook his head, amazed at the turns his life had taken. He couldn't even be upset that Gene had a lot to do with those curves because he'd ended up with Pepper and EllaJayne. No regrets in either case. Maybe one small regret that EllaJayne's mama wouldn't know her wonderful daughter. Some women just weren't cut out to be mamas.

"I could hear you stewing from the house," Pepper said.

He turned and smiled because, well, he was happy as a bull in a field of heifers. Well, one heifer and he was a smart enough cowboy to not share that thought.

"Not stewing," he said to her. "Thinking about how lucky I am."

"You think you're getting lucky tonight?" she asked with a secret smile as she walked up to him and snuggled into his side, despite the lingering heat of the day.

"I didn't think tonight would be about luck. Thought that was a sure thing." She poked him in the ribs. He laughed. "I meant lucky that Gene decided to play matchmaker. Lucky Suzy would take money over motherhood. And, luckiest of all? That Angel Crossing is allowing us to rent to own Santa Faye Ranch."

"I don't know if I believe Daddy Gene had any plans for you and me," Pepper said seriously. "I'm just going to say EllaJayne couldn't have a better daddy than you, and Suzy is going to miss out on knowing an awesome person. But I hope if she ever changes her mind on wanting to see her daughter, you'll think about it."

"She doesn't deserve—"

"It's not what Suzy deserves. It's what EllaJayne might want and need."

He squeezed her hard because that was Pepper. Thinking about others. "You're right, of course."

"I like the sound of that." She squeezed him close, then said with a hint of jealousy and humor, "One day I'll want to hear all about your sordid past. But not tonight."

"Good. It's a lot less sordid and a lot more ordinary than you think." They stood arm in arm watching the furballs find a comfortable place to settle. Faye and EllaJayne were spending the night with Grammy Marie. He'd cut off Faye when she'd tried to give him advice on how to spend the evening.

"Faye told me that our astrological charts indicate we will make beautiful babies," Pepper said.

"I don't know if I'll ever get used to her…how she… Aw, hell…let's go to bed." He didn't want to think about the future. All he wanted to focus on was Pepper and letting her know again how much he loved her. She pressed her soft breasts against him as she pulled his head down for a kiss, saying softly, "Bed. My favorite three-letter word."

Pepper's lips were petal-soft under his. When had he gotten addicted to them, and to her? He lifted her against him, wanting her supple heat. He deepened the kiss until both of their breaths jerked in and out.

He pulled away, slowly, reluctantly. "I love you."

"I love you, too," she said, cupping his face, her brown gaze locked on him, shining. His chest swelled. He gave her a quick kiss, then pulled her toward the house, his feet moving faster and faster. Pepper's laughter rang out as they ran into the house, landing on her bed with a bounce.

He wanted her now and he knew he'd want her in ten years…twenty, fifty. That was heady stuff. He took her lips and his hand loved her curves as he quickly stripped her. When he got down to her plain white panties and bra, he thought they were sexier than any lace and silk. They made what was under them a mystery that he needed to discover. He buried his face between her breasts, his hand slipping into the cup of her bra to tease her nipple "Yes," she gasped, her hands holding his head in place as she moved under his lips. Her responsiveness sparked his own scalding need.

AJ's mouth tasted the sweet skin as his hands slipped

her bra from her breasts. When he shifted for a moment, Pepper shuddered and whispered, "You have too many clothes on." Then she wriggled out from under him. Her hands, small and competent, opened the snaps on his shirt and pushed it off in one motion. She went for his jeans and he reached for her, clasping her butt and making her jump. He wanted her to hurry or this would all end before it had even started.

"I want you naked and I want you on that bed," she said, her voice rough. She bent over to take off his boots. As she shook her fanny at him, a deep-from-the-gut groan broke from behind his clenched teeth. She had to know the sexy power she had over him.

She stood and turned. "Your pants. Take them off. No, wait," she said, a gleam in her eyes that made him wish he had a whole case of condoms. "That's my treat." She brushed her fingers along his shuddering abs, dipping her fingers under his waistband before opening the metal button. He reversed their positions, kissing her while he stripped her and him of the final barriers of their clothing. No more teasing. He fumbled his condom on and slid into her. Finding a thrill and contentment that he hadn't known he'd been chasing.

"I love you," she said, holding him still for a moment before moving her hips and sending them both flying.

"I love you," he whispered as he tucked her already familiar curves against his body. They were both where they needed to be now and forever.

AJ looked out over the dusty parking lot filled with pop-up canopies and plastic tables. He refused to panic. His daughter was here somewhere. He could find her.

She hadn't done a disappearing act like this in a while. He looked over the large lot that had been empty just yesterday. Today was a big party, where the town was celebrating the weekly farmers market, planting for the new year and the second grant they'd gotten from a big foundation that understood Pepper's vision.

Darn it. Where was his daughter? Where was Pepper, who was wearing a bright lime-green hat today. She said it was easier to see her, plus her mother had given it to her for luck with the new planting season. Faye had told him it was to increase their fertility. EllaJayne was enough for them right now, thank you very much.

"You missing something, cowboy?" Chief Rudy asked, catching AJ off guard.

"Not missing, exactly."

The older man squinted at him from under the brim of his cowboy hat. "They're over there by the mayor's tent." He gestured with his chin.

AJ nodded and headed that way. He got waylaid twice by members of the Community Garden. He hurried on and managed to avoid the ladies who used the furballs' fleece. They were trying to convince him the spinners and knitters needed Santa Faye Ranch to get "just one or two angora goats." That's what they'd said when they'd talked him into increasing the number of alpacas—two more in a buff color, which turned into six because otherwise they would've been put down. He'd told them firmly they were not running an alpaca rescue group.

AJ checked at the mayor's tent, but Danny said he hadn't seen Pepper or EllaJayne for at least twenty minutes. AJ scanned the crowd again, looking for Pepper and his daughter. Soon to be *their* daughter. The adoption process was nearly complete.

Where the heck were they? He got stopped a dozen more times, turning down tastes of dishes being created for the Best Potluck contest. Everyone had just seen Pepper. Finally, he got pointed in the direction of the old movie house that hadn't been in operation since the 1970s and hadn't been grand even in its heyday. Everyone had been wondering how much longer it would stand. That sort of headache was for his friend Danny. AJ had his work cut out for him at Santa Faye Ranch, running herd on the furballs and setting up a website, Lord save them all. Pepper still worked at the clinic because she loved it and the town needed her. That meant the running of the garden had fallen to him and Faye, who was surprisingly sharp when it came to the farm. Of course, she'd grown up in a commune. She knew how to get people to work for free. She was organizing tonight's feast, even though it included meat. She said next time they would do an all-vegetarian potluck. He didn't think the meat-eating residents would go for that, but he was learning Faye could accomplish anything.

He heard Butch barking. EllaJayne couldn't be far behind. The two of them were attached at the hip. She still called him Boot, even though her nearly three-year-old vocabulary had gotten so much better. "Baby Girl," he shouted. "Butch. Come here now." He waited for an answer. Nothing. Darn it. He might just have to go back and ask the chief for help finding—there they were. EllaJayne was walking down the sidewalk toward the old theater with Butch keeping watch at her side. Where was Pepper?

EllaJayne screeched in joy. He followed the sound into the abandoned movie theater. Great. Creepy old theater with rats and who knew what else.

"Baby Girl," he yelled, as he walked in, blinking when he noticed it wasn't dark.

"Darn it, EllaJayne," Pepper said. "You were supposed to stay with Grammy Marie."

"Oops," his daughter said, her new word for getting out of any mischief.

"Pepper," he said.

She turned around, looking even guiltier than his daughter and the dog. The three of them stood in the theater's lobby, lit well from a duo of chandeliers.

"I was going to surprise you."

"Surprise me?"

"Danny found an angel donor and more money from somewhere—he's a genius with that. We—Angel Crossing, I mean—bought the theater. We're going to turn it into a permanent, undercover Farmers Market for our extra produce and for the urban gardens in town and for all the items the ladies make from the furballs. It'll take a year or so, but won't it be great?"

He could see how much work it would be. He'd trust her on this, but he figured it'd take much more than a year.

He hugged her. "'Great' might not be what I'm saying in a couple of months. Who'll be running this project?" She was quiet and he got suspicious. "No. I already have the new fields laid out and the chickens ordered."

"Chickens? You got me chickens?" She kissed him hard.

A year and a half ago he'd never have imagined a

passel of hens would get him a lip-lock. He squeezed her butt for good measure. "That was supposed to be my surprise for…later," he said quietly with a waggle of his brows.

"You thought laying hens would get *you* laid," Pepper whispered for his ears only. "You do know your woman." She gave him another deep kiss.

He liked the sound of that. He wished he could thank his cousin for his matchmaking. *Damn right, and you'd better do right by her*, Gene's voice rang out in his head.

"What?" Pepper asked at his expression. "I know the theater's a lot to take in." She turned and gave the narrow, dusty space a loving look, exactly like the one she used on the fields of beans and kale.

"I'm just trying to figure out how you turned a cowboy into a farmer," he answered.

"*S-e-x.*"

He laughed until he heard Baby Girl singing, "*S-e-x. S-e-x. S-e-x.*"

"You're going to explain that to Grammy Marie."

"No problem. I'll just tell her it's Grana Faye's fault." Now, his daughter added Faye's name to her chant.

He held Pepper again in his arms and watched his daughter move little piles of nuts and bolts around the lobby, while Butch trailed behind her. In these kinds of moments, he realized he was happy, beyond happy. He wasn't sure exactly when that had happened. He knew it would last until the next time the furballs got out, but he couldn't imagine his life any other way.

"You told him," Faye said from where she stood at the entrance to the small old-fashioned theater.

"She told me," he answered, not moving away from

Pepper. "But she still hasn't told me who will be running the project." He tried to sound stern.

"Me and you, of course," Faye said. "I'm a water sign."

"Of course. Makes total sense." It did in some weird Faye way. "When will you start?"

"The mayor and I are discussing that. I need to cleanse the building, then we'll be ready. We have great plans. Gene would be so happy." Faye's smile wavered a little. She still obviously missed him.

Pepper pulled away from him and went to her mother. "He would. He'd like what you've helped us do at the ranch, too."

"He would not like that you've turned his ranch into a farm, but he'd do it for you." Faye hugged Pepper. He saw tears in both women's eyes. His own chest tightened.

"Don't cry," his little girl said as she hugged the women's legs. Butch sat on Pepper's feet in sympathy.

He couldn't take the tears. He knew they would flow. They were women who felt deeply but their tears cut him down to the soles of his boots. "Enough of that. Gene's good in cowboy heaven and there's a potluck to judge."

"*S-e-x, s-e-x, s-e-x,*" EllaJayne sang.

He joined the women's laughter, catching the happy glint in Pepper's gaze along with the promise for later. Yep. Sex. It was a good thing.

If Pepper saw another pie, she was going to throw up. The Potluck Contest had been more popular than she'd expected. Next year—if she survived tonight—they needed more judges. She thought even AJ was feeling a little queasy from all the tastings. She pulled EllaJayne tight against her where she sat listening to Danny read off the winners. She hoped by later tonight her too-full stomach wouldn't be still making her feel a little green around the gills because she had lots of plans for her cowboy. She glanced over at AJ again. He leaned back in a lawn chair, looking as comfortable there as on the back of his horse Benny who'd found his way to the ranch to live happily among the furballs. She smiled to herself. Santa Faye Ranch was more ranch-like than she'd ever imagined even with the gardens. She was content. For now.

She felt more than saw AJ sit up. What had happened? What was going on? She looked around and noticed everyone staring at them.

"AJ and Pepper, get up here," Danny said, motioning for them to approach the stage. Grammy Marie whisked EllaJayne from her arms.

"Go on," the older woman said, a huge grin splitting her face.

What was Danny up to?

AJ grasped her hand and she figured she could face anything. As they walked by smiling faces, she mouthed to him, "What's going on?" He shook his head, for once not covered by a hat. She needed to cut his hair. That warmed her from stem to stern. She liked giving him a haircut.

"Stop the lollygaggin', folks. We've got dancing to do," Danny said, giving them a mock glare.

She and AJ stepped onto the low stage with the band now set up.

"Up here to the microphone, so everyone can hear you."

AJ pushed her a little forward. He might be a big brave former bull rider but speaking in front of a crowd made him a palm-sweating mess.

"Faye," Danny said into the mic and her mother magically appeared on stage.

AJ squeezed Pepper's hand hard. With Faye involved, this could be anything. Everyone in the crowd were smiling. They were listening.

"All of you have been touched by my daughter and her cowboy. We're all here because of them. Look at this amazing event and what's planned for next year. Who would have imagined her idea for a garden to provide us all with good wholesome food would end up with a weaving circle and a soon-to-be Angel Crossing Market, where we can sell what we grow and make, no matter the weather and more than one day a week. Gene would be so proud." Faye's voice broke a little but she went on immediately. "So how do we repay that sort of commitment and kindness? The pie was great, as were all the other dishes, but we—the women of Angel Crossing—decided we needed to do more."

Oh, crap. She glanced at AJ and saw a similarly worried look on his face. She started forward to tell Faye she didn't need to do anything. Her mother went on before she could take one step.

"With the help of the ladies—"

"And the men," one of the cowboy-hatted guys who hung out at the diner piped up.

"And men. We laid out the foundation for a house of your own at Santa Faye Ranch. We've got the plan and most of the materials. It's time you and AJ and, of course, that darling EllaJayne started a home of your own. Plus my place is too small. I looked at your tea leaves, and you'll have at least five children."

Everyone cheered and laughed, while Pepper gasped in surprise. She and AJ figured they would make do with the cobbled-together, too-small ranch house until they could afford to build what they needed. She'd never imagined they'd have the money to move into a place of their own for years and years.

"Oh, my, they are speechless." Faye laughed. "We did it."

Pepper looked over the crowd of smiling faces. She saw patients. She saw people who needed her help. But what she also saw were friends, who would do this for AJ and her because they cared. It didn't matter if anyone saw her tears. This was such an amazing day. She looked at her mother, who was openly crying. She ran into her arms for a hug. "Faye. Mom. Thank you. Thank you."

"Don't thank me. Thank Angel Crossing. They love you almost as much as I do."

Pepper gathered her wits and wiped at her eyes. She went to the microphone and knew AJ was beside her without having to see him.

"Thank you," she said into the microphone. "I thought today couldn't get any better. We had this amazing potluck, and everyone had a good time. And we even had a few healthy dishes. We are so on our way. That was thanks enough for me. Honestly. This house. Well, I never expected or would have asked—" She couldn't say anymore because of the tears.

AJ stepped forward and wiped his palm on his jeans. "When I stopped in Angel Crossing to pay my respects to my cousin, I expected to stay one night, maybe two. I was a bull rider with a baby. I had no real plan. Then I met Pepper. She took us in...even if she didn't want to." Everyone laughed. "In less than two years, I went from cowboy to farmer. You know what that's like." More laughter.

Pepper stared at her cowboy. How could she ever have imagined he was selfish and uncaring?

"What I'm trying to say is I am the one who wants to thank all of you. Without this town, we wouldn't have the ranch and we wouldn't have EllaJayne safe with us."

Pepper listened to the silence and went to the microphone, finally sure what she needed to say, "AJ is right that we owe everyone here thanks, but I've learned that allowing others to help is also a gift. So, we thank you for your help on getting our new home started. Thank you for coming out today."

Shouts echoed around the open lot.

Then Danny took over as AJ pulled her in for a hug and a kiss into the top of her hair. "You always know what to say or do. Must be why I love you."

Danny said, "Will you two lead us in our first dance?"

"Hell," AJ said. "I can't dance."

"You weren't a farmer either and look how well you've done at that."

"Guess so. Come on, honey. Let's show them how it's done."

Pepper snuggled into AJ's chest, allowing him to rock her around the dusty lot to the slow crooning of the band. She didn't care what happened next because this was all she needed.

Then a little girl voice carried over everything, singing to her own tune: "*S-e-x, s-e-x, s-e-x.*"

Everyone laughed. AJ said, "That's our girl."

* * * * *

"The Joshua trees and saguaros sure are pretty," Jack
said reflectively. "This sort of looks like the land west
of the Three Rivers Ranch house. Where you showed
me the North Star, remember?"

Remember? Those moments had been burned into
Vanessa's memory. Even if she never saw him again
for the rest of her life, she'd always have those special
moments to relive in her mind.

The thought unexpectedly caused her throat to
tighten, and she wished the waitress would get back
with their drinks. She didn't want Jack to think she was
getting emotional. Especially because she could feel
their time together winding to a close.

"I do. And I just happen to know a place not too far
west of here where there's another special view of the
evening star."

His eyelids lowered ever so slightly as he looked across the table at her. "After we eat, you should show me."

Did he expect her to look at him in the moonlight and not feel the urge to kiss him? Or maybe she'd get lucky, Vanessa thought, and the moon would be in a new phase and the light would be too weak to illuminate his face.

Damn it, Vanessa. Who are you fooling? You could find Jack's lips in the darkest of nights.

Thankfully, a waitress suddenly approached their table, and the distraction pushed the mocking voice from her head…but not the idea of being in Jack's arms again. She was beginning to fear she'd never rid herself of that longing.

Don't miss
The Other Hollister Man *by Stella Bagwell,*
available August 2022 wherever
Harlequin books and ebooks are sold.

Harlequin.com

Love Harlequin romance?

DISCOVER.

Be the first to find out about promotions, news and exclusive content!

Facebook.com/HarlequinBooks

Twitter.com/HarlequinBooks

Instagram.com/HarlequinBooks

Pinterest.com/HarlequinBooks

YouTube.com/HarlequinBooks

ReaderService.com

EXPLORE.

Sign up for the Harlequin e-newsletter and download a free book from any series at **TryHarlequin.com**

CONNECT.

Join our Harlequin community to share your thoughts and connect with other romance readers!
Facebook.com/groups/HarlequinConnection

HARLEQUIN

HSOCIAL2021

HARLEQUIN

Heartfelt or thrilling, passionate or uplifting—Harlequin is more than just happily-ever-after.

With twelve different series to choose from and new books available every month, you are sure to find stories that will move you, uplift you, inspire and delight you.

SIGN UP FOR THE HARLEQUIN NEWSLETTER

Be the first to hear about great new reads and exciting offers!

Harlequin.com/newsletters